PARALLEL LIES

RIDLEY PEARSON
PARALLEL LIES

HYPERION
NEW YORK

Library of Congress Cataloging-in-Publication Data
Pearson, Ridley.
    Parallel lies / by Ridley Pearson—1st ed.
      p.   cm.
    ISBN 0-7868-6564-4
    1. Railroad accidents—Investigation—Fiction. 2. Widowers—Fiction. 3. Sabotage—Fiction. 4. Revenge—Fiction. I. Title.
    PS3566.E234 P3   2001
    813'.54—dc21   00-047227

FIRST EDITION

10 9 8 7 6 5 4 3 2 1

Betsy Dodge Pearson

For holding us together all these years. For leading the way with grace and creativity. For the neighborhood art fairs in the back-yard. For all those things too big and too small to mention. Support is a tiny word when laid at your feet. You hold the world sometimes. And all of us with it. You are the best. The only. The Betsy.

ACKNOWLEDGMENTS

This novel was edited by Leigh Haber (Hyperion) and my agent Al Zuckerman (Writers House).

Special thanks to William Eder, Nick Gilman, C.J. Snow, for reading with a trained eye. Matthew Snyder, for the film work. Nancy Litzinger, Debbie Cimino, Mary Peterson, Louise Marsh, for everything you do at the office. Heidi Mack for creating and maintaining the web site. Courtney Samway for being our cyber-space mail courier. Thanks, too, to Ellen Archer and Bob Miller.

Marcelle, Paige, and Storey—as always, yours.

PARALLEL LIES

CHAPTER

1

The train charged forward in the shimmering afternoon sunlight, autumn's vibrant colors forming a natural lane for the raised bed of chipped rock and the few hundred tons of steel and wood. The rails stretched out before the locomotive, light glinting off their polished surfaces, tricked by the eye into joining together a half mile in the distance, the illusion always moving forward at the speed of the train, as if those rails spread open just in time to carry her.

For the driver of that freight, it was another day in paradise. Alone with his thoughts, he and his brakeman, pulling lumber and fuel oil, cotton and cedar, sixteen shipping containers, and seven empty flatbeds. Paradise was that sound in your ears and that rumble up your legs. It was the blue sky meeting the silver swipe of tracks far off on the horizon. It was a peaceful job. The best work there was. It was lights and radios and doing something good for people—getting stuff from one place to another. The driver packed another pinch of chewing tobacco deep between his cheeks and gum, his mind partly distracted by a bum air conditioner in the bedroom of a mobile home still miles away, wondering where the hell he'd get the three hundred bucks needed to replace it. He could put it on the credit card, but that amounted to robbing Peter to pay Paul. Maybe some overtime. Maybe he'd put in for an extra run.

The sudden vibration was subtle enough that a passenger would not have felt it. A grinding, like bone rubbing on bone. His first thought was that some brakes had failed, that a compressor had failed, that he had a lockup midtrain. His hand reached to slow the mighty beast. But before he initiated any braking—before he only compounded the problem—he checked a mirror and caught sight of the length of her as the train chugged through a long, graceful turn and down a grade that had her really clipping along. It was then his heart did its first little flutter, then he felt a heat in his lungs and a tension in his neck like someone had pulled on a cable. It wasn't the brakes.

A car—number seven or eight—was dancing back there like she'd had too much to drink. Shaking her hips and wiggling her shoulders all at once, kind of swimming right there in the middle of all the others. Not the brakes, but an axle. Not something that could be resolved.

He knew the fate of that train before he touched a single control, before his physical motions caught up to the knowledge that fourteen years on the line brought to such a situation.

In stunned amazement, he watched that car do her dance. What had looked graceful at first, appeared suddenly violent, no longer a dance but now a seizure as the front and the back of that car alternately jumped left to right and right to left, and its boxlike shape disintegrated to something awkwardly bent and awful. It leaned too far, and as it did, the next car began that same cruel jig.

He pulled back the throttle and applied the brakes but knew it was an exercise in futility. The locomotive now roiled with a tremor that shook dials to where he couldn't read them. His teeth rattled in his head as he reached for the radio. "Mayday!" he shouted, having no idea why. There were codes to use, procedure to follow, but only that one word exploded from his mouth.

The cars rolled now, one after another, first toward the back then forward toward the locomotive, the whole thing dragging and screaming, the beauty of its frictionless motion destroyed. The cars tilted right and fell, swiping the trees like the tail of a dragon, splintering and knocking them down like toothpicks, the sky littered with autumn colors. And then a ripple began as that tail lifted briefly toward the sky. The cars, one coupled to the next, floated above the tracks and then fell, like someone shaking a kink out of a lawn hose.

Going for the door handle, he let go of the throttle, the "dead man's switch" taking over and cutting engine power. He lost his footing and fell to the floor of the cab, his brain numb and in shock. He didn't know whether to jump or ride it out.

He would later tell investigators that the noise was like nothing he'd ever heard, like nothing that could be described. Part scream. Part explosion. A deafening, immobilizing dissonance, while the smell of steel sparking on steel rose in his nostrils and sickened his stomach to where he sat puking on the oily cab floor, crying out as loudly as he could in an effort to blot out that sound.

He felt all ten tons of the engine car tip heavily right, waver there, precariously balanced up on the one rail, and then plunge to the earth, the whole string of freights buckling and bending and dying behind him in a massive pileup.

He saw a flatbed fly overhead, only the blue sky behind it. This, his last conscious vision, incongruous and unfathomable. For forty long seconds the cars collided, tumbled, shrieked, and flew as they ripped their way through soil and forest, carried by momentum until an ungainly silence settled over the desecrated track, and the orange, red, and silver leaves fell out of a disturbed sky as if laying a blanket over the face of a corpse.

CHAPTER

2

Six Weeks Later

Darkness descends quickly in December. In the flaming blue light of a camp stove, a man's breath fogged the chattering boxcar as he struggled to warm a can of Hormel chili, the aroma mixing with the smell of oil and rust. The faint vapor of his breath sank toward the planking and then dissipated.

Umberto Alvarez thumped his fist onto the floorboards, the feeling in his fingers lost to the cold, and then cupped both hands around the small stove, wishing for more heat. The train rumbled. The can danced atop the stove. Alvarez reached out and steadied it, burning himself. *Be careful what you wish for,* he thought.

The train's whistle blew and he checked his watch. Nearly ten o'clock. The last significant slowing of the freight train had occurred ten minutes earlier, in Terre Haute. Alvarez had taken careful note of this, for at that speed, a person could get on or off the moving train—important to know for any rider. His reconnaissance almost completed, this trip, Indianapolis to St. Louis, would be his last ride for a while. *Thank God.*

Behind him in the boxcar, Whirlpool dishwashers were stacked three high, their cardboard boxes proclaiming *Whisper Quiet* as the rattle of steel-on-steel shook his teeth.

Alvarez's fatigue-ridden eyes peered out from beneath a navy blue knit cap that he had pulled down to try to keep warm. Still, unruly black hair escaped the cap in oily clumps. A brown turtleneck was pulled up over his unshaven chin to keep out the cold. It protruded from beneath a rat-holed sweatshirt. Over that, a faded fleece vest that had once been turquoise.

The stacked dishwashers occupied half the boxcar, secured by tattered webbing straps held together by cast-iron buckle clasps. The rhythm of the wheels on rail—two loud bumps followed by whining steel, followed again by the two bumps—contributed to Alvarez's pounding headache, a sound that would remain with him for days, on or off the lines, a sound that lived in any rider's bones: *cha-cha-hmmmm, cha-cha-hmmmm.*

Pale blue light from the fire ring limited his vision. He could barely see to either end of the forty-foot boxcar. There was spray paint graffiti there, if he remembered right, or maybe that had been another car, another day, another line. It all blended together—time, weather, hunger, exhaustion. He'd lost track.

The train could move him physically from one destination to another, but it couldn't change the way he felt. The weary darkness that surrounded him had little to do with the dim flicker of the stove. It lived inside him now. His grief was suffocating him.

Minutes earlier the open cracks at the edges of the boxcar's huge sliding door had flickered light from a small town. The train's driver sounded the locomotive's horn on approach. Through the car's rough slats, street lamps cast shifting ladders of light throughout, reminding Alvarez uncomfortably of prison bars.

The train had clattered through the crossing, the warning bells ringing and sliding down the musical scale, driving Alvarez further into depression. Any such crossing was an agonizing reminder of his past. The minivan carrying his wife and kids had been recovered nearly a quarter mile from a similar crossing, flipped onto its side and shaped like a barbell—flat in the center, bulging at either end.

He felt only a sharp, unforgiving pain where he should have felt his heart. Nearly two and a half years had passed, but still he couldn't adjust to life without them. Friends had comforted him, saying he would move on, but they were wrong. He'd lost everything and now he'd given up everything. To hell with sleep. To hell with his so-called life. He'd turned himself over to the grief, succumbed to it. He had purpose, and that purpose owned him: Payment for atrocities against him and his family would be made in full. If not, he would die trying.

For the past eighteen months the media had reported a string of derailments: a freight train in Alabama; another in Kansas; still others west of the Rockies. Drivers were blamed. Weather conditions. Equipment failures. As many lies as there were train cars torn from the tracks. He had not begun with any grand plan, but somehow one had evolved. He had not awakened one morning to think of himself as a terrorist, although the description now fit. He had a meeting with a bomb maker scheduled for the next day. He had never followed a script, and yet he now found himself with a clear mission: nothing short of destroying the huge Northern Union Railroad would do. David versus Goliath: he'd assumed the role effortlessly.

While one hand stirred the chili with a red plastic stir stick, a shadow drew his attention. Shifting shadows were routine in a boxcar; it was the shadows that did not move that attracted one's attention. But this shadow was caused by something—someone—on the *outside* of the boxcar; it—he—moved slowly, boldly negotiating on the outside of a moving freight. Alvarez alerted himself to trouble—some drunken or crazed rider, no doubt, catching a whiff of the chili. It was no easy feat, what this man was doing—inching along the boxcar's exterior; it implied someone strong, or hungry enough to risk life and limb for a can of chili. Alvarez rose to block the door, but too late. The heavy door slid open—a one-handed move!—another near impossible feat.

Alvarez stepped back. The faceless visitor, silhouetted in the dark opening, stood tall and broad, a big son of a bitch, with a football player's neck. This man reached for his belt and a flashlight came on, blinding Alvarez, who felt another wave of dread: maybe not a rider but a security guard, or even a cop. The feds had cracked down on riders since one recently had been arrested for butchering people in seven different states. *Hobo Homicide!* one of the headlines had read. *The Railroad Killer,* on the TV news.

"Smells good," the visitor said in a friendly enough tone, the voice low and dry. He did not sound winded by his effort.

The comment confused Alvarez slightly, lessened his anxiety. Maybe this guy was just trying to invite himself to dinner. But then again, that flashlight was oddly bright, too bright. Sure, some riders carried penlights, even flashlights. But one with fresh batteries? Never. Not once had Alvarez seen that. Discarded batteries were scrounged out of Dumpsters, the last few volts eked out of them. If a rider had two bucks in his pocket it went to booze, cigarettes, reefer, or food—usually in that order. Not batteries. The crisp brightness of that light cautioned Alvarez. Heat flooded him. Finally warm.

"You alone?" the visitor asked.

Alvarez had long since learned to keep his mouth shut, and he did so now. Most of the time people tended to fill the dead air, and in the process they revealed more about themselves than they intended.

The bright light stung his eyes. Alvarez looked away, the chili boiling at his feet.

"You Mexican?" his visitor asked. The man's round face was now partially visible. A white man, with the nose of a boxer and the brow of a Neanderthal.

Riders beat the stuffing out of one another for the damnedest reasons. Most of the time it had little to do with reason—just the need to hit something, someone. Maybe this guy rode the rails looking for Mexicans to pummel. Again, Alvarez glanced down at the simmering chili.

"Or maybe," the visitor suggested, "your father was Spanish, and your mother, Italian."

As a part-time rider, Alvarez had learned to live with fear, had learned to compartmentalize it, shrink it, rid it of its power to seize

control. You couldn't be fighting fear and someone else simultaneously, so you learned to let the fear roll off your back. But what he
felt now wasn't fear, it was terror.

He knows who I am!

There was little he could do about terror. Terror, once allowed
inside, owned you. There was no fighting off real terror. Survivors
could harness it, redirect it, but could never be rid of it. Terror had
to be dealt with quickly or it would freeze every muscle.

Alvarez bent down and launched the boiling chili into the visitor's face. He charged, hoping to drive the man out the open door.
But behind the ghoulish scream, as his face burned, the man produced a nightstick or a sap, connecting it with the side of Alvarez's
face. He felt his nose crack and he spewed blood. Alvarez faltered,
regained himself, and turned, diving for the small stove. Coming to
his feet, he waved it as a weapon, prepared to strike.

This would be a fight to the finish. Alvarez knew it before the
next blow landed.

A lvarez awoke to the jarring sound of a garage door being hauled open, a pickup truck starting, and the sharp smell of engine exhaust. He quietly moved a garden spade and peered down through cracks in the garage loft into which he had climbed the night before, weary and soaked in another man's blood. Dried blood, now brown, caked and cracking. If he were spotted, it would mean the police. He couldn't allow that. Not after working at this for eighteen months.

He shook from the cold and from his memory of the night before, realizing that he had probably killed a man, whether in self-defense or not. By the time Alvarez had thrown the intruder from the freight car, his attacker had lost so much blood that under the glare of the flashlight he'd looked ghostly pale. Even the man's lips had been white. And now . . . now he felt forced to question his own motives. He'd been accused of killing his own attorney, Donald Andersen— a phony accusation that had caused him to flee in the first place. The thought that he now indeed might have killed a man could add weight to that earlier accusation. With their relentless pursuit of him, they may have turned him into a killer. Now resentment and anger overrode his initial self-questioning. Northern Union Railroad would cease to exist. This, for their lies and endless atrocities.

His position up in the garage loft afforded Alvarez a view of the truck's steering wheel and two large male hands gripping it. Alvarez lay down flat just in case the driver happened to look up as he backed out. As a precaution, he remained still, even after the truck cleared the garage, and this paid off because the driver left the vehicle to manually pull the garage door back down. Alvarez listened to the truck pulling away, waited another half minute, and then moved the ratty blanket and canvas tarp off himself, grateful that the owners had left a hot lamp going all night for the cat. The lamp had taken the edge off the cold and had probably kept him from freezing. It was the glow from the lamp that had called him to this garage: a beacon seen through the woods.

A train whistle sounded, reminding Alvarez again of last night's horror and that he had to keep moving. They might not find the body for weeks—or perhaps as soon as that same day—but whatever the timing, he needed to put as many miles as possible between himself and southern Illinois, and fast. The man in the boxcar had known his birth heritage—had teased him by saying "Mexican" first, then waiting and identifying Alvarez's Spanish father and Italian mother. It meant that Northern Union Security was closer to capturing him than they'd ever been. He'd obviously screwed up—had allowed himself to be seen or recognized, or worse, he'd become predictable. Had they known which train he was on, or had it been random chance, a lucky guess? Had they determined his next target? Did they know he'd sabotaged the bearings? Had they finally made this connection between the various derailments?

He climbed down from the loft, all his joints aching, cold to the bone, passing a small bicycle hung on the wall and catching a glimpse of his own face in the bike's tiny rearview mirror. His wife had claimed he looked more Italian than Latino, citing his olive skin, thin face, and sharp features, but he saw his father's face in the mirror, not his mother's. He gingerly touched his nose. Bruised, but not broken as he'd originally thought. Like the rest of him, his face was crusted in blood and dirt. He needed a shower, or at least a facecloth. He had a small tear in the skin above his slightly swollen left eye, the cut clotted shut. It would clean up and eventually recede beneath his thick black eyebrows. His dark skin would go a long way toward hiding the discoloration. Now he needed to get back on schedule: he had a plane to catch. But he couldn't even walk out in public looking like this, much less hitchhike. He glanced around the dimly lit garage, the morning sun just burning the edge of the horizon and sparkling off the fallen snow. Panic struck him: snow. Footprints. A trail to follow. *Them*—right behind him.

For eighteen months he'd been running, and though in a way he was accustomed to it, he still broke out in a sweat at the thought of capture. He clung to his purpose, confident that God would protect him.

Ultimately he blamed William Goheen, CEO of Northern Union, for killing his family. But his revenge was no longer focused solely on Goheen. Not only did one life not equal three, but Goheen had not acted alone. The institution, the corporation, had killed his wife and children, intentionally or not. There was no halfway in this.

A change of clothes—and fast! he thought, still looking out at the carpet of fresh snow. Time seemed always to be working against him.

He edged up carefully to the frosted window behind the cat's bed and peered out at the two-story farmhouse not twenty yards away. Gray smoke spiraled from a brick chimney. Icicles hung from the gutters. A yellowish light glowed from the downstairs windows.

The kid's bike hanging on the wall suggested a family, not a single guy gone off to work in his truck. It meant there were others inside: a wife, at least one child old enough to ride a bike. Maybe others, too—perhaps a mother-in-law, more children, houseguests. But he needed a closer look. He wouldn't get anywhere in his bloody clothes. He could only hope that school might take the mother and child away to catch a school bus, or that the wife was still asleep, a heavy sleeper. He watched the house carefully for ten long minutes, evaluating his chances of crossing the open space unseen. If there was movement inside, he couldn't detect it: he decided to make his move.

He elected not to crouch or sneak. He would run openly. If

confronted, he would act as if he were in shock. He would claim there had been a horrible traffic accident, that he couldn't remember where, or even how he'd gotten there, but that he needed a telephone quickly. He needed help. He would play on do-gooding Midwestern values. From there, he'd see.

He opened the garage's side door and started running. All kinds of thoughts went through his head. How had he come to this point? He didn't belong here. Eighteen months ago he would have laughed at the notion that he would be running across a yard of freshly fallen snow in bloody clothes, with the intention of stealing fresh clothing from complete strangers. He'd been a schoolteacher—eighth grade science and computer science; he'd loved his job, his wife, the twins. To have told him then that the threat on his life would be so high just a few years later; he would never have believed it. And yet here he was.

He reached the house unnoticed. Perhaps he would not need any elaborate story. He crept up the back porch. A forgotten withered black pumpkin frowned monstrously at him, its jaw frozen, wearing a crown of ice.

He saw someone inside. An attractive woman in her early thirties, she wore green flannel pajamas, the top unbuttoned enough that she wouldn't want a strange man gaping at her. Short, but not skinny. Hearty Midwestern stock. Dull hair that hadn't yet been brushed out. She left the kitchen and returned a minute later cradling a pile of sheets. Alvarez ducked under the window and moved in tandem with her to the far end of the small back porch where another window looked in on a pantry, a laundry room. An ironing board stood on all fours next to the window.

The woman bent over to remove a load of clothes from the dryer, exposing her breasts to him, and he thought how there had been a time when that might have had an effect on him. Now he felt no stirring, no interest whatsoever. He thought of his wife, the crushed car. It strengthened his resolve. He focused on a pair of men's jeans strung over a clothesline rack in the far corner. The woman lifted a pile of darks to the top of the dryer. He spotted a flannel shirt, some heavy socks. Alvarez leaned back from the window as the woman unloaded the clothes. He sensed that she was about to look out, that she had felt his presence.

She moved some clothes from the washer to the dryer and then stuffed the sheets into the washer. He glanced around, making sure he wasn't being watched. He briefly considered entering the kitchen right then—he felt certain the back door would be unlocked—surprising the wife, perhaps tying her up, and stealing some food and clothing. But any such encounter would put him at greater risk. Cops would be called in—his trail would be easier to follow. He began to feel impatient, but the cold in his bones was gone, replaced by hot adrenaline.

She reentered the kitchen. Alvarez moved cautiously to another window and took a position nearer the porch stairs but still with a view inside. The woman measured out water into a pot and turned on the stove. She pulled down a box of Cream of Wheat and set it on the counter. Morning rituals. He recalled them with longing.

Then she hurried out, disappearing into another room.

He was guessing three to five minutes for the water to boil. How accurately did she have such things timed in her head? His wife would have known *exactly*. Three minutes would be plenty for him to get in, grab the clothes, and get back out. He made his move, pulling his hand into the sweatshirt's sleeve so as not to leave fingerprints on the doorknob as he turned it.

The door opened. He stepped inside.

The kitchen smelled like a home. God, he missed that smell. For a moment it owned him, the poignant feeling carrying him away, and then the distant sound of shower water caught his attention. It was warm in here, the first warmth he'd felt in days. Was she just warming up the shower, or getting in? Each option offered a different scenario. He crossed toward the laundry room. He wanted to stay here; he wanted to move in. He pulled the jeans into his arms, stepped to his left and reached for the flannel shirt in the pile of dry clothes.

The buttons plunked against the surface of the dryer. He stiffened, though he thought the noise from the washing machine would conceal this much tinier sound. But in rising up abruptly he bumped the ironing board and now watched as the iron, just out of reach, began to rock, first this way, then that, teetering back and forth. At that moment, the wife, her flannel pajama top now fully unbuttoned, pants off and left back in the bedroom or bath, crossed the kitchen to where, had she looked to her right, she would have seen a panicked stranger reaching out to stabilize her iron, which was about to crash to the floor.

The iron started to fall.

Alvarez caught it, reaching out just in time. He then remained absolutely still, aware that the iron might have just presented itself as a weapon, if needed. Could he bring himself to use it that way? he wondered.

He couldn't hear her over the noise of the appliances. He pictured her measuring the Cream of Wheat and carefully stirring it into the boiling water. That was when he realized she had used hot tap water, not cold, which had shortened the time it took to boil. He moved a bit in order to remain hidden, all the while keeping one eye on the kitchen.

The woman's pale bare bottom shifted hip to hip as she left the room.

Alvarez returned the iron to the ironing board, grabbed a few more pieces of clothing—a T-shirt, several mismatched socks—and made for the kitchen. Here, he heard the shower water still running. This woman had her morning routine all planned out.

He took two steps toward the back door and changed his mind. He returned to the pantry, deciding to take some canned food while he had the chance. A clock ran inside his head; he had maybe another minute or two.

"Mommy?" a tiny voice called from behind him.

Alvarez flattened himself to the wall. Dead still.

"Mommy?"

He rocked his head to see, with great relief, that he was partially screened from the kitchen by the open pantry door. Through the crack he saw a small six- or seven-year-old boy with red hair, freckles, and a blue stuffed dog tucked tightly under his arm. The boy crossed to the fridge and pulled out a carton of orange juice. He moved around the kitchen comfortably, reaching for a glass on tiptoes and then filling it with the juice.

The plumbing pipes to Alvarez's left rumbled and went silent. The shower had ended. He stood there with his bundle of clothes and cans of tuna not knowing what to do next.

She'd be drying herself off now. Just from having observed her, Alvarez knew she'd already decided what clothes to wear, if in fact she hadn't already laid them out.

The boy gulped the orange juice. Alvarez felt himself tighten, not over his predicament, but at the sight of the boy—a living, breathing boy, in a joyful moment of drinking orange juice. A child. Innocent. Loving. Waiting for his mother. Alvarez's vision blurred. Nothing would bring his twins back. He'd revisited their loss countless times. He pushed his anger deeper inside and locked it away, though only temporarily. It owned him. Possessed him. But he could not work with it in the forefront of his thought, he could barely move. He had learned to tame it but feared he would never be rid of it.

What to do? he wondered, silently urging the boy to seek out his mother. The Cream of Wheat would burn in another minute or so. Mom had to be just about fully dressed by now. His worlds were colliding. He had to get out.

The boy seemed to be debating whether to leave the kitchen, but Alvarez needed to take action, now.

The window . . .

There appeared to be some home-fix-it caulking plugging its edges. Could he get out it with his arms full? Slip off this far end of the porch? He could taste his freedom.

The boy remained in limbo, hugging his blue dog and staring off into space, but he faced the laundry room, preventing Alvarez from crossing the pantry's open door and making for the window.

"Nate, honey?" called Mom, sounding close, though not yet into the kitchen.

"Yeah?" the boy called in response.

"Stir the cereal for me, would you? Turn it off first! Use a pot holder! And watch out for the bubbles. They're hot! I'm going to get your sister up."

A second child!

The boy crossed to the stove.

Alvarez moved back to the ironing board. He set down his loot on the dryer and gently moved the ironing board out of his way. Would she remember how it had been sitting? If he could get out without setting off any alarms in her, he might buy himself more time—*freedom.*

He unlocked the window, the washer's motor and churning water providing cover. One firm bang with an open palm jarred the window loose. The weather stripping, long strings of soft caulk, pulled from the jamb. He was in a full sweat now—hands, armpits, brow, the back of his neck. He tossed his haul out into the snow, slipped his legs out, and reached to pull the ironing board back into place, dragging it.

His mistake was attempting to stand the iron itself back up as he had found it. He stood it up fine, but in his final effort to get out, he once again nudged the ironing board. This time, he took no notice. As he ducked his head out the window, he heard the iron strike the floor.

He pulled the window shut and scooped up his stolen possessions.

The woman heard the noise. Sounded like something falling. With Samantha cradled in her arms and Nathan standing on a chair stirring his hot cereal, she stepped into the confined space. She thought it felt cold, but this laundry room never heated well in the morning. Northwest side of the house and all.

The iron lay on the floor. She stared at it, puzzled. Then the washing machine shook, going off-center, as it was prone to do with sheets and towels, and the room vibrated so much she was surprised every shelf hadn't fallen down along with the iron. Just another thing that needed fixing. Like most everything in this place.

His name was Peter Tyler, and he drove a beige, front-wheel-drive Ford convertible that smelled of spray can deodorant, courtesy of Avis. The rental agent could not understand his insisting on a convertible in the middle of winter. Tyler gripped the warm plastic steering wheel a little too tightly, thinking that if the snow didn't let up, he would never make it to the rail yard on time. Not the best message to send back to Washington on the first day of a new job.

He adjusted the mirror and briefly caught sight of his own dark eyes and knitted brow, his worry overriding what was normally his more lighthearted expression. He needed this job, both financially and emotionally, even if it was only freelance work. He knew that rebuilding his life would not be accomplished in leaps and bounds but in small, determined steps. And as hard as it was for him to adjust to this, adjust he must. For the past decade, he had formed his identity around his work as a homicide detective. With that now behind him—stolen from him, by his way of thinking—he needed something to hold on to. Anything. This job, however temporary, seemed a place to start. A beginning. An opportunity he could not squander. That it also felt a little like the first day of school was simply something he would have to overcome. Change never came easily.

The snowstorm had left St. Louis in slop—wet, thick, and sticky. Tyler rolled down his window and reached outside, snagging the wiper just long enough to dislodge some of the ice from the blade. A three-inch clear arc appeared through the muck on the windshield, about chin height, requiring Tyler to either sink in his seat or meet his chin to his neck and try to look out through the steering wheel. He sank. For a moment, he could actually see outside.

Cars and trucks had spilled off the road to both sides. Flashers flashed. So did tempers. He saw two different lame attempts at fist-fights, comical for the winter apparel. A tow truck, also off the high-way, convinced him road conditions were serious. He slowed and tried the wiper again. A truck horn sounded behind him. Tyler cursed a blue streak inside the fogged rental and then, unable to take it any longer, unfastened the two clasps, hit the button, and put down the convertible top while under way. Surprisingly, even with the top down, not much snow hit him; it was being carried back by an airfoil created by the windshield, but this required a certain speed to be effective, so he sped up and threw caution to the wind.

He hadn't explained his acute claustrophobia to the rental clerk, doubting the man would have wanted to hear that the car's interior was going to be exposed to winter conditions. Peter Tyler had been driving ragtops for over a year.

With the lid down, people waved at him from cars and the side of the road. This was a country that celebrated personal expression. There would no doubt be talk around the suburban dinner tables that night of the crazy man in the beige convertible doing forty on I-70 in freezing weather with the top down.

Tyler stopped the car outside the rail yard, put the top back up— first impressions were important to him—and took another moment to brush the snow off the wet shoulders of his trench coat. Homicide cops wore trench coats—lined in the winter months, but still trench coats—and Tyler had been a homicide cop for eleven years prior to the six or seven minutes that had changed his life. Now he felt like a cheap imitation. He wasn't sure he even deserved the trench coat. Life was a bitch.

With the car's lid up, his heart beat fast and his palms sweated. He took a deep breath and calmed himself. This affliction was relatively new, and growing worse: perhaps it came from a fear of jail time—a real possibility for a while there. The so-called assault, and the resulting charges, had changed everything. Now he felt lucky just to have a job, any job, and he was not going to screw it up. He certainly wasn't going to let some stranger's first impression of him be in a snowstorm, in a convertible, with the top down. He still hoped that a strong performance on this investigation—his first assignment for the National Transportation Safety Board, or NTSB—might lead to a more permanent position. He needed the work, the income, the stability. He needed this.

At a few minutes past three in the afternoon, with the storm still raging, Tyler parked and climbed out. The rail yard smelled of petroleum—grease, fuel, and cleansers—even in a snowstorm, a rusty bitterness in the back of the throat that reminded him of overheated electrical sockets.

A ruddy-cheeked man approached and introduced himself as Hardy Madders, rolling his eyes at the joke of his own name. An overweight man with loose jowls and a jovial disposition, Madders shook Tyler's hand vigorously, introducing himself as the yard's superintendent. He led Tyler across railroad tracks buried in six inches of wet snow, pointing out where to step to avoid tripping on the buried rails. The yard held freight cars, tankers, and flatbeds. Red, black, gray. Dozens of tracks, perhaps thousands of cars. According to Madders, a man who plainly liked to hear himself talk, the yard hands sorted the arriving trains, redirecting groups of cars to various tracks and to trains on other routes. An interline train from the east or south would carry one "package" of several cars headed to the northwest, another package intended for the southwest, and several more bound for the West Coast or Canada. Here, at the St. Louis switching yard, these cars were separated out and rerouted—

"repackaged"—connected to engines and sent on their way. "Twenty-four, seven. No holidays here," Madders added.

"And the car I'm supposedly interested in?" Tyler asked.

"Oh, you're interested all right," Madders assured him. "Why would the NTSB send an investigator all the way from Washington if there wasn't something to be interested in? Don't you boys have regional offices?"

"I'm new," Tyler answered, not wanting to give this guy too much information. He carried NTSB credentials but did not feel like a federal employee, a federal agent. For the last eleven years he'd distrusted the feds. Now he was one.

Madders replied, "Which means you're some kind of expert, right?"

"I wouldn't exactly say that."

"Homicide," Madders said. "You gotta be some kind of expert in homicide. Am I right?" They walked a few more feet—it was treacherous going—when Madders said under his breath, "You'd better be."

Lit by a number of battery-powered fluorescent lights, the boxcar in question held crated dishwashers. A St. Louis Police Department uniformed patrolman stomping his cold feet together was at a step-ladder leading up into the car. Tyler showed the man his credentials.

"Feds are here!" the cop announced.

Inside the car were two crime scene technicians busy with stain-less steel tools and plastic bags. They had attached little flags of various colors around the car. Supervising the two was a detective by the name of Banner, or Bantock—the man was so cold his jaw didn't move properly and Tyler missed the name. The detective was short and stocky and wore a gray wool overcoat. His street shoes looked wet all through, and his face was a florid pink, from either temperament or the cold. Clearly he didn't want to be here—it was written all over him, from his hunched shoulders to the squinting eyes that conveyed resentment.

"Blood?" Tyler asked. The floor, the boxes, the walls appeared sprayed in it. The air smelled sour.

"No lie," the detective answered.

"It was a question," Tyler explained. He'd attended hundreds of crime scenes, most of them bloody, but this was among the worst.

"The cold helps us," one of the technicians explained. "If the fluids hadn't frozen, nearly on impact, they would have been absorbed, spread out. Instead, we got some real good splatter indicators here."

The other tech added, "We're thinking two people. Both bleeders—we'll know for sure when we type the blood. If either one's still standing I'd be surprised, but this one—" he said, indicating the boxcar wall behind his partner, "—this one's a couple quarts low. He's either dead or wishing he was."

"Have we identified that?" Tyler indicated the brown mess on the boxcar's floor.

"We were thinking fecal matter or vomit," the first tech answered. "But now I'm guessing soup. Frozen chili, maybe."

"Chili," Tyler said curiously.

"Go figure," the technician said.

"These riders will fight over anything," Madders said from outside the car. Snow covered his head like a thin handkerchief.

The detective, plainly suspicious, inquired, "What's NTSB care about a fight in a railcar?"

Tyler nodded. He'd been expecting this. "The homicides and the subsequent arrest—"

"The Railroad Killer," Madders interjected.

Tyler continued, "—have everyone in Washington oversensitive about reports of blood in railcars. If we've got a copycat out here, the sooner we shut him down, the better."

Madders said, "Good riddance to all riders—these two included. We chase a dozen out of here every day."

Both the detective and Tyler turned to face Madders. His breath fogging in the cold boxcar, the detective asked, "You chase any out today?"

Tyler in turn asked Madders, "Who do you mean by 'we'?"

Madders answered the detective first. "None that I saw. Listen, we got bums coming and going, twenty-four, seven. The ones who know anything know to jump way before they ever reach the yard. It's only the dumb ones we see here. You trespass onto company property, that's a crime. We see the same face two, three times, and we arrest 'em."

"Who's 'we'?" Tyler repeated.

"Northern Union *Security,*" Madders emphasized.

"They got their own company, their own security guys, their own *investigators,*" the detective answered, beating Madders to it. "And it sucks, as far as I'm concerned—the whole damn arrangement."

"Security guards have authority to make arrests?" Tyler asked, incredulous. He was thinking *rent-a-cops,* but he didn't say it.

"You bet they do," Madders answered, jumping in. "Do it all the time."

The detective answered, "They dump 'em off with us. We house 'em until their hearings."

"And these security guards," Tyler said. "Where are they now? We'd like to talk to them."

"It's a big yard," Madders replied. "We got six guys total. Two guys each shift. They're around here somewhere."

"I've already asked," the detective told Tyler. "One of our guys is rounding them up."

"They ever hear of radios?" Tyler mumbled.

"We got radios," Madders told him.

"Use 'em," the detective barked. "Get those guys over here!"

"The ones on duty, or the ones on day shift? 'Cause that's gonna be a problem," he said, checking his watch. "Three-thirty. Shift rotates real soon."

"Find 'em!" the detective ordered.

Madders hurried off into the storm, cursing under his breath. Not a minute had passed before he reappeared with two security guards. "Already on their way," he said proudly.

"I thought you said there were two," Tyler said, observing a third.

Standing between two football-player types who made their plain blue uniforms look undersized stood a tall black woman who wore a long chic overcoat with the hood up. The hood was trimmed in faux fur meant to look like a tiger's tail. The whites of the woman's eyes showed from within the shadow of that hood, her lips pursed in concentration.

"Who's in charge?" she asked, her delicate voice rising above the clatter of a nearby train. Then she caught sight of the flags and the enormous quantity of blood in the boxcar. Her eyes wandered over to Tyler's. "You?" she asked.

Jurisdiction had not yet been discussed. Tyler answered, "It's his crime scene." He considered introducing the detective, but he still wasn't sure of the man's name.

"John Banner," the detective told her. This time Tyler caught it clearly. "Detective. SLPD." Either Banner didn't like blacks or he didn't like women. Or maybe it was that he didn't like black women, but an attitude change came with the introduction. "And you are?"

"Here to observe and help out if I can," answered the woman as she approached the stepladder. "Nell Priest. Northern Union Security, corporate." Tyler felt she had sized up Banner immediately, and this impressed him. "You don't have a problem with that, do you, Detective?"

Tyler's live-in companion for two years, Kat, had walked out at the height of his legal problems, leaving him alone and despondent. He blamed the media's invasion of their privacy rather than his own inability at the time to communicate. He'd put Kat behind him now, along with nearly everything else of his former life. But Nell Priest had Kat's spunk, reminding him of her and winning his spontaneous admiration. Not every woman could hold her own with self-important bastards like Banner.

The two forensic technicians observed this exchange without moving. Clearly Banner came with some baggage that his co-workers were aware of. For a moment the air seemed unusually still. "I'd rather not contaminate the scene," Banner answered, looking right at her.

She looked to Banner, back to Tyler, seemed to consider the situation, and elected to answer with a faint nod. Some snow broke from the faux fur and flew around her face.

"He's federal," Banner said, pointing to Tyler, as if that explained something.

Tyler introduced himself. He stepped toward the edge of the boxcar and reached down to shake hands—gloves actually—with her. "I'm working for the NTSB."

"Meaning you are regular army or a recruit?" she inquired. "I know most of the NTSB investigators."

"My guess," Tyler said, not quite answering her, "is that my bosses are afraid of a copycat, or that maybe they locked up the wrong Railroad Killer. They'd tell you we have to investigate any serious crime that involves interstate transportation. And that's true, of course—"

She said, "Meaning you suspect that whatever happened here began in another state." She added, "And that makes it yours."

"Not mine," Tyler corrected. "I'm here to observe and write a report. Gotta love government work. As long as there's a paper trail to follow, my bosses are happy."

"Well then, we're not so different," she said. "My report gets filed with Northern Union Security. Maybe we can cheat and look over each other's shoulders."

She had nice shoulders to look over, Tyler was guessing. She didn't want this blowing up on her bosses any more than he did. It seemed as if everyone had learned some lessons from the Railroad

Killer case, namely, that a small, localized investigation could mushroom exponentially and make the company or department, or the
agency, look bad.

Banner suggested, "Maybe you two could get acquainted somewhere else and let the rest of us finish our jobs and get out of this
cold."

Tyler ignored Banner and asked her, "You're based out of
where?"

"New York." She then said to Banner, "No one's challenging
your authority here, Detective. But technically, your crime scene is
on my property. I'm here representing Northern Union, so I'm the
go-between. That's all. You need our people for anything, we're
happy to cooperate."

"So go-between somewhere else for the next half hour, okay?"
Banner said dismissively.

"Ladies!" Tyler said, looking squarely at Banner. "Let's not spill
any more blood, it'll only confuse the technicians."

"Got that right," one of the lab men said.

Nell Priest suppressed a grin, and Tyler knew he had scored. She
said, "I'd like to step aboard my company's property and observe
whatever it is you've got."

Snow had collected on the shoulders of her coat and the very
top of her hood. It clung delicately to the fake tiger fur. The two
Northern Union security guards with Madders were doing the cold
foot shuffle nearly in unison. They looked like poorly trained dance
partners.

The air hung with expectation, everyone waiting for Banner's
response to her request.

Tyler said, "Why don't I step out and make room for Ms. Priest?
You've seen one bloody boxcar, you've seen 'em all."

Banner grimaced.

"Thank you," Priest said, backing away from the ladder so that
Tyler could climb down. She climbed up and stuck it to Banner by

removing her glove and extending her hand and forcing him to shake hands with her. "That's Banner with two n's?"

He looked like a man sorting garbage as he touched her. "You want a business card?"

"Yes, that would be good. Thank you." Priest slipped her hand back into her glove and asked the technicians a few questions about "impact velocity," "major vessel disruption," and whether they worked in centimeters or inches.

"So, let me give you my card," Banner suggested, perhaps a little intimidated or even impressed by her knowledge. He handed her a card and she pocketed it.

Standing in the snow, Tyler asked the two security agents if they had been on duty all day.

"Since eight this morning," answered the first, who must have once played college fullback.

His black partner replied, "Yes, sir. On at eight. Off at four. We hauled a couple guys outta some cars on line two. But nothing on this line. This car here . . . it was already sorted off line and had been tugged over here onto line twelve before our receivable guys opened her up and saw . . . this. They called us over. We informed the super, Mr. Madders, and he—"

"Called New York," Madders interrupted. To Priest he said, "At which point they sent you, I suppose."

"I suppose." Nell Priest clearly didn't want everything on the table. Tyler understood corporate paranoia, but she wasn't helping her case with Banner any by playing coy. She struck him as being new to this. There was protocol to follow; the evidence collection was Banner's show, the investigation Tyler's, like it or not.

"So why'd no one call us?" Banner injected.

"We called you," Priest informed him.

"But if I've got my timing right, not until they already had you on a plane," he said to Priest, "and you on your way out here, too," he said to Tyler. Banner asked, "What's with that?"

She answered, "If corporate took their time notifying you, it wasn't my doing. My guess is it was nothing more than a mix-up, thinking that Mr. Madders here had already done it."

"No one told me to do nothing!" Madders complained.

"You see?" Priest fired off, "a mix-up."

Tyler wasn't buying it, and neither was Banner. "Corporate," Tyler quoted her. "Is that the railroad or the security company? Or are they all the same?"

"Separate entities," she replied. She apologized and said, "I was referring to the parent company—the railroad, as you called it. They're top-heavy with decision makers. Everything requires a meeting, a committee. It doesn't surprise me if they were a little slow."

Still, it didn't compute for Tyler. The police should have been called immediately. He wrote it off to Railroad Killer paranoia: "corporate" had wanted one of their own—Ms. Priest—on the ground and running before the police got too far out in front. And then another thought occurred to him: who the hell had called NTSB, for they clearly had been given a head start as well?

"Anyone here want what we got so far?" inquired the lead technician, a sharp-nosed man with beady eyes, small and frail in appearance, even bundled in winter clothing.

"With you," Tyler said, hoping to quiet things between Priest and Banner, who also looked on with interest.

"First, you need to know the difference between the various kinds of wounds we deal with." His tone was definite, almost impatient—the person at the cocktail party who's the expert on everything. "We have cutting wounds, stabbing wounds, and blunt force injuries that include lacerations and chopping wounds. You might think these would all bleed the same, but they don't. To offer any kind of accuracy, I need a look at whoever did this dance, but if we lose this weather, we lose this evidence—it's gonna melt—so bear with me while I make a few educated guesses."

No one objected.

"Give us the abridged version, Doc," Banner complained, feeling the cold. "God damn witch's tit out here."

Tyler reached out and shook the hand of the forensics technician, having not been formally introduced. The man's name was Greistein. He didn't seem to feel the weather.

"To determine the events, we follow flow pattern. We categorize blood evidence into three groups: low-velocity impact, medium, and high. At almost any scene like this we have splashed, projected, and cast-off blood." Greistein pointed to the portable lights. "Fluorescent, because we want as little heat in here as possible. All of us standing in here, breathing—we want to make it quick. We're incredibly lucky to have this cold because it literally froze our crime scene, like taking a picture only minutes after the assault." Tyler noted the dozens of numbered flags attached to pins stuck into various bloodstains. More white flags than yellow. Only a dozen or so pink flags, which was where Greistein pointed first.

"We're guessing chili, not regurgitated but thrown from a can or pan." He allowed everyone to think on this. "Two individuals," he stated. "One sitting—we'll call him Low Man. Another we'll call Mooch, because maybe he wanted some of that chili."

"Who the hell cares what this guy was eating?" Banner complained.

"We care because judging by the viscosity, that chili was hot when it was projected."

"Not spilled?" Tyler attempted to qualify.

"Very good," said Greistein. Banner bristled. "Quite the difference, isn't there? Not spilled, projected. Thrown. Definitely hot at the time. We know this by the angular impact. We have a lot of exclamation points and tapered stains. The chili was thrown from low to the floor," he said, indicating a thick area of his little flags near the boxes of dishwashers. He made a throwing motion from low to high. "Judging by volume, it was most, if not all, of an eleven-ounce can. It struck Mooch here," he said, using a small laser pen to indicate another grouping of flags. "Mooch was standing at the time." He fended off doubts by explaining, "Mooch created a spray shadow—a void behind him—that suggests he was standing at the time. When you find him, an examination of his clothing will reveal the projected food and will substantiate these findings."

"Low Man there," Tyler said, accustomed to such briefings, "probably sitting. The other guy, Mooch, standing about there."

"Exactly." The doctor added, "And the chili was thrown before any blood was shed. We know this as well because of coverage."

"These guys knifed each other over a friggin' can of chili?" Banner questioned.

"Not knives, no," the doctor replied.

"Weapons?" Tyler asked.

"Low Man, for whatever reason, projects the chili, hitting Mooch in the upper chest and face. But it's Mooch who lands the first blow. Probably a sap or a stick. I'm guessing he inflicts a nose wound onto Low Man because Low Man's blood spills over here. Mooch rears back and strikes again. Let me explain that any blunt force object produces very little cast-off blood following the first blow. It's typically the second blow that collects the blood and sprays it off in predictable arcs. These arcs are seen as medium-velocity spray patterns, and we have just the one. A knife does not cause such a spray pattern." His laser light, a small red dot, traveled up the ceiling of the boxcar.

"But Mooch was cut, too," Priest offered. "The flags indicate the blood of two men."

Greistein grinned; he appreciated attentive students.

"Hurry it up!" Banner pressed.

Greistein continued. "If Low Man is right-handed, the movement was like a tennis backhand, and quite frankly, judging by the blood loss, I'm amazed that he was even standing at this point. Those first two blows from Mooch were convincing. At the very least, Low Man's nose was probably broken. But now, Low Man strikes out with one defensive blow. A backhand. Delivered quickly." He looked at them all. "I'm guessing he grabs his portable stove and lashes out. Maybe Mooch takes a metal fin to the neck. Low Man gets lucky— he probably severs the carotid artery. Whatever, he unleashes some serious bleeding." Now the man's little red dot from the laser pen was jumping flag to flag in a hurry. "Mooch gets off another blow but misses, spraying cast-off blood here in another medium-velocity arc." The pen's bead of red light danced across the dishwasher boxes. "He drops the weapon here," he said, indicating a small pool of frozen blood, "and grabs for the neck wound. His pressure against that wound causes low-velocity patterns, here, here, and here." He pointed out a variety of wide stains on the boxcar's floor.

"A defensive blow," Tyler repeated, echoing the man.

Greistein allowed a wry smile. "Someone's listening," he said.

Tyler continued, "Mooch is the bleeder, but Low Man took the first blows."

"Exactly. I have no doubt—no doubt whatsoever—that Mooch struck first."

"It's speculative," Banner complained. "These are two homeless sons-of-bitches who could have been arguing about who got the chili and who got the green beans, for Christ's sake. Low Man cuts his pal out of the chili, and they duke it out."

"Maybe," Greistein said confidently, "but then why was the door open this whole time?"

"What?" Banner muttered.

"The car door," Greistein said. "I have solid evidence that the freight car's door was open exactly thirty-three inches throughout this whole ordeal. And you didn't let me go on to explain the fight that ensued. In my opinion, a hand-to-hand fight, that suggests the two men wrestled, both bleeding." His penlight traveled back and forth across the car. "We have tracks. I can practically show you the dance steps. First, there. Then, there. And the whole time, Mooch is bleeding out."

"And Low Man is waiting for him to pass out," Tyler said. More may have been said. Tyler wasn't sure. He traveled back to his own battle in that grungy apartment months earlier. He had relived those few minutes of horror repeatedly, to where he wasn't sure if they were real any longer or if he had embellished or augmented them or even diminished them in some desperate attempt to understand them more clearly. But as always they consumed him, and he missed whatever Greistein added as his conclusion.

"I'm going to leave our guards here," Priest informed Banner. "They'll protect the property after you and your people have wrapped. Is that okay with you, Detective?"

"Dandy," Banner replied.

To Tyler, she said, "You want a cup of awful coffee?"

Tyler hesitated. "I want the bodies that belong to this blood. I want to hear that this is a confined incident. That'll close it for us, and I can get down to abusing an expense account."

She grinned. Her teeth were perfect, which he guessed pretty much described the rest of her as well. She said, "Mr. Madders, can we find someplace warm and out of this weather?"

"Yes, ma'am." Madders pointed toward a weather-beaten trailer some distance away.

Following the footprints in front of him kept Tyler's feet dryer on the way back across the yard, though Priest took long, determined strides—matching her long, determined legs—and she walked fast, a woman with purpose. Tyler wondered about that, about her company's attempt to outflank local police. Risky politics at the very least. The snow fell in wet flakes the size of quarters, practically splashing as they hit the ground.

Halfway to the distant double-wide trailer, Priest stopped and turned around. "We need to find these bodies ahead of the evening news," she announced.

It took Tyler a moment to realize that they had just joined forces. "Is that what this is about?" he shouted through the snowfall. But Priest was walking again, and she didn't answer.

CHAPTER 5

Tyler kept the convertible's top up for the long drive east to Terre Haute. In the fading light, the remnants of the storm left sugar-coated hills that reminded Tyler of the jagged Maryland countryside and the life he had so abruptly lost. He saw the legal system now as something that expected the worst of people, as more comfortable jumping to conclusions than discovering the truth. He had beaten a man nearly to death, but the guy had been a drunken child-beater and Tyler had thought of it as being in the line of duty. What hung him was that the child-beater was black and he was white, and for that he had paid with his career. Five minutes of terror and rage had erased a dozen years of dedicated service.

Repeatedly, he tugged the wheel sharply, fishtailing left or right, to prevent the icy highway from spilling the rental into the ditch. A convoy of sand trucks had failed to improve the road, and now, as temperatures dipped, the highway surface froze into a black ice peril.

Nell Priest was up ahead somewhere, her rented four-wheel-drive Suburban more stable than his convertible. Northern Union Security provided well: she had flown private into St. Louis. Tough life, the corporate expense account.

He didn't want her to get ahead of him. If the Terre Haute yard held any information about the two riders who had caused that blood-bath, he wanted it, and without any filtering on her part. Whatever relationship had quickly formed between them, it felt more like com-petition than cooperation. She had been sent to determine if there

was a fire, and if so, to quickly put it out. His role here was to
discover the source of that fire, and their two goals seemed in direct
opposition—too bad, since he liked her spark.

He had always denigrated the world of rent-a-cops and tin
badges, but now that he saw the perks of private security, he wondered if Priest might put a good word in for him with Northern
Union. With his house on the auction block, private security work
suddenly seemed okay.

Tyler's concern over the possible loss of his house grew daily.
At first, suspended without pay, and then, months later, removed
from the department, he had missed five mortgage payments and his
home was now in foreclosure. Having already lost Katrina, his girl-
friend of two years, to the calamity of the assault, having lost contact
with his colleagues, and having been stained by the racist accusations
of a headline-driven press, he now struggled to hold on to the one
last vestige of his former life: his home. His touchstone. It wasn't
so much that he needed the house; he'd sold most of his possessions—a stereo, a dining room set—so that a bachelor apartment
would do just fine. But he had fixed the place up from a weed-
encrusted, paint-peeling dilapidated wreck in a borderline neighborhood to a gentrified Cape, thanks to an incentive program from the
mayor's office that encouraged police to settle in neighborhoods
where their presence and guidance were most needed. Never mind
that his was one of only five mowed lawns on the block; he hadn't
moved there to be a hero but to get a good deal on a piece of real
estate. Never mind that his neighbors had turned their backs on him
thanks to the racial accusations that accompanied the assault. After
all the sweat and hard work, it was still his home, and it seemed
inconceivable he might lose it. With little else left in his life, he had
made holding on to his home more important than it should have
been. He knew this yet could do little to lessen its importance. He
thought perhaps that focusing on this job might free him up some.

He placed a late-night call to an attorney friend, Henry Happle,
who was leading the charge against the bank. The idea was to es-

tablish a plan of repayment for the missed mortgages and use the carrot of Tyler having gotten a job to convince the lender that he could make current and future mortgage payments—all of which was a stretch. His current job came with no contract, no agreement beyond a few days of freelance work, even though his boss, Loren Rucker, had generously offered to speak to the bank on Tyler's behalf.

In the course of the phone call, Happle attempted to sound encouraging, but it was just that, a halfhearted ruse to buoy a friend's sagging spirits, and one that left Tyler more depressed than ever.

He eased the rental car a bit faster on the glare ice, worried that Priest might conduct the worthwhile interviews ahead of him. He didn't appreciate racing her for the next lead, like a hungry journalist. It wasn't the way law enforcement was supposed to work. Besides, it had been his question to Madders, not hers, that had led them to jump into their cars: *Where would the bloody boxcar's last stop have been?* An obvious enough question—establish the point of origin. Priest certainly would have asked it if he hadn't. And now, as a result of that, here he was fishtailing along the interstate. Despite Priest's explanation for her presence, Tyler wasn't buying it. He sensed something else going on. Flying an investigator out on a private plane over the discovery of a bloody boxcar? Railroad Killer or not, it seemed unnecessary. So why *was* Priest there? he wondered. And though he didn't want to face it, he also had to wonder why Rucker had offered him the chance to pick up three or four days' work instead of sending a regular NTSB investigator. His explanation had been simple enough: Tyler's expertise set him apart. But curiosity got the better of him now and encouraged him to drive faster.

It was after 9 P.M. when he arrived at the Terre Haute yard, another massive area of rust, rails, and parked railcars. He spotted Priest's Suburban already parked. He touched the hood of the vehicle and found it barely warm. She had beaten him here by at least a full half hour.

Bothered by having to play catch-up, Tyler entered the office of Max Shast, night foreman. Nell Priest occupied one of the two free chairs, her full-length coat draped over the other. This was the first time Tyler had seen her with the coat off, and it had been hiding plenty. She wore a light gray wool suit with a dark blue silk blouse unbuttoned at the collar. The skirt was probably above the knee when she stood, because it was well above the knee when she sat. To look at her, his first reaction was cover girl or supermodel. In her early thirties, she was a little too perfect for him—fine to look at but nothing to mess with. Women that beautiful carried baggage, they had lived with too much of the wrong kind of attention. Her hair was pulled back severely from her face and held with a southwestern-style Indian-bead-and-silver clasp. She wore her watch on her left wrist, suggesting she was right-handed, and a plain silver ring on her right hand. Her wrist was so slight the watchband fit her loosely like a bangle. He figured her for a tattoo tucked in a provocative place on her body, a tiny rose maybe. He indicated her coat. She dragged it off the chair and folded it across her lap.

Shast came around and hung the outer garment on a coatrack outside. Tyler sat down. The room smelled of corn chips and coffee.

"We were just wrapping up," Priest said in what sounded to him like an imperious tone.

"How did I guess that?" Tyler asked.

She smiled her best smile.

Shast said, "Ms. Priest tells me you're looking for a pair of riders, maybe boarded here, maybe somewhere between here and St. Louis."

"One or both of whom may have subsequently been beaten pretty badly," Tyler reminded him. "A description of one or both wouldn't hurt us any."

Shast responded, "As I was explaining to the lady, boarding here is a possibility, of course, but more typically these guys jump the trains out in the countryside."

Priest said, "Mr. Shast says that it's a busy line. Lots of traffic coming through at all hours."

Shast said, "We toss some guys, sure we do. I mean, if we find 'em, we toss 'em. But it's not a top priority."

Priest added, "Dozens come through a week, even in the winter, he's guessing."

"No names, no faces," Tyler suggested, sensing a dead end. "A parade of the homeless."

"You got it."

"We need more than that," Tyler encouraged the man. "One of these guys is either dead by now or close to it. That can't be left to stand." He, Tyler, had done something awful to another man, and it was to be left to stand for all time.

Priest said, "Mr. Tyler and I are feeling the pressure of time, Mr. Shast. You can appreciate that, I'm sure. These two people in the boxcar bled badly. They need medical attention. St. Louis hospitals report no such admissions. We need some help here."

Tyler found her beauty distracting—maybe that was part of her technique. Shast, too, could barely keep his eyes off her.

"It's not like I know these guys personally," he complained. "I'm telling you: dozens, a hundred or more maybe, come through here every week."

Tyler pressed, "We believe it possible that one or both of them might have reversed direction. The storm has backlogged the St. Louis yard. Trains were moving east in three times the numbers of those moving west."

Priest added, "One or both may have traveled back through your yard."

"It's possible, but unlikely," Shast protested. "This time of year, riders spend as much time under bridges and in shelters as they do on trains. Your guys could be anywhere."

"No rail company," she stressed, for the benefit of Shast, who did not work for Northern Union but might prove sympathetic, "wants or needs the rumor mill to get going. Am I right? We have *all* suffered enough bad publicity lately. A fight between a couple of hobos is a nonevent."

This drew a heated look from Shast. "Another killer out there?"

"You see!" Nell Priest said. "People will jump to the same con-clusion, and what's important here—to both Mr. Tyler and me—is that we get to the truth of what happened in that boxcar just as quickly as possible."

Tyler understood that Northern Union would have a public re-lations nightmare if their property proved to be where a second killer had surfaced. Priest had apparently been assigned double duty: to quickly determine the extent of the crime and to keep a lid on it. In this way, their purposes were not in line. Tyler was barely worried about the public relations aspect. A crime had occurred. He wanted a suspect in custody.

Addressing Shast, Tyler said, "The NTSB, quite frankly, has a slightly larger agenda. It involves the recent derailments of several Northern Union trains." Priest stiffened. Tyler consulted her: "What's it been? One every six to eight weeks? Six over the last eighteen months? They're in the paper, on the news, all the time."

"One has *nothing whatsoever* to do with the other," Priest argued.

"We can't rule out a possible connection," Tyler replied. "The NTSB hasn't, and I doubt very much your superiors have either, Ms. Priest." He turned to Shast, using the man as his forum. "Why else fly an investigator out private?"

Shast looked confused.

"Listen, the experienced riders know to stay away from here. We catch 'em, we gotta lock 'em up. Company rules. No trespassing of any kind—it's an insurance thing. The kids too. God damn spray cans. And, on top of that, we got the junkies trying to steal anything metal not tied down."

"So you don't see that many experienced riders," Tyler stressed. "They must get on and off these trains somewhere." If whoever had fought that fight in the boxcar had reversed directions, Tyler doubted he, or they, would have been in any condition to make it too far. The survivor was probably somewhere between here and St. Louis. But it was a lot of track to cover.

"They jump the trains west of here," Shast announced. "They know enough to stay away from our yard. East of here, it's flat for a long ways, and the riders need the long grades or the ungated town crossings to slow the trains to where they can make the jump."

"Can you provide us possible locations?" Tyler inquired.

"We've been over that!" Priest protested.

"Some of us," Tyler reminded her.

"Well, I, for one, am all done here," Priest announced. She offered Shast a look that seemed to caution him against sharing much more with Tyler.

Priest stood.

"I'd like you to stay," Tyler suggested. He didn't want her gaining yet another head start on him. He felt they'd be more productive together; he needed to explain to her his own dislike of the feds, despite the fact that he was now one himself. And he didn't want her thinking she could run this investigation. His boss at NTSB, Rucker, wouldn't appreciate hearing a woman rent-a-cop had taken the case away from the federal agency running it. Besides, he wanted this case in his win column, not hers. She already had her corporate plane and Suburban. As a detective he had rarely played second fiddle. He was in no mood to start now. But she left anyway, and he watched her go. Her brash independence stirred his interest—he appreciated her nerve and resolve, though he didn't like being on the receiving end.

One eye still on the door, he said to Shast, "I need those locations. You're not going to make me beg her, are you?" Shast hesitated. Tyler raised his voice. "Are you?"

Shast also glanced toward the door.

As a cop, Tyler knew when to play his trumps. And, as a fed, those cards were larger, more powerful. "Do you want to face obstruction charges?" He didn't win Shast's full attention. "The worst *she* can do to you is make a phone call, get your hand slapped. Weigh your options carefully, Mr. Shast."

Shast nervously directed Tyler to a wall map. "There are three spots we tell all the drivers to watch. Right past the yard, as the trains are still gaining speed, and then," he said, standing and point-ing to a location on the map well outside the city, "here, where the grade slows down the longer rigs, and again here, about twenty miles on up the line before she crests and gains steam heading for St. Lou. Both those two areas have camps. Homeless camps. Transients. Rid-ers. State cops move 'em out every now and then—you should check with the staties—but those boys move right back in."

"Hobo camps."

"Riders," he corrected. "Listen, you're new to this. By the sound of it, and the *look of her,* she is, too. So, a heads up: Half those boys are crazy, and I mean clean out of their gourds. A fair percentage are on the run from people like you. They can get downright nasty. Knives mostly, but to a man, they're good with their fists. They're boozers and addicts. Losers. It's not a happy place, one of them camps. I'd go in careful, and I'd go in armed. I'd shoot first and ask questions later."

Tyler thanked the man, asking him to draw him a map with mileage. "How much of what you just gave me—the warning—did you give her?" he asked.

Shast shook his head. "She's a talker, not a listener. She wants it her way. You know the type."

Tyler left at a run, trying to stop her, to warn her.

He saw Nell Priest's taillights receding into the dark and a white plume of exhaust mixing with the cold night air. She was hoping to beat him to a suspect or a witness. He had a feeling she was going to get more than she bargained for. Considering how pretty she was, things might well get ugly.

CHAPTER

6

Tyler's Ford caught up with Priest's Suburban six miles west on a state "highway," a two-lane road that had a three-digit number for a name: 376. The moonlit countryside was cut into geometric blocks—snow-covered fields that in the growing season were devoted to feed corn. The dead stalks stuck out of the snow in regimented rows, like beard stubble.

Tyler switched on the car's interior light, so he could be seen, and pulled out into the empty oncoming lane as if passing. He drew alongside Nell Priest's huge Suburban, signaling her to pull over. She finally obliged.

Tyler climbed out and came up to her window, his breath white fog, his temper hot. "What the hell are you doing?" he blurted out, releasing some of the anxiety he'd felt in trying to catch up to her.

"Pursuing leads, same as you," she said a little too casually.

"You're going to drive into these homeless camps and just say hello, are you?" He shook his head, frustrated. "Do you think *anyone* will stick around if they see a pair of headlights approaching?" He met eyes with her. Hers were luminous. "And if you go sneaking in there, a woman, alone . . . this time of night—"

"Oh, please! Don't give me that crap!"

"—the keys to a thirty-thousand-dollar car in your purse." That seemed to register. "What the hell are you thinking?"

"I need you, do I?"

"You need backup, yes. You need a plan, certainly."

"And you think I don't have one?"

The temperature was somewhere in the thirties, but it felt below zero to Tyler. He shoved his hands deep into his pockets. "You're aware that state troopers clear these camps on a regular basis?" She nodded. "That animosities may exist over that?" She shrugged, seeming not to care. "We—yes, we—both need either a witness or someone in custody. That's what we're here for." He glanced around, feeling as if he were on the dark side of the moon. "We blow this, maybe we don't get a second chance. Maybe whatever happened in that boxcar goes unexplained. That hurts both of us, especially once the press gets it. And they may have it already, courtesy of our friend Banner, or Madders, or someone looking for a free meal or a future favor. The men in these camps are not the most stable." He banged his feet onto the icy pavement. "I suggest we team up. I suggest we get a good solid plan and do this once and do it right."

"Are you done cheerleading?" she asked.

"You know, I don't care if you botch this up for yourself," he said. "You have a nice, steady job. Cushy even. But my situation is a little more precarious. I *need* this one in the win column, okay?"

"Chester Washington," she said, revealing that she knew all about Peter Tyler and his unfortunate past. Mention of that name hit Tyler hard. He hated that she'd run a background on him. *When? During the drive from St. Louis?* And why hadn't he thought to do the same for her?

She added, "Don't you find it amazing that a black woman such as myself would even exchange words with you, much less contemplate working a raid, at night, with possible weapons involved?"

"It wasn't like that," he blurted out. The media had painted it all one way, had painted *him* as a racist, a bad cop, and a man with a violent temper. None of it true, but he would live with it forever. Her comments were proof.

He stepped back from the Suburban, wounded. He motioned for her to drive on, but he never took his eyes off her. He was struggling for his dignity.

"It's warmer in here," she said, indicating her passenger seat.

"You do whatever it is you planned on doing," he said. "Just tell me which of the two camps you're hitting. I'll stay well away, believe me. And I'll take the other one."

"Hurt your feelings, did I?" she asked in a teasing tone that infuriated him. She maintained eye contact. "Chester Washington was a pig," she said in a hoarse whisper. "What happened to you was reverse discrimination. It was unfair and inappropriate. I bet you've heard this before, but if you'd killed the son-of-a-bitch, none of this would have happened."

"I've heard it before," he confirmed.

"You don't have to tell me if you don't want to," she said.

"There's nothing to tell."

She turned up the car's heater, the cold air from the window beginning to bother her. "Get in the car," she said again. Tyler circled, lit silver by the headlights, and climbed in.

"Talk," she said.

"No, thanks."

"I'm a good listener." She added, "How many chances have you had to explain this to an African American?"

"Another time, maybe."

"These camps," she said, seeming disappointed. "How would *you* do them, exactly?"

"Get either the local law or the staties to help us with a roundup. They've done it before; they know what to expect."

"At eleven o'clock at night?"

"We at least tell them we're going in there. If they want to provide backup, fine. If not, at least they'll come looking for our bodies tomorrow morning."

"Very funny."

To his embarrassment, Tyler's authority as a federal agent failed to rally the Illinois State Police. The desk sergeant, answering his call, proved unwilling to wake up anyone in a position to do any good, and the one lieutenant Tyler reached informed him that the homeless camps were "pretty much deserted" in the winter and that, in any case, the staties seldom raided a camp with fewer than four uniforms and a supervising officer, which he didn't have to spare.

"Probably all parked under bridges with their heaters running, waiting to give out speeding tickets," Tyler complained. He was inside the Suburban now, welcoming the warmth.

"No doubt."

"And if we wait 'til morning," he added.

She interrupted him, "Another half dozen trains will have passed through. Another half dozen chances that anyone who knows anything about that boxcar will be long gone."

"Yes." Feeling frustrated, he decided to challenge her. "I take it that we're both in agreement that what happened in that boxcar was more than a fistfight."

"Two of the Railroad Killer's nine victims died at the knife. Are you aware of that?" she asked.

"Painfully."

"We never gave that to the press."

"No. But the NTSB has it."

"So we can cut the crap," she said. "We both know why we're here."

"They've got the right guy in lockup," Tyler said, attempting to sound certain.

"But a copycat couldn't possibly know about those two who were knifed. So there could have been two guys out there all along, and the Bureau has only arrested one of them."

"The point is, the focus of what we're doing—that was way too much blood in that boxcar. Given that no hospitals are reporting similar wounds, someone either died there or has bled out since." He added, "So what we're really looking for in these camps is a body."

"And someone who can tell us who did it."

"That would be nice," he agreed.

"Bleeders draw attention," she said.

"Or they wander into a cornfield with a pint and they freeze to death," he said.

"The victim does. The killer climbs back into a freight car, climbs back into his own bottle, and that's the end of it."

"In which case we've got a killer riding the rails," he pointed out, "and a body that's freezing solid, if it hasn't already."

She informed him, "The question you failed to ask back there at the yard was whether or not car eleven-thirty-six had been inspected there or not. If it had been, and it was found clean and empty of riders, then we know whoever boarded did so between the depot and the St. Louis yard. That increases the chances of discovering a potential witness at one of these camps."

"You give seminars, do you?" he asked a little bitterly, because she was right, he had in fact failed to ask. She had rushed him, which had been her intention—and he hated the fact that she might have thrown him off his game.

"A little upset, are we?"

"What you failed to take into account, Ms. Priest, was the weather," he advised. "Ahead of that storm, temperatures across the Midwest were in the forties. According to the forensics team, that blood froze on contact. The storm hit this area the night before— ergo, the fight, or whatever happened in that boxcar, also happened the night before, *after* the temperatures had dropped. The storm is a real slow mover—that's why the big dump. So, whether I asked that question or not, I figure we're in the general area of where whatever happened, happened: four to six hours by slow freight train out of St. Louis."

She looked impressed. The way she fiddled with the car's heater, he thought she was trying to think of a comeback. She asked, "Would you have killed him if your partner hadn't stopped you?"

The car's interior suddenly felt the size of a Volkswagen bug. Once again he saw she'd done her homework. He fished for the door handle. He'd had enough. He heard the pop of the automatic door locks. She wanted an answer.

"Leave it alone," he said. He popped the locks back open. She popped them shut.

"I've got a little problem with enclosed spaces," he confessed. He popped the door open and climbed out of the Suburban. The cold cut through his clothes.

She put down the window and spoke loudly, "I'd like to know about your temper before I enter those camps with you."

"The man was slamming a seven-month-old baby girl against a wall, turning her skull into sponge cake. He'd done it before, and we knew it—the doctors, us, even the girl's mother—but no one could prove it. The mother was too afraid of him to bring charges. And there I was—on surveillance. The mother had agreed to let us wire the house. My partner and I *heard* that sound—her head, those cries." He felt breathless, a little dizzy.

He couldn't see Priest; he saw only those long dark arms clutching that little girl and driving her against the wall. The stream of blood running from her ear, her eyes so filled with tears he couldn't see them. The child's sweaty head. He looked up and saw the stars. All he ever needed was a little space. He recovered and stepped farther away from the car.

She climbed out, came around the front, arms crossed in the headlights against the cold. "You okay?" she asked him.

"Guilt," he answered. "Or at least that's what the staff psychologist says."

"If you're putting me on . . . ."

"I lost my shield, my car, I'm about to lose my house. You did your homework. You probably know all that. So you might think twice about reminding me of my situation. I think I'm pretty much aware of it."

She asked, "Are you going to puke, or can we get back in the car?"

"We go into the camp without headlights. We use the Suburban because of the snow. We hike the last quarter mile or so. We roust whoever we find. Are you carrying?"

She nodded, the shadows and light playing across her features like fire.

"You have a permit for Illinois, or only Missouri?"

She told him, "We have agreements with everyone but Louisiana. I'm licensed."

"So if one of these bozos runs, I'll pursue. You'll get your back against a tree and your weapon out."

"And if two run, I'll pursue the other one," she clarified.

"Fresh snow," he reminded her. "We can track them. We don't need to turn this into more than it is."

"If that statie you talked to is right, then there's no one out there anyway."

"He's not right," said the ex-policeman. "When are the cops ever right?"

It won a grin. She asked, "They gave you how many days—on the taxpayers' payroll—to make a determination on this?"

"Three."

"Typical government excess. If we strike out here, there isn't much to follow."

"More time, if needed," he informed her. He felt better now. He didn't know if it was the air or this woman.

"Park that thing somewhere it won't get stuck," she stated.

Tyler headed back toward the convertible, wondering what he'd gotten himself into. With the state police as backup, he would have felt a lot safer.

They walked down a farm road through a cold slice of a midnight moon and the spindly silhouettes of trees, leaving the Suburban far behind. The car's ignition key was hidden inside Tyler's sock, placed there on the off chance they lost whatever confrontation was ahead and that Tyler's pockets were searched. The key lay alongside his ankle, cool and scratchy, where it was unlikely to be discovered. If things went wrong, they didn't want the Suburban stolen. It was cold going on colder, and Tyler's Ford was two miles away.

The tree-covered terrain rose to their right, and it was here that the long-haul freight trains slowed, giving riders a chance to jump them. Tyler expected the camp to be close to the tracks but on level ground. Nell picked up the smell of the burning wood first. Tyler switched off his flashlight—they would navigate by moonlight; they didn't want to be seen.

Priest was also the first to pick up the yellow light of the distant campfire—an oil drum stuffed with broken limbs and flaming like a smokestack fire. They approached in silence, the air so still that the crackling of the fire sounded incredibly near. They began to detect voices through the woods and then, finally, less than a hundred yards off, the faint silhouettes of four figures standing close to the upright barrel. Tyler pointed at her and to the right; he pointed to himself and indicated the left.

Far off in the distance, he heard a train approaching. Tyler pointed to his ear, and Priest nodded. He gave her a thumbs-up, and he took off at a run. He glanced back to see Priest running as well. They would use the sound of the train for cover.

The clatter of the train grew. Tyler again glanced over at Priest and ran faster to synchronize their arrivals.

The close cry of the train charged his system. These four hobos could be harmless, or they could be wanted men. His lungs stung with the cold.

The train roared past.

One of the homeless looked up toward the train. His head tracked left, and he spotted Tyler. The man said something sharply to the others, turned, and ran, his attention on Tyler and not on the woman in the trees who stood nearly directly in his path.

Tyler shouted, "Federal agent!" his voice lost to the roar of the train.

Priest stepped out of the shadows, her gun raised, and the one attempting to escape dove into the snow, face down, his hands already on the back of his head.

The others turned, looked around, and in drunken contemplation took in Priest and Tyler. They seemed to be callused to such raids, shaking their heads and chatting among themselves.

Tyler spotted four discarded cans of Colt 45. None of the recent snow had collected on them. "Federal agent," he repeated. The haggard men wore multiple layers of ragged clothing. All three had teeth missing and streams of mucus frozen beneath their noses. *A matched set,* Tyler thought. He'd seen plenty of similar homeless on the streets of D.C. and in Metro's lockup.

"You lock us up, you'd be doing us a favor," their spokesman said.

"Some questions is all," Tyler answered. He lowered his weapon and approached the three. Her gun aimed at the man's head, Priest patted down her captive, removed a pocketknife, stood him up, and led him over to the fire. One by one, Tyler singled out one of the three and patted him down for weapons. All three carried knives. None were bloody.

"We're going to divide you up into pairs," Tyler announced. "A couple questions, and we're all done." None of the men showed signs of a fight, nor did he see even trace amounts of blood on their clothing—and there was no doubting that *any* of this clothing had been worn for a long time. They smelled ripe.

Priest pushed her guy up to the fire barrel. Tyler studied the nearby shelters—some of cardboard, some plastic sheeting. "How many others?" he asked the spokesman.

"One. Not doing so great."

"Passed out?" Tyler asked.

"Going on dead," answered the toothless man.

That won both Tyler's and Priest's attention. "Hurt?" Tyler asked.

"You could say that," answered the shortest of the three. "A nigger," he said, eyeing Priest. "In that first lean-to over there."

All four were white. They looked to be between forty and sixty.

"I've got them," Priest said. "Go have a look."

Tyler headed over to an arrangement of fogged plastic sheets, some twine, and at least one large truck tire. There was a lump inside, vaguely the shape and size of a human being. It was buried beneath jackets, a dark tarpaulin, and a torn orange flotation vest that was stenciled in silver with USCG—Coast Guard. Tyler kicked the lump, trying to wake it. He kicked again, and the lump moved and groaned. "Fuck off," came a weakened, sickly voice.

Erring on the side of precaution, and not trusting his source, Tyler inspected the three other makeshift structures and found them empty. No surprises. Five men, in a camp that in the summer might have held three times that.

He heard Priest begin to question the other three. Tyler rousted the lump—he smelled of urine and something much, much worse. "Get up!" Tyler ordered. The lump groaned. He didn't want to search this one, didn't want to touch him.

"Can't get up. Bad foot," the man complained, still face down, straining to see Tyler.

"Bad?" Tyler asked.

"Cut it."

Cut? Tyler wondered. *As in knife blade? As in bleeding?* "Cut it how?" was all that came out of him. He tried to get a decent look, but the lump wasn't cooperating. Tyler's heart was somewhere in the middle of his throat and straining to get out. He had a feeling he was looking down at one of their two suspects.

Tyler called out loudly to the others. "How'd this guy hurt his foot? Or did he show up here with it that way?"

"Chopping wood," one of the drunken three called out from the fire.

"Was not!" the shorter man objected. "Someone done it to him!" he shouted.

Any kind of bad cut could explain the excessive blood in the boxcar. Maybe Priest was to get her wish; maybe this was going to be a brief one after all.

Tyler nudged the lump again. "Who did this to you?" He toed the layers of covering and flipped them off the man's leg. The odor was nauseating. His stomach retched, and he nearly vomited. This, from a homicide cop with a decade of dead bodies under his belt. Dead was sometimes easier than living.

Priest and the others stood in a tight group. She appeared to be shining a penlight on something in her hand. She glanced over her shoulder—had she sensed him?—and turned her back just slightly toward him. *Was she blocking his view?* he wondered. *Or trying to stay warm?* When she turned again, the penlight and whatever had been in her hand were put away.

The lower extremity of the man's left leg looked half frozen, swollen and busting out of itself, like an overcooked sausage. The pant leg was torn to accommodate the swelling, but the boot remained on, split down the middle of the toes in a horrid, blackened wedge. If anything matched the carnage they'd found in the boxcar, this foot was it.

Tyler stepped away and took in some fresh air. He approached Priest and signaled her away from the fire drum. She stepped off a few feet so they could speak, but she never took her eyes off the four, even as Tyler spoke.

"Could be our boy," he announced.

"Not according to our witnesses. They're claiming his injury happened here."

"Covering is all."

"Maybe," she said.

"What was that," he asked, "you and the light?"

The fire flickered across her face, and for a moment she seemed frozen—and not by the cold air. She answered, "My ID? Just now? I was trying to convince them that I wasn't any kind of cop, just a security guard accompanying you out here. That they could tell me stuff without worrying about getting arrested." She added, "I showed them my corporate creds, but I'm not so convinced they can read anything beyond 'No Deposit, No Return.' "

He liked that.

"Guy's foot is cleaved in half. Could easily explain the boxcar."

"They say it happened here," she repeated. "In camp."

"Chopping wood, I suppose," he proposed to her.

"That's right."

Raising his voice, Tyler addressed the four. "So where's the axe?"

The bewildered men looked between themselves. Their spokesman said unconvincingly, "Snow musta covered it."

"Sure it did," Tyler said to Priest. Indicating the shelter, Tyler said, "We can't leave him." He added, "He's dying, going on dead. Besides, he'd like a beer."

"You're kidding, right? You want to baby-sit this guy?"

"I want answers from him. How his foot got that way, and who did it to him. Having him alive to give us those answers would help."

She said, "So call him an ambulance."

"You think they'll prescribe a six-pack of beer?" He added, "That beer is the quickest way to our answers, and you know it. Or would you rather wait around in an emergency room all night while they clean up that wound and knock him out with sedatives?"

"We are *not* taking this guy out in the Suburban," she protested.

"I'll drive. I'll even clean it up, if need be," he suggested.

"And if he dies on us?"

"He's not going to die on us. He's made it this far."

"I don't know, Tyler. An ambulance is the right way to go."

He shrugged and said, "Then you get what you can get out of

the Four Stooges. Visitors to the camp? How many? When did club-foot arrive? Let's find where he did the foot with the axe, and let's find some blood, or the axe, or *anything* to support it."

Surprising him, she reported immediately, "They all four claim to have arrived just this morning; one from Cincinnati, one from Pittsburgh. The others wouldn't say from where. Found that guy, just the way you did. They're all headed south—to warmth. They heard the storm had closed the westbound lines. They're holed up here until tomorrow, by which point they're sure the tracks will be open again."

"How much of it do you believe?" he asked, impressed by her.

"They want to distance themselves from that guy," she said pointing back to the lean-to. "Maybe they did it to him. Maybe they don't know anything about it."

"Some kind of life," he said.

"You got that right," she agreed.

"Try them again."

"Or you could," she suggested.

"Which leaves you helping our guest into your car."

"He's not going in the Suburban," she repeated, less convinced.

Tyler indicated the shelter. "Your call."

"I'll try them again," she agreed.

"Good choice," he said. He walked back over toward the wounded man, wondering if a six-pack would do the trick.

Tyler drove Priest's Suburban so that she didn't have to suffer the smell. She had made no mention of car insurance this time around, no protest to his driving. He had both the front and backseat heaters going full blast and all four of the Suburban's windows down in an effort to dilute the stink. She followed in the Ford, a quarter of a mile or so back.

The lump was now a person—or what remained of one.

"You got a drink?" the man asked. He was lying across the backseat.

"I'll get you a couple beers," Tyler replied, "but I need a little information first." He put the driver's window up a little, in order to hear the guy. "We're heading to a hospital."

"I don't want no hospital."

"You want the beer?"

"You a cop?"

"A fed. NTSB. Transportation agent." If he misrepresented himself, then he might later lose whatever information this guy might be able to provide.

"Just let me out here, would you?"

"No, I don't think so. I'm buying you a drink. Remember? But we gotta talk a minute."

"The hell you say."

"How'd you do that to your leg?"

"Chopping wood. Right there in camp." The man sounded tentative.

"When?"

"Two days ago."

"Two days ago?" Tyler questioned. "The doctors can confirm this, you know?"

"Maybe three days ago. I been sleeping a lot."

That didn't fit with the boxcar timing. If the wound proved that old, then this guy hadn't been part of the bloodbath. "There's a gas station in a couple miles," Tyler said. "Passed it on the way here. Maybe I stop for that beer there, if you're being cooperative."

"Yeah?"

"I'd have to believe your story," Tyler said. "And I don't."

"You *are* a cop, aren't you?"

"I'm a fed. I told you." He waited. "You want that beer or not?"

He informed Tyler, "The guy needed to make an example. I was the example."

"What does that mean?"

"He was asking questions that none of us wanted to answer."

"Who was?"

"Big prick. I thought he was a cop, but shit, even a cop wouldn't put a hatchet through your foot for wising off."

Tyler took a moment to digest that. "What questions? Who was he asking?"

"Wouldn't mind that beer about now."

"It's another mile or so." Tyler repeated, "What kind of questions?"

"Wanted to know 'bout some Latino. Didn't even offer a bottle or nothing. What the hell is that about? Since when do we rat out a fellow rider . . . for nothing?"

"What about this Latino?"

"How the hell should I know? He put that hatchet to me because I was black. Wasn't about to hit no white boy."

"Who else was in camp with you?"

"They're all long gone. Believe it. A rider gets hurt like I did, you split. Plain and simple."

"There were four others."

"New guys. The small one—he don't like people of color. Kicked the shit outta me when I was just lying there. The others? They just watched him do it."

"The big guy. The guy who did this. White?"

"Damn straight. Lumberjack, he was. Wide as this car. And he weren't no rider, though he came off a westbound freight and wanted us to think he was."

"Why do you say that . . . about his not being a rider?"

"Believe me, you know. He was one of you, not one of us."

Tyler pulled into the gas station and bought a six-pack of Bud. The guy hit the first can too hard, especially lying down as he was, and threw up before Tyler had the car moving.

Tyler ran around the car and heaped snow onto the pile of vomit and got it out of the car as quickly as possible. The wounded man had pulled himself up on his elbow, enough elevation to work more of that beer down his throat. "Sorry 'bout that," he said, burping foully into the enclosed space.

Nell Priest wouldn't be happy about the hygiene. But Tyler was positively beaming. They had a witness and descriptions of two men, a lumberjack and a Latino.

According to the forensic tech, two men had battled in that box-car. Tyler finally had a pair of suspects. And this time it would be him telling Priest, not the other way around.

CHAPTER
7

Alvarez, sitting in the plane's window seat, row twenty-seven, would never have been mistaken for a hobo. For the flight from Chicago's O'Hare to New York's JFK, he wore fresh jeans, a black T-shirt, and a thin, black leather jacket that didn't quite help enough against the cold. Only his boots remained the same—and these he had cleaned of the blood while changing in a bus station's men's room. He wore a pair of Ray-Bans, his face trained away from the other passengers and out the small, cold window. He would not be remembered on this flight.

The fresh clothes had been recovered from a duffel/backpack left checked a week earlier at Chicago's Greyhound station. The bag now carried the blue jeans and the red-and-gray flannel shirt he'd stolen. He'd thought better of disposing of those in the bus terminal's trash—no reason to leave the bastards easy evidence to follow. He had soaked his own bloody clothes in lawn mower gasoline from the garage and burned them in a hole dug in the snow, deep in the neighboring forest. He'd stayed with that small fire until every last thread had burned. He was taking as few chances as possible.

A second snowstorm had tracked in from Canada and had buried Chicago, less than twenty-four hours after St. Louis had been hit. This most recent storm had delayed his flight three hours. Hours spent anxiously with one eye on Airport-CNN and the other on the busy concourse. He'd hardly slept. He had a massive headache, and he was hungry. If he took the Carey bus from JFK to Grand Central and then the Lexington subway down to Bleeker, if everything went right—no more delays—maybe he could still make his meeting with McClaren, a meeting he needed if he were to pull off his larger plan.

No rest for the wicked, he thought, an ironic smile playing over his slightly bruised face as he gazed out at the endless clouds. There had been a time in his life when that vast sameness would have felt peaceful. But no more. He saw only lies heaped upon lies. Butchers in blue suits and boardrooms. Anything but peaceful. Now he, too, had contributed to that lack of peace—he had single-handedly derailed and destroyed a half dozen freight trains. The news reported them like clockwork, attributing them to maintenance problems or driver error.

But the biggest prize of all was yet to come. And for this, he hungered.

It seemed out of context to be meeting an Irishman in Chinatown, but then again, this was New York. Alvarez climbed out of the Bleeker street subway station carrying the duffel bag, which he knew would be a problem. He, and it, would be thoroughly searched. He'd been warned that Randy McClaren and his Irish hooligans took no chances. Precaution had kept them alive this long.

McClaren built bombs. Alvarez's deposit had been wired weeks earlier; the remainder of the fee had to be transmitted once Alvarez had the device in hand. The joys of the Internet.

Taking precautions to ensure he wasn't followed, Alvarez walked eight blocks into the heart of Chinatown and located the address he'd received by placing a phone call from Grand Central. He climbed four flights, pain and fatigue weighing him down. He was met in the hallway by one of McClaren's soldiers—a kid of eighteen or nineteen with already lifeless eyes. The delivery of the explosive— postponed twice by McClaren's people for "security reasons"—was critical to Alvarez's plans. His heart beat wildly as he approached the top of the stairs. McClaren's expertise was undetectable explosives—no dog could sniff them, no machine sense them—essential to Alvarez and well worth the exorbitant price. With this small bomb, he'd have the final piece to derail Northern Union's prized F-A-S-T Track bullet train, a passenger train. He hoped that just the threat of that derailment would prove enough to finally win the truth, as well as a public apology from the company's CEO, William Goheen. Eighteen months of hard work was about to pay off. McClaren's explosives were crucial to his task.

He had been right to worry about the duffel bag. McClaren's child-goons forced Alvarez to leave it out in the hall under the watchful eye of the skinny kid who'd met him at the door. In the first room off the hall he saw the guys standing guard with their guns right out in the open—mean-looking weapons.

One of the guards ran a wand over him like the ones at airports and then forced him to empty his pockets and remove his boots, which had steel shanks in them. Alvarez walked in stocking feet.

This first room was a pigsty: chipped paint, a bare bulb, and steel-reinforced windows, this latter feature an obvious recent modification, and one that loaned the room the look of a jail. Scattered on the floor were pizza boxes with cigarette butts, beer bottles, and scores of empty Coke cans. The place smelled sour. He saw no TV and only upside-down plastic milk crates for chairs. Alvarez was hustled to a door, upon which was written in spray paint: TURN YOUR CELL PHONE OFF NOW! NO CELL PHONES OR PAGERS BEYOND THIS DOOR!

When Alvarez entered, McClaren was typing at one of three computers, his head down, his shoulders arched.

The room looked like an electronics lab, or a computer repair shop. Large sheets of brown Peg-Board occupied two of the walls, supporting wires of every description. The air smelled of solder and cigarettes, acrid and bitter. A trio of wooden doors placed on top of file cabinets held the computers and created a U-shaped office area for McClaren, directly in front of Alvarez. To his left, behind the computer where McClaren sat, a cluttered workbench filled the corner.

The thugs pulled the door shut. Alvarez heard himself be locked in. He took notice of two pipe bombs rigged on the inside of this door. Alvarez felt out of his element. The only sound came from a very small TV that ran CNN. A black rubber mat, with a wire running to the wall, fronted the workbench.

Randy McClaren had blown off the last three fingers of his left hand as a teenager in the IRA, and yet he was able to work his thumb and index finger so that he typed with dexterity. He did not look up. He spoke with a thick brogue. "Wanking Internet, I'm telling you. God's good and gracious gift to his Christian Soldiers. Pass information in an instant, trade stocks, check the bank, and no fucking FBI listening in." He turned and faced his guest, his freckles and carrottop hair making him look younger than his thirty years. But the coldness in his vivid green eyes left little doubt that he'd seen many horrors.

"The FBI will be listening in one of these days," Alvarez warned.

McClaren typed the last few characters and clicked the mouse. "You're new, so I'll tell you this, but only once. You checked out or you wouldn't be here. Doesn't matter, mate: don't *ever* come here, don't *ever* attempt to make contact with me without calling your friend. I'll kill you if you do."

"I'm prepared to make payment," Alvarez said, his throat dry. He was intimidated, even afraid. He had no idea what was in this room, but he had a feeling it was a powder keg.

"Was just checking the accounts." McClaren nodded toward the computer. "Have a seat."

"Are we all set then?" Alvarez inquired.

McClaren indicated a small gray box. He handed it to Alvarez, who nearly dropped it.

McClaren nodded. "Nervous?"

"Uncomfortable," Alvarez admitted. "Explosives are new to me."

"Mine are safe. Nothing to worry about."

Nonetheless, Alvarez felt no safer. This wasn't his world. He'd been a science teacher, a father. Bomb makers? He wanted out of there.

McClaren stood and indicated his seat. Alvarez sat down, spent a minute at the keyboard, and electronically transferred the remainder of the money due.

"We wait for the e-mail," McClaren said. Confirmation could take anywhere from five minutes to an hour or more. He glanced down at his socks. He wanted his boots back.

Alvarez studied the small polished aluminum box. It was about the size of a cigarette pack. "It's enough explosive to break that steel pin I described?" Alvarez questioned. This was the only time his plans included explosives.

"The pin you described is most commonly used in high-speed train couplers, ehh, Laddie? Not bank-vault hinge pins, as you wanted me to believe." His information stunned Alvarez: he had figured out the purpose of the explosive. McClaren warned, "If they catch you, they'll ask you where you got it, and I could care less what you tell them as long as I'm not mentioned. If I am mentioned, Laddie, a box this same size will be shoved up your ass and detonated."

The e-mail notification chime rang on the computer. McClaren leaned over the keyboard and liked what he saw.

Alvarez slipped the box into his front pocket. McClaren caught this out of the corner of his eye. "You be careful of those switches. First the toggle, then five seconds, then the button. You'll have ten minutes exactly, from the time you push the button. You can't stop it. And if that magnetic connection is broken, she'll blow as well."

"Got it," Alvarez declared.

"Get out of here."

Alvarez wanted his boots back. He wanted away from there.

McClaren would take his own head off someday—a bad wire, a missed switch.

Ten minutes later he was walking the streets of New York, a box of undetectable explosives in his pocket. He had work to do on the computer board he was assembling, and he needed the final details of the bullet train test run. He intended one last derailment as a diversion before the bullet train. There was much to do.

If he threw those two switches, the box in his pocket would blow, taking his own life, along with a couple dozen pedestrians.

New York. What a city.

CHAPTER

8

Riding a bicycle uptown on Madison Avenue in December, Alvarez both sweated and shivered as he kept his eye on the cell phone antenna on the black Town Car he was following. He pedaled hard at times, managing to stay within a half block of the car, grateful for New York's bumper-to-bumper evening traffic. The fact that she was riding in a Town Car confirmed for him that this was a business trip. When Daddy sent for her, it was always a stretch limousine, sometimes, an extended stretch. *Never* a Town Car.

After five hours of sleep he'd left his loft apartment with a feeling of destiny swelling in his chest. McClaren's box could help him to roll the bullet train; this woman, and her secrets, could cripple William Goheen. He had designed it as a one-two punch, and so he followed her, intent on gaining access.

He'd stopped at St. Bart's Church, lit three candles—one for each of his departed—and said prayers for thirty minutes before taking confession, where he had informed the father only that he had "a bad thing" planned, and though he would not seek forgiveness, nor absolution, that it relieved him to speak of it even in the abstract. The priest had given him twenty-five Hail Marys and some scripture in St. John to review, small penance for the deeds to come.

The bike was a brutal choice in this weather but a useful tool given that there was no cab driver to remember his face. A bicycle could jump a sidewalk and head the wrong way down a one-way street or quickly switch lanes in almost any traffic. At red lights, he could jump off and cross with pedestrians. On the streets of New York, a bike was the vehicle of choice for surveillance.

The Town Car turned right on 64th Street.

Alvarez followed, pedaling hard and pulling closer. That was another plus: cabbies and limo drivers paid little attention to such cockroaches in their rearview mirrors. Bike riders were nonpeople.

Alvarez caught sight of the back of her head through the Town Car's rear window—blonde hair tonight, her own, not a wig, parted so that one side fell to her ear, the other to her neck. Always a different look. Always provocative. She could get a man's juices going from fifty yards. Always just enough makeup to conceal her real face. If she had been a spy instead of a call girl, she could have brought down governments. As it was, she brought down Japanese businessmen—brought them down to their knees, begging, as they volunteered fifteen hundred dollars an hour.

Alvarez needed a name and a phone number. The two hundred dollars in the pocket of his jeans was for the driver of the Town Car.

Upper East Side, the city's old-money neighborhood—her John had to be some tycoon or dot-com dad here on a business trip; the Japanese favored the hotels near Times Square.

This was only the third time he'd followed her like this. The first had been a black-tie affair, and he'd thought she was simply attending, not working—but he'd stayed with her *after* the event. Her two-hour visit to the Essex House, the somewhat shaky gait to her wide-legged walk as she'd left the hotel, picked up there by the same Town Car and delivered to her doorstep, had suggested otherwise. The second time the same car again was involved; she was delivered to a Japanese half her height and twice her age. All doubt disappeared.

Stopped behind the Town Car at Park, waiting for a light, he briefly glanced back at the line of traffic, propelled by a nagging, nervous feeling. He mentally clicked off images of the string of cars behind him, including two city cabs, a Mercedes coupe, a Lexus

SUV, a light blue four-door that had seen better days, and a green Ford Taurus.

The traffic light changed to green.

The Town Car turned onto 63rd and pulled over in front of a small luxury hotel, the Powell, where a uniformed doorman came around and opened the door for the stunning young woman. She carried an oversized purse—no telling what sex toys might lie inside. The doorman held the hotel's door open for her and sized her up as she passed. Alvarez marked the time: 10:09 P.M. The Town Car waited out traffic and then backed up to claim a parking space—a rarity in this neighborhood. To check if he'd been followed, Alvarez circled the block and came back up 63rd.

He walked the bike up the sidewalk on the west side of Park and rounded the corner, back onto 63rd, the Powell's flags a half block ahead. He stopped, leaned against a wall, and studied each and every car in sight. Although there were plenty of cabs to confuse him, he didn't see the Lexus, nor the Mercedes, nor any of the others he had registered when that sense of dread had hit him at the stoplight. Convinced he was okay, he walked the bike up the sidewalk, preparing himself for the bribe he had in mind.

The Town Car was empty. The driver apparently had been given time off. Alvarez cursed himself for being so paranoid. He had wasted several minutes circling and scouting 63rd. Now he would have to wait for the driver's return.

He glanced up and down the block, searching for a place to light. The narrow street, lined with immaculately maintained four-story brownstones that were fronted by high wrought-iron fences, spoke of the wealth and privilege of the Upper East Side. Opposing rows of mature maple trees, their bare branches like delicate pen-and-ink drawings, offered an overhead canopy. An old man with a stoop walked his Dalmatian. An elegantly dressed couple strolled arm in arm, chatting privately; she carried Prada while he wore a cashmere overcoat.

The Lake House, a restaurant attached to the Powell, offered an opportunity, but Alvarez didn't want to risk that the woman might be flirting at the bar with her client. He couldn't afford to be seen by her. He spotted another restaurant directly across the street. It appeared crowded but worth a try. He walked the bike across, slipping between car bumpers, and chained it to an ALTERNATE PARKING signpost. He shed his zippered sweatshirt, exposing a more stylish, Italian black leather jacket. Spotting two empty tables through the window, he headed inside.

Murals and mirrors. The smell of olive oil and freshly baked bread. He checked and confirmed a good view of the Town Car, hoping he might be here but a few minutes.

The women inside, the waitresses as well as the patrons, all appeared under thirty, very Euro. Maybe employees from the chic boutiques just around the corner on Madison. Maybe this was just another one of those New York anomalies—chic and trendy in a starched-collar neighborhood. Alvarez's Mediterranean looks drew some attention as he moved to a window seat with a view of the Town Car. A pale young woman with free-weight arms, nut-hard nipples, and Stairmaster buttocks led Alvarez to the banquette, passing him a wine list.

"Your server will be right with you." She sounded German, not French. The Stairmaster did its stuff as she retreated.

With his attention divided between the Town Car and the front door of the Powell, Alvarez missed his server's introduction.

"Excuse me, sir." A creamy, youthful voice, this time with a hint of Paris in the inflections. He glanced in her direction but only briefly. Pale skin. Red lips. Haunting gray-green eyes. Black top. Black pants. Black shoes. Looking back out the window, he ordered a Pinot Noir that she quoted at eight dollars a glass. He looked up at her once again, his mind working to place her—for suddenly he knew that face and, most of all, that cream-filled voice. But from where and how? His excellent memory briefly failed him. And now, as he sat there awaiting the wine's delivery and the driver's return to the Town Car, half lost in the past, half consumed by the present, he found himself straining to place her. What was she doing there, inside his thoughts, occupying him like an unsolved puzzle? He wanted her out.

He blocked her out temporarily, concentrating on the hotel and the black car across the street.

"Are you staying at the Powell?" His waitress again, delivering the warm bread and olive oil. He found her accent enchanting and knew full well it was her voice he recognized, more so than her looks. That told him he'd known her when they'd both been younger, and suddenly he placed her. He didn't want her placing him, and yet he was a man intent on proving himself in all situations. He couldn't stop himself from saying her name. "Mariam?" he questioned. "Marianne?"

"Jillian," she answered tentatively.

"Umberto. Bert," he abbreviated, returned to his college days. "Fredo and I—we were roommates. I came to your family home a couple of—"

"Oh, my God!" she exclaimed.

"You were . . . smaller . . . younger—"

"I was . . . twelve!"

"Much younger," he said, once again dividing his attention between her and the Town Car. "You live here? In the city?"

"God bless rent control."

"Fredo?" he asked. "Belgium, isn't it?"

She nodded. "Married. Three children."

He lost her then. Lost the whole room, the street, the hotel. Lost everything to memories of the twins and a life not too far removed. A nearby server banged two plates together, and Alvarez returned.

She grinned. Her hair was jet black and cut with bangs like a Chinese doll. Her two front teeth were stained faintly yellow, indicating a smoker. He wondered if her eyes could possibly be that

shade of green, or if she wore pigmented contact lenses. A silver
charm bracelet adorned her left ankle. She had long, elegant feet. In
the last eighteen months, he had learned to quickly assess people this
way. He looked for lies. He looked for *them*—the Northern Union
Security agents like the one in the boxcar.

She caught him staring back out the window. He explained,
vamping for a lie of his own, "My wife—my ex-wife—" he was
already off to a lousy start, "went into the Powell a few minutes ago.
Dressed to the nines."

"You're following her?"

"Pitiful, isn't it?" He hoped this might send her running, angry
at himself for identifying himself to anyone. Anyone! To his surprise,
this seemed to have the opposite effect.

Jillian said, "Let me catch these other tables. I'll be right back."
Harmless enough words, but her eyes betrayed a definite attempt to
maintain the connection with him. She had been twelve going on
twenty, as he recalled. She'd had an obvious crush on him that
amused her older brother but had made Alvarez uncomfortable, because even at that age she'd been too much woman and too little
child. Women of all types, all ages, were attracted to his dark looks.
"It's the charisma, not the skin tone," his wife, Juanita, had once
told him. She claimed that he charmed women simply walking into
a room and smiling, and that for the sake of their marriage he had
to learn to control it. Control it, he had. Through eleven years he
had never entertained a single unfaithful thought—at least he chose
to remember it that way. These last two he'd been celibate, focused,
even consumed, with the truth. Settlement. Restitution. His chest
knotted and he caught himself tightly gripping the stem of the wine
glass. He was ten years older than Jillian, he reminded himself. He
had no interest in women. And yet he had to force himself to relax,
amazed it could be so difficult.

But he tensed again, this time Jillian's sultry eyes the farthest
thing from his mind. What caught his attention was the uniformed
limousine driver approaching the Town Car. Alvarez left a ten-dollar

bill on the table and hurried for the door. He cut across traffic and caught up to the man just as he unlocked the driver's door.

Alvarez fished out the two hundred dollars and gripped it in his fist. Distracted, he caught sight of Jillian standing by his table and cupping her hands to see out the glass.

"Excuse me," Alvarez said, a world away from his hobo existence.

The driver stood up, his dark eyes evaluating Alvarez, who had donned a pair of sunglasses. "Help you?" He sounded Eastern European.

Alvarez took the driver by the arm and forced the two hundred into his fist. The driver resisted, until he saw it was money.

"Listen," Alvarez said. "It's really simple. I saw your . . . passenger, and if I read it right . . . then you can help me. It's an escort service, right?"

The driver attempted to hand back the money. "Hey, buddy—"

"No, no, no! You keep the money whether I'm right or wrong. If I'm right, you have a first name for her and a phone number I can call. That's all I ask. No addresses, nothing personal." Alvarez glanced over his shoulder at the hotel, as if longing for her. "Her manager. Whatever. I don't need anything more than that."

The driver considered. "I just drive them. I don't know their business. It's my business *not* to know their business."

"So make an exception," Alvarez said. He grabbed the man by the hand and made him squeeze that money. "Special circumstances."

"It's an exclusive service, my friend."

"I can tell that just by looking," Alvarez replied.

"You need references—referrals. It's *very* exclusive."

"Mr. Takimachi's my referral," Alvarez pressed. He'd done his legwork. Takimachi was the man she had entertained the second time he'd followed her.

"I do not know this name," the driver lied. "Besides," he said, burdened by a tongue that didn't appreciate English, "if you have a referral, then you have everything you need."

"Mr. Takimachi does not like to share. Not *that,* anyway," Alvarez said, indicating the hotel. "Who can blame him?"

The driver simply stared.

"Please," Alvarez pleaded. "So sue me for being male. My name is Cortez," he lied. "I'm a conqueror."

The driver grinned at that. "You request Gail," he said. He recited an Internet address.

"No phone number?"

"You request Gail. Mention Takimachi. They will e-mail back to you."

"The Internet?"

"These people are careful," the driver said. He added, "You should be, too."

Alvarez flushed with heat, set off by the warning. He didn't need to compound his problems. He nodded, glad for the heads up.

He had accomplished what he had come to do. Even so, in a moment of weakness, he returned to the restaurant and his table by the window. It took him a moment to realize the glass of wine had been cleared.

"You're back," Jillian said. A coy grin.

Indicating the hotel, he said, "She's not my ex-wife."

"Okay."

"She's a woman who owes me something. Her father, actually ... The details aren't important. He'd rather put me in the hospital than repay that debt." He invented this as he went along, wondering if any of it sounded credible and reminding himself that short lies worked better than longer ones. "I've just discovered I'm being watched. The father, I think. I can't go home tonight."

"That's understandable." She seemed to be looking through him, to have expected something like this from him. It left Alvarez feeling disconcerted.

"I'll take a room ... in a hotel, but running into you just now ... I'd love the company, a friendly face, if you're not busy after you're done here." He went for broke; he lowered his sleepy gaze, wandering from her eyes to her ankles. "Would you have any interest in that?" He wasn't sure why he lied, why he wanted the company—in celebration perhaps. He'd had two major successes. He tried not to face the real reason he pursued her—if caught in the next week, he would never have such company again.

"My roommate and I, we usually go clubbing."

"Whatever."

"I won't let you take a hotel room," she informed him. "That's ridiculous."

The couple at the next table were listening in. Alvarez gave the guy a dismissive look and won back their privacy.

She said, "It's a studio down at Sheridan Square. Small. We share a double bed," she addressed the customer at the next table, "and *not* the way you're thinking." To Alvarez she said, "We'll work something out."

"The hotel," he said, "is not a problem."

She grinned. "Let me check with her when I get a minute."

Alvarez adjusted his position, affording himself a view of the hotel.

The Town Car had once again double-parked in front. The blonde left the hotel, leaned in, and spoke to the driver.

Alvarez checked his watch—perhaps her John had stood her up. At the same time, he chastised himself for allowing Jillian to distract him. The blonde now headed across the street toward the restaurant. He'd been sloppy, and this realization hit him hard.

She looked angry. The Town Car pulled away.

"She's coming over here," Jillian said softly.

Alvarez spun around. "Yes."

She met eyes with him. "Quite a looker, that one." She added sarcastically, "You're sure you're not stalking her?"

He said, "Write down the club for me, would you?" The napkins were linen. He searched for something to write on. Jillian produced a notepad and leaned down, putting pen to paper.

"We can go together from here," she encouraged, "or meet you there."

She handed him the name and address of a club. "We stop serving here at midnight, which means we're usually out by one, one-thirty. We'll be there around two." She pulled out a twenty-dollar bill from her bank and folded the president in on himself. She turned the folded edge to face Alvarez. "The guy at the door . . . hand him a twenty folded in half, the fold facing him. Just like this, or he won't let you in." She added, "We'll be inside."

Alvarez pocketed the address. The blonde came through the door. Again, Alvarez adjusted his chair, this time, away from the door. He felt trapped. He couldn't afford to be seen by this woman—there was a possibility she might know his face. He reached out, took Jillian by the hips, and moved her into the line of sight, blocking him.

"Another wine?" she asked. She clearly liked the contact.

He wasn't sure what to do. He glanced around Jillian, the blonde's back to him. She was shown to a table and was seated partially *facing* the restaurant's door.

"Another wine," he said.

The blonde pulled a cell phone out of her enormous shoulder bag and immediately began complaining to someone on the other end. Her whole body conveyed anger. A coffee drink was served to her.

Alvarez caught eyes with Jillian, who now stood at the bar awaiting his wine. He cocked his head in the direction of the restaurant's rear exit.

The couple sitting next to him continued to take this all in like a pair of theater patrons.

Jillian negotiated her way past several tables. She looked over at him and nodded. Alvarez understood then: she was providing another screen for him.

He carefully watched the huge mirror behind the bar, knowing that if the blonde happened to look in that direction, their images would meet. He stood and walked slowly, not wanting to attract attention. Jillian's eyes met his in the mirror—she was smiling, proud of herself. He allowed his eyes to smile back, and then he carefully made for the rear exit.

"They've found a body," Tyler said, pounding on Nell Priest's motel room door. They had taken rooms in a cheap roadside motel a few minutes' drive from the center of the small town. Bone weary and cold, Tyler had gone to bed in a foul mood. He was using up one perfectly good night of expense account living on a hole-in-the-wall. Two beers into the six-pack, he'd gotten an even better description of the lumberjack who'd put a hatchet through the rider's foot—this time, added to the man's broad shoulders was the color of his hair, "sandy," and the sound of his voice, "southern cracker." The Latino whom this man believed had passed through the camp was never described beyond his heritage, "Spanish, maybe a little Italian." But Tyler reveled in this information. It amounted to the first solid leads in what now, with the discovery of a body, appeared a likely murder case.

He had not slept well, wondering if he might have done something different in order to keep his relationship with Katrina. For some reason, Nell Priest made him think about Kat, and he warned himself not to mix pleasure with business. Priest had her own agenda. Northern Union's interests were not necessarily those of the NTSB. On the practical side, the shower water had been tepid and with no water pressure to speak of. He'd left a layer of soap on his skin that had dried to a persistent itch.

"Do you have hot water?" she called through her motel room door.

"No."

"Yeah? Well, I can't live without a shower! I'm waiting until the water heats back up!"

"Don't count on it." He didn't want to waste time, but he also didn't want to leave ahead of her and renew their competition. A truce had settled between them, and the raid on the camp had united them. He didn't want to mess with that. "We've got to go. Right now. We're closer to where they found this body than anybody else. We could get a jump on this."

"How'd you hear about it?"

He sensed she was dressing on the other side of that door. It provoked distracting images in his head. "State troopers," he answered. "Believe it or not, that desk sergeant actually wrote down my cell phone number."

"A double skinny latté," she said. "I'll be ready by the time you're back."

"In this town? Don't count on it," he answered. "Dunkin Donuts, maybe. High-test?"

She cracked the door, standing back so he couldn't see the rest of her. Again, his imagination ran away with him, and he filled in the blanks. "You're kidding, right?"

"Cream-filled, or jelly?" he asked.

"You *are* kidding?"

"High-test with Coffee-mate," he repeated, altering her order, "no sugar, no pastry."

She caved in. "One of those braided things. With almonds, if they have them."

"We're going to get along fine," he said. "You have exactly ten minutes. After that, I go without you." He headed down the sorry excuse of a hallway toward the sorry excuse of a lobby.

She called after him, "Why didn't you?"

Tyler turned. She was leaning a little farther around the door, and he could see an expanse of smooth, dark amber skin. Maybe more than she would have wanted him to see.

She completed her thought, "Leave without me?"

He fought back the smirk, but it crept onto his face in spite of his efforts. "Ten minutes," he repeated.

Less than an hour later, the empty coffees in their respective cars, Tyler and Priest parked alongside a perfectly straight two-lane road, surrounded by fields and distant woods. There was an ambulance and a couple of state police vehicles pulled off the road. They followed the trail of many boots in the snow as it paralleled a lone set of cross-country ski tracks.

The crystal clear air smelled only of the snow, so pure, so fresh, that in fact it held no smell whatsoever, the way clean water has no taste. The only sounds were those of the woods—the clicking call of squirrels, the lonely, plaintive song of wintering birds, the gentle rattle of a few determined leaves that had stayed behind.

They approached the nightmare, and for an instant Tyler wished he could turn back: from this point forward there would be no return. As a former homicide investigator he knew this. A body. A bloody boxcar. An outsider intruding into the hobo camps with an angry hatchet. Homicide cases always reminded him of his own mortality, his vulnerability, the fragility of life. A few breaths. A blade here. A bullet there. The snap of a neck. Nothing romantic about it, no matter what the writers of films and books had to say. He felt sorry for Nell; she was about to learn a hard lesson.

The various tracks led through a stand of trees that took them ten minutes to walk. These trees led to a rising, snow-covered railbed that held the twin tracks. The snow was disturbed in a curving arc that led from the tracks to the frozen body. It was face down.

The state troopers had run enough yellow tape around tree trunks to contain a herd of wild horses. They probably didn't get the chance that often to play with their toys. A man and woman in plain clothes—detectives—poured coffee from a steel thermos for a young woman in her early twenties whose cross-country skis were leaned up against the tree, snow melting off them in silver lines. Her ski tracks cut through the area now cordoned off by the yellow tape— she must have come very close to the corpse. Tyler could see that she had stopped there in the snow and shuffled a little closer—perhaps not believing her eyes—moving her skis to the right and tamping down the snow in the process. Then she had pushed hard and fast and had skied away in a hurry. If he had it right, she had vomited only a few yards later. Had fallen over, gotten back up, and fallen over again.

"She skis with a cell phone in her pocket," Tyler told Priest as the two stood studying the area, still too far away to see the corpse. "We'll need to know who else she called about this. And if she won't tell us, then we'll need to check her phone records."

"Why?"

"Because we don't know why she was out here," he explained. "She'll tell us it was morning exercise. But look where we are! It could have been us on those skis, right? You. Me. Out here looking. So who knows why she was out here, or who she is? And we *need* to know. It's our job to know. We don't need any media leaks on this—it'll only send our boy deeper under."

"Are you always this paranoid?"

"Most of the time." He added, "And impatient, too. One of my better qualities."

"Maybe the hatchet guy did this," she stated, suddenly very solemn. "When do we get a look at the body?"

"We get their permission," Tyler said, indicating the detectives. "Even though we don't need it, it's how we do it." He asked, "Are you scared?"

She answered, "Should I be?"

"Yes," he told her. "Hatchets are no fun at all."

Tyler and Priest followed the route through the snow and stopped several feet short of the frozen corpse. It wasn't a hatchet—not unless the blunt end had been used. Tyler spotted the problem immediately. He called back to the detectives, "I need to look a little closer."

Priest looked at him like he had to be out of his mind—*closer to that!* her eyes said. "Oh . . . shit," she moaned.

"Don't touch anything!" the male detective hollered back.

Tyler stepped toward the corpse and squatted. Lacerations covered the man's bloodied face, but it wasn't like any knife fight Tyler had ever seen. The skin above his eye had been ripped open a good inch or two so that the eyeball hung partly out of its socket, and though the wound was frozen shut now, it appeared to have been the primary source of all that blood. A bunch of loose ends came together for Tyler: so much so that he cautioned himself not to jump to any conclusions. The dead man was big—real big—and seemed to fit the lumberjack description provided by the wounded rider in the hospital bed. The dead man's hair had been cut by a professional—albeit, a while ago—not by gardening shears. No rider, this man. He'd lost enough blood through the various tears in his skin to drain him of all color. Enough blood loss to account for the boxcar they'd found. But his face had been burned as well, the frozen skin bubbled and raw. He thought back to the frozen chili. Tyler studied more closely what had drawn him to his knees in the first place. He asked Priest, "What do you want to bet this comes back as canned chili?"

"As in the boxcar?"

Tyler called back to the detectives, "Will your photographer bring a Polaroid with him?"

"With her," the woman detective answered. "As in *me*. Yes, she will. The gear's in the trunk. Give us a minute."

No local law enforcement ever welcomed the feds' involvement.

Priest looked shaken. It didn't surprise him. The dead man was a mess. He had a broken neck and shoulder—probably from the fall from the train—so that he lay in an awkward, impossible way that one saw only in broken dolls or crash-test dummies.

"You okay?" he asked.

"No," she answered.

"Your first body?"

"First, in person," she corrected. "Listen, Tyler . . . ," she said, looking past him at the corpse.

"Yeah?"

She seemed to snap out of it. "Nothing." But she had wanted to tell him something.

"I'm listening."

"Another time," she said.

"Sure," he answered. "Whatever." He wanted to roll the body and search it for ID. He wanted fingerprints, any body markings or piercings. He wanted a name. A history. A story to follow.

He wanted whoever had done this, even though he found himself already leaning toward self-defense as an explanation. This was no longer about expense accounts or trying to win a better job—the crime scene made it real to him. It was about a death now, a murder. A manhunt.

"This is our hatchet man," Tyler announced, a bit prematurely, but confidently.

"You think?" she asked.

Tyler nodded. "And that begs an even bigger question," he said. She raised her eyebrows, awaiting his explanation.

"If this is what happened to the one wielding a hatchet, then what the hell does the other guy look like?"

A state trooper the size of a Sasquatch approached Tyler and Priest, who sat on a frozen log awaiting the evidence report from the technicians. Their interview with the cross-country skier had confirmed that she was nothing more than an innocent outdoorswoman who had happened upon a frozen horror.

"You Tyler?" the statie asked.

"Frozen and accounted for," Tyler answered.

"You got some ID?"

Tyler showed him the credentials provided by Loren Rucker, the NTSB deputy director who had hired him. The trooper studied the creds and handed them back to Tyler.

"You want to talk in private?" he asked Tyler, eyeing Priest.

"She's with railroad security," Tyler said.

"Word is," the officer told him, "that our guys came across a report they thought might interest you."

Tyler had requested a statewide Be On Lookout for reports of thefts and break-ins, knowing that a killer on the run might steal a vehicle, or cash, or even provisions. He nodded. "I'd be all ears, if mine hadn't frozen off," he said.

"An individual reported a possible break-in with clothes stolen."

"Men's clothes?" he inquired.

"Don't know, sir. Can't answer that. My commander—I guess you've already spoken with him—radioed that I was supposed to tell you 'bout it, and that if you needed more, you should be in touch directly. Much as I know."

"Same number I called last night? State police headquarters?"

"Commander Marshall," the man answered.

Tyler thanked the man, who then walked away without another word. Tyler asked Priest, "If this is something that bears looking into, are you willing to work with me on it? Are you willing to *share* it?" She looked inquisitively at him. "Because I don't dare let this body out of my sight—as attractive as it is—for fear these guys'll mishandle it. Not that I don't trust Iowa farmers in blue uniforms."

"Illinois," she corrected.

"My point exactly," he said. "Whoever did this to our frozen friend left behind hair and fiber evidence. Count on it. Maybe prints on the clothing. That body is our ticket to close this case."

"Would we still be sitting here if I didn't already know that?"

"But these stolen clothes," he said. "That could be just as good, even better."

She encouraged, "I'll share anything I find."

"Everything," he corrected, emphasizing the word.

"You don't trust me?"

"A private security officer with her company's reputation and market image to protect. Should I?"

She grinned. "Probably not."

He said, "You've been itching to tell me something since we showed up here."

"I'm cold is all."

"I don't think that's all," he contradicted her. "You're agitated. Restless. What gives?"

"I'm cold," she repeated. "I didn't dress right for this." She indicated her pair of city slacks, wool, but thin.

He nodded, though he didn't believe her. Her body language indicated an impatience. She wanted to be rid of him but didn't want to make a scene. He felt this most of all: she was worried about something. "Officer!" Tyler called out, stopping the state trooper. "The location of this break-in? Anywhere near here? Anywhere near the railroad tracks?" He was thinking that the killer would have jumped the next time the train slowed enough. He might have made a few miles before daylight but not much farther. Not in this cold, not looking the way Tyler imagined he must look. They might pick up a trail. How far could he have gotten?

"Town of Jewett," the state trooper shouted back. "Ten, twelve miles west of here."

They were outside a small town called Casey.

"Near the tracks?" Tyler shouted.

"Forty and I-seventy both parallel the tracks from Terre Haute to St. Louis. Jewett's right on the rail line."

The big man waited for another question but then turned and went on.

"You want me to visit Jewett?" Priest inquired.

"I *have* to stay with this body. If you feel like it, why don't you call this Commander Marshall. Interview the individual who reported the theft. Check the place out. Protect the scene and ask for a forensics unit." He nodded toward the crowd around the corpse. "Probably these guys will handle it. You know what we're looking for. Tracks in the snow. Blood. Discarded clothing. *Do not* follow those tracks, if and when you find them. Keep me posted. Are we in agreement here?"

"I don't work for you," she clarified. "If I want to follow the tracks, I'll follow the tracks."

"Not alone you won't," he corrected. "A uniform or detective accompanies you at every step. If not, we can lose the chain of custody for any evidence you find, and that'll make it useless."

"Understood." She didn't sound convinced.

"We need every scrap of evidence if we're going to have any hope of finding whoever did this."

"Understood."

"Something's still bothering you," he said.

"You are," she answered. "Who put you in charge?"

"I did," he answered. "The feds did," he added.

Priest didn't say a thing, but her eyes hardened. Then she glanced over at the frozen body, and that same, penetrating sadness he'd felt before seemed to overcome her again.

"We need to do this by the book," Tyler encouraged her. "We don't need any more bodies."

Priest shook her head. She seemed ready to cry.

Tyler informed Priest, "They've moved him to Paris—Illinois, not France." He smirked, thinking himself funny. "The victim remains unidentified, but that may change. Currently he's thawing out in a morgue there. Paris lays claim to the nearest pathologist."

"Change how?" Priest inquired.

The two stood on a plowed road outside a gray farmhouse, a mile from the tiny town of Jewett. This was where the break-in had been reported. Tyler had caught up to Priest following his phone discussion with the pathologist, who had no intention of touching the frozen victim until he had thawed. Tyler drank a lukewarm coffee bought from a vending machine at a gas station down the road. Two state police cruisers were parked with their engines running, their tailpipes belching plumes of gray exhaust. One was occupied by a uniform behind the wheel; one was not, the engine left running to keep the car warm.

Jewett was deep in Midwestern farm country—stark and barren in winter's grip.

Tyler answered, "What we *do* know about the dead guy is that he was a smoker—he carried a pack of Marlboros—he was a former Marine, judging by the mock tag he wore around his neck, and, more important, he apparently carried a piece because he had an empty belt holster strapped to his back. The weapon's missing—a nine millimeter. The geniuses are guessing that it was probably stolen by whoever opened up his face." Tyler affected an ignorant-sounding accent. "He weren't no hobo." He returned to his normal voice. "So, who was he? And what was he doing on that freight train, and what got him killed?" He lowered his voice conspiratorially, despite the fact that no one was around. He said, "Have you people had reports of an axe-wielding maniac traveling your lines? Is that why they sent you out here in such a hurry, Ms. Priest?"

"Why Paris? Why not—" Priest changed the subject, clearly not wanting to answer his question.

"I argued for Champaign but lost—they just love federal agents around here," he quipped. "They'll get some heaters going. This pathologist gets a poke at him, and maybe then I can get him moved."

Pointing to the farmhouse, she spoke in a professional, almost clinical tone, and he wondered what she was up to. Something had changed. Perhaps nothing more than that she didn't like playing second fiddle. "I talked to the resident, a Mary Ann Gomme. She's positive about the missing jeans. She thinks maybe a flannel shirt was also taken. Maybe some canned goods. The window frame had been winterized with some kind of putty, and the husband noticed the putty was busted up. I asked the forensics guys to work that laundry room as a crime scene." She added, "And don't get mad at me about those tracks in the snow, because it was the husband that followed them out into the woods, not me. Not at first. I called you, as per our agreement."

"And?"

"And when you told me to get out there ahead of the staties, I did."

"And?"

"I found a fresh burn. A hole in the snow, deep in the woods. Probably clothes, by the look of what's left. Fabric, at any rate, not paper, not wood ash. It's south of here, toward a stream called Muddy Creek. The husband called the sheriff. The sheriff called the staties."

"Our corpse fell off that rail rolling east to west," Tyler recalled.

"That's right."

"We're west of there, meaning the dead guy didn't steal these clothes."

"Okay. Agreed."

"So I already don't like whoever this is," Tyler said. "Breaking and entering an occupied home. Burning evidence. Nerves and brains—bad combo."

"Ms. Gomme has two children. And this guy was *inside* her house. And that's got her pretty shook up."

"You have kids?" Tyler asked her.

"None of your business." She softened then, as if she heard her own tone of voice too late. "No. You?"

"No. And I'm not married."

"Me neither," Priest said.

Tyler asked, "And where exactly are we in all of this? Other than out in the cold, yet again?"

"Waiting for these guys," she pointed to some arriving vehicles.

Four bloodhounds arrived in a minivan that had a child's seat in the middle row and a pair of sunglasses hanging from the rearview mirror. The local vet was a man named Acker. He wore a full beard, a down jacket, and big rubber boots with felt liners. They were his dogs. He knew the troopers on a first-name basis and they talked for a few minutes until one of them signaled Tyler, and then the search was on, dogs in the lead.

"Have you noticed how much time we spend walking around in the snow?" Tyler asked Priest. But her humor had still not returned. He asked, "What color flannel shirt?"

"If they have it right, it's a rose and gray plaid. Husband wore it a couple days ago, and now they can't locate it."

Tyler flipped open the phone. The battery was indicating low. "If the cold kills this thing," he said, "I'm screwed. Can't live without it."

"We're screwed anyway, Tyler," Priest said sharply. "You think Davy Crockett and company are going to find this guy? Forget it. He's gone."

"I know that," he said. "A guy like this with a decent lead and a fresh change of clothes?" He dialed a number as they followed the bloodhounds and the local vet. "But as long as he gives us pieces to follow—like this clothing—we'd be stupid not to run with them."

They followed, well behind the dogs and the staties. The suspect's tracks had been partly disturbed by only one other set—the husband as he had followed earlier. Thankfully, he'd returned to the house staying well clear of the trail, just as the dogs and everyone else did now in an effort to preserve possible evidence.

Priest pointed. "Judging by the gait, the long strides, this guy was running. In a hurry, not taking his time. He knew we'd be on him soon enough. You're right: he's a thinker."

The cell phone call connected. Tyler continued walking at the same pace. He asked for Commander Marshall. After a brief reintroduction, Tyler requested, "We're going to want any and every video security camera for twenty square miles. Our guy's wearing a plaid shirt and jeans. Convenience stores, grocery stores, banks, ATMs in particular, department stores, train stations, bus stations, airports, rental cars. I know it's asking a lot—maybe too much—but this bozo is leaving crumbs, and we'd be wrong not to pick them up and follow 'em." He paused and listened. "I know that. . . . I understand that. . . . Yes, it's a hell of a lot of phone calls. Absolutely. Maybe cadets, trainees, doesn't matter how professional these requests are. The important thing is that some, if not all, of these surveillance tapes are loops; they re-record over themselves, and we've got to catch them, stop them, before they do that." He listened. "Uh-huh. . . ." He thanked the commander.

Still walking, Priest said, "You're good at this." She thought a moment. "Is *that* why you won this assignment? You're a man hunter?"

"The cold's getting to you," Tyler said dismissively.

"But you actually must think we're going to catch this guy," Priest called over her shoulder to him, "or you wouldn't be doing all this."

Tyler answered calmly, "If he isn't dead or dying, if he isn't bleeding out, then of course we'll catch him. We've got the boxcar, the body. In terms of a crime scene, it was sloppy as all hell. The thing that worries me?" he asked rhetorically. "He *knows* we're going to catch up with him. Someday, sometime. Just ask Ted Kaczynski. So what does that pressure do to him? In his head, I mean."

"I'm with you."

"More important: what's his next move?" The dogs started barking excitedly. They had found the fire hole in the snow.

CHAPTER

10

Alvarez awakened in a state of arousal, at first believing it to be a dream, but then realizing Jillian was responsible. He reached down under the sheets and tugged on her, drawing her up and on top of him. She knew exactly what she wanted. He remembered this from their encounters of the night before. He appreciated a woman who went after her own pleasure first, knowing his would follow. She didn't want him getting ahead of her. Maybe it *was* a dream, he thought. "Good morning," she said in a hoarse, smoky voice.

From the moment he had entered the club at two in the morning, Jillian had treated him with obvious interest, no longer the proper waitress he had met in the restaurant. At first, he attributed the change in her to the drinking, or perhaps a pill or two. But as the late night wore on, Jillian and her roommate continued dancing together, always within sight of him, and he saw a young twenty-something aware and in control of herself. Boundless energy and a simmering sexual urgency drew him to her. For her part, whether a holdover of a crush begun a decade earlier or an attempt to make a statement about her age and maturity, there had been no secret about her physical attraction to him. When they reached her apartment, hours later, she had shared herself without reservation or conditions.

Youth! Juanita and he had taken their time to get physical, despite the immediate attraction. They'd met at a Cinco de Mayo festival, both in their mid-twenties. Despite the beer and the dancing, he'd not dared to kiss her that first night, realizing he had stumbled upon a gem of a girl and not wanting to scare her away as he had others before her. Following that chance encounter there had been family dinners at her aunt's place, the occasional film or bar date, and only a rare make-out session, awkwardly in the front seat or quickly on the front steps to an apartment house she shared with three other nurses. She'd been the only woman, in a long string of many, who had openly held him at bay, sticking firmly to her Roman Catholicism and not wanting to go too fast. But she'd also been the only one to open him up about the loss of his parents as a teenager—his mother to alcohol, his father to points unknown—his parenting of a brother, Miguel, who had been born with fetal alcohol syndrome, and Alvarez's struggle through college juggling his two lives of student and older-brother-turned-guardian. As a nurse, she had wanted to meet Miguel, and upon doing so had advised Alvarez to move his brother out of the state institution, despite the cost. She had completed endless paperwork to win Miguel financial assistance in a private care facility through the age of eighteen. They had formed a sense of family before they'd even gone to bed together, by which time he had known there would never be any woman but Juanita. He had dated for the last time.

But circumstances had changed all that. Northern Union Railroad had changed all that. A few precious seconds, a faulty crossing gate, and a freight train had changed all that. A long string of lies had changed all that. He pulled himself up and out of his memories and tried to enjoy the moment, but his involvement with Jillian, his first of any kind since the accident, proved as distracting as it was exciting.

Breakfast arrived an hour and a half later, in the Star Café on Bleeker. He picked the restaurant because of its proximity to the Lexington subway line, and he walked his bike at her side while a city of eight million people attempted to sort itself out. In a surreal, dreamy way that he put off to a complete lack of sleep, it felt incredibly natural to be with her—this woman whose last name he knew only because he'd known her brother ten years before. *Jillian Barstow.* To her credit, she asked nothing of him—even breakfast together had been his idea, not hers.

He ate *Eggs Mexicana* but was disappointed by the cheese's lack of flavor and a need to smother his plate in Tabasco sauce to find any punch. Juanita's aunt made her scrambled eggs with garlic, shredded chicken, fresh tomato, and diced jalapeno. It took the roof of your mouth off and landed in your stomach with intense satisfaction.

"What kind of work is it you do?"

Alvarez thought about this long and hard. "Demolition," he replied, not knowing exactly why he said it. His usual response was "sales." Uninteresting enough that no one ever asked a follow-up question.

He explained, "I work freelance. Mostly for the film industry. They shoot a lot of shows here in the city. I'm working on one in the Midwest right now."

"Who's in it?" she asked. "Any actors I'd know?"

"Sure," he answered. "But we sign nondisclosure agreements—you can't believe how paranoid some directors are." He waited for her to say something, but she didn't. He said, "Antonio Banderas and Harrison Ford."

"Not really!"

"It's a train picture. Railroads. But you didn't hear it from me." He smirked, proud of himself for this invention.

She held tightly to his arm. "Is this okay?" she asked.

"No problems here," he answered.

Throwing that body off the train had changed things forever. No matter that the man had come looking for him—had intended to kill him—the blood, the battle, the man's face lacerated and gushing as Alvarez blindly wielded the hot stove like a mace. These images did not leave. He'd seriously injured a man—perhaps *killed* him—whether in self-defense or not.

But the lies had started too long ago to stop now. He had to keep up the pretense, to continue to be the kind of person he had come to hate.

"Are you going to tell me about the woman last night?" Jillian inquired.

"I told you: she owes me something."

"Money?"

"More like a favor. I'd rather not discuss it."

He felt tired, nearly crippled with fatigue. Their night together, added on to the brutal night in the boxcar, had taken its toll.

"I may not see you again," he told her.

"I know that," she answered. "No strings, no complications— it's how I want it, too." She smiled confidently, and said, "But I have a feeling you'll be back."

"You may be right."

She liked that. "Maybe by then you'll feel comfortable enough to tell me the truth about what you do." Her voice never wavered. "Harrison Ford's on a shoot in Vancouver," was all she said.

Breakfast between them was quiet. Alvarez had met his match.

The discovery of a bloodied frozen corpse along the Midwest corridor rallied southern Illinois law enforcement, whipped up a media feeding frenzy, and set hundreds, if not thousands, of residents along Midwestern rail lines on edge, as the public envisioned the second coming of the Railroad Killer. When FBI investigators in Champaign stepped in, it created a heightened sense of urgency.

While Nell Priest sat in on FBI briefings, representing her corporation's interests, Tyler found himself in Charleston, Illinois, working with a masters criminology class at Eastern Illinois University, to where all the various security camera videos from nearly two dozen retail establishments had been messengered. For the time being, the existence of these tapes escaped the notice of the FBI and others bent on hammering out jurisdictions, which was just fine with Tyler.

"We've received a total of twenty-two tapes," Professor Ted McCaffery explained to Tyler. McCaffery wore his graying beard trimmed close, a pair of half glasses perched on the end of his nose. The tips of his button-down collar were frayed, and one of the small buttons was missing. Those videos had been sent in from convenience stores, groceries, and bus and train stations, all within a fifty-mile radius of the farmhouse. "We're expecting a like number from the banks—the ATM tapes you requested. We put two students per tape," he explained, "on the theory that two heads are better than one."

"A plaid shirt—"

"And blue jeans. Yes," McCaffery said. "I wouldn't have bothered Don Marshall unless I was pretty damn sure of what we've got. I put in twenty-four years with state police," he added proudly. "Then the university scooped me up on retirement, probably because I'm one of the few with twin masters—criminology and forensic sciences." He was bragging now. "Had never even *considered* teaching before this. Look at me now!"

The large audiovisual lab smelled of institutional disinfectant and bore the groan and hum of dozens of VCRs and television monitors, where students sat fast-forwarding through grainy black-and-white images, alert for men wearing plaid shirts and jeans. The randomness of chance was not lost on Tyler.

"Let me show you why I called you." McCaffery pointed to a freeze-frame on one of the monitors, where a man stood at a ticket counter, his face obscured in shadow. He wore a large-pattern plaid shirt, blue jeans, and work boots. Tyler stepped closer, his heart doing a dance in the center of his chest.

It was their boxcar killer. He felt certain of it.

"I need to borrow your plane," Tyler told Nell Priest through a pay phone, his cell phone batteries having died an hour earlier. His thumb rested on a Yellow Pages listing for an electronics superstore on the fringes of Charleston. He hoped to find an automobile charger for the cell phone on the way out of town.

"I beg your pardon," Priest said.

"Thumbnail sketch: we've got a guy on a security video in Effingham: plaid shirt, jeans, work boots. The individual is scruffy, thin, early thirties maybe—no clean look at his face. Granted, he could be anybody, including our suspect. It's not much to base a decision on, but those jeans have the legs rolled up into cuffs and they look a little big on him. Maybe they aren't his jeans."

"Where's Effingham?" she asked.

"We drove through it. Twelve miles from Jewett. Hell, he could have walked it, not to mention hitchhike, jack a car, steal a snowmobile. The bus station is a McDonald's. The restaurant's security video is time-coded. He bought a Happy Meal and waited for the bus, which is how come we've got him on tape. That bus, that time of day, is an express to Chicago."

"And?"

"Greyhound has pulled the Chicago terminal's videos for us. They're reviewing them using the scheduled arrival time, awaiting our arrival up there. It's a four-hour drive. Less than an hour in your plane." He hesitated, "Listen, I know it's a lot to ask."

She said, a little breathless, "Does the FBI know about this?"

"My cell phone's dead. I'm not wasting anybody's time until I know we're onto something here."

"You're withholding from the FBI?"

"I'm following a possible lead. We'll report it if and when it looks good. The plane, Nell. It's available or not? If not, I'll put the pedal to the metal and hope for the best."

"If you get the plane, you've got me for company."

"No argument there."

"Tell me your nearest airport," she said. "I'll call the flight crew in St. Louis."

The security firm hired to police Greyhound's Chicago terminal proved surprisingly capable and cooperative. Tyler's standing as a fed may have put off the state troopers, but civilians treated him like God. Priest's King Air had been met at Midway by a black, chauffeur-driven Town Car, also courtesy of Northern Union Security. On the ride to the bus station, Tyler had shown Priest still photocopies of their suspect lifted from the McDonald's security video as well as those of three other possible suspects, two of whom had been taped at convenience stores, one from a rifle shop in Marshall. Both the convenience store shots showed men using their credit cards, and Tyler believed their killer was too smart for that, though he didn't mind the idea of passing these suspects along to the FBI for follow-up. "Throwing them a bone," he called it. The plaid shirt from the rifle shop weighed in well over two-fifty and just didn't have the look that Tyler envisioned.

"We'll want to get this picture at the McDonald's to our Mrs. Gomme," Nell said. "Hopefully she'll recognize her husband's shirt."

"Already ahead of you. McCaffery, at the university, is faxing this to Marshall at state police. They'll send a car out there and run it by her."

"If they're going to that trouble, then we should fax all the photos we've got," she said.

"Point taken." Tyler used his cell phone as it recharged in the arm- rest cigarette lighter. He made the call to McCaffery and arranged it.

When Tyler hung up, Priest asked, "What, if anything, have we found out about the victim?" Her voice sounded tentative, and it drew his attention.

"They've thawed him out slowly for the sake of tissue preser- vation. They printed him and are running those prints through every known database. Nothing criminal kicked."

"What do you mean by every database?" she asked, slightly irritated.

"You know, federal government employees, military, state em- ployees—every state east of the Mississippi. Anything to ID him," Tyler clarified. "If that gun was registered, then some state could have his prints on file." Until that moment, Peter Tyler had never seen a black person go pale. He'd seen his colleagues on Metro PD flush, even blush, but never pale. This in turn forced a second real- ization: he'd stopped thinking of her as black, or African American. He'd been constantly aware of her color in their early dealings, had even altered his own demeanor—walking on eggshells to avoid committing a faux pas—but somewhere in the blur of the past twenty-four, or thirty-six, hours, her skin color had lost its impact. Only now, as she paled, was he once again reminded of her color, and for no explainable reason, he felt embarrassed.

"You're staring at me," she complained.

"You're hiding something from me," he said, digging. His instincts rarely failed him. "You've been a changed person since we found that body along the tracks. Why?"

"Don't be ridiculous," she fired back, but weakly. She wouldn't make eye contact with him.

Tyler felt hurt, and he realized Nell Priest and her friendship now owned some small part of him. Or maybe not so small. "Am I being ridiculous?" he asked. He *felt* ridiculous.

"I tried to tell you," she whispered.

"You tried to tell me what?" he asked, unable to conceal the concern in his voice.

The Town Car pulled to the curb and hit the brakes. Tyler felt a pit in his stomach that had nothing to do with the driving. Nell Priest thanked the driver, completely ignoring Tyler, and popped open her door. "We're here," she declared, hurrying toward the bus station and away from him and his prying eyes.

"Tell me what?" he asked her on the run through Chicago's bus terminal.

"Later," she whispered in a gravelly, sexy voice, an obvious attempt to try to mollify him.

"Tyler?" a loud male voice called out from across the cavernous station.

Tyler whispered at her, "You can't leave me hanging."

"Sure I can," she answered.

Tyler fumed.

The inquiry came from a gray suit. Maybe a football or hockey player once upon a time. If so, it had been a long time ago indeed. He had buzz-cut gray hair, a round face, and spongy jowls. Probably not his own teeth, judging by the bite and their whiteness. They stood near a water fountain, not far from the men's room. Tyler would have preferred an office to the bus station's central concourse, but he took the lack of any such offer as a good sign. Perhaps time was of the essence.

"Eleven cameras in all," the private security guy said, rushing his words and failing to introduce himself. "The system is old but competent." He began dishing out photocopies of stills from the security system like a man dealing impossibly large playing cards. "We have him disembarking—" Another photocopy. "Pulling a dark duffel bag from storage bin two-seventeen." Another. "Entering the men's room. Nearly lost him here but caught the duffel bag going back over things. That's him. Leather jacket, pretty sharp dresser, you ask me."

"Same guy?" Priest asked.

Tyler didn't trust the lousy photocopies, but his heart raced at the prospect of their suspect being caught on tape. He inquired, "Are the video images any clearer than these?"

"Not much better, no. The cameras and recorders are old and we reuse the tapes. Kodachrome, this ain't."

If it was the same guy, Tyler realized he had wetted and combed his hair, switched clothes, and reappeared as a very different man. "He looks more comfortable as this guy," he muttered, believing they no longer needed the farm wife's confirmation of the plaid shirt. They had their suspect. Who but their suspect would have entered the men's room in ill-fitting clothing that matched the description of the stolen clothes, only to leave a few minutes later, rid of the costume? Again, Tyler felt elation. But at the same time he kept an open mind. The worst thing they could do was waste time chasing the wrong guy. "Could have handed off the duffel bag to an accomplice. We'd follow the bag then, instead of the guy."

"No," Priest contradicted, leaning across him and affording too much contact. She pointed to the boots. *Only a woman would notice the guy's shoes,* he thought. She tapped Tyler's pocket as if he would understand the signal—and then of course he did; he withdrew the folded photocopy from the McDonald's.

"Same boots in both shots. It's the guy," Tyler said under his breath. He wasn't sure he ever would have caught that.

"That's all I'm saying," Priest said confidently. Repeating, "Same boots, both photos."

"The guy changed everything but his boots." To Priest he said, "Nice work."

"Thank you." That time, it was a blush for sure.

"We'll need the tapes," Tyler told the security agent.

"Already arranged," the man informed him.

"So he's in the Windy City," Priest surmised.

The big man asked Tyler somewhat sheepishly, "If I may?"

"Go 'head."

He handed Tyler a series of four more shots. None revealed a face, nor did they come any closer to identifying the man—no accomplice, no pay phone. The security man pointed to the suspect's back pocket—the only shot of his ass in the whole group. "That right there," he said strongly, as if of great importance to him.

Tyler studied the back pocket, Priest leaning over his arm. She said, "A notebook?"

"A timetable?" Tyler guessed.

The big man waited until he had their undivided attention. He looked first to Priest and then to Tyler.

The security man said, "You ask me, it's an airline ticket."

This time Tyler's strides matched hers as they raced through the bus terminal for the Town Car. "Midway or O'Hare?" he asked.

"Divide and conquer?" she inquired.

"I'll take O'Hare," he said, glancing toward the waiting taxis.

"You could spend a month at O'Hare looking at one day's videos."

"I'll take my chances."

"A black leather jacket and blue jeans? It's a wild goose chase."

"A black leather jacket, jeans, and those boots. He's going to step off that airporter bus," he reminded her. "Unless he thinks to change clothes en route, we've got him. It may take us a couple hours, but we've got him."

"Do we tell the FiBIes now?" she asked, meaning the FBI.

Tyler's recharged mobile phone rang and he answered it before replying. He listened a moment and stopped dead in his tracks. "Repeat that," he said.

Priest stopped, too.

His eyes bore into her, hard and distrustful. And judging by her wounded expression, she knew what this call was about.

Tyler closed the phone, his jaw muscles tight, his eyes burning. "You kept that from me?" he asked her.

"I was going to tell you. . . ." A whisper. A shudder. A trembling lower lip. "I was on orders not to, but—"

"Northern Union Security, LLC," he stammered. "The dead guy—the pleasant guy with the hatchet and the temper—was one of your company's security agents." He looked her up and down. "And you knew it all along, didn't you?"

Alvarez, the black duffel/backpack at his side, stood reading a *People* magazine beyond the security check in the lobby of the massive high-rise at 471 Park Avenue South, as if awaiting a friend. He eyed each and every person who departed from the bank of elevators marked for the floors twenty through thirty, acutely aware that these housed the Northern Union Railroad's corporate offices and that therefore every person departing any of these cars was likely an employee. He waited for the right look, the right face, the right target. It wasn't his first time here, though he hoped it would prove to be his last. With McClaren's explosive in his possession, his final derailment was all but in place. He needed up-to-date information on the F-A-S-T Track to ensure success—this risky foray into the corporate headquarters of his enemy promised that information, and therefore an increased chance of success.

He had stolen into these offices on four previous occasions using a cloned NUR identification tag. This time would have marked his fifth visit on that tag, his first in December. He worried that given the start of a new month, the firm's security computer might have detected these earlier visits, all in November. Afraid to push his luck, he lay in wait for a new target—a new ID tag to clone.

The encounter with Jillian remained in his thoughts, her phone number on a piece of paper in his pocket. If he needed something from her, if she could help, he would call her. Otherwise, he'd relegated her to the past, along with everything else in his life.

He took each minute separately, and though a compulsive planner, he had learned to adapt and adjust his plans to suit the moment. He rarely knew what the next hour would bring. *The only constant is change*—his personal mantra. He did not spend a lot of time worrying; he left that for others. Instead, he focused almost single-mindedly on bringing Northern Union to its knees.

For now, he concentrated on the task before him. His target should be a man, the closer to his own age, the better. He knew he ran a risk each and every time he penetrated the enemy camp, but ironically, their reliance upon the technologically advanced credit-card-like identification tags made them all the more vulnerable. One of the devices he carried in his backpack/duffel was a credit card read/write that connected to his laptop. Intended to accommodate retail sales on the road, the device needed only a single swipe of any credit card for the computer to read all the digital information stored on the card's magnetic stripe. Alvarez's expertise was computers. For eleven years he had taught the subject. He used to joke that if he hadn't been a teacher, he'd have been locked up for hacking. The same slotted credit card reader was also capable of writing digital information back to the magnetic stripe, allowing Alvarez to clone any magnetically encoded card. A stolen ID tag was no good, as it would be reported and instantly made invalid. But a cloned card provided endless access—as he had proven in November—as long as the person to whom the ID belonged was not inside the building at the same time. If such an overlap were to happen, the security server would detect the double-up and alert the guards.

Alvarez finally spotted his target—an accountant or an engineer by his looks: bargain-basement suit, rubber-soled shoes, heavy black plastic glasses, cheap leather briefcase. He stood nearly six feet with dark hair, dark eyebrows, an unkempt beard, and little or no muscle.

Women tended to carry the plastic IDs in their purses or a handy pocket; most men preferred the badge look, hung around the neck on a strap or key chain necklace. They used the tags to log themselves in and out in the lobby, as well as to unlock doors on various floors. Alvarez selected the nerdy accountant because the man had carelessly slipped his ID into his back pocket after he'd logged out. A loop of the beaded-metal necklace spilled out of his rear pocket. Perfect for pocket pinching.

The next few minutes would dictate Alvarez's tactics: what mode of transportation his mark selected—cab, foot, bus, subway. Alvarez strapped on the small duffel as a backpack and followed the man, keeping a decent distance, disappearing into the herd of rush-hour pedestrians. He unchained his bike and walked it along the sidewalk. Alone, in a sea of bobbing heads, Alvarez kept his attention carefully on his mark, knowing how easily he could lose him. At last, the mark crossed at a traffic light and headed for Grand Central Station—along with a few thousand others.

Alvarez quickly chained his bike to a post and followed.

The incident in the boxcar stayed with him, a nightmare he couldn't shake. Northern Union Security—NUS—was run by a smart bulldog of a man, Keith O'Malley, a former Boston cop, and Alvarez put little past the man. He believed that O'Malley had attempted to corrupt Andersen, Alvarez's attorney, into accepting a settlement in the lawsuit filed on behalf of his family, and that when this failed, for whatever reasons, accidentally or intentionally, O'Malley had murdered the man, framing Alvarez and leaving him no choice but to run. O'Malley had again shown his cleverness by assigning an NUS agent to the Terre Haute line. How many other agents were currently out there looking for him, he wondered. A dozen? A hundred? Were they on the New York streets? Around the next corner?

His mark surprised him as he walked right past the 42nd Street entrance to Grand Central and continued into the Hyatt next door. With a drink at the bar more expensive than the minimum wage, Alvarez had a hard time believing his eyes as this man pushed through the hotel's doors. The lobby was white marble with brass light fixtures, a black registration desk at the far end, and a noisy bar to the right amid a jungle of potted plants. The bar was jumping. Alvarez had performed a break-in to steal his previous ID tag, so this effort seemed simple by comparison.

He hurried through the crowd—his black leather jacket and black backpack making him look enough like a New Yorker to draw no undue attention—and approached the mark with deliberate speed. He intentionally collided with the man—bumping into his back—and apologized as he reached out to steady himself. He pressed a hand down onto the man's shoulder and gripped. The hand proved enough of a distraction for Alvarez to slip the ID tag from the man's back pocket.

Tag in hand, Alvarez headed for the men's rest room and locked himself in a stall, his heart racing, his hands busy. It was only a matter of minutes before the magnetic strip was read into the laptop. The ID card itself showed a poor photo of one Robert Grossman. Alvarez collected himself, his gadgetry repacked, and returned to the bar, again searching out Grossman. He saw him sitting at the bar, his hand wrapped around a clear drink of gin or vodka, his eyes on the overhead television and the Wall Street report. A drink and the market before heading home.

Like taking candy from a baby. . . .

Alvarez approached the teeming bar, the voices at shouting level. He leaned in close to Grossman and dropped the ID tag onto the floor while at the same time calling to the bartender for a book of matches. The overwhelmed bartender pointed to the end of the bar. Alvarez walked off in the direction of the hostess, grabbed a waitress by the elbow, and pointed out the fallen ID tag. "I think that guy may have lost something out of his pocket," he said, making sure she identified Grossman at the bar.

She thanked him, the Good Samaritan that he was.

"No problem," he answered. *None at all,* he was thinking.

Alvarez transformed the data into an ID at a high-tech copy shop nearby on 42nd Street. He worked sitting on a metal stool at a counter that looked out onto the bustling street. He first created a digital graphic image that matched the NUR format and copied it to a disk; he then transferred the data stored on Grossman's magnetic stripe to a blank card; the copy shop printed his disk-based graphic onto the blank card for a total charge of three dollars. Within fifteen minutes, he had an NUR corporate ID tag bearing Grossman's name but his own photograph. The man behind the counter barely spoke English and did not question any of this. He was nothing more than a hardware clerk duplicating a key.

At 6:20 P.M., knowing Grossman was in a bar or headed home, Alvarez reentered 471 Park Avenue South, now wearing a four-dollar tie beneath the partially zipped leather jacket, the backpack on his back. The security guard barely looked up as Alvarez ran his ID through the slot and the red light turned to green. Alvarez walked with increasing confidence to the bank of elevators and selected the twenty-second floor. Once inside the offices there, he would be greeted by a huge banner announcing Northern Union Railroad's foray into the new millennium, the ultimate target of all of Alvarez's striving:

Northern Union Railroad
THE *F-A-S-T* TRACK
Express New York to Washington, D.C.
2½ Hours!
Now Taking Reservations!

The banner was only an ad agency mock-up. The train, still in its testing phase, was approaching its final test—a glorified publicity stunt—an event that Alvarez intended to sabotage, now less than a week away.

If he proved successful, that banner would never see the light of day. And not only the train—the high-tech marvel—but Northern Union itself would be in ruins.

He lived for that moment.

CHAPTER 13

The pieces came together for Tyler just as the lights of Long Island appeared beneath the right wing of United Airlines, flight 670.

Priest's demeanor had changed the moment they had seen the dead body. Tyler had taken this as a sign of a weak stomach—the guy's face had been lacerated, badly burned, and then frozen. Now he understood that it hadn't been a queasy stomach so much as her recognition of the dead man as a Northern Union Security agent. Tyler had also seen her at the hobo camp showing something to the men there. He had even asked her about it, and she had told him it had been her ID credentials. He suspected now that she had been showing them a photo of the dead agent. She had been withholding information all along. Northern Union had apparently rushed her to St. Louis because they had lost contact with one of their agents. Word of a bloody boxcar matched with their agent's route. Her cover story of a copycat Railroad Killer had proved a clever invention because it dovetailed so well with Tyler's own mission. Leaving her behind in the Chicago bus station, her words of apology trapped inside quivering lips, had done little to satisfy his outrage. He'd jumped a cab and left her on her own.

The surveillance video work with O'Hare's airport police had indeed proved time-consuming—he'd spent nearly four hours in a chair staring at replays—but ultimately had been successful. The suspect had indeed been spotted departing the shuttle bus wearing that same leather jacket and work boots, a baseball cap snugged down obscuring his features. Camera by camera, sorted by time stamp and location, airport security, watched by Tyler, had pieced together the suspect's journey through the enormous airport. When one camera lost him, another picked him up. Camera by camera, they tracked him. Making the work more difficult, three hours of weather delays had crowded the already jammed concourses and gate waiting areas. Tape by tape, Tyler and airport security followed their mark. When the suspect was seen boarding a flight for JFK, Tyler booked the next plane, an 8:45 P.M. departure. To the annoyance of his fellow passengers, he worked the airphone for most of the flight. JFK airport police obtained a passenger manifest for the suspect's flight, and all 273 names were run through the databases of both the Illinois Bureau of Investigation and the FBI. One name kicked out, but it was a woman who had been arrested five years earlier for check fraud. Nothing for a male suspect.

His jet touched down at 11:41 P.M., Tyler's head thick, his tongue dry, his clothes soiled, his energy sapped, his infatuation with expense-account living worn thin. The travel bureau that worked for NTSB booked him a room at the Empire, a midtown hotel where he was kept awake for two hours by traffic on Broadway. Falling sucker to a conspiracy perpetrated by Northern Union Security—he couldn't think what else to call it—left him in a distrustful, foul mood. Nell Priest had stung him. Loren Rucker, his new boss at NTSB, would certainly have already been told about the dead man's identification. Tyler would look like an idiot. He seethed.

At 7:30 the next morning, Tyler caught Rucker at his home, and the two discussed the investigation.

Rucker said, "We're playing catch-up now. Northern Union knows more than we do."

"Don't think I'm proud of this."

"On the contrary, Peter, you've done better than any of them, following this guy the way you have. You're getting the job done, in spite of them. Our biggest problem now is that it's not our job to track murder suspects; we're supposed to identify the cause of transportation accidents."

They had discussed this at his hiring. His presence could be justified by the NTSB, but loosely.

"The Bureau isn't thrilled you're on the case. They want you off."

"And what do you want?" Tyler asked.

"Credit for a job well done. A suspect in custody. Some trophy to justify your working this," Rucker answered. "Asking too much?"

"Harold Wells worked for Northern Union. He evidently mentioned a Latino at the hobo camp. He died a few hours later. Anybody could have killed him, but I've got to think that Wells not only was looking for someone in particular but died at that person's hands. We have to ask who, and we have to ask why."

"Yes. Agreed," Rucker said.

"Maybe this Latino *is* a threat to public transportation," Tyler suggested, attempting to give his boss the ammunition he'd need to keep Tyler on the investigation.

"I could make that argument," Rucker agreed. "But it would be better if you asked Goheen first why you were kept out of the loop."

"Goheen? As in Goheen, Going, Gone?" Tyler asked. *Time* magazine had done a cover story on Northern Union's CEO and chairman, the illustration depicting Goheen riding a bullet train with money spilling out of every pocket, the provocative title referring to rumors that he might enter national politics.

"You've been invited to meet Goheen at a reception in the Rainbow Room."

"Not exactly the kind of meeting I had in mind," Tyler responded.

"It's the only one you're going to get. He made the invitation

personally, Peter. And that says something, right there. Not a secretary, not a personal assistant, but Bill Goheen himself. His dance
card is full. This is a gift he's giving us. We take it, or we wait a
month to see him." Rucker paused and said, "It's black tie, Peter, so
rent something and we'll cover it."

"He's worried," Tyler said. "Obstruction of justice comes to
mind."

"Tread lightly. He hits a long ball."

"He has to be worried, or he'd pass this off to a minion."

"Bill Goheen takes responsibility, even for other people's screw-
ups. This was Keith O'Malley's mistake, not letting us in on the
identity of Harold Wells. Count on it. But O'Malley works for Bill,
and so Bill takes the heat. It's just the way he is."

"You know him," Tyler suggested.

"Know him well. Yes."

"If I sit down with William Goheen, it's going to be a shouting
match. Choosing a party like this—this is his way of diffusing that,
nipping it in the bud."

"You represent the U.S. government, Tyler. No shouting matches."

"They used us, me, your department. They lied, they kept secrets,
obstructed justice, and they still haven't explained themselves. Or
have they?" he inquired. "Did you happen to ask your friend Goheen
what one of his undercover security agents was doing on that train
out of Terre Haute?"

"His job, I would hope."

"You didn't ask."

"I did not," Rucker answered. "It hardly seemed appropriate."

"Appropriate? The blood in that boxcar belonged to one of Goheen's own agents! What was his job, exactly? Who was he looking
for and why? And why did they fly Nell Priest to St. Louis in the
first place? I'll tell you why: because they'd lost track of Harold
Wells and it scared the hell out of them. And that means they had
something, someone, to fear. They knew Harold Wells was close.

Close to what? To whom? I'll tell you: a Latino. The same guy he was asking questions about at the hobo camp. And if that's the case, they're *still* holding out on us, because I don't hear them volunteering any names."

"Diplomacy is part of this job, Peter. Keep that in mind. A *big* part of this job. We're the federal government, not some homicide squad attempting to round up suspects. You step on toes—especially William Goheen's—and I'll end up in the filing department."

"Harry Wells put an axe through a hobo's foot. Is that standard investigation procedure at Northern Union? I'll tell you what it is: it's frustration. I've been there. That's a whole string of dead ends. That's some perp doing the dance a little quicker, a little more surefooted, than you're capable of. And you start doing stupid things. Harold Wells is dead because he'd become impatient." He wondered if Rucker had hung up on him. "If William Goheen tries to tell me Harold Wells was the victim of a random inspection, I'm going to lose it! Diplomacy—I don't exactly hit long balls in that department, to use your own metaphor."

"We don't know what Bill will say," Rucker complained. "How 'bout we give him a chance?"

"I'm telling you—"

Rucker interrupted him. "Don't tell me unless you *know!* Don't go tossing out accusations like that to Bill Goheen. Lose the street cop thing, would you, Peter? It won't play in these circles. I'm telling you: this is a different league."

"Then you should have sent one of your own guys."

"I did send one of my guys," Rucker reminded him. "Help me out here, Peter, and you help yourself."

His pulse drummed at his temples. It was everything he could do to sound calm. "Listen, Loren, I appreciate this work. You know I do. We play Saturday ball together, we're not exactly what you'd call close friends, and you took a chance that was risky and probably unpopular. But you hired me for this one for my homicide experience, and if we're going to capitalize on that then I've got to follow the leads where I see them. Goheen and company played some bad cards, and I've got to call them on it. It's why you hired me."

"Rent a tux. Talk to Bill Goheen. Be polite. Remember everything that's said. Get a meeting with Keith O'Malley. Report back to me—I don't care what time it is."

"What about the FiBIes?" Tyler asked. "Have we told them we believe our suspect flew to New York?"

"I haven't. I'd hate to waste their time until we have more substantial evidence."

Tyler hesitated a moment. Rucker was supporting him. Fully. "Thank you, Loren. Okay. I can live with that."

"Diplomacy," Rucker reminded him.

"Message received."

At the Empire Hotel's registration desk, an Armenian woman with dark, brooding eyes handed Tyler a fat manila envelope marked with his name. It had been messengered from CBS TV and contained a videotape marked "*60 Minutes*—William Goheen." Rucker obviously took his job seriously.

The tiny hotel room smelled of cigarettes and room deodorant despite its nonsmoking classification. The bathroom's pipes whined when the plumbing was in use. Management's lack of trust in its clientele meant the TV's remote was chained to the bedside table, where the clock radio was glued down as well. The room's only window offered a view of a concrete block wall. If he strained to look beyond the wall he could make out a row of Dumpsters some twenty stories below. He inquired after a possible tuxedo rental with a concierge for whom English was probably a third language.

Tyler arranged for a VCR to be brought up, and while a maintenance man struggled with the wires, Tyler reflected on his talk with Rucker. Granted, Northern Union Security was a subsidiary of

Northern Union Railroad, and so it seemed possible, even probable, that William Goheen might not have been kept informed of daily events, might not have known that Nell Priest had been sent to St. Louis to gather information without sharing any. But Tyler kept coming back to Harold Wells entering that hobo camp looking for a particular individual—a Latino, the only description Tyler had. If true—and he couldn't be sure it was, given his source—it implied an active manhunt. For whom, and why? These were the questions Tyler wanted answered.

The *60 Minutes* reporter, in coat and tie, sat in a captain's chair, an enlarged image of William Goheen's face serving as a backdrop. The title, "Goheen Goes for It," and the producers' names filled the left half of the screen. The reporter's voice, steady and conversational, reminded Tyler of someone speaking across the table at a dinner party.

Seven years ago, William Goheen, heir to a trucking fortune and CEO of the largest fresh produce shipping company in the world, was tapped for the head job at the nation's fifth largest railroad. Five years later, after three successful mergers and five hundred million dollars in research and development, Mr. Goheen chairs the most profitable freight lines in the industry. The newly named Northern Union Railroad has seen passenger miles increase by thirty-seven percent in an industry that is otherwise shrinking. Freight tonnage has also increased by a whopping one hundred and seventy percent. Northern Union's stock price has nearly tripled during Goheen's tenure, making the CEO's golden parachute worth an estimated three hundred million dollars and propelling some to believe this man with the Midas touch might just seek public office—quite possibly a cabinet post or even the vice presidency. *60 Minutes* caught up with William Goheen in his Manhattan penthouse on the eve of his announcement of a new bullet train, dubbed "F-A-S-T Track," to run the lucrative northeast corridor. This French-built, Japanese-designed one-hundred-and-eighty-mile-an-

hour technological marvel will run on existing track and shorten
the New York to Washington, D.C., trip to just two and a half
hours—a trip Goheen himself may be taking soon, if the pundits
are reading their tea leaves correctly.

The report lasted fourteen minutes. Tyler studied Goheen's on-
camera personality: strong and confident but just short of arrogant,
the kind of man who could convince voters to punch the card or pull
the lever. He looked rich—his strong features, graying hair, dark
eyebrows and captivating blue eyes complemented his crisp white
shirt, red, white, and blue tie, and tailored double-breasted suit. One
could imagine him sailing a yacht or skiing Aspen, chairing a fund-
raising event or pacing the Oval Office. He clearly had it all, including a gorgeous daughter—a Princeton graduate and fellow New
Yorker—who, the report went on to say, had taken on the role of
first lady of the Goheen empire when her mother had died of breast
cancer, six years earlier. Gretchen Goheen was given only a minute
or two, but in Tyler's opinion she stole the show away from Papa.
Poised, slightly irreverent, almost flirting with the camera, she delivered glowing remarks about her father. She was clearly at home in
the limelight. And why not? he wondered. Her supermodel looks had
no doubt held her in that spotlight. At twenty-two, she had a rich
father and a face that could stop traffic.

The hotel concierge interrupted Tyler's viewing of the tape with
a call saying he'd arranged a tuxedo fitting. Tyler walked the few
blocks to the tailor, his mind still on *60 Minutes*. William Goheen
didn't seem like someone who would be cajoled or bullied into volunteering information. Tyler needed explanations about the murder
of Harry Wells but knew he faced an uphill battle. He would have
preferred Priest's boss, Keith O'Malley, to Goheen. O'Malley had
certainly known that Harry Wells had been riding Midwestern trains
in search of a Latino. Was Goheen's intention to soften him up,
downplay the events of the past few days? Tyler accepted that NUS
would place undercover agents in the field. Hobos were insurance

risks, vandals, and unpaid passengers. He accepted that NUS would pull surprise inspections in yards, stopping trains and rousting the hobos. But none of that explained the actions of Harry Wells in that hobo camp.

The tux fit fine. Now it was time to try it out.

Tyler rode the elevator to the Rainbow Room amid a half dozen different perfumes and colognes, the provocative whisper of women's satin slips, and the silence of strangers confined in a small space.

His imagination ran wild: the salaries . . . the expendable income. He had stepped into a world of the rich, a world he'd only viewed in film and television, a world so far from his own that he felt slightly intimidated.

Again, he considered Goheen's motives in extending this invitation—the man *wanted* Tyler off-balance. And William Goheen got what he wanted.

Bright-eyed, blue-suited hostesses greeted each guest just outside the elevators. One of these women, twentysomething and handsomely dutiful, hooked Tyler's arm, requesting his name as she guided him over to the registration table. She announced him to her colleagues behind the table. There would be no crashers. When a rehearsed warmhearted expression met Tyler, he beat her to the punch by explaining his name would have been added late this afternoon. That drew her to another list and, this time, a throaty invitation for him to enjoy himself.

The volume of the people in the room, the social energies given to shouting and gesticulating, laughing and cheek-kissing, conveyed an air of overindulgence. The crab hors d'oeuvres and bubbling flutes of champagne added to this first impression of his.

A college-aged fellow with broad shoulders grabbed Tyler's coat from behind, helped him to slip out of it, and handed him a check stub. Orchestrated and well rehearsed—nothing here was left to chance. He felt determined not to allow the environment to run him but to remain businesslike and professional. This, despite the opulence of the Rainbow Room, an NUR publicity event, and William Goheen's scripted world.

Tyler accepted a glass of champagne, a stuffed mushroom, and a party napkin as he threaded his way through the melee of white-toothed smiles and stretched skin. Black velvet, diamonds, and pearls appeared the favorites for the ladies. The gentlemen leaned toward Christmas red and green for their bow ties and cummerbunds. Tyler overheard discussion of politics, the stock market, and world travel. Chins were held high here, shoulders square, backs straight—everyone postured, posed, ready for the society pages. He raised to his toes and searched for Goheen. Like searching for a specific penguin.

The room roared with conversation. Floor-to-ceiling windows looked out on glittering towers of glass and red streams of taillights, strung together like a Chinese kite. Two dozen Christmas trees had been overdecorated, their boughs sagging under the weight of gold balls and strings of twinkling lights. Lavishly wrapped decorative boxes, empty of presents, were piled in stacks beneath the trees. Sprigs of mistletoe had been hung in doorways, though few seemed to notice.

"Agent Tyler?"

The voice came from a man in his late thirties. He reeked Ivy League and old money.

"Mike Campbell," he introduced himself with a vigorous handshake. "Northern Union."

Tyler shook the man's firm hand.

"Mr. Goheen has been expecting you."

"Fine." He looked for a place to put down the champagne. He'd drunk it a little too fast.

"Mr. Goheen appreciates that, like him, you're a busy man."

"In other words, you're with public relations," Tyler stated.

Campbell recoiled at being so easily pinpointed. He nearly dis-connected a woman from her drink. Apologies all around. These people were so damn polite, it was almost sickening. "Well, yes," Campbell confirmed.

"Lead on," Tyler instructed, wondering how many other eyes were watching him. He pictured the high-rise's security room with a half dozen black-and-white monitors and a pair of tuxedo-clad NUS guys sitting in. They had located him quickly in a crowd of hundreds. He kept that in mind: they were good at what they did.

"What do you think?" Campbell asked over his shoulder, taking his time through the gathering.

"The mushroom was a little salty. The champagne not quite cold enough." They stopped abruptly, to make room for a big woman with a bigger walk. Tyler realized that few of the women he'd seen could be considered even a few pounds overweight. In this crowd, if you couldn't lose it yourself, you had it tucked or liposucked.

"The event in general," Campbell corrected, still civil.

"Either these guys in the tuxes are treating their daughters to some holiday cheer," Tyler said, "or there are more trophy brides per capita in this room than I've ever seen."

He won a genuine smile from Campbell. The guy leaned more toward women-and-sex jokes.

Tyler tried again, "There's more breast in this room than a turkey shot with hormones." Another chuckle from Campbell. He was gain-ing ground, breaking the ice. He raised his voice to make sure he was heard. "Mr. Campbell, do you know why Harry Wells was aboard that train?"

Campbell stopped, and Tyler collided with him. They held each other by forearms, eye to eye. Tyler squeezed. Campbell tensed.

"I don't know any Harry Wells, Mr. Tyler. So I certainly don't know what train he might be on, if any."

"Since when is a fireman unaware of the fire?" Tyler still held him by the forearms. "If you'd said you didn't know what he was up to, that would have been one thing, but a complete denial? No one has briefed you on the murder of one of your company's security agents?"

"Security is a separate company," Campbell said strongly enough to sound almost convincing. "Maybe that explains the confusion."

"Nothing explains the confusion," Tyler corrected, "except a cover-up, and that's a word that someone in your department must certainly recognize. I'm a federal law enforcement officer, Mr. Campbell. Maybe I should have reminded you of that fact up front. Lying to the federal government is not generally considered a good idea."

"It's a big job," Campbell said. "Maybe I did hear something about a Harold Wells."

"Maybe so," Tyler replied.

"I'm in the executive offices."

"A PR department just for the corporate officers?"

"For all employees, including corporate officers, yes. If a guy's volunteering Little League, or mentoring, or if one of our female employees has qualified for the Olympics—any of those help our company image."

"As long as others hear about it."

"Which is why it's a big job. We have over four thousand employees."

"And what did you hear about Harold Wells?"

Campbell struggled free of Tyler's grip.

Campbell said, "Mr. Goheen is over there. I see him now."

"Your job, Mr. Campbell, is to make your CEO look good. Am I right? Your job in particular?"

Campbell made sure he met eyes with Tyler. "I wish I had that job. Nothing could be easier. Unfortunately for me, Mr. Goheen doesn't need any hand-holding when it comes to public image. I make sure the office looks good, Mr. Tyler. I make sure the CEO of Northern Union Railroad is seen as a community leader and one of the good guys, and as I've said, it's a no-brainer when you work for somebody like Mr. Goheen."

"So you're one of the lucky few going to Washington with him," Tyler said.

"Providing he goes, I'm hoping to be a part of that team, yes."

"Congratulations."

Campbell never broke eye contact and said, "You beat an African American by the name of Chester Washington nearly to death. You've lost your badge, your salary, and all benefits."

"Shield," Tyler corrected immediately. "Badges are for cowboys and Indians." He added disdainfully, "And security guards like Harry Wells."

Campbell wasn't easily ruffled. "You've survived a criminal trial, but a civil suit still remains. That civil suit could cost Washington, D.C., over two million dollars in damages. Mr. Goheen knows all that, and more, about you, Agent Tyler. I offer that as a heads up. You will find him polite, knowledgeable, and generous. Brilliant, even. He feels bad that this boxcar investigation was apparently handled inappropriately by our security company. I believe he intends to correct that tonight. But make no mistake, he will not be badgered. NUR has always cooperated fully with the NTSB. He hoped to speed up that cooperation by inviting you here tonight."

"And for that I thank everyone involved." *Diplomacy,* Tyler reminded himself.

"This is a public event, Mr. Tyler. I ask you to keep that in mind. People will be hovering about—they always do where William Goheen's involved. If Mr. Goheen seems to be avoiding certain language, you might want to keep that in mind."

"Point taken." Tyler was reminded of Loren Rucker's similar admonishment. Since the Chester Washington assault, and his expulsion from the department, a bitterness had taken root inside him, surfacing at the most unexpected times. He had yet to find a way to contain it, but he knew he had to. It would eat him alive otherwise.

The money, the artifice in this room had set him off. Or maybe the champagne. When his anger surfaced, it took over, it owned him. He searched for control as he stepped up to the man of the hour and stuck out his own hand.

William Goheen was a commanding presence—the deep golfer's tan, the salt-and-pepper gray hair, the piercing blue eyes—and yet *Agent* Tyler sensed reservation in the man, not quite fear but a caution that Tyler typically associated with a suspect. They shook hands and made introductions. It seemed that even the economically mighty felt a bit of knee tremble when confronted by police. Tyler had heard his civilian friends explain this before: even innocent motorists feel a nervous twitch, an acceleration of the heart, when a cop car pulls up behind them at a light.

"Listen," Goheen said, as if in the middle of an explanation, "I appreciate this is neither the time nor the place, but I wanted us to make contact as soon as possible. This job keeps me on a pretty tight leash. It's a busy time for us."

"I appreciate the opportunity to meet you."

"I understand there's been some confusion concerning this investigation, and that our security subsidiary is at least partly to blame. I wanted to assure you, face to face, that I'm personally on it now, and that we're going to clear this up. Apologies where apologies are due." He added, "I take it that neither you, nor our people, have shared everything with the FBI. They're certain to question me in the next day or two." He was pointing out the similarities of Tyler's handling of the investigation with that of Northern Union. "As I understand it, you believe our suspect is in New York," Goheen said. "If I'm asked about it, I'm going to have to share that with the FBI. And I will, as it's my duty to do. Just so you know where things stand."

Goheen obviously knew that Tyler had still not informed the FBI.

Tyler felt off-balance. "I appreciate that, sir." He had come here not wanting to like the man, but men like William Goheen could win converts out of anyone, given a tuxedo and ten minutes.

"I need access," Tyler urged. "A meeting with Keith O'Malley. I had actually hoped that meeting could have taken place before this one."

A tic in Goheen's left eye. Fatigue, or reaction to Tyler's request? Tyler was aware of people swarming around them trying to get to Goheen. Several of the tuxedoed males at their elbows were security guys acting as bodyguards. Tyler could feel his time was nearly up.

Lowering his voice, Goheen said, "One of our investigators has met with unforeseen circumstances." Tyler had heard murder called many things, but never unforeseen circumstances. "We've never had anything like this. I thought that a man in your position would want direct access to the top. And you have it. Day or night, Mr. Tyler, you call. I'll take those calls—you have my guarantee of that. And now," he said, scanning the crowd, "you'll get your wish."

"Harry Wells was pursuing a Latino," Tyler stated bluntly. "He assaulted a homeless man trying to get information on that individual. Are you going to tell the FBI about that as well?"

Goheen maintained his composure. If he knew anything about the Latino, it didn't show on his face. Guys like this practiced composure, however. They hired composure coaches. Tyler wouldn't rule out that he'd known.

"The NTSB is not authorized to conduct criminal investigations, are they? So what are they doing hiring you?" Goheen stood close to Tyler now.

"I'm fact-finding," Tyler replied. "That way, the NTSB knows which department to refer this to."

There were just the two of them in the enormous room then; the swirl of partygoers surrounding them seemed almost like an artificial backdrop.

"Perhaps the FBI will buy that explanation. Perhaps not." He added, "When do you plan to involve them?"

"I'd rather just catch this Latino and be done with it," Tyler pressed. "Wouldn't hurt to know who he is, of course. Wouldn't hurt to keep this from becoming a full-scale FBI investigation." He lowered his voice, "The NTSB doesn't want that any more than your company does. It's our job to keep the rail lines safe. This bastard is nothing but trouble for us."

"Agreed," Goheen said.

"It was you who mentioned involving the FBI, not me," Tyler reminded him.

"Maybe that can be avoided for a day or two."

"Why don't I talk to O'Malley?" Tyler suggested. "Get things moving."

Goheen turned and pointed across the crowd. "We have an agent who can help you with that."

Tyler searched out the person that Goheen was attempting to indicate. It took him a few seconds. The agent was a woman. A familiar woman.

From across the room, Nell Priest met eyes with Tyler and nodded.

For a moment, he wanted to turn and run.

"You get here ahead of me, brief them on what I know and don't know, and your people prep Goheen," Tyler said. "How am I doing so far, Nellie?"

"Don't call me that," she protested. She wore a black cocktail dress that looked better on her than the haute couture gowns did on the trophy brides. "I requested this assignment. I *asked* to be here tonight," she corrected. "I wanted to apologize for not telling you about Wells. I was on orders. For what it's worth, it tore me up. I didn't enjoy withholding information from you." She stood absolutely motionless, only her chest moving behind anxious breathing.

"You used me," he said.

"Not by choice."

"It's called obstruction of justice. Conspiracy." He added, "Goheen wants to soften me up, make it all seem like it resulted from simple confusion." He sniped sarcastically, "Sure it did!" He added, "I can direct the FBI to bring charges against you and the corporation, Nell. He knows that! He's using me again."

"We're all on orders around here to cooperate. I think you're reading this wrong."

"So tell me about the Latino," he said. "Right here, right now. Who is he, and why was Harry Wells after him?"

"That homeless camp was the first I'd heard about any Hispanic."

Tyler didn't buy it.

"Listen, Harry Wells was one of O'Malley's personal team. He calls them the Special Response Unit—'the Unit' for short. He uses them to vacate the hobo camps when state or locals don't. In the summer, most of them are rail riders; they sweep trains at random, clearing riders, making arrests for trespassing."

"Bullies."

"More like Marines or mercenaries. If these guys were ever busted, they would never, and I mean *never,* reveal the source of their orders. They'd take full responsibility. They'd say they were rogues, acting solo. You have to see these guys to believe them."

"Kneecappers." Tyler had visions of that homeless man's cleft foot courtesy of a hatchet. "How many of them?" he asked.

"Seven or eight. Ten, at most." She added, "I can't confirm any of this, Tyler, except that the Unit exists, and we all know what they're used for, whether it's written down anywhere or not."

"The Latino," Tyler repeated, still doubting her.

"The guy could have robbed Harry the day before, out on the line somewhere. He could have lied to him. Who knows? Harry

Wells could have been pissed about something that had nothing to do with his assignment. Keith O'Malley said nothing about any Hispanic to me. Nothing. I think we read this wrong."

"And me?" Tyler asked rhetorically. "I think the forensics will reveal black hair in that boxcar. Harry Wells had brown hair."

"So he caught up to the guy. So it got ugly. It's an ugly assignment—chasing freeloaders on the freight lines."

"And that's all this was?" Tyler questioned. "A confrontation that turned ugly?"

"I don't have any information or evidence otherwise," she said. "Do you?"

"I need to talk to O'Malley," he pressed.

"I can work on that. Where are you staying?" she asked.

"The Empire. But I mean now, tonight. I'll be down in the hotel bar. Tell your boss that if he sees me tonight, I'll make a lot less noise. I think our guy came to New York for a reason. We have to consider your company a possible target here—that Harry Wells knew that and was pursuing the man for that reason. Time could be running out: it's a big city and he's got the jump on us."

"You're making more out of this than it deserves."

"The guy who killed Harry Wells was no hobo—no rider—and you know it. He stole those clothes. He had an escape route that included a bag left in a storage locker. He took a jet to JFK. Does that fit the profile of a *rider?* Don't discredit Harry Wells, and don't underestimate this other guy. He's had half of Illinois law enforcement on the run for two days. He's good."

"O'Malley will meet you in the bar." She looked scared.

As hard as he tried, he found it hard not to like her.

A commotion from behind them forced them both to turn. There were few people, aside from celebrities, who could create a buzz by simply entering a room, but Gretchen Goheen proved the exception. The crowd passed news of her coming as if royalty had arrived. Tyler caught only a glimpse of her—translucent skin, like bone china; a self-possessed presence. She commanded the room as she walked directly to her father, where she was welcomed with open arms and a kiss on the lips.

"Have you met her?" Tyler asked in a whisper.

He turned when she failed to answer. Nell Priest was gone.

A short, stocky man with a severe brow and tight stride entered the hotel bar and studied the room's inhabitants like a general reviewing his troops. Tyler identified Keith O'Malley by the man's grim expression—so in keeping with a former Marine, a former Boston cop, a father of five, a baseball fan, and a beer drinker. Rucker had provided Tyler a quick profile in a five-minute phone call from the lobby. Tyler had also caught Rucker up on his conversation with Goheen, Rucker satisfied for the time being that Goheen had provided access.

Tyler had been waiting in the hotel bar for over an hour and had just been contemplating leaving as the man arrived. Following on O'Malley's heels, Nell Priest wore a game face that revealed nothing of her thoughts.

"Tyler?" O'Malley inquired. They shook hands. The man had the muscled hands of a day laborer.

"Keith O'Malley, Northern Union Security," he introduced himself.

"Loren Rucker sends his regards," Tyler said.

"Is that right? He tell you he can't swing a bat for shit?" He signaled the bartender, who relayed it to a waitress. O'Malley was one of those guys that bartenders, waitresses, and doormen kept their eyes on. He had a demanding demeanor that warned of an explosive nature simmering beneath the surface. The waitress was tired but cordial. O'Malley ordered a Heineken. Tyler did the same. Priest ordered a vodka gimlet, up. O'Malley said, "Loren and I were in the Corps together. He probably left that part out." He smiled. A few of the teeth were his, though not many. "Rucker was a little too much brain, not enough brawn for the Corps. Know what I mean?" He glanced in the direction of the bartender to make sure his needs were being tended to. "You know Ms. Priest."

Tyler felt troubled over why Rucker would have left out this personal connection to O'Malley and Northern Union Security. It could not have been an oversight. He shifted in his chair, now uneasy.

Nell Priest glanced at him, smiled, and returned her attention to her boss.

"So," O'Malley said, "gloves off, Tyler. What's eating you? I'm told you don't like the way I run my shop. Maybe that matters to me, maybe it doesn't. We work within the letter of the law. All my people are licensed law enforcement in forty-nine states. Fucking Louisiana still thinks they're French." He smiled again but was growing impatient for that beer. "We cooperate with the feds anytime they ask. You're asking. However, the way I hear it, at no time did you *ask* Ms. Priest anything about the murder victim's relationship to this company. The way I hear it, you were basically *telling* her the way it was. You were leading her. And I have yet to instruct my people to start volunteering information to the feds. Know what I mean? You used to be police. You know what I'm talking about."

Tyler still felt himself to be a policeman, no matter that he was off the payroll, off the roll call. It was something inside him that couldn't be controlled with a switch. He bristled, fighting off the urge to set the record straight on the Chester Washington assault. The thing followed him around like a shadow. Instead, he said, "Harry Wells put an axe through a homeless man's foot looking for information. Is that part of your policy?"

"If Harry did anything close to that, I can promise you it was provoked. You've been out there. You've seen these guys. Harry . . ." Nostalgia clouded his eyes. "He'd worked here, off and on, for the last ten years. The guy knew the rails, I'll tell you what. Chances are, this incident to which you refer, it wasn't Harry at all but another squatter. The lies these guys tell. . . . Most of 'em can't remember an hour ago, much less a couple days. But, regardless, what's your point?"

"My point?"

"Yeah, your point. Harry's dead. It's a tremendous loss to us. We lost a soldier. You can understand that! A brother. What, you want to reprimand me for something a dead man, one of my guys, may or may not have done? What colors are you wearing, Tyler? What if that had been one of your guys?"

Tyler glanced over at Nell Priest, but her full attention remained on O'Malley. The drinks arrived. Everyone seemed relieved. O'Malley did a third of the beer bottle on his first pull.

Tyler said, "You send undercover agents out in the dead of winter to ride Midwestern lines looking for riders? Why does that strike me as a little strange?"

O'Malley lit a cigar that was a little big for his face. "Are you listening to me, Tyler?" O'Malley asked. "You got your ears turned on?" He had lowered his voice, either out of deference to the smoke or for privacy.

"I'm listening," Tyler replied.

O'Malley sat back and regarded Tyler over the length of his cigar, a plume of gray smoke rising toward the ceiling. "You don't look like you're listening. You look like a man whose mind is already made up. So what's the point of this?"

"I'm listening."

"Because I don't care one way or the other. And you couldn't get any of this out of me with anything short of a nutcracker. So either there's a sense of cooperation here or not. Personally, I don't care. I'm not the one who asked for the meeting."

"Maybe you train your people to beg, Mr. O'Malley, but it's not my style. You want me to get a court order, you want me to air this out in the media—something I already *could* have done but did not— you just go on playing General Patton, or George C. Scott, or whoever the hell it is you think you are. I'm here trying to help you guys, something I explained to Mr. Goheen earlier. I followed a possible suspect here to New York. Ms. Priest and I have already discussed that this particular individual's behavior would hardly classify him as a hobo, a rider, a freeloader—whatever. He's smart as hell. He has killed one of your men. He created an escape route for himself, and he took it. That route led here to New York, which is, coincidentally, the site of your corporate headquarters. Do I think this was a random act of violence? No. Do I think the Latino that Wells was pursuing in the camp was some homeless guy who lifted his wallet?" He directed this to Nell Priest, then returned his attention to O'Malley. "No, I don't. You don't want to work with any of this, fine. You want to attribute it all to coincidence, also fine. Then I make my report to Loren Rucker and he passes it up the line and someone involves the Bureau. At that point, the chips fall where they may."

O'Malley's Irish face flared scarlet, and for a moment Tyler worried he might have pushed him too far. O'Malley worked the cigar to a bright orange bead, burning the tobacco a little hot and probably ruining the rest of its smoke. The beer went down like water. Tyler wasn't drinking his.

O'Malley sat forward and wheezed in a whisper. "According to Ms. Priest, you've already made the jump, am I right?" Tyler could only guess at what the man might be referring to—he and Priest had covered a lot of possibilities. He kept quiet, and let O'Malley talk. "Every six or eight weeks—there's no real pattern to it—one of our freight trains derails. Six trains to date. We lost one engineer, one driver to disability. Our insurers and their underwriters have lost tens of millions. Hundreds of millions is more like it. We've followed a half dozen leads across twice that many states—"

"Enter Harry Wells," Tyler whispered back across the table. His heart raced.

O'Malley nodded. "Harry was assigned one of our more promising leads. A Latino had been remembered by a rider who was rousted in a yard in Indianapolis. He'd been hiding on a car, and he remembered this Latino because, believing he was alone, the man had been constantly checking the scenery against his watch and making notes. That won our attention, to say the least.

"Harry was handy, already in Kansas City," he continued. "We bumped him over to Terre Haute, and it was the last we heard from him."

"I've read about those derailments. They supposedly resulted from mechanical problems or the conductors or engineers on drugs and alcohol."

"We retire a few guys early, it's cheaper for everyone than turning this into a three-ring media circus. We have customers, Mr. Tyler. Stockholders. Merger partners. Some maniac gets us in his sights, it's not something we're going to broadcast, especially since we can't even prove it's all the same guy. You know what I'm talking about?"

"Is it the same guy?"

"We have no evidence, if that's what you're asking. That's why Ms. Priest was put on orders not to share. We don't know shit, quite honestly. Only that our trains keep rolling over. And now Harry Wells."

"Sabotaged tracks? Explosives?"

"I meant what I said: no solid evidence. None. Zero. They look mechanical. When bearings fail on a freight car, the axle shears. We've been seeing a lot of bad bearings lately," he said sarcastically. "Like six different sets. My job—at least one part of it—is to determine if foul play was or was not involved. When Bill Goheen took over this company we went five years without a single accident. Now six derailments in eighteen months. What do you think a bookmaker would do with that?"

"Disgruntled employees; people you didn't hire but thought they deserved to be; fired workers at another company angry over a merger." Tyler rattled these off but saw the enormity of the task. "It's a big job."

"Huge."

"You've told Loren Rucker?"

"Your guys have investigated right alongside ours. No evidence of foul play. Just bad bearings." He spoke a little louder, though still half voice. "But maybe, I mean what if, this is some wacko who didn't get enough time with his Lionel set as a kid. You know? We got real serious about this investigation about a year ago, when our third train rolled over. Harry . . . Harry Wells I'm talking about . . . he was living with some of that frustration. I don't believe he did what you said he did, but if he got tough with some of these guys, I can understand it. You lose too many in a row and the guys in the dugout get kinda restless." He looked Tyler in the eye. "You know about losing your patience. I don't have to tell you."

Tyler felt his skin warm and his fist clench. He controlled himself and said, "He's here in New York. At the very least, he passed through."

"Ms. Priest filled me in. Rounding up the security videos—some quick thinking. I'd sure as hell appreciate any of those tapes when you can make them available. This guy's been without a face for us for a long time."

"And he still is," Tyler reported. "Maybe video enhancement can help, but it's doubtful: the cameras are typically mounted high, to see over heads, and the tape seems like it's always a year or two old, grainy and full of dropouts. You won't be matching him to any mug shots."

"You got further with this than my guys did," O'Malley said, with a hint of respect. "When you make your report to Loren, treat it however you have to, but on the report to the Bureau, I'd sure as hell appreciate it if this particular conversation was left out. That said, I'm not telling you how to run your show. You do what you have to do." He added, "After you make your report, if Loren's too dumb to keep you on, and you're looking for a place to hang out your shingle—"

Tyler felt a surge of relief, both from O'Malley's job offer and the information the man had provided. The offer did not feel under-handed nor an attempt to manipulate him. Just an offer put on the table—and a tempting one at that. He clarified, "I won't be making any written report until someone ties me down and makes me do it. I think you're safe there. The verbal reports? They're for Rucker to deal with."

O'Malley looked genuinely pleased. "So you plan to continue?"

"Absolutely." He glanced over at Priest. She looked at him; she seemed pleased to hear this.

O'Malley clearly had believed Tyler's work was over. "It's a city of six to ten million, Mr. Tyler. We have over a dozen agents out there looking for him around the clock. Have had, for months. You really think you're going to find him here?"

O'Malley had slipped—perhaps he'd drunk that beer too fast. Tyler wondered how they could have been looking for someone for "months" when mention of a Latino had only recently come in. Tyler considered pointing this out but then said thoughtfully, "No. I don't think I'll have to find him. My bet: he's going to find *you*."

CHAPTER 14

Terre Haute, Indiana, held closely to the eastern banks of the Wabash River and steeped under a brood of winter clouds. The small Midwestern city had given birth to a socialist leader, Eugene Debs, who'd been jailed for participating in a railroad strike, its river had been the source of a folk song or two, but for Alvarez, its importance was that it was home to several rail yards. Terre Haute served as a rail intersection, a nerve center, and as such it was the logical jumping-off point for Alvarez's final freight derailment.

By contractual arrangement, these tracks carried trains belonging to dozens of other carriers, including Northern Union. Fees were determined by tonnage and number of cars. Of the four regional companies, CIE and Louisville-and-Nashville were under contract to Pinkerton for their security. The smaller carriers worked with lesser-known firms. Northern Union, CSX, and the big nationals kept security work in-house. Consolidations and mergers had left many companies traveling over the same shared rails, sharing yards, sharing maintenance, and yet oddly, all being managed by different security companies. In terms of security, Terre Haute was a model of confusion; for Alvarez it was a thing of beauty, a place where jurisdiction was unclear. A derailment would necessitate dozens of meetings and phone calls—a time-consuming process that would benefit Alvarez's escape. His encounter in the boxcar had shown him that NUS agents were out looking for him. But NUR controlled more than thirty thousand miles of track. Even O'Malley could not effectively police a network that size.

Alvarez's purpose that night in the boxcar had been to establish location. That research now returned him to Greencastle, Indiana. Shipping manifests that he'd studied inside NUR's New York headquarters had provided him with both scheduling and equipment assignments.

Somewhere in the darkness, freight car AJ5-6729 awaited him. Once he found it, he needed only minutes to ensure its derailment.

He was distracted by erotic thoughts of Jillian and cautioned himself to maintain a clear head. New York had been a success: he had gained access to the escort service's Internet site and had won confirmation of a "date" with the same woman whom he'd followed to the Powell. Jillian was not needed, not necessary, and he knew better than to involve himself with *anyone*. Even so, she lingered in the back of his mind invitingly: sensual and understanding—a near lethal combination for a man in his current situation.

In Greencastle, five lines of CSX track met with a north/south spur of the Louisville-and-Nashville, meaning that all freight trains slowed to a crawl when passing through this small town. Some interline trains exchanged cars, others off-loaded freight. Despite all this activity, Greencastle was considered insignificant real estate by the conglomerates that controlled these tracks. In all of Greencastle, there was not a single security agent for any of the rail companies. Yard employees were encouraged to keep an eye out for riders and throw them off, but only the local police had authority to arrest or detain, and the police here seemed more preoccupied with Depauw U. kids than with the rusting tracks left behind by the mining boom nearly a century earlier.

At midnight, in forty-one-degree temperatures and near total darkness, Alvarez wore four thin layers of insulating clothing, including black jeans and his black leather jacket. He carried the duffel containing two hydraulic car jacks, each weighing about fifteen pounds. He also carried a box filled with a dozen round bearings intended for equipment half the weight of a freight car. All those bearings would quickly fail as they overheated. He slipped into the area of intersecting tracks west of South Jackson Street. Using an alias, he had flown two flights to get to his spot: Newark to Cincinnati; Cincinnati to Indianapolis. To reach Greencastle, less than thirty miles from Indianapolis, he had avoided trains altogether, electing to take an airport cab to Putnamville and then walking a series of country roads three miles north to Greencastle. He'd begun that walk at ten-thirty at night, and not a single car or truck had passed him during the entire forty-five-minute journey. Umberto Alvarez loved the Midwest.

The yard was dark, and Alvarez was taking no chances that NUR had stationed someone here. Upon his arrival, he had stood perfectly still, waiting for his eyes to adjust to the darkness, only to realize they already had: he could hardly see any distance at all, given the cloud cover and lack of city light. He watched and waited for a half hour, his nerves wired by coffee and adrenaline—not a movement out there. Finally, he braved it, using a red bandanna as a filter over his mag light, creating a faint red ray that he followed. Red light did not carry well past a few yards and therefore would be difficult for anyone to spot, even from nearby South Jackson Street. He worked the long line of rail cars sidetracked in the yard, some hitched to others, some orphans, all the while alert for the unexpected rider or unscheduled guard who could be lurking. He remained attentive for the smell of booze or cigarettes. He crept quietly alongside the cars, pausing at intervals, his dull red flashlight beam seeking out the control numbers on the sides of the cars and flatbeds.

There she was: AJ5-6729. He touched the side of the car with reverence. It was a messenger, this car, destined now to deliver destruction to the doorstep of William Goheen, one last effort to draw O'Malley's attention away from the bullet train, however briefly. AJ5-6729, a flatbed listed in the NUR manifest, was scheduled to depart Greencastle today. The smell of success filled his head like the glow from a good wine. He felt giddy. He carried no notes, all necessary information had been committed to memory. His laptop, his mechanical brain, was secured through passwords. He read the stenciled numbering—AJ5-6729—one last time. It was scheduled to be interlined that same morning. The full train, owned and operated by NUR, would travel on CSX tracks through western Indiana— Brazil and Seelyville—on its way to Terre Haute and St. Louis beyond.

Its ultimate destination was Albuquerque, New Mexico—a destination that would never be reached. AJ5-6729 would lose its axle and roll somewhere this side of Terre Haute. It would carry the rear cars with it.

Alvarez circled the flatbed. Convinced he was alone, he tossed the duffel beneath the car and followed under himself. With the proper equipment, a trained maintenance crew could switch out journal bearings in minutes. Train truck axles were secured by nothing more than gravity. With bad bearings and lubricating wood waste removed, Alvarez could create a "hot box" in virtually no time. Later he'd ride a different freight to the town of Brazil. There, he would waste the morning awaiting the only foolproof mode of transportation out of the area: Amtrak. His research into the speed of this train and the timing of "hot box" failure suggested that sometime before Terre Haute, the driver or engineer would notice an unexpected shimmy, a buckling, a rumble, which would pass up the steel like a cold shiver. AJ5-6729 would begin to fishtail. Then the train would roll, car after car. A lazy, slow roll that would snap a coupler well before the forward cars—and the locomotive—were threatened. A few thousand tons of steel would roll off the track, skid, and crawl through the landscape, ripping up the rail in its wake. An investigation would begin that would distract, if not consume, O'Malley and the NTSB—all players that Alvarez needed out of the way in order to give him room to work his magic on the bullet train.

CHAPTER 15

Tyler might have had his first decent night's sleep had it not been for the thoughts patrolling inside his head. The talk with O'Malley had both intrigued and upset him. Information had been kept from him, by NUR and possibly by Loren Rucker. O'Malley's unwavering confidence and arrogance got under Tyler's skin and festered. The man's opinion that Tyler had little chance of success irritated but somehow also inspired him.

He tossed and turned, sleeping poorly, with the hotel's bedside clock shining a dull green light onto his face and through his closed eyelids. He woke himself up with a start in the middle of making love to Nell Priest, an erection beneath the sheets, and realized that she, too, had gotten under his skin. He had been away from home just a couple of nights, but it seemed much longer.

Tyler placed another call to his attorney, Henry Happle, who related that the bank was unwilling to negotiate repayment of the missed mortgages. They took the stand that if Tyler repaid all his current mortgage debts in a lump sum, as well as a $527 penalty fee, and was able to keep current with future payments, the foreclosure papers would go away. They might as well have suggested he fly to the moon.

He told Happle to put his 1953 Norton Model 7 on the auction block, something he had steadfastly refused to do, for to him it represented his last chance at freedom. If the house and all its contents *did* go, then his backup plan was to escape reality for a while on the back of the Norton. Some gas money was all it would take, and not much of that.

Little by little, the Chester Washington assault claimed all he held dear. The importance of this boxcar investigation increased daily. He grabbed onto it for dear life. It represented not only his sole chance at some income but also, by his way of thinking, the only real possibility for future employment, whether with the government or with the likes of a Northern Union. (A horrible thought, but not one he could completely rule out.) No one was exactly beating a path to his door to offer work. The headhunters had yet to call.

He worried about updating Rucker on the meeting with O'Malley. Given O'Malley's disclaimers, he wondered if Rucker would now pull him from the assignment? The investigation was not over, but it might take a strong argument to win that point. Furthermore, if what he had was passed along to the FBI, then he had little doubt it *was* over. And what then? Take a job with O'Malley? Work side by side with Nell Priest? None of this sounded too bad.

What was the sense of returning home to a foreclosed house and a woman who wouldn't return his phone calls? He had little, if anything, to go home to, and he found the prospect of this more than a little terrifying.

He took breakfast in the hotel's dining room at 8 A.M., wondering why he hadn't heard back from the security group out at JFK and hoping they hadn't bypassed him or, worse, neglected his request outright. He'd had a great success working the security videos, and he clung to his belief that the suspect was in the city and had not simply boarded another flight. He leafed through a copy of the *New York Times* but couldn't focus, worrying more and more about O'Malley's suggestion that in a city this large the case was essentially closed: they weren't going to find him.

By 9:00 he was back in his room watching *Headline News* and wondering if he should call Nell Priest. At 9:20 his cell phone rang, and he answered it hungrily, like a lover awaiting a call.

"It's me." *Nell Priest.*

"What's up?" He tried to sound casual. In fact, his chest felt tight, and he found it hard to breathe.

"We lost another one. A derailment."

At that same moment, *Headline News* broke away to a helicopter shot of freight cars lying on their sides, the cars jacked up against one another, a fire burning. Tyler had muted the sound, but the caption read, LIVE BREAKING NEWS, TERRE HAUTE, INDIANA.

"Oh, God," he heard himself say. Indiana—less than a hundred miles from where the frozen corpse of Harry Wells had been found. "CNN has it live," he told her.

"Driver and engineer are both fine, same as the others. There's some kind of gas leaking from one of the cars that's requiring we evacuate the area. It's a mess, Peter. I'm going out there with O'Malley—on the company jet this time—and he offered you a seat, if you want to come. We can land right in Terre Haute. It'll be much faster than commercial." He could hear in her voice that she wanted him to come.

"You know how it is: I can't accept gifts from the private sector."

"You took that flight with me up to Chicago."

"That was a favor from you and one made at my request, not the other way around. I trusted you not to make it an issue. O'Malley knows better than to even offer."

"Call your boss. I'll bet he'll make an exception. Maybe he can bend the rules a little."

"Give me the particulars, in case it works out," he said.

"We leave from Teterboro," she said.

Tyler started writing.

Riding on the company jet with O'Malley was making Tyler anxious, despite Loren Rucker's okay. It wasn't exactly sleeping with the enemy, though that thought also distracted him—Nell Priest occupied one of the cushy leather seats directly across from him. He

doubted the invitation to ride along had come from O'Malley's generosity—that concept didn't fit with the man Tyler had met in the
hotel bar—and if not generosity, then it was a calculated effort on
his part. O'Malley either wanted Tyler within arm's reach or wanted
him out of New York. Both possibilities troubled him. So Tyler had
booked his own rental car before leaving New York and therefore
politely refused the offer of a ride in either of the Suburbans that
O'Malley had rented for himself and Priest. Tyler drove a two-door
Oldsmobile—a convertible—that made a joke out of him with its
sporty lines and neon crimson purple paint. Within a few minutes,
though, he'd have the top down.

"What's the plan?" Priest called him on his cell phone as the
three cars drove away from the airport.

"This is my first derailment." He meant it as a joke, but she took
it seriously.

"You don't like O'Malley," she concluded. "But I'm telling you,
Tyler—"

"It's not a matter of liking. It's a matter of trust."

"And me?" she questioned.

How did he answer that? he wondered. "I need information. Inside information. And O'Malley isn't giving it to me."

"You're testing me? Tyler, I work for the man."

"No test," he said. "How many agents is he putting on this?"

"Buckets. Six guys we had out in the field are all on their way."

"I think our Latino is going to want to see the wreck," Tyler
said, nervous to share this thought.

"Based upon?"

"A few shots on *Headline News* aren't going to cut it for him.
He'll want a front-row seat."

"Suddenly you're a profiler, too?"

"An opinion is all. If he's gone, he's gone."

"You're talking in circles."

"Listen, we know that twenty-some hours ago he landed in New
York. So we have to make a judgment call. Did he rig this derailment

before Wells got to him, or did he come back? Both scenarios offer completely different tactics, in terms of how we investigate."

"I like your pronouns," she said. "Keep talking like that."

"I don't know what O'Malley has planned, but my instincts say to investigate it as if he returned, because if not, he's so far gone by now we're chasing a trail, not a person."

"What's the information you need? How many agents we're using?"

"We need to know where this train stopped in the last twenty hours. Where, why, and for how long? We need to know if this stretch of track was inspected by your people recently. Same with the individual cars. Where were they? When were they last inspected? It's all stuff O'Malley will cover, I think. But if not—"

"I can do this," she offered.

"I'll need comparison photographs of this scene, as well as shots of the other derailments. Aerials, if you can get them. Rucker can put those shots in front of a forensics engineer and plot similarities, if any."

"I can handle that as well."

"I'd just as soon O'Malley not know what I'm requesting, though I understand if that's impossible."

"Nothing's impossible," she declared. "Some things are just trickier than others."

"Why help me?" he asked. "Did O'Malley put you up to this?"

"I'll pretend I never heard that," she said. Returning to their earlier discussion, she asked, "What about our guy wanting a closer look?"

"You brought video gear?"

"Of course."

"Whoever's shooting the video should shoot the crowds as well. Watch the crowds, Nell. You'll never spot him just standing there. The trick we always used on homicide was to *approach* the crowds—making it nice and obvious—and look for the ones attempting to quietly slip away. One of those is our guy," he stated.

"You've just given me goose bumps," she said.

She gave him more than goose bumps, as he recalled from the night before. He wondered what a relationship with her would be like. He'd never been with a black woman. How far apart were their worlds?

He said, "Hold any and all of those guys for questioning and let me know about them, if you can."

"And you? What are you up to?"

"I'm going to gamble that our boy's human. And if I'm right," he added, "it'll be me calling you, not the other way around."

Tyler used logic to play a simple hunch: anonymous airline travel was no longer possible, every passenger had to show a picture ID. Granted, every detail of a driver's license was rarely examined by the airline employee, but they did match the picture with the face and the name on the license with the name on the ticket. The suspect had flown from Chicago to New York, presumably on a fake ID. But how many fake IDs did he possess, and how many was he willing to use? Typically, IDs were hoarded, saved for use when all else failed. A perp stuck with an ID as long as possible. Would their guy run through his IDs needlessly by using them freely? Tyler thought not. The smart money said to run with that one ID until its use became risky and then move on to another, if available. To test his theory required only a single call to Rucker's office.

"I have some homework for your minions," Tyler began the call.

Rucker countered, "I have an official request from the FBI on my desk. They're wondering if we're investigating a criminal activity, and if so, why?"

Tyler stayed true to his needs. "Compare the flight manifest for the United flight our suspect flew to JFK with the manifests for every flight flown in the last thirty hours into Indianapolis. I'm betting a name will kick. When it does," he said confidently, "pull the security videos at baggage claim, taxi stands, buses, rental car counters, and the appropriate arrival gate in Indianapolis. Then back up and do the same for the gate and check-in counters at the originating airport. The computers time-stamp check-ins. Those time stamps can help—"

Rucker interrupted, "—determine which security video to check. And maybe we get a face to frame on our walls." He hesitated and then allowed, "Impressive."

"Airports are not on twenty-four-hour security tape loops. They hold theirs for thirty days before recording over them. But just in case, we'd better hurry," Tyler pressed. "Some of those may get recorded over." He added, "How much should I worry about the FBI pulling me?"

"The boxcar could be related to this derailment. We're in charge of the derailment. I'd say not to worry. Ironically, the derailment just saved you your assignment. I'll monitor the situation."

"Work those flight manifests," Tyler encouraged.

"Consider it done."

Wearing an NTSB windbreaker over his winter coat, his teeth biting down on the mouthpiece of a special gas mask that had been provided, Tyler stood off from the other investigators and rescue workers. It was not an easy site to reach; he'd had to park the rental out on a road and walk nearly half a mile through slush to reach the derailment. He couldn't take his eyes off the twisted and torn metal of the derailed train, a curving S of rolled freight cars. The derailed cars had been thrown up an embankment, some fifteen yards or more from the broken tracks, rails and ties scattered in all directions, bent and twisted and broken in an ungainly display. The sight made him sick to his stomach, or perhaps the gas mask and his claustrophobia had something to do with his nausea. He couldn't take his mind off the fact that had this been a passenger train, dozens, perhaps hundreds, might have been injured or killed. Certainly this was the greater concern of William Goheen and Northern Union: *what if he targeted passenger trains?* Interestingly, the public barely paid attention to a few thousand tons of freight train jumping track. Within a day or two there would be no mention of it in the news.

The site was crowded with local law enforcement and firefighters. O'Malley and Priest scoured the rubble. Everyone wore some form of respiratory protection against the escaping gases, the car responsible for the leak was crusted in a fire-retarding white foam. The word from NUR was that those gases were benign and posed no health risk, but no one was taking any chances. Wearing the gear, Tyler felt a little like an astronaut. About the only real solid benefit of that escaping gas was that it kept the media at bay—behind barriers erected three-quarters of a mile off—and Tyler was thinking that they could have used some gas at some of his homicide crime scenes in D.C., where the initials of their city had evolved into a Disneyland Circus—a perfect description of how the media treated crime scenes. The other benefit of the masks was that no one talked much because it required shouting, and even then words were lost to the plastic hoods. That gas was so beneficial, in fact, that for a moment Tyler considered the possibility that O'Malley had arranged for it. He put little past the man.

Tyler didn't know enough about derailment investigation to be effective here, but he had wanted to see it for himself, to record his own mental images, to *feel* the devastation firsthand, and also to run off a few Polaroids to advance to Rucker. It was an impressive, disturbing sight—some piece of human engineering so massive, incongruously at rest on its side.

Priest came at him through the mist of a fire hose used on car thirty-six, which was thought to contain flammables. Unlike the others, who had jobs to do, Tyler stood upwind of the wreck. As she approached, he pulled off the gas mask. Nell Priest followed his lead.

"You've never been to one of these, right?" she asked.

"Shoe's on the other foot," he said, shaking his head no. She had never been to a homicide.

"Most everybody here has a specific assignment. Fire suppression, communications, medical. The biggest job for everyone involved is keeping the chain of command straight. Ironically, you're in charge, did you know that?"

"Because I'm NTSB?"

"Exactly."

The National Transportation Safety Board had investigative authority in any such transportation-related disaster.

"Our guys—the *real* guys—are on their way," he corrected. "It's an Emergency Response Team."

"You're still in charge for now. Even the FiBIes are second to you until your cavalry arrives. It's not just a technicality; it's the way it works."

"I've never even seen one of these," he pointed out, "much less investigated one. I think I'll pass."

"The smartest move you can make is to hand it off to the locals," she advised. "Your ERT guys will take it back when they arrive, but you're a hero if you give it to the locals for a few hours."

"Not your guys," he tested.

"Listen, the biggest mistake you could make is to give it to O'Malley, though you never heard that from me. He'll expect it of you. I'm sure it's why he offered to fly you out here. Not only did he want you, an NTSB guy, to be on the scene, mandating the hierarchy, but he'll think you owe him one. He wants control. You're his ticket."

"Got it."

She dug into a pocket and offered Tyler a handwritten list of the towns where the various cars of the derailed train had been parked and for how long. "Maybe this gives you a head start," she said.

"Maybe," he agreed.

"What's wrong?" she asked. "I thought you'd be grateful for that."

"I am," he replied, though unconvincingly.

She picked up on this. "Listen, Tyler, I objected to you being left out of the loop on Wells. For what it's worth, I made a stink about it before I ever headed to St. Louis. But Keith O'Malley operates on eighty percent paranoia. He's extremely distrustful where the feds are concerned. He compartmentalizes information so no one person ever has the full picture. And I don't think I have the full picture even now. I don't think you do."

"This Latino?" Tyler asked.

"I would bet O'Malley knows more than he's letting on, yes. And flying you out with us? Keith O'Malley doing the feds a favor? Since when? All I'm saying is watch your back. With your recent history, you make a pretty good target if someone's looking for a scapegoat. Maybe O'Malley's doing you favors for the wrong reasons. And I don't want *anything* to do with that." She added, "I like you."

He thanked her for the list.

"Thank me later," she said. "And keep your phone on. If anything comes up here—which it won't—I'll let you know."

Attempting to retrace the movements of the saboteur, to find evidence or establish an escape route to follow, Tyler visited the derailed train's last stop.

The train tracks in Greencastle had once been used to ferry hundreds of millions of tons of coal from the mining pits of Appalachia to every city and town in both the central and northern states and parts of western Canada. Judging by the lack of rust on the rails, Tyler determined they were still in use, though today's traffic no doubt paled in comparison with what had traveled here a hundred years earlier. This group of side-by-side tracks now couldn't even be considered a yard, and yet NUR and several of its competitors used the Greencastle spur as a holding area and pickup point, by-passing Indianapolis's Big Four yard and its higher fees. This was all explained to Tyler by a heavyset black man in his mid-fifties who must have felt exceptionally cold in his oil-stained overalls and well-worn lineman's boots, but he behaved like a man standing on a beach, all smiles and sunshine.

"Kind of a bother, moving some of these cars," he explained, "as we ain't necessarily set up for it. A lot of push-and-pull, you ask me. The Big Four yard, northeast of here, would be a hell of a lot easier."

"What about the N-nine-ninety?" Tyler asked, naming the de-railed train.

"We added three cars earlier this morning. Yes, sir."

"When would that have been?"

"Around sunrise, it was. Frost was on. Steel has got a mean bite in these temperatures."

"You see anyone? Strangers? Anyone like that?"

"No, sir." He smiled like a jack-o'-lantern. "And I know 'bout everyone in Greencastle . . . *including* the strangers."

"Did you check the cars?"

"Inspect 'em? 'Course we did."

"No, I mean for hobos."

"Riders," he stated, shaking his head at Tyler's ignorance. "Not me, no, sir. A man fool enough to ride a car in these temperatures, who am I to stop him? You gotta be some kind of desperate. 'Round here we see riders more in the warm months, but it wouldn't make no difference to me, no how. Not my job to police these cars. I just push 'em and pull 'em, and the pay ain't great at that."

"And if someone *was* on one of these cars—in them, whatever—at what point could he get off? When does the nine-ninety stop again?"

"For most of the Northern Union trains it's Terre Haute."

"Somewhere before there," Tyler encouraged.

The man looked a little confused.

"Someplace a person could jump on or off?"

The big man looked at Tyler strangely. "What you got in mind, anyway?"

"I'm running an investigation into the derailment," Tyler reminded him, impatient now.

"Plenty of places to jump from the N-nine-ninety, if you got a mind to do it. It ain't no high-speed train, you know? The N-nine-ninety runs once a week, Tennessee to Michigan. She carries brake hubs, mostly . . . from the Street Brothers foundry in Chattanooga. Been making this run for fifty years."

Tyler felt trapped under a weight of frustration. The suspect was a planner. He had known where to hit the 990 and he would know how to flee the area. If the man's encounter with Harry Wells had been a dry run, then he'd already jumped another train bound for St. Louis. O'Malley was certain to cover that possibility. Tyler's hope was that the suspect either had delayed leaving the area to get a look at the wreck in daylight or changed his escape route due to the attention Harry Wells had brought him. If so, he would have had to improvise or rethink his getting away. If he'd stayed, he could still be close by, or just on his way out. Tyler felt discouraged but not beaten. "Plenty of places to jump, eh?" he said, echoing the big man.

"Yes, sir. I figure that's about right."

Tyler asked the next logical question. "If a person doesn't have his own car, how does he get out of these towns? Bus? Train?"

"Sure thing. There's both, but nothing from here that'll help you. Closest Gray-dog is down to Cloverdale." He glanced over at Tyler's rental car. "Amwreck is up to Crawfordsville," he said, self-amused. "Right here, you're kinda in no-man's land. This here is freight-hauling track. This is the real railroad."

"Other tracks, other trains someone could jump—*riders,* I mean," he said, using the proper terminology.

"Plenty." He rolled out his thick fingers from his cold fist as he counted. "Amwreck, CSX, NUR, Indiana, Indiana Southern, Louisville-and-Nashville. Take your pick. They all work these same rails."

"But the wreck of the nine-ninety has closed the tracks," Tyler reminded him. "Right?"

"Not Amwreck, it hasn't." He addressed Tyler like a teacher to a student. "Amwreck runs on the northern tracks, not these. Fact is, every damn freight line out of Indianapolis is going to have to be rerouted to those northern tracks. Me? Unless they call me down to that wreck to lend a hand, I'm out of a job for the better part of the next week. Mark my word."

Tyler tried putting himself in the mind of the suspect and considered his options. The man had about a six-hour jump on them—much less if he'd stayed to admire his work, as Tyler believed he would. If the derailment had been set up four or five days earlier, just prior to the boxcar assault, then all was for naught, but Tyler doubted it. According to O'Malley, the derailments resulted from bad bearings. It seemed likely, if sabotage, it would have been carried out just prior to the derailment.

North or south? Train or bus? Tyler doubted the man would steal a car or charter a plane. Either option could be too quickly chased down. He could *feel* his time running out, *feel* the man escaping as he stood there in the cold talking to this yard hand. "Which runs more often, Greyhound or Amtrak?"

"The Graydog only runs twice a week anymore," the big man replied, "Tuesdays and Thursdays, I believe it is. Time was when it ran every day."

"And the Amtrak?" Tyler asked, more hopeful.

"On through to Chicago once a day. From Indianapolis, more often than that."

"Once a day," Tyler said, breathlessly.

"Afternoon," the man said.

Tyler felt awash with relief. It was not yet noon. He saw a flicker of possibility: the Amtrak to Chicago could be their suspect's backup escape route. Glimpse the wreck, get to Crawfordsville. He'd used O'Hare in Chicago once; would he use it again?

Tyler thanked the yard hand, already at a full run back toward his rental.

From the front seat, his cell phone pressed to his ear, Tyler attempted to navigate not only the streets of Greencastle but Amtrak's automated phone system. By the time he reached state highway 231, he learned that Crawfordsville, an unmanned Amtrak station, offered two choices, not one, as he'd just been told: a "motor coach" to Bloomington, Illinois, and then an Amtrak to St. Louis, or an express Amtrak to Chicago. Both departed Crawfordsville within the hour.

Tyler's choice was the express, because it departed first. A long shot, he made the drive anyway, believing it worth the try.

He brought the car up to eighty-five. He had a twenty-five-mile drive to make in seventeen minutes.

The flat Indiana farmland streamed past, broken only by intersections with smaller roads so straight they reminded Tyler of railroad tracks. Everything reminded him of railroad tracks. His cell phone rang. With the top down, Tyler had to slow to hear. It was Rucker.

"Since when do you have a crystal ball?" the NTSB man asked him.

Tyler felt a little dance in the center of his chest. He'd put Rucker on cross-checking passenger manifests. He had thought it might take a day or two. A week. He hadn't been sure. "Did we kick a name?" he asked incredulously.

"You'll appreciate the irony," Rucker said. "The guy actually has a—"

"Please, cut to the chase."

"A sense of humor."

"I'm all laughs."

"Kevin Christopher Jones is listed both on the United flight from Chicago to JFK, and again last night on a ComAir flight from Cincinnati to Indianapolis. His ticket originated in Newark."

"I'm missing the humor," Tyler said, his blood pumping so quickly that he felt light-headed. *A name!* Alias or not, it was a start.

"Kevin Christopher Jones. Initials, K. C." Rucker paused. Tyler still didn't get it, and said so. "K. C. Jones. Casey Jones! Now do you get it?"

The car swerved and lost its rear tires, briefly fishtailing. Tyler regained control. "You're kidding me. The guy's making a joke out of this?"

"We should have a gate photo shortly. We may get a good look at his face."

A photograph! "Do you have it in your power to delay an Amtrak express at a station stop?" The thought had only then occurred to Tyler—he worked for the *government* now.

"What do you need done?" Rucker asked.

Tyler grinned. Government work wasn't so bad after all.

CHAPTER 16

When the Amtrak bound for Chicago failed to leave Craw-fordsville on time, Alvarez's stomach turned. If the train had arrived late, it would have been one thing, but to his surprise it had clocked in right on time. Instead, it was late *leaving* the tiny station, and he began to second-guess his backup plan. Having aborted his original freight route because of the boxcar incident, and fearing Northern Union would be crawling all over the various freight lines, he had killed the last six hours in a crummy motel room in Brazil, using the down time on the Internet.

His backup escape, an Amtrak from Crawfordsville to Chicago, avoided St. Louis.

He had two credit cards and two driver's licenses under matching names that had been both expensive and hard to get some months earlier. He had never used either—he used yet a third driver's license for air travel: Kevin Jones. He saved the two alternates, reserving them for only the most dire circumstances, knowing they could safely be used only once.

This, he believed, qualified as a dire circumstance.

Northern Union knew they were dealing with a saboteur, though that had never reached the press (each derailment had been attributed in public to a different cause). Their security people would believe that he was in a hurry, desperate even, to get away from here. His confidence in this had allowed him to delay by a few hours, thus doing the unexpected. Any car rental made in the area would be, or already had been, examined by NUS. So his current plan called for riding the Amtrak to Chicago and then renting a car from there. Distancing himself from southern Indiana meant everything.

Alvarez had trained himself to contain his anxieties. And yet, as the seconds ticked off, he debated abandoning and getting off the train. But what if that, he wondered, was expected of him? What if the train was being watched, waiting for someone to make a run for it? He had no idea if a company like Northern Union had the power to delay an Amtrak, but it did seem possible. The derailment would allow all sorts of exceptions.

He felt boxed in. There were precious few ways out of southern Indiana, discounting freight trains and buses. He started second-guessing himself, wondering if he should have stolen a car or found an abandoned farmhouse in which to lie low. Then he chastised himself for getting distracted. He had to make some decisions, and quickly.

Settling his nerves, he elected to stay on board, all the while keeping his attention focused on the station platform, waiting to see if anyone would board or if the delay was simply Amtrak-oriented. He sorted through possibilities about what to do if someone did board. Conductors would be coming around to collect tickets of the recently boarded passengers—three, including himself. That ticket collection would identify him. Sweating now, he checked his watch: eleven minutes late. It felt like an eternity.

He craned to get a look out of the opposite windows, alert for activity. Then back to the platform. Then out the other side again.

The woman next to him studied him closely, growing as uncomfortable as he was.

"Do you think there's something wrong?" she asked.

"Yes," Alvarez answered. "I think quite possibly there is."

"God bless the Internet," Loren Rucker said.

His cell phone once again held to his ear, Tyler pulled the rental car to a stop, the Amtrak's dull aluminum siding wet with a cold winter rain that turned the snow to white cement. The long train snaked back down the track intersecting with the horizon, an ominous presence of steel and glass and power. He'd never had a train held for him before.

A uniformed conductor stood on the platform thumping his gloved hands against his legs to fight off the cold. Tyler wished there might be some way to board anonymously, but it was too late for such tricks. He felt lucky just to have the train, never mind that most of the passengers on the platform side would see his face. He carried an overnight bag that held his laptop and some paperwork and what was to have been three days of clean clothes, all of which were soiled and needed laundering. He wished he had a baseball cap or something to pull down over his face, but his baseball caps all hung on pegs back in a house that had been foreclosed upon.

"I'm kinda in a hurry, here. There's a train waiting for me," Tyler said. He climbed out of the car and opened the door to the backseat to grab his bag.

"We have a gate photo of our suspect as he arrived in Indianapolis," Loren Rucker announced proudly. "It's not the best quality, nor the best angle. He's wearing a black leather jacket and carrying a black duffel. No decent look at his face."

Tyler found this interesting but not groundbreaking—they already had the jacket and duffel from the O'Hare security videos. He asked Rucker to e-mail him the photo. He could dial up from the laptop, once he was on the train. He added, "Okay? Can I call you back?"

"There's more," Rucker said. "The airline recovered his boarding pass in Cincinnati. The local lab there fumed it for prints and developed five latents of various sizes."

"Boarding passes move through a lot of hands," Tyler cautioned.

"They scanned the five prints and beamed them out to every god-damn print database out there. That's why I mentioned the Internet—this is moving at light speed. Literally. All this in the last two hours. It's a prioritized request, so we move to the front of the line. By now those prints are being checked against national and state felony arrests as well as Northern Union's own database, so we may be able to eliminate airline employees and narrow the search. Within hours, they'll run through databases for the military, state and federal employees, medical workers, teachers, day care workers—you name it." Rucker paused for a breath. Tyler caught his heart racing, and it had little to do with his running toward that train. Rucker added, "We're going to ID this son of a bitch." He paused, "Tyler? You hear me?"

"Send me that e-mail," Tyler repeated, reaching the conductor, who was already signaling for the train to roll.

Alvarez looked on as a man climbed out of a two-door convertible and approached the conductor, who then ushered him aboard. A moment later the train was rolling and Alvarez's eyes were briefly pinched shut committing that face to memory. The enemy had just boarded; he felt certain of it. His mind reeled. What now? Was it possible O'Malley's people had tracked him to this train? Had he somehow left crumbs to follow, all the while working so hard to avoid making any? Or was this blind, random luck—O'Malley playing every hunch? It was at that moment his eyes landed on various multicolored paper stubs snugged into the seats in front of each passenger—the conductors' means of keeping track of who had paid and who had boarded where. The conductors would make their rounds any minute. What he had to do was pilfer one of these, and then he wouldn't be asked for his ticket. Two things could work in his favor: the train was crowded, and he had chosen a seat in the middle cars, allowing him movement in either direction.

The train rattled and lurched as it started down the tracks. Alvarez excused himself and sneaked his legs past the older woman sitting on the aisle. He left his duffel in the overhead rack; he didn't want it to look like he was changing seats, didn't want to attract attention. He tried to quiet the alarm that sounded in his brain, ringing there, out of control. He would try to buy himself a few minutes; then, at the first opportunity, he would jump. Hopefully, with no one the wiser.

Tyler reached out for balance as the train began to move, wondering if this wild-goose chase was worth it. He had no idea how one would calculate the odds that his suspect might be riding this same train, but he couldn't see letting it get away without him. Why hang around the crash site with a dozen other investigators all vying for control? He knew law enforcement well enough: talk now, act later.

He pushed through a heavy door and into a quiet, but crowded, train car. A *Latino,* he reminded himself, walking forward, one row at a time, as he searched the car, face by face.

The new arrival had boarded behind him, and so Alvarez moved toward the front, quickly, not looking back but feeling the presence of the man behind him like a sharp pain. He shoved the car's door open and stepped through to the loud, mechanical roar of that familiar rhythm that now seemed part of his bones. *Cha-cha-hmmmm, cha-cha-hmmmm.* Down the tracks it raced, a hundred tons of steel and human beings. He needed a seat stub. He punched through to the next car and spotted a possible: a man—a boy, really—in his late teens or early twenties. He wore a green baseball cap and was slumped against the left wall of the car fast asleep. Alvarez spotted the dull green stub. Perhaps green meant the kid had boarded in Indianapolis, or someplace further east. It didn't matter; he needed that stub. He picked the boy in part because he seemed so typical. The train was crowded with such kids—probably heading home for Christmas break. He picked him in part because he imagined that college-aged kids tried to duck tickets all the time. Would the conductor remember this one in particular? He hoped not. Would the kid have kept his receipt? Possibly, but it was also possible he'd tossed it and would have no proof he was a legitimate passenger. No matter what, the resulting confusion had to occupy the conductor's attention for a few minutes.

He didn't want the conductors figuring out that a seat stub had been stolen until he, Alvarez, had already jumped.

Alvarez walked up the center aisle, purposely unsteady, alternately placing his hands on the back of the seats to steady himself, his fingers only inches from those stubs. As he closed in on the kid, he took in his surroundings. His eye caught movement up ahead. He glanced up to see through the distant window of the car's end door, and through it beyond and into the next car and a conductor just finishing up looking for new passengers. The man was heading toward him. A quick check over his shoulder revealed a second conductor. He was sandwiched!

Demanding of himself that he stay calm, Alvarez focused on the task at hand. He needed that stub—and he needed it before either of the conductors reached him.

He staggered again, slipped, and fell to one knee. As he did so, he captured the green stub. He owned it. He looked quickly in both directions attempting to judge his situation. The conductor ahead seemed likely to enter first. He slipped into the first empty row of seats, tucked his stub into the space for it on the seat ahead and slouched into a napping position, his eyes open but dazed with fatigue—a passenger ready for a quiet trip to Chicago.

The forward conductor entered and began inspecting stubs and looking for unstubbed passengers to ticket. Alvarez felt a bead of sweat trickle from his forehead. His ears whined. He doubted that on close inspection he would pass for a passenger intent on napping.

The conductor stepped another row closer. And another. His heart began to swell painfully in his chest, its drumming ferocious.

Behind him, he heard the car's rear door open: *cha-cha-hmmm,* said the train. This would be the other conductor, quite possibly accompanying the stranger who had boarded late.

"Ticket?" It was the conductor looking down at him.

Alvarez swallowed dryly. "You already—" He glanced up to see his green seat stub was not where he had just put it. Panic seized hold of him. He blinked rapidly, his eyes stinging.

The conductor leaned in toward him. Alvarez prepared to fight back. The man said, "Never mind. Sorry to disturb you." He bent and retrieved the green stub from where it had fallen to the car floor.

Alvarez thought that in a way this had worked out even more in his favor, for now he and the conductor had a connection. He would be remembered as a ticketed passenger. "No problem," Alvarez said.

The conductor moved on. The pain in Alvarez's chest slowly subsided. He tried to steady himself.

Voices from behind, as the conductor rousted the sleeping kid, asking for a ticket. The kid protested, claiming he'd already given the man his ticket. The conductor was heard asking for a receipt. Alvarez watched in the reflection on the inside of the window as the kid pulled a ticket receipt out of his wallet. A *receipt!* Sweat dripped down and blurred Alvarez's vision.

The other conductor and the man who had boarded in Crawfordsville approached from the rear. The two conductors talked while one dropped to a knee, no doubt looking for the missing green seat stub. Alvarez couldn't hear them, but he didn't have to. No matter what they were saying, it was trouble.

"This here is Agent Tyler. He's interested in anyone who boarded at Crawfordsville. I told him I counted two."

"I saw three," the other conductor corrected. His name tag read

Charles Daniels. Tyler's conductor was tagged Felix Ramone. "I punched two in car three. Haven't hit the third yet."

"I started in five and worked forward. Didn't punch no one. Six through nine weren't open."

Tyler had noticed that at Crawfordsville only three cars had been open for boarding. He had a little trouble maintaining his sea legs with the train's movements.

"I seen two ladies," Ramone told his partner.

"Me? I seen them and a guy."

"You get a look at him?" Tyler asked Daniels.

"If I did," the man replied, "I didn't pay him no mind."

"So we have one unidentified male on board who has yet to be ticketed," Tyler suggested. His skin itched. The hair on the nape of his neck felt prickly.

"Probably somewhere in six through nine. More seats back there anyway."

Tyler spoke softly, "Here's what I want to do. Mr. Ramone, you're going to go check six through nine. If you ticket the guy, you do nothing unusual. Complete your rounds and come back up the train and find me." Ramone nodded. He looked a little excited, which bothered Tyler. "Mr. Daniels, you and I are going to have a talk with the two women who boarded at Crawfordsville. We'll ask a few questions. Maybe get a description. Nice and quiet, nothing showy."

"Got it."

"What's this guy done, anyway?" Ramone asked.

The other conductor paused as if remembering something, and then said, "You know, come to think of it, I shoulda checked that guy's receipt." He turned slowly toward the front of the car.

"What guy?" Tyler asked, his throat sour and dry.

The man pointed. But the seat where Alvarez had been sitting was now empty.

Car number three, two cars forward of where Alvarez had left his duffel, was packed. He carried his green stub with him and knew that there would be a receipt or two for the picking, tossed as litter, since few passengers, other than businesspeople, held on to their receipts once punched in by the conductor. The trick was to locate one of today's, and quickly.

Alvarez bent and scooped one off the floor, but it carried a shoe print, and that bothered him. On closer inspection, it had been punched yesterday. This train evidently had come from the East Coast and had already run more than twelve hours without cleaning.

The door thumped closed behind him as he moved into the next car. He was getting too far away from his duffel, too disconnected from his plans.

He scooped down, again collecting receipts, this time a pair. One was clean and punched as an Indianapolis boarding. He pocketed it. He took a minute to collect himself and dab off some sweat with his forearm.

He didn't want to cross paths with the conductor—especially not with the man who had boarded late—but he was running out of room at this end of the train, and his duffel was now three cars behind him. If an NUS agent, this guy was likely to know his face. He tried to settle himself. Calm won the day.

The public address system announced that the dining car was open. Several people came out of their seats at once. Alvarez saw an opening: the dining car was midtrain. If he could group himself in with the others . . .

Tyler had three hours until the train reached Chicago, plenty of time to isolate the one man who had boarded in Crawfordsville.

The conductor, Daniels, came alive as they entered the next car. "There," he said, indicating two women. One of the women stood and headed away from them. "Excuse me!" the conductor called out loudly. The woman didn't turn. She stepped out of the way of a thick group of several people, apparently heading for the dining car.

Tyler rose to his toes, trying to keep his eye on the woman. As they reached the vacated seat, Tyler said to the conductor, "You take her. I'll talk to this one." He turned, stepping out of the way of the other passengers in the crowded aisle. His cell phone rang, and he was distracted as he answered it.

The man ducking his head in that group behind him was Umberto Alvarez.

"Nothing on this end," Nell Priest told him over the phone. "It'll be weeks before we know exactly what rolled this train, but it could have been an axle shear. It could have been a hot box from bad bearings."

"The same M.O."

"Yes."

Tyler debated telling her what he knew. He gave in. "Rucker has a gate photo and prints. He's closing in on an ID."

"And you?" she asked.

"I'm on an Amtrak to Chicago."

"Do we have a face?" she asked.

Tyler was about to mention the black leather jacket. For privacy, he turned while cupping the phone. As he did so, he saw the backs of two black leather jackets among the group of passengers that had just squeezed past him. Granted, there were probably other such jackets in this car, but these two walking away nagged at him. He kept his eye on that group.

"If you want to be part of this," he said, "get yourself to Chicago by tonight. I gotta go." He disconnected and followed that group—those two jackets—an unexplained sense of dread overcoming him. The interview with the woman could wait—she looked to be in her eighties; she wasn't going anywhere fast.

The conductor pounded his fist onto the door of the car's only lavatory and called out to the woman inside. "Madame! Excuse me! We'd like a word with you in a moment."

The sense of dread in Tyler built to a higher level. He moved more quickly now. He stepped into the loud passageway between cars, watching the group through the glass in the end door. As he entered this car, the group was just leaving. He hurried, walking more quickly. He didn't want to run—to attract that kind of attention—but he did turn it up a notch. He reached the far end in time to see through both door windows and into the next car.

One of the two men wearing the black leather jackets was tall, with wide shoulders. *Strong,* Tyler thought. Dark haired. All at once, this man reached up into the overhead rack and, without breaking his stride, snagged a piece of luggage.

A small black duffel bag. The kind that doubled as a backpack. The description fit.

It was hardly definitive—the ubiquitous black duffel—and yet the cop in Tyler sensed this was a person worth confronting.

He pushed through the rear door, adrenaline coursing through his system. The suspect simultaneously exited through the far end of the next car.

His instinct drove him. A veteran, he survived the street because of it, cleared investigations, and won cases. And Tyler knew he had it. He moved down the next car's center aisle with confidence and determination. He prioritized. He wanted to talk to this guy. That was all. No violation of rights, no violence. Nothing whatsoever like the afternoon with Chester Washington that had ruined his life. *The bag and black leather jacket could easily be coincidence,* he reminded himself. *But enough for probable cause.* The investigator felt energized. This particular train made sense as an escape route. There weren't a hell of a lot of other options.

Another possibility remained—that the sabotage had been done days or weeks earlier, and that the suspect was nowhere in the area, but this seemed unlikely given that Rucker had turned up the matching flight manifests. What else explained the arrival of K. C. Jones at Indianapolis?

As he approached the rear door to the next train car, the suspect out of sight, Tyler kept the image of Harry Wells firmly in mind, that deep cut from earlobe to eye, the bleed-out that left the man "as pale as a polar bear" as one of the techs had put it. This guy was dangerous, and the tight confines of a train were no place to come to terms with that. This thought was followed by a twinge of anxiety—a weightlessness in the center of his chest. The train car suddenly felt as if it were shrinking, and Tyler sensed the early warning signs of his particular brand of claustrophobia. *Not now!* he pleaded, but the car continued to shrink, an esophagus ready to swallow him. His head pounded and the train car continued to constrict. When a sudden *whoosh* rocked the entire train as an eastbound express passed, the jolt broke his anxiety. He pulled open the car door and stepped out into the noisy passageway that connected the two cars. He spun abruptly as he caught sight of a man to his right. The man's back was turned, a thin spiral of cigarette smoke rising. Tyler caught himself reaching for the man as he identified that the black jacket was not leather but Gore-Tex or nylon, and that there was no duffel to be seen.

He glanced into the next car, but it was the dining car—nothing but a narrow aisle with a turn to the left, as seen from this end.

The smoker's partner, a woman with short hair, freckles, and thin lips, stared at Tyler contemptuously.

Tyler stammered, "A man. Just now." He added, "A black duffel." The woman pointed to the dining car.

Tyler tripped a bright red bar and waited for the automatic door to slide out of his way. He paused by the car's only lavatory. OC-CUPIED, the indicator read. He knocked. A woman's voice answered. Tyler moved on.

The automatic door wheezed behind him. It was the same woman with the ultrashort haircut. She slipped past Tyler, who hurried and followed her. The small counter area was stainless steel. The thin woman ordered a Diet Coke. Tyler now pushed past her, facing twenty or more people, all standing with drinks and packaged sandwiches, cookies, and candy bars.

No black leather jacket. No black duffel.

His suspect was no longer here. *He's running from me,* Tyler thought, encouraged.

Tyler's legs buckled. The train slowed noticeably. An express to Chicago, there were no scheduled stops after Crawfordsville. This was merely a slowing—a turn up ahead, or a slight grade, an approaching town, or a control light being observed. *Slowing.* He hurried through the small crowd thinking:

He's going to jump!

Flight. Escape. The cop knew with absolute certainty that this was his suspect, and that he was about to lose him.

He recalled Harry Wells's broken body after being knifed and thrown from the train.

He lost his balance again.

The train dragged considerably.

Tyler punched the door's red bar, and the door *whooshed* open.

Noise. Wind. Through the passageway, an open side door on the left. The brown farm fields and slanting rain blurred past.

"Federal agent!" he announced, going for his gun. The duffel appeared as a huge black wall and knocked him back on his heels.

His head banged against the steel wall and he swooned. Dizzy. He squeezed his trigger finger, but nothing happened. He had dropped the gun. He struggled forward, suddenly off-balance again as the train slowed further. He lowered his vision, looking for his gun, and something connected with his chin. His head snapped back and he heard a crack. And then he heard it, like a bird taking flight— the rapid flutter of clothing. And then it was gone, absorbed in the wind and the rain.

The train lurched once more, this time regaining speed.

Tyler found his weapon and grabbed it. He leaned his head outside, the rain stinging his face, the wind whipping his hair. "Sweet

Jesus," he mumbled, knowing he had to jump, had to follow. He looked down: a wet, auburn blur of winter's monochromes streaming past. He took a tentative step forward, his face wet and cold, his vision partially blinded. He held on tightly, leaning further, knowing what had to be done—he had to jump, tuck, and roll.

The train's rhythm increased in tempo, the song of steel wheels picking up speed.

Jump! he commanded himself, first shutting his eyes, then opening them again. That blur like a long brown ribbon. Jumping down into things he couldn't even see.

His toes hovering on the edge, Tyler finally stepped back and away from the open door. He couldn't do it.

Alvarez came to standing, already brushing himself off. He tested the right ankle. Sore, but he could walk it off. He located the duffel—twenty yards behind him. He'd thrown it ahead of his jump. He watched the train, waiting only a second or two for the agent to jump, fearing the man would be armed.

Then he cleared his head, turned for the duffel, and ran. Ran, as fast and hard as his body would carry him.

CHAPTER 17

The pristine carpet of unplowed snow confirmed to Alvarez that the farmhouse was empty. A dead giveaway. Either the owners of this farm had left on Christmas holiday prior to last week's snowstorm, or they had abandoned the farm for winter to snowbirding in Florida or Phoenix or some other such spot. Alvarez approached the nearby barn without fear of being spotted. Typical of these Midwestern farms, he found the barn doors unlocked. A large tractor occupied the structure's main area. He discovered a room filled with dozens of tools of every description but still nothing to assist his escape. But inside the attached shed, essentially a two-car garage, he found a robin's-egg blue, vintage Buick with white walls and a spit-polish shine. With no activity at the farm since the storm, the car seemed unlikely to be reported stolen. In the end, the only tracks in the snow led from the garage to the two-lane road.

The incident on the train from Crawfordsville had left Alvarez's head spinning. For over a year and a half he'd wondered how long he might maintain his advantage of surprise, might continue to stay one step ahead. Now he knew: not much longer.

He felt a sense of urgency unlike anything he'd yet experienced. He couldn't change the schedule of the bullet train, so he would have to adjust.

His right elbow and ankle ached. He'd been lucky the other guy hadn't followed, because he'd landed in an open expanse of farmland. He'd have been caught or shot in minutes. But God had been looking down on him: the agent hadn't jumped. Alvarez took it as a sign—he was meant to continue. David had withstood another test from Goliath.

He made the trip to Rockford, Illinois, on farm roads, never exceeding the speed limit and always using his turn signals. He couldn't afford to be arrested now, although many a fugitive had hidden from the system by going *inside*—being arrested under an alias on a lesser crime and doing a year or two while the search for them, the manhunt, ran out of steam. Alvarez kept this ace in his back pocket—a contingency plan, there if needed. If they drew too close, a breaking and entering or assaulting an officer would earn him a year or two in prison and would ironically shelter him.

Rockford, Illinois, was a necessary detour, and though a long way from New York, it was a trip he had to make, wanted to make, and one he had made often over the past eighteen months.

The Bennett House, on Arcadia, only blocks from Rockford Memorial Hospital, was an imposing brick colonial with wooden black shutters and a gleaming black door with a brass knocker. There was a trace of old snow shoveled and plowed into sand brown lumps of decomposing ice, and the thick air held a bite that burned his skin as he climbed the short wheelchair ramp to the door. He rang and let himself inside.

He was met by Mrs. Dundell, a woman of great energies and deep compassion, a registered nurse for twenty years before turning her talents to the management of Bennett House, with its staff of eleven and its client base of ten live-ins and dozens of outpatients.

"Ahh . . . Mr. Alvarez. So nice to see you! Is that knee bothering you?" Always the nurse.

"Slipped on some ice."

"Yes, it's that time of year."

"Miguel?" He pronounced it in the Spanish.

"I wish you'd called," Mrs. Dundell said, leading him by the elbow to a small sitting room peopled with antiques, dried flowers, and out-of-date magazines. "He's having a bit of a challenge today.

A cold, I hope. Flu's possible. He's in his room." She changed tone. "But I'm glad you're here. Your visits always cheer him up."

"His lungs?"

"Better, I think. His spirits have been good. We want this cold over as quickly as possible."

"The job?"

"Everyone at the library loves him. He's been very earnest and dedicated. I've heard nothing but glowing reports."

"Attendance?"

"Yes, he's been fine on that, ever since your last visit. Well done, whatever you said to him. Not one unexcused absence."

"I told him I'd kick his butt," Alvarez teased.

"Yes . . . I'm sure you did." When Mrs. Dundell grinned, a room felt warmer, a window brighter. "It's good you've come. Are you sure that knee's okay? I could have a look at it."

"Just banged up a little. I'll live through the morning." He grinned at the irony.

The bedroom was small and sparingly decorated in a slightly frilly, Victorian motif. The wall-mounted television played the Cartoon Network.

At nineteen, Miguel still had not graduated past Elmer Fudd or the Road Runner. He could keep up with most of *Sesame Street* though tired of it quickly. It had been explained to Alvarez that the alcohol in their mother's blood had poisoned his brother's brain to the point of scarring, to where transmitted signals became lost and wandered inside their chemical confines until dissipating. The blessing was that he seemed so happy in his limited world. He laughed, and smiled, and, on a good day, was able to carry on a conversation at the level of a ten-year-old. Despite the continuing efforts of Mrs. Dundell and her staff, Miguel had never crossed this ceiling. But his unusual ability in mathematics allowed him to conceptualize the

Dewey decimal system of card-catalog filing and made him the perfect reshelfer. His lungs were a constant worry. He'd suffered five
bouts of pneumonia while under the state's care. Once he'd been
moved, through Juanita's arrangements, he'd vastly improved. At the
age of eighteen, the insurance funding had been cut in half, with
Alvarez paying the balance. In his mind, the private care at Bennett
House had saved his brother's life, and it was worth every cent.

Ironically, he had Northern Union to thank indirectly for the
money. Having cashed in a modest amount of retirement funds, he
now played the market. If he ended up in jail or dead, he wanted the
boy taken care of for life. He'd built up a sizable trust to that aim,
though he was counting on the derailment of the bullet train to put
him over the top. He desperately needed to stay out of trouble
until the bullet train was yesterday's news—Miguel's future counted
on it.

Miguel continued watching the cartoon as his older brother entered the room, though he had clearly sneaked a look at the door.
"Bert!" he said, a grin widening across chapped lips. His nose was
runny, his eyes watery.

"Who's winning?" Alvarez asked, his throat tightening with the
sight. It always took him a few minutes to adjust to his blood relation
in this condition.

"The wabbit," Miguel said, inflecting an Elmer Fudd accent.
"Twicky wabbit."

"You've got a cold."

Miguel shrugged it off. "This is where the wabbit goes down the
hole."

Not a good day, Alvarez realized immediately. There wasn't going to be much of a conversation. But he had felt required to come
here, to pay this visit; if anything went wrong with his plans for the
bullet train, this might be his last visit.

Umberto Alvarez pulled up the room's only chair, rested his
elbow on the bed, and held his hand in the air, as was their custom.

He sat back, facing the television and the mindless drivel that so entertained his little brother. A moment after holding this pose another, weaker hand came up to join it. Their fingers entwined, the two hands sank back to the cotton sheets. "Miguel," Alvarez said softly, "your hand is so cold." And he held on, all the more tightly.

Their date turned into a working dinner and consisted of pizza delivered to Priest's hotel room while their two cell phones as well as the line into the room rang constantly. Together, they monitored and attempted to orchestrate a multiple-state manhunt that had begun within minutes of the man jumping from the Amtrak train. The manhunt grew by the hour.

O'Malley had left on the private jet, preferring to brief William Goheen in person. Rucker had obtained a poor printout of the suspect's face—in profile, gleaned from the Indianapolis airport gate area. They anxiously awaited word that the prints had produced a name.

"This guy's slippery," Tyler said, working the laptop, e-faxing the airport photo to a string of truck stops along I-70 and I-74. The work was slow and frustrating.

"We're making headway," she said. "Don't lose sight of that."

Tyler had not seen the man's face during his Amtrak pursuit—the guy had been quick to jump to prevent that. Tyler said, "He's long gone. We're not going to catch him so fast."

"You were close, Peter. Very close. Closer than we've been." She added, "How'd the NASDAQ do today?"

Tyler checked the laptop. "Up fifty. Dow transports are off, following the derailment. Surprise!"

"There go my options."

"I'm in debt," he said. "And trouble. Mostly trouble."

Truckers were on alert via CB radio to be on the lookout for male hitchhikers. News radio listed Kevin Jones as an escaped convict believed loose in the area of the border between Indiana and Illinois. Every resource was being tapped. Checked. Rechecked. And checked again.

Tyler had a plastic bag filled with hotel ice cupped under his chin. He was bruised, but the swelling was down. Pizza had not been the best choice; his jaw hurt with the chewing. Priest was some kind of vegan.

"No meat, no cheese," she had requested as Tyler placed the pizza order.

He had the phone and said, "A pizza without cheese? That's a Bloody Mary without vodka."

"Then call it a virgin pizza, I don't care. Just don't put any meat or cheese on half of it. Or if you do, it's okay, but I won't eat it."

"Then it's *not* okay," he told her.

She shrugged, indifferent.

Tyler had printed out the gate shot of the suspect by faxing it to himself at the front desk, and he'd taped it to the hotel mirror. He looked up to it from time to time and even talked to the man. Priest didn't comment, though she raised her head a couple times as if to interrupt.

CNN ran from the television, the volume low but discernible. When mention of the manhunt caught their attention, she turned up the volume. The photo ran, but it looked even worse on TV—as if this manhunt had been launched to arrest an ear, part of a forehead, and some dark hair. Only that black leather jacket—European, smooth, and void of stitching lines—and the carry-on, a hybrid back-pack/duffel that met airline carry-on requirements, seemed to offer any ray of hope.

She turned the television sound back down when the story shifted to a sick panda in the San Diego Zoo.

"I should have jumped," he said.

"Yeah," she snapped sarcastically, "two broken legs would have helped a lot."

"Come on," he pleaded. "I had him. I lost him. How long before CNN has *my* identity? I might remind you, there may be some law against jumping from a train, but at this point, this suspect cannot be connected in any way, shape, or manner to this or any other derailment. It's all speculative."

"So, you should have jumped," she acknowledged. "But I'm glad you didn't. And here we are."

"Here we are," he echoed.

She turned her head to face him, and they were practically kissing. The thing of it was, Tyler *wanted* to kiss her. She didn't even seem to notice him.

A look transpired between them. Then her face changed, and she, too, finally realized how physically close they were.

Tyler had never kissed a black woman. Fearing she might reject him, he nonetheless found himself leaning to kiss her. He paused a moment to allow her to object, but her huge eyes simply stared back in wonder. It began softly and mostly all his doing, but then she caught up and kissed him back. She stared into his eyes with an enticing combination of playful mischief and an intensity that to him seemed to be asking a question. "Yes," Tyler answered, "I'm sure."

An enormous smile filled her soft face and she chuckled. "Me, too," she told him, her fingers working down the buttons of her own blouse.

Tyler freed an arm and they slipped off the chair and onto the floor. As he untucked his own shirt, her blouse fell open, her bra some kind of shiny stretch fabric nearly the same translucent amber tone as her skin.

He kissed her breasts through the fabric and she raked his shirt off his back, her nails ringing through him.

He went dizzy with warmth and wet and scent. They stopped short of a full union, but neither went wanting.

Sweating, and smiling at the ceiling, they lay side by side, he with only his socks left on, she, with her underwear still around one ankle.

"Oh, my," she said.

"Should I apologize?"

"You had better not! I'd say you should take a bow. I don't usually . . . that doesn't usually happen to me without—" She reconsidered. "I think I'll stop there."

He nodded. "Good idea."

She giggled. "Oh, my God," she said, laughing harder and covering her face. She pulled some clothing over her, and Tyler pulled it back off and drank her in with his eyes. She blushed and pushed him away, and he rolled over then and was quiet for a while. She said softly, "No comments about brown sugar, please." Tyler said nothing. "Is it a first for you?" she asked.

"Not my first woman, no," he answered truthfully. After a long pause, he said, "Yes." He added, "Can we leave it at that?"

"Are you okay with it?"

"I could ask the same thing," he said.

"No pretending." She rolled and reached over him and took his hand. They lay on the carpet like two spoons. "One day at a time?" It was a suggestion, not a question.

"For now," he said. "Then a week. Then maybe a month."

"That makes me feel some pressure," she said.

"Good," he told her, squeezing her hand, not letting her off the hook. "I want you to feel *something*. We'll start there." He kissed her hand and held it to his face. Several minutes passed in silence, the only sound the whine of the laptop's hard drive. They spoke with their eyes.

"Tell me about it. About *him*. Please," she said. "How can I know you, if I don't know your side of it?"

There was no need of an explanation. Tyler knew exactly what she was asking. "All I remember of that day was his huge hands. First, holding that little girl and driving her head against the wall.

Later, it was my own throat, and for a minute I thought maybe my last breath. But always those hands. When I busted into the room, those hands let go and he just dropped her. Discarded her, you know? Like a picture he'd been hanging on the wall, and he just let go. He was a big man. Huge, really. Intimidating. And when he turned on me . . . I froze."

Tyler propped himself up on an elbow. "I've been in dozens of similar situations, never had a problem. Maybe it was the baby on the floor. Maybe it was her crying. Maybe I was just afraid of him. But when he hit me, he knocked me sideways. He clocked me. I must have dropped my weapon. Crime Scene Unit found it under a chair. Unfired, of course. His second blow missed, or I probably wouldn't be here right now. And if he'd been a little more sober, or I'd been any slower, then my first punch wouldn't have landed, and maybe everything would be different. But it landed all right, and so did my second and my third. He got me in the ribs and the gut, and then those hands on my throat. Those damn eyes of his. Dead, as any dead I've seen. Something came over me. Maybe it wasn't my time to check out. I don't know what it was. But after that, it was all me. I found this rhythm. Some shrink called it rage, but it wasn't that. Not for me. It wasn't so much anger as it was this rhythm. One-two to the face, one to the gut; over and over. Over and over," he whispered. "That little girl lying there on the floor like that. And there was nothing in this world to break that rhythm, like when you get a jingle stuck in your head, only for me it was my fists—this rhythm. I don't remember him, or his face . . . nothing. Only that rhythm. It felt so damn good. So damn right. And I just never stopped. Never could stop. I was too damn scared to stop. Of him. Of what he'd do to me and the little girl if he came back. And so I didn't stop until they pulled me off."

She had glassy eyes. He said, "It's not that I was enjoying it, though that's how the prosecutor painted it. The papers. The media. They fed on that idea: white cop beating a black man to a pulp. It fit something they believed. But it wasn't that. Had nothing to do with that."

"But you had a trial," Priest said. "If it was self-defense—"

"My attorney wouldn't have any of that. Said it would hurt us, maybe really badly, to go that route. And who am I to complain? He got me acquitted. He focused the defense on the child abuse. Said a jury can handle only one concept. That if we put that image of the child into their heads, that it would be enough to justify what I did. And it was."

Now she seemed mad. "But it was at the expense of your reputation, your career!"

"He got me acquitted," Tyler repeated. "That's what he was hired to do. It wasn't a popularity contest; it was a criminal trial. And we won. We still have the civil trial to go but—"

"It was self-defense!" she complained harshly.

He nodded thoughtfully. "Yes, it was. And maybe it was self-defense in that boxcar as well. And if so: who's guilty, and who's innocent?"

Tyler's cell phone rang. The pagers and phones had been ringing all evening, but this time the phone surprised them and caused Priest to quickly redress. "Wait a second," Tyler spoke into the phone, attempting to pull some clothes on. To make matters worse, his pen had run out of ink. He signaled Nell for the hotel's freebie. The thing wrote dashes instead of lines, but Tyler scribbled out a name while Priest zipped and buttoned. "We're sure? Absolutely sure?" He listened, thanked the caller, and hung up. He felt the wind knocked out of him.

"Peter?"

"That was Rucker."

"The prints kicked?" she guessed.

"Running those latents through the FAA database identified four of them as belonging to airline personnel—probably whoever collected the tickets at the gate. We can rule them out. The one remaining print just kicked from an Illinois state employee database."

"We've got an ID?" Priest said, leaning forward, straining to see what he'd written.

"Up until a couple years ago, the guy we're calling K. C. Jones taught computer science at a school in Genoa, Illinois. A science teacher! Can you imagine?"

"The name, Peter?"

"Umberto Alvarez." He met eyes with her. "Get it?"

"Get *what?*"

"The name's Latino."

"So it fits," she declared. "What's the problem here?"

Tyler maintained his eye contact with her. He said, "If Harry Wells came looking for a Latino, then someone—probably O'Malley—either already had a description of the suspect, or—"

"A name!" she answered for herself, bewildered by the implication. She mumbled, "O'Malley has known this guy's identity all along."

Tyler nodded gravely.

She moaned, "They lied to me."

Tyler whispered back, "They lied to all of us."

"We've got more problems," Tyler said, pointing to the screen of his laptop and the Internet search site Northern Light. The unspoken problem was that over the last several hours they had leaned against each other, rubbed up next to each other, laughed, and broken bread together. He tapped the screen, where the search engine had produced dozens of hits—newspaper articles and Internet news pieces— for the text string "Alvarez+railroad."

"Go ahead," Priest said, hanging up the phone by the bed.

"Two and a half years ago, a Juanita Alvarez and her two children, four-year-old twins, were killed in their car at a railroad crossing in . . . guess where?"

"Genoa, Illinois," she answered knowingly.

He nodded, "The town where Umberto Alvarez taught science."
He returned her attention to the screen. "A freight train crushed the
family car and moved it a quarter mile down the track before dump-
ing it into a ditch. Any guesses who owned the freight train?"

"Oh, God. Northern Union," she whispered. Her cheek now was
nearly to his as she read over his shoulder.

"One of the papers has the nine-one-one call placed by an unidentified male who, close to hysterics, claims the crossing's barrier
arm did not lower, that the lights didn't work." He scrolled down
and pointed. "But get this, the same story says that law enforcement
found both barrier arms in place, suggesting the car had gotten
stuck—mechanical problems—out there on the track, putting the
blame, the responsibility, squarely with the driver. The 'alleged'
nine-one-one call should have been taped, but the tape was never
recovered. The story doesn't mention the husband by name."

"Doesn't have to," Priest said. "We have his prints on a boarding
pass." She placed her hand on Tyler's shoulder, and for him, the
contact seemed to burn. His heart raced. His eyes and throat felt dry.
She instructed, "Click on the next ten searches."

Surprising himself, he obeyed.

She scanned the titles faster than he. "Second to last."

Tyler clicked on the title. It would cost him three bucks to view
the article. He clicked "OK."

"Bingo," she said. Umberto Alvarez's name appeared in the first
paragraph. She must have taken speed reading at some point in her
youth. She summarized the first few paragraphs well before Tyler
had the first few sentences read. "He sued, claiming Northern Union
negligent. But without that nine-one-one tape—" She moved around
the chair and hip-checked him, stealing half of it as she sat. This
contact put Tyler over the top. He found it difficult to read, difficult
to breathe. She, on the other hand, seemed absorbed by what she
read. Their hands brushed as she took over the laptop's roller ball.
She scrolled, effectively taking Tyler out of the picture as he lost
two paragraphs. "You know what this means?" she said.

He had his own ideas. "I don't even know what it says," he commented.

"O'Malley has been orchestrating a cover-up."

"Has he?" He needed to find his focus. He sat perfectly still for several minutes while she clicked through articles.

She maintained a running monologue, like a play-by-play announcer. "Alvarez sues NUR for negligence, and apparently the attorneys drag it out for nearly a year. Probably were trying to settle out of court." She'd found an article in the *Chicago Sun.* She scrolled faster than he could read, her dark eyes racing back and forth. "Not possible!"

"What?" He nearly slipped off the chair.

She leaned back and pointed, her breathing hurried and excited. The headline read, DEAD IN HIS TRACKS! ATTORNEY IN GENOA CROSSING CASE MURDERED.

Alvarez's attorney, Donald Andersen, had been found dead of a broken neck in his office. His client, Umberto Alvarez—his last known appointment—had been wanted for questioning. Tyler scanned the piece, this time faster than Priest. *Assault . . . broken neck . . . arrest warrant . . .*

"No way," he gasped, marveling at the similarity to his own recent past. That image of Chester Washington beating the baby against the wall suddenly filled the screen. The room felt small. He felt hot.

She added, editorializing, "Six months later the derailments began. Every six or eight weeks. Signal failures, engineers drunk at the controls. Every excuse O'Malley could fabricate. But he must have known all along it was Alvarez."

"Of course he knew! And he sent Harry Wells out to catch him," Tyler added. "Kill him, if possible."

She whispered, "And he sent me to find Harry Wells before you did."

"Yeah? Well, that backfired," Tyler pointed out.

She leaned back against Tyler, practically into his arms. She tapped the computer. "They don't want us knowing any of this, or they would have told me in the first place."

"And that begs a larger question," Tyler suggested, rhetorically. "Why, if you know a particular person has cost you a hundred million dollars, don't you want every cop, every fed, looking for the guy?"

A cavernous silence hung between them. She said tentatively, not really believing it herself, "Maybe they just don't want the press knowing the connection, dragging the Alvarez deaths into the national press."

"You don't actually think that?" Tyler asked.

"No."

"More likely, Umberto Alvarez has been a victim all along. They were responsible for that crossing accident and of course *they know it*." Tyler knew something about what that felt like. "They can't afford to have his side heard. It's business as usual for them." He added, speculating, "What if Alvarez didn't kill this attorney Andersen? What if that was intended to put him into legal problems?"

"Isn't that just a little bit paranoid?"

Tyler answered, "Is it? This guy had turned into a nightmare for them. What if Harry Wells was supposed to end their problem once and for all?"

CHAPTER 19

"I didn't expect to see you again," Jillian whispered into Alvarez's ear as she poured him a glass of red wine.

Following his visit with Miguel, Alvarez had driven nearly six hours to Toledo, Ohio, in time for the 12:33 A.M. Amtrak for New York. The train actually left from Chicago, but he feared the Union station would be crawling with *them*. He had retired the black leather jacket and blue jeans to the duffel in favor of a sweater and down vest because he'd been seen in the other clothes. His only concern came from driving the stolen car, but at night, keeping within the speed limit on an interstate, and with the car less than a day in his possession, it had seemed a risk worth taking. He slept lightly on the train and arrived in New York that same afternoon at three o'clock, somewhat refreshed.

The test run of NUR's bullet train was scheduled to take place in four days, departing New York's Pennsylvania Station for Washington, D.C. Everything Alvarez had labored for now came down to these next four days.

The bistro across from the Powell hummed with conversation and the bell-like percussion of tableware against Breton pottery. The aromas were of dill and rosemary and a warm, sweet chocolate from the soufflés. Jillian stood at attention, pencil poised as if awaiting his order.

"I wanted to see you again," he told her, looking down at his wine glass as he spun it by the stem.

Jillian glanced around the room, ensuring privacy, and maintained a stiff posture that imparted none of the intimacy they had once shared. "And here I am."

"I wanted to apologize," he said. "I'm not sure for what, but I feel one is owed."

"I'm a big girl, Bert. No apologies necessary. I'd wanted to do that since I was thirteen." She grinned. "Another of life's little conquests taken care of."

He toyed with his place setting and ordered food.

"The baked sole would be nice. With the spinach, if you have it."

"Who was that woman the other night?"

"I told you."

"Yes. But I didn't believe you."

"Perhaps I shouldn't have come back."

"Then why did you?"

"Some potatoes if you have them, and pâté to start."

"Don't do this."

"Goose pâté," he clarified. "None of that vegetarian crap. You don't serve that, do you? Not a place like this."

"You need a place to stay," she theorized. "You can stay with me."

He said, "I've a room of my own. I'm fine."

She leaned in close and whispered angrily, "First you sleep with me; then you feel guilty and come back. You're limping. You're hurt. You're in trouble, judging by that limp and your reluctance to tell me about anything that's going on. And now you want me to simply put up your order?" She turned on her heel and stormed off back toward the kitchen.

Alvarez felt he should leave before she returned. Complications. He had hoped for a pleasant dinner. He'd made a mistake by coming here. She must have caught on to his intentions, for she cut back across the room, her purse in her hand. A waitress carrying her purse was somehow an unusual sight. He was standing by the time she reached him.

"Have you ever had one of those moments where everything suddenly seems so clear? So sharp? So right? Don't ask me why, but when I saw this in the paper . . . I thought of you." She dug out a torn newspaper article from her purse. When he declined to accept it, she placed it on the table. The photo showed an aerial of the Terre Haute train wreck. She said, "I know about your family. The tragedy. And then the way you were with me, so . . . jumpy . . . the other night. Mysterious and all. And then this." She leaned in and lowered her voice to less than a whisper, a warm wind on his neck giving him shivers. "What's going on, Bert?"

Alvarez crumpled the article. He found it hard to breathe. "This has nothing to do with me."

"No?"

"Forget this!" He looked around. Some customers were staring. He felt cornered.

"Explain it to me," she pleaded.

"Nothing to explain." He pushed past her for the door.

"Yes, there is!" she called out loudly enough to lift every head in the restaurant.

Alvarez reached the outside and ran.

An hour later, Alvarez adjusted the doors to the hotel room's hand-painted armoire, holding one of the doors open with the back of a chair. Opera played from the radio built into the television. Big lungs. He sat back and attempted to enjoy the moment, but the encounter with Jillian had shaken him.

The Plaza Hotel room cost $380, and yet it felt cheap to him. He had a little over three thousand in cash split between two pockets and the sock of his right leg. With everything ready, he waited impatiently as a teen before the prom, sitting first on the edge of the bed, then in the chair at the desk, and finally on the toilet. Dinner hadn't agreed with him, his nerves were frayed.

He felt giddy with anticipation. If this proved successful, he believed he would gain the leverage to crush William Goheen, whether or not he managed to derail the bullet train.

As a student of science, Alvarez deemed data the most powerful tool, information, the most powerful weapon. This premium on information accounted for his risky forays into Northern Union's offices, as well as the hundreds of hours he'd spent in surveillance of both Goheen and his daughter, Gretchen. He knew their day-to-day lives as well as they did, their routines, the exceptions to those routines, their preferences for travel, their friends. He checked his watch: she was late. Elation briefly gave way to anxiety. He had severed all ties with his past other than with Miguel. He had no place of his own except a sparsely furnished loft south of the Flatiron Building that he rented by the month. For a while, this nomadic lifestyle had been tolerable, exciting even, his hunger for revenge so overpowering, but now it dragged him down. Jillian's discovery had shaken him. She knew about him! Knowledge was just as dangerous as it was powerful.

The ringing of the room's phone jolted Alvarez. He answered it quickly. "Hello?"

"Mr. Cortez?" a woman's smooth voice inquired.

"Speaking."

"It's Gail. May I come up to the room?"

"Twelve-seventeen."

"Twelve-seventeen," she repeated. "See you in a minute."

Alvarez hung up, his chest tight, adrenaline casting aside any lingering fatigue. Gail. Even the sound of her voice gave him a shiver. He had played roles for the past eighteen months, but none as exhilarating as what was required of him over the next hour. This woman, too, was playing roles. He pushed Jillian from his thoughts as he studied the room, reminding himself to keep his back to the armoire and the video camera it concealed. He reminded himself that for this performance he'd have to make demands of this woman that would not come easily to him. Fifteen hundred dollars, and he wouldn't use a cent. He wondered how far he could go.

He looked into the mirror at the man he had become—the tired eyes, the oppressive sadness, the slightly discolored broken bridge to his nose that was still healing, a few scars that interrupted his own recollection of that face. His body, like the soul inside him, was worse for the wear. He felt like a train wreck himself when he compared whom he'd become with the eighth grade teacher who had once taught Buckminster Fuller's mechanics to eager minds. That former Umberto Alvarez could no longer be seen in this mirror.

When the knock came, Alvarez checked the security peephole. His heart misfired in his chest at the sight of her. Even distorted by a wide-angle lens, this woman's perfection spoke of high society. Escort or not, she was no street urchin. Black hair, cut in bangs, framed her oval face. She wore blue pigmented contacts and enough makeup for the theater, including a haunting application of eye shadow. In an unusual twist, the cosmetics hid, instead of emphasized, her high cheekbones. Her small Roman nose perched haughtily above sensual, pouty lips painted rose. Those lips held his attention. Captivating. He drew in a deep breath, opened the door to a wind of lilac and French soap, and faced a welcoming smile. She could have been a woman of Paris, London, or Milan.

"Gail," she said, her voice now husky and raw. She intended to earn every penny.

"Fernando," he lied. They shook hands, hers frail and delicate, not at all what he had expected. She kissed him lightly on the cheek and walked past him, the scent more intense. She wore a tailored, blood red jacket, buttoned to emphasize her chest. Her pleated black skirt reminded him of a schoolgirl, except for the smooth curve of her hips.

She placed her handbag on the bedside table and turned to face him. "In town for long?"

"A couple days is all."

"You flew in from?"

"Train, actually," he said, waiting to see her reaction.

She smiled, amused. "I love trains."

"Last romantic way to travel," he said.

"I couldn't agree more."

He couldn't have scripted it any better. He said, "Do I pay you now?"

"No business, please. Your credit card was charged when I confirmed you were in your room. You *are* a regular on the site?" she asked suspiciously.

"A friend of Takimachi," he answered.

She smiled. "Oh, yes. Fine."

"Ohio," he said, answering her initial question.

"Do you live in Ohio?"

"No, I don't live there. It was business. Same as New York." He moved toward the minibar. "Drink?"

"No, thank you. But go ahead. I'll just take a minute." She pointed to the bathroom.

"While you're in there, please lose the wig," he instructed her, "and remove the eye makeup as well. I like the feel of a woman's hair." He added, "I like a woman plain. God given. I'd like to undress you, if that's all right?"

"This is your time, Fernando. I'm here for you. Whatever you like. However you like it." She didn't look or sound the least put off by his request. *Probably hears a lot worse than that,* he thought. She nodded obediently. "We're going to have fun, Fernando."

He found her confidence disarming.

"Leave the bathroom door open," he told her.

"Excuse me?" Again, surprise.

"I want you to leave the bathroom door open. I want to watch. And remember: I want to undress you."

"I need a private moment, Fernando."

"Then take one, but with the door open."

Now she looked troubled. He wanted her on her heels. "I beg your pardon?" she said.

"Listen," he answered, "it can't be disrobing that bothers you. Not even using the toilet—you must have freaks who like that stuff as well."

Her brow knitted, but then she forced it smooth and she relaxed, letting the customer have his way.

"And if it's drugs . . . you should know that the idea of that turns me on: a woman giving up control of herself like that. Not that I want any. Whatever it is, do it in front of me. Right here," he pointed to the bed. A puzzled expression gave way to submission. She nodded reluctantly. "Never mind the bathroom then." She slipped a small glass bottle from her purse and spooned a substantial amount of cocaine up her nose, her eyes nearly constantly on him.

"I will undress you now," he said. "Remove the wig." He motioned to the room's mirror. "And also the contact lenses."

She snorted even more cocaine and put away the small vial. "Fine." This word she had at the ready.

He took her by the hips from behind and turned her so that she addressed the mirror. She carefully lifted the wig and pulled it off her head. She shook out her hair and asked if he wanted her to comb it out. Alvarez stepped behind her, told her not to worry about it, and then helped her out of her waist-length jacket. He carefully unfastened a hook and unzipped her black skirt. He pulled it down around her ankles, revealing a red garter belt over a red lace thong that disappeared into her cheeks. He sensed no nervousness in her whatsoever, a woman accustomed to others undressing her. His own heart rate had doubled.

"Would you like me to hang it up?" he asked.

"If you don't mind. Yes, please." She toyed with her hair, again trying to improve its look. "I can brush it out," she offered again.

"No," he said, clipping the skirt to a hanger. He returned, reached around her, making contact with both breasts, and slowly unbuttoned her cream-colored blouse. "Just like that is fine."

"I'd prefer to leave my face on," she said. "I made myself pretty for you, Fernando."

He slipped the blouse off her. "I prefer an honest face to one adorned," he explained. *And I want the camera to clearly see you.*

"What do you mean by an honest face?" she asked, clearly troubled. "Are you insulting me?"

"Insulting? I'm complimenting you, Gail. This face of yours isn't close to your real face, is it? I think not. Not in the slightest. You're probably a much more beautiful woman without all of that. Do you use warm water or cold?" He pointed toward the bathroom.

"I'm afraid it's not negotiable," she protested. "My face stays as is."

"How long to redo it? An hour? I'll pay for the extra hour." He pulled out a wad of bills. "Cash," he added.

"One cloth hot, the other warm," she answered.

Alvarez returned with the two washcloths, and she began working through layers of color, the accents to her cheeks, the highly decorated eyes. "It's a strange thing to ask," she said, mostly to herself.

"Have you never been asked this before?"

"Never." Clearly uncomfortable to discuss such things, she gave in to her client's questioning and informed him, "Oh, sometimes I add something. Some men prefer a certain look, you know?"

"I like a woman to be herself, not an invention." He made sure she heard each word that followed. "Except for the occasional party, my wife never wore any makeup at all. None." He had hoped she might fish for more information, but not this one. She'd been well trained, well schooled. "My use of the past tense was supposed to incite curiosity on your part." The bra was black satin. He unhooked it and slid its straps down her arms. No gooseflesh; no response on her part whatsoever. His blood pressure now chased his pulse. His mouth was dry. Her pupils were dilated from the coke.

"Was it?" she asked.

"Absolutely."

"Then I've disappointed you," she apologized. "I'm sorry. Shall I ask you now?"

"She's dead, you see," he explained, interrupting. "It was ruled an accident, but to me it was murder."

"Murder?" She frowned, disturbing her practiced smile. Alvarez fell to his knees and gently drew the garter belt and the red silk thong slowly down the length of her tan legs. His head came even with her waist. He took her by the hips and turned her around slowly so that she faced the camera in full frontal nudity. The transformation complete, it was no longer a fifteen-hundred-dollar-an-hour call girl with a captivating face and million-dollar body. It was Gretchen Goheen.

She lived for the way they worshiped her, the way they physically responded so quickly to her. She loved this sense of dominance, of total control. They became putty in her company. Grown men. Some of the most powerful—certainly the richest—men in the world. For an hour or two they placed her above all other women on the face of the earth. And though the hour was theirs, ironically most would do anything she asked.

He knew nearly everything there was to know about Gretchen Goheen. She had been educated at Choate and Princeton, afforded privileges—the private jets, the presidential suites, the limousines, nannies, maids, and kitchen servants—that only a handful of children ever saw. She had lost her mother to alcoholism, although the press had reported the death as cancer, when she was just fifteen. Alvarez assumed that Keith O'Malley, who played cleanup hitter for his boss, had skillfully kept Leslie Goheen's drug and alcohol abuse hidden inside the walls of private clinics. Reading her *New York Times* obituary, one heard of the philanthropic socialite. It had taken him some digging to discover the Midwestern adolescent swept off her feet by the Machiavellian husband who knew nothing but work, competition, and excess. And girls. Alvarez believed her husband's philandering had probably driven Leslie Goheen to the bottle in the first place.

Gretchen's experimentation with drugs and alcohol had begun during her junior year in prep school—she'd received a two-week suspension, as well as a two-week vacation with friends to Amsterdam. He could imagine that the boys had always lined up for her, falling at her feet. Perhaps she'd developed an addiction to their desire that proved stronger than her own ability to resist them. No doubt she had slept with dozens of college boys, always aiming for the older and more experienced. She had learned how to please. With an absentee father, who she knew took women on the side, Gretchen had became overcome with a need for more partners, more attention, more adoration. When they became complacent—even a whiff of complacency—they were out the door.

Some event had precipitated the move to professional call girl. One of her father's glamorous parties where some drunken executive had cornered her, only to offer her money to keep silent about it? A drug habit that needed financing? A sex addiction that went bad? Blackmail? There was no evidence to explain this, and Alvarez was no psychologist. But the adoring, rich, absentee father certainly played a big part in this transformation of socialite into elite escort.

Perhaps her psychiatrist (she had seen him twice a week for nearly a year) had said she was trying to hurt her father through her actions. Whatever the case, she had stopped the sessions.

Alvarez believed that sometime around the summer before she headed off to Princeton, Gretchen Goheen had accepted gainful employment as one of the most sought after call girls in New York City. Five years later at the ripe age of twenty-three, she had checked in to an exclusive Arizona "spa"—a treatment center—probably for a cocaine addiction. Alvarez believed that Keith O'Malley had been Gretchen's savior throughout. Perhaps O'Malley himself had slept with her, or still did, though Alvarez could find no proof of this connection. What seemed obvious was that O'Malley shielded Goheen from as much as possible, including his own family's problems.

It suggested a liaison between O'Malley and Gretchen that Alvarez hoped to exploit.

With Gretchen Goheen stripped naked and standing in front of him in nothing but a pair of black heels, Alvarez briefly felt tempted to help himself to her wares. He told himself that any male would feel the same, despite his moment of self-loathing for being so predictable. Grabbing her wide, sumptuous hips, as if ready to explore her, he instead backed her up to the bed, gently sitting her down on its edge.

"Whatever you like, however you like it," she said in a warm, womanly purr. "My time is yours."

He stood, intentionally blocking her way to the door. He stood so that he towered over her, gaining a psychological advantage. He swallowed, clearing his throat and gaining his courage, knowing that if successful this oratory might save hundreds of lives. Lives that would otherwise be on his conscience forever.

"Ms. Goheen," he said, immediately having to reach out and force her back down to the bed, preventing her escape. "I'm not the police." She continued to struggle, so he stepped aside and let her jump to her feet. "If you leave," he called out loudly to her as she freed the skirt from the closet, not bothering with the underwear, "your father's life is in your hands alone. I can't help you." That won a reprieve. She looked even more sexy to him, with her flushed, bare chest and the skirt cockeyed on her waist. Her rapid breathing was audible. Her lips trembled, and he realized she was trying to speak. He wanted this to be a soliloquy, not a discussion. He continued, "My name is Alvarez. I'm the one your father and O'Malley are after. I'm the one whose wife was killed at the railroad crossing in Genoa, Illinois. You know about this, right?" He saw no indication that she had heard so much as a word, but he stayed with his plan. "Your father and O'Malley must confess the truth of my family's tragedy. That is all I ask—all I've ever asked: the truth. It's not money I'm after, only the truth—and for all the world to hear. I have tried to get through to your father. I have failed. He has lost a great deal of property, and still he doesn't listen. But he may listen to you."

"Oh, my God." Said like a person coming awake.

"I would listen to my daughter, I can tell you that. But my daughter is dead. Dead because of policies initiated by your father and carried out by O'Malley. You *must* make him listen. Do you understand? If there is no apology, I am going to derail this final test of the bullet train. You can tell him that. No matter what he plans, I will succeed—and with all the press and all the dignitaries aboard. With your father aboard. I will ruin him, ruin you, ruin anyone who stands in the way of the truth. You win that apology, a public apology, and no one will be hurt."

"Who are you?"

He hoped that she had heard him, hoped the shock of his knowledge of her identity had not caused a blackout. He leaned into her, so their faces nearly touched, and raised his voice for the first time. "Do not test me!" He saw where his spittle clung to her cheeks. Numb, she was unable to move.

He crossed to the armoire, knocked the hotel's notebook onto the floor, and quickly seized the small video camera that hid behind it. He held it out for her to see, for her to take it all in. "You see? You will go down with him, if it comes to that. I have no desire to bring you any harm. Yours is a pitiful life. The fate of that train, and all aboard, is in your hands, Ms. Goheen. The truth. Genoa, Illinois. Talk to him." He reached into his pocket, counted out fifteen one-hundred-dollar bills and dropped them to the floor. The bills fluttered and rolled and made a carpet at his feet. Her eyes never left his face. She was crying now. Fear, he thought, not empathy.

"Whether or not he will listen to you is a test of your father's love and trust. You *must* prevail, or accept the consequences."

Alvarez turned his back on her.

"Wait!" she called out, as he reached the door.

He faced the small sign that showed a floor plan of the hotel hallway. A red dot indicated their room. He turned the brass door-knob and slipped out into the hall, already running, in case she phoned security.

New York was a claustrophobic's nightmare. The streets and avenues, crowded with high-rises, at times felt to Tyler like the floors of deep, granite crevasses. The United flight back from Chicago had been at capacity, and Tyler had agonized the whole way, longing for a drink to calm him. Having completed the requisite paperwork to carry a weapon and ammunition on board, Tyler was therefore forbidden by law to drink. Priest, who had checked her unloaded weapon, drank a vodka and tonic, basically torturing Tyler.

It took only the one drink before she admitted, "I'm not so sure this can work."

"Us?" he asked, "or my idea?"

"The idea," she answered. "Us?" she echoed, bewildered. "I don't even want to go there, not now, anyway."

"If there was, or is, a cover-up," he pressed, "then chances are some personnel have been—"

"Promoted, transferred, or retired ahead of schedule," she interrupted. "I got that the first time you explained it." She added, "Incidentally, it made more sense to me the first time than it does now."

"The company is too big," he rationalized. "One man, even a Keith O'Malley, cannot keep something like this crossing guard accident buttonholed."

"This company has been good to me, Peter. They've given me advancements that others might not have."

"You've already chosen sides," he reminded her. "They sent Harry Wells after Alvarez. They told you only half the story."

"There might be explanations for that," she said tentatively. "Need to Know. Fear of media leaks. Not wanting to put me in a position to lie to you—the feds."

He didn't want to get into a shouting match with her over whether withholding truth constituted a lie. To him, it did. O'Malley's explanations in the hotel bar had been concise and well thought out but ultimately evasive and unconvincing. He said, "All you need to do is get me inside your Personnel department."

"Human Services," she corrected.

"I'll ask the questions," he said.

She didn't look convinced.

"I don't want you to lose your job," he reminded her.

"No," she snapped. "You just want me to help you bring down the whole company."

God, how he wanted that scotch.

Northern Union Railroad owned the Art Deco, sixty-story office high-rise erected in midtown Manhattan nearly seventy years before. The lobby ceiling had been repainted by the WPA—a mixture of God, sky, and the Worker. The corporation retained twenty stories for itself and leased out the rest.

Tyler cleared NUR security, registering as an NTSB agent and a guest of Nell Priest. He rode up to her floor and drank a cup of surprisingly decent coffee while Priest got stuck on the phone.

Tyler wanted words with O'Malley about the Alvarez identity but knew he was unlikely to get any such meeting. His purpose instead was to do some quiet digging in Human Services in search of personnel changes in and around what Tyler thought of as the Genoa, Illinois, cover-up.

When Priest hung up, Tyler said, "If you help me with this, and they find out, and I'm right—" He didn't bother to finish.

"I know," she said.

"You want to think about that. They'll either promote you to keep you quiet or fire you without benefits." He recalled his own fate at the hands of Metro police.

"They promoted me," she informed him.

"Already?" he said, surprised.

"Better salary, better bennies."

"But you're off the Harry Wells case," he guessed.

"Not at all," she contradicted him. "I receive a full briefing this afternoon from O'Malley himself. He wants me on the task force to bring in Alvarez."

"There's a task force already?" This felt much too fast for Tyler; he had underestimated O'Malley's savvy.

"Apparently there will be by the end of the day."

"So I need to work quickly," he said. Then he sensed her reluctance. "You're not going to help me," he suggested.

"I want to hear O'Malley's side of this first."

"I don't," Tyler said, suspecting the worst. "He's doing the Slick Willy, Nell. He's probably got Rucker convinced he's a team player. Believe me, he is not."

"You smell conspiracy," she said. "I'm thinking more like corporate bureaucracy. We were back on our heels after the Railroad Killer—same as everyone else in this business. Share price is *everything* these days, Peter. And it all turns on public opinion. The stock market is no longer just the engine of the economy, it's *everything*. Cabbies are trading stocks on Palm Pilots; my hairdresser talks about valuations and IPOs. We were hammered by those killings—twenty-six percent off at one point. This, when we're betting everything on F-A-S-T Track, our new bullet train. Over a hundred million dollars! Goheen's pumped everything we have into this— he's out on a limb, betting we can bring people back to mass transportation if the service improves. The country *needs* this. Who could afford to imagine that Alvarez was behind these derailments, that NUR, and NUR *only*, was a target of some bereft widower with a vengeance? You can see that, right? There's no evidence, Peter. It's all speculation. All I want is to hear O'Malley's side."

"I think I just did," Tyler quipped.

She scrunched her nose, snorted, and crossed her arms.

He said, "If Alvarez is just some wacko, and there's actually no evidence that he's behind the derailments, then your point is taken. But if there was malfeasance, criminal negligence in that crossing accident, if that has been covered up to protect your sacred share price, what then? Umberto Alvarez loses so that the country gains? No, I don't think so."

"You're just speculating!"

"So prove me wrong. Get me into Human Services and show me that no personnel changes were made soon after the crossing accident. Or better yet, get me the record of investigation for that accident. The file. I'll bet you can't find it. I'll bet it was pulled by O'Malley before it ever reached whatever filing cabinet or computer directory it should have reached. Call me a skeptic. Get mad at me. But first, prove me wrong. That's all I ask: prove me wrong."

"I will," she said, "after the meeting."

"O'Malley's going to get me pulled from this, Nell. He's going to get his whitewash task force in place, and he's going to get me pulled. I promise you. Your promotion is the first step. By the time your meeting is over, I'm out of here. And by tomorrow, he'll be offering me a job. Guaranteed. I need this information," he pressed. "Now."

She clearly considered all he had said. "Okay," she said, at first tentatively. Then repeating herself, she said sincerely, "Okay."

NUR's lower few floors were typical corporate rabbit warrens—office cubicles, interconnected like a maze in a French formal garden. Computers. Phones. Headsets. Wall calendars. Plastic travel mugs courtesy of Starbucks. Pictures of the kids. Felt pennants for the New York Yankees on thin wooden sticks. An election pin proclaiming Dave Barry for President. The only distinguishing feature was the preponderance of train memorabilia. Photos. Models. Posters.

Priest, self-conscious, concerned about the company's security cameras, moved erratically and with her head down. She had no reason to be down in Human Resources and didn't want to be answering embarrassing questions on the same day as her new promotion. She explained that where Goheen had a TV in his office constantly tuned to CNN, and another to CNBC, O'Malley had CNN and a display of six black-and-whites, each of them changing screens every few seconds, tracking the dozens of security cameras in the NUR work environment. She went on to explain that the security room—with eighteen monitors—conducted round-the-clock surveillance of the building and its employees and was currently on an even higher state of alert due to possible security breaches of late.

Hearing this, Tyler asked, "Alvarez?"

The inquiry briefly stopped Priest. She pulled Tyler to the side of the hall and kept her voice low. "It would explain the paranoid attitude," she admitted. "Since I didn't hear about Alvarez until yesterday, it hadn't occurred to me they might *know* who was behind these security breaches." Again she cautioned him, "No matter what, O'Malley finds out we're down here asking questions, he won't be thrilled."

"He's just a little bit busy today, Nell. I doubt he's watching a lot of tube."

"The things remain on all the time."

"Got it," Tyler said. They continued on, toward the cluster of offices ahead. Tyler kept his head down, if nothing else, to humor her.

"It's not as if he can arrest you or something," Tyler replied, walking alongside her.

"He can fire me," she reminded him. "And he could do worse to you."

"The Unit?" Tyler didn't take this threat too seriously. It sounded to him as if O'Malley considered himself some kind of CIA Op instead of the chief rent-a-cop he was. Playing a version of the short-man complex, he'd clearly put the fear of God into his employees, but Tyler wasn't one and would not play along.

She replied, "Let's just say I wouldn't want to see Keith O'Malley pushed into a corner."

Tyler experienced a brief but convincing chill. She was right: rent-a-cop or not, O'Malley's Irish temperament and Marine personality were nothing to mess with. In a dry whisper of a voice, he said, "Given what we now know, what choice is there but to keep pushing?"

"You can't say I didn't warn you."

"No," he answered. "I can't."

They entered Human Resources, arriving at an office occupied by a coffee-skinned woman named Selma Long. She had the bright face and booming voice of a southern Baptist, the body of a sumo wrestler, and looked to be somewhere between forty and sixty.

Tyler took a chair. Priest slid an in-box out of the way and perched herself on the corner of Selma's desk, her legs facing, and distracting, Tyler. Priest handed the woman a piece of paper on which he'd written the date of the Genoa, Illinois, crossing accident. Priest said, "Selma, this is Peter Tyler of the National Transportation Safety Board." Tyler half stood and shook the woman's meaty hand across the desk. "Northern Union Security prides itself in cooperating with both local police and federal agencies, and Mr. Tyler had a few questions that I couldn't answer and that I hoped maybe you could."

To Tyler, the deep-voiced woman said, "Little Nell and I attend the same church. She tell you that, Mr. Tyler?"

"No ma'am, she did not."

"She tell you she a choir girl? Voice like an angel, this one."

"I can believe that," Tyler replied, watching as Priest's neck flushed below her ears.

"Selma—" Priest teasingly scolded.

Tyler said, "My agency is interested in which, if any, NUR employees may have received bonuses, added benefits, early retirement, or promotion in the month period that follows that date."

Selma Long considered him thoughtfully. "Uh-huh," she replied.

Tyler held his breath, every nerve alive and tingling. He believed this information key to the investigation, and there was no way he'd ever win a court order to obtain it. His future on this case, and the case itself, rested with Selma Long.

She started typing.

Tyler exhaled audibly.

For the first time since they had come into the office, Priest turned her head and made eye contact with Tyler, hers filled with the excitement of their success.

Selma Long caught this exchange, stopped typing, and said to Priest, "What are you two up to here?" To Tyler, she said suddenly, "I believe I should have asked for your credentials, sir." She offered Nell Priest a disapproving expression.

Tyler produced his creds and passed them across.

"This is in regards to—?" she asked Priest. She reached for the phone. "On whose request?"

Nell Priest stared at the phone. She looked down at the woman. She lowered her voice and said, "This is something that needs to be done, Selma. It's best left at that. It's best that you don't know any more. For your sake."

"But I could get in trouble here? Is that what you're saying, girl?"

Tyler said, "We're trying to keep this low profile, Ms. Long. To avoid the subpoenas and court orders that, by necessity, attract the press."

Priest interrupted. "To keep our stock options worth something."

This seemed to hit Selma Long where she lived. She looked back and forth between the two and settled on Priest. "Are you taking advantage of our friendship, girl? And don't you lie to me!"

Priest hesitated and then answered, "Yes."

Selma Long nodded gravely. She looked again to Tyler, then back to Priest. "Well, okay then. At least the cards are on the table." Collectively, Priest and Tyler sat perfectly still, hanging on the woman's every breath, her every twitch.

She began typing again. After a minute or so she began mumbling to herself and stabbing at the keyboard. She cocked her head at the screen and said to Priest, "I've got three that fit what you're looking for. All three, men. Left the company within a month of this date. Two white. The driver's a black man."

"A driver?" Tyler inquired anxiously. "As in locomotives?"

She looked at him as if he knew nothing. "A driver, a man from engineering, and a bean counter—an accountant. Milrose, Stuckey, and . . . ," her finger ran across the screen, "Markowitz."

Tyler and Priest both took notes, asking for spellings.

"Nice packages. Made out okay, all three of 'em," the woman said. "Maybe a little too okay, if you know what I'm saying. Milrose and Stuckey are pulling their full salaries." She eyed Tyler, "That's not unusual for the linemen; it's unheard of. Markowitz, too. He's not only drawing his salary, he took home an option package that's going to make him a rich man." She smiled up at Priest, "F-A-S-T Track's going to make us all rich, right, Nell?"

Tyler scribbled down: *F-A-S-T Track?* Both the *Time* cover and the *60 Minutes* piece had mentioned Goheen's high-tech gamble. Selma Long's reference to this in the same breath with the unusual retirement packages aroused Tyler to the possibility of the bullet train being Alvarez's ultimate target. What greater revenge than to derail Goheen's dream? Still, the answers—if there were any—seemed to lie with these three men who had received golden parachutes immediately following the crossing accident.

"Addresses?" Priest asked, pen ready.

Selma Long scowled. "You people going to tell me what's going on here?" She directed this to Tyler.

"No," he answered her bluntly, their staring contest continuing.

She nodded. "Yeah? Well, I didn't think so." Directing herself to Priest, she said, "Mr. Markowitz has relocated overseas, to Israel. Mr. Milrose . . . all his information is now under a woman's name—Louise—same last name. You could go asking accounting, but when we see that here in HR we're thinking widow."

"And Stuckey?" Tyler asked intensely.

"Following his early retirement, his mailing address changed from Pittsburgh to Washington, D.C."

"Washington," Tyler mumbled. Not his favorite town right now. "Wouldn't you know?" He glanced over at Priest.

Priest asked the woman, "You said he was an engineer, right? But then why Pittsburgh? That's a *maintenance* facility. Can you check his title again?"

Selma Long didn't appreciate repeating her work. She met eyes first with Priest, then with Tyler. Hers were not smiling. She typed, checked the screen, ran a finger along it, and said, "My mistake. Not that kind of engineer. It's *electrical* engineering. Pittsburgh maintenance facility. That's right."

Priest slid off the edge of the desk and pulled the in-box back in place. To Tyler she said, "Electrical." She questioned, "As in crossing guards?"

Tyler jumped up and shook hands with Selma Long. "If we can keep this in confidence, we'd be grateful."

Nell Priest was already out the door.

CHAPTER 21

Tyler's return to Washington, D.C., was under the cover of darkness and made him feel like a criminal. He wanted to visit his house, to see what was left of his friends. But there was no time for that. After only a few days away from the city, it no longer felt like home, and he found that both puzzling and troubling. His face had been in the papers for months, off and on, making him into a celebrity of sorts, a person that others stared at but could rarely place. More often than not, these strangers believed they knew him and would invent the wildest places where they thought they had met. Ironically—it seemed to him—his return here came courtesy of the Metroliner, a direct competitor to Northern Union. After having seen the wreckage outside Terre Haute, he wasn't sure he'd ever view trains quite the same way again.

His goal was twofold: to find out what the recently retired Sam Stuckey knew about the Genoa crossing accident, and if possible to review with Rucker the NTSB file for the same accident. The more he learned about that accident the greater he believed his chances were of not only finding Alvarez but also unearthing NUR's role in all of this and their guilt, if any.

The train trip took two beers for him to overcome a mild bout of claustrophobia. Nell Priest slept in the seat beside him, a few minutes into which she settled her head against Tyler's shoulder, nestled in for the long ride. He felt a bit like a schoolkid in that he tried not to move, to the point of being uncomfortable himself, not even getting up to relieve his beer-bloated bladder.

Having been surprised by her at Penn Station, Tyler had asked how she could simply pack up and leave on such short notice.

"A half hour after you left, I got called up to O'Malley's office," she answered. "Before I went, I called Selma, and she told me that O'Malley had called her personally and asked about our visit."

"And Selma told him?" Tyler did not like the sound of this.

"She wanted to save her job. Yes."

"And?"

"I ignored him and headed here, my pager and cell phone turned off."

"You'll have to check in," he said.

"Sure. And when I do, I tell him that at the very last minute I found out you were heading to Washington, D.C., to question Stuckey about an accident in Genoa, Illinois, and that I thought it better to keep an eye on you than to run upstairs to a meeting. They'll praise me."

"Playing both sides is a lot of risk, Nell," he cautioned.

"It's worth it." After a brief hesitation she admitted, "The Genoa accident is not on file, just as you said. I want to hear what Stuckey says when a federal agent challenges him for the truth. You need me there, just as I needed you with Selma Long. Your creds got her to talk. Listen, if an NUS employee tells Stuckey that it's all right to talk to you, he just may buy it, he just may talk. And if he does, we may have ourselves a witness. But if you're alone—a federal agent asking questions—he's going to clam up and call either O'Malley or an attorney. That's guaranteed. And that's the end of it."

Washington's Union Station had undergone a multimillion-dollar re-model in the late 1980s, converting it into a "multiuse retail facility,"

part rail station, part urban shopping mall, complete with upscale restaurants. So the enormous stone structure held far more people than just travelers. It was teeming with shoppers and restaurantgoers even as late as 8:00 P.M., as Tyler and Priest disembarked and climbed the broken escalator into the central lobby, which was a vast expanse of marble and granite with a forty-foot ceiling.

As a result of their discussion, Tyler arrived nervous, even a little paranoid, and that held on as the two of them followed a huge parade of full-length winter coats, down jackets, backpacks, and Coach overnight bags. The details of their meeting with Selma Long had long since reached O'Malley. If the man had anything to fear from a former electrical engineer talking with him, then O'Malley would have tried to prevent the meeting, either by moving Stuckey or somehow impeding Tyler.

Tyler took a cursory look around the station, wondering if O'Malley had thought to place agents here, to try to keep tabs on him, and perhaps on Priest, too. Was Reagan Airport being watched as well? To what lengths would O'Malley go to intercept him? It depended on how much was at stake.

He and Priest were both scouting the terminal, and she was the first to sound a warning.

"On your right," she said, turning her head left and giving nothing away. "I'm pretty sure I spotted a woman named Sumner. One of ours."

"The Unit?"

"I told you before: I don't know who's in the Unit. I don't even know if there *is* a Unit." They walked slowly, looking like a couple in casual conversation. She added, "I bet I've never formally met half of our people. You see them around the coffee machine, but that's about it."

"So we split up," he said softly.

The crowd shoved outside into the cold as people jockeyed for position in the taxi line. It was damp and slippery underfoot. Tyler saw his breath as he said, "You stay behind and confront the woman. Stall her. It'll buy me time to get in a cab."

"But you need me with Stuckey. Believe it."

"Warn me as soon as you can if you think there are more than her—if they're following me. I'll take precautions in any event." He added, "When you can manage it, we rendezvous at Stuckey's. But take care to make sure they're not following you. Don't lose your job over this."

"I don't like it," she protested.

"Suggestions?"

Nell said nothing.

Tyler said, "The Sumner woman is going to tell you it's a co-incidence to meet like this in a train station. She was waiting for someone else. That's when you play dumb and ask to bum a ride downtown to the Jefferson. At some point she'll have to cave in because no one else is going to show up. She'll use her mobile. That'll be to tell whoever else is here that I got away. It'll happen fast, and it'll be a little edgy, but if you play it right, you sink her with her own story."

"And you'll wait for me," she encouraged.

"I'll play that as it comes. Maybe they've warned him already. Maybe they weren't going to warn him until they knew I was here."

"You need me, Peter."

"I'd rather do it with you than without you." He paused. "I'll wait as long as I can."

Nell Priest turned around and walked with long, determined strides back toward the terminal.

Despite having called it home for the last twelve years, Tyler didn't like being back. Too many troubled memories. The Chester Washington assault had ruined it forever. As a victim of a legal system that had used racial bias to nail him for excessive force, he had been hurt by this city in ways that could never be reversed. Tyler would never again call this place home.

The December rain was falling more heavily, switching before his eyes to a wet snow with flakes the size of nickels. The cab's wipers swept them aside, pushing them into lines of slush. Twice, Tyler directed the cabbie to take him fully around a huge city block—four consecutive right-hand turns—as he watched for headlights following. Deciding they were not being tailed, he directed the cabbie to a location within walking distance of Stuckey's apartment building, not wanting to land at the exact address.

He'd probably driven past this twelve-story condominium dozens of times without noticing it. A blight of similar housing had been constructed in the early '70s, ruining the charm of a brownstone neighborhood with boxy, concrete blandness. For a cop, and for the residents, too, the District was a city of contrast—a few blocks this way or that and one crossed into dangerous neighborhoods. More often than not, these same street boundaries were along racial lines as well. He had phoned Stuckey from New York, identifying himself as a telemarketer for a long distance phone company, his intention merely to confirm that the man was at home, that it was worth the trip. If the man now wasn't at home, he would wait. Inside a small lobby used for mailboxes, he approached the columns of apartment call buttons and found Stuckey as 5B. His finger found the buzzer but did not push it, honoring his pact with Nell to wait for her. It was warmer inside than out, so he stayed in the small foyer, awaiting a call from her or her arrival.

Five minutes passed.

Ten.

As he was debating what to do, a pizza delivery boy hurried inside and buzzed an apartment.

Tyler, seeing a way inside, said to the delivery boy, "You'd think she could hurry it up a little, knowing I'm down here. Probably stuck in front of a mirror."

The pizza boy was buzzed through. He held the door for Tyler. "So surprise her," the kid said.

Tyler's claustrophobia demanded the stairs. He reached the fifth floor, feeling good about the pounding in his chest. Passing apartments F, E, and D, he turned left past C and finally arrived at B. The hallway smelled strongly of cigarettes. In front of the apartment door, he stepped onto a thin, rubber-and-felt welcome mat and rang the bell. The mat felt spongy—wet—beneath his shoes.

Tyler looked down, lifting a foot. It wasn't wet, but tacky. It wasn't water, but *blood!* He stepped back off the mat immediately, a detective's response to resist contaminating a possible crime scene. Both of his shoes tracked and smeared the blood onto the worn hallway floor. Tyler's pulse quickened. He reached for a handkerchief and turned the doorknob, ever the cop. The door opened to the smell of blood and excrement, and he thought: someone's dead. He knew that this involved him—stepping into blood and leaving his shoe prints on the hall carpet was only a part of it. He knew immediately that whatever had happened here tied directly to his and Nell's questions at NUR, knew immediately that Nell had been right to fear those security monitors, knew immediately that O'Malley was sticking not thumbs but whole fists into the dike. It wasn't exactly guilt he experienced so much as responsibility. His actions had caused harm to another human being, whether he had drawn the sword or not. Regret stung him.

Tyler eased the apartment door open but did not step inside, his cell phone already in hand at the ready. He briefly considered the address here because unlike other major cities, Washington, D.C., was policed by four large-scale police departments and another half dozen smaller ones: D.C. Metro, Capitol Police, U.S. Parks Police, and the FBI. Jurisdiction was a constant concern and occasionally a battleground. The cop in him immediately thought he should call Rhomer or Vogler or Vale—a fellow homicide cop with whom he could work without prejudice. The NTSB agent in him wanted to call Nell or Rucker.

I should have waited for her! he thought.

A bloody path led from the doorway. Tyler didn't need a road map. A lamp had been knocked to the floor. There was blood on the ceiling, blood on the walls. He saw a smear on the carpet—Stuckey had either dragged himself across the floor or been moved after the beating. The body was a swollen mass of contusions. Tyler had seen worse, and yet always the same. DOA. The man's nose had been pushed back into his head, his right eye collapsed under a jigsaw of broken bone, and Tyler knew one of those blows had killed him. He didn't bother checking for a pulse—the unmoving open-eyed stare told the whole story. Out of habit, Tyler was already processing the scene.

The attack had been immediate—no hellos, no small talk. A man answers the door, gets shoved back into his own apartment, and gets a blow to the head.

Now his gut twisted as he absorbed the blame. With a cop's attitude he'd gone charging into NUR despite Priest's warnings. *Damn them all,* he'd thought at the time, not seeing far enough ahead to realize it was a man like Stuckey who would be damned, not the people he'd hoped for.

Tyler looked around for a possible weapon. And there it was: dark, round. Wood or metal. Lying by the victim's left leg, as it was, and with the light in the room only from the open door, Tyler leaned to move his own shadow out of his way.

The dark stick had a knurled handle and a loop of leather. His chest knotted in pain. It felt as if all the air had suddenly been sucked from the room. That shape, that length of stick, was too familiar. Any cop knew that shape: a nightstick, a billy club. Standard issue for any cop. Tyler's vision dimmed, and his head swooned as he caught a closer look at the very end of that club where every rookie cop carved his initials.

Unsteady, he reached out and supported himself with the door-jamb, jerking his hand back as he felt something cold and sticky between his fingers, only to see them smeared in blood. He'd left a handprint behind. His *own* handprint.

He glanced back at the stick—the murder weapon—and the initials carved into its end: P. T.

He recognized them only too well.

He had carved them himself in his rookie year on Metro.

"Where are you now?" Tyler asked her. He faintly heard Nell speak to her cabbie, and she answered that she was less than a mile away.

"You were right about O'Malley playing hardball," he informed her. He wondered how much to share with her. O'Malley had made it personal, had made Tyler the scapegoat—Tyler the cause and the effect. He seethed with anger, for failing to see his own vulnerability and how he might be taken advantage of. But O'Malley had leveraged it all only too cleverly. The stakes had changed. It was no longer an assignment, a job opportunity, a chance for income. O'Malley had singled him out, made him a target, had capitalized on the Chester Washington assault, and in doing so had picked the wrong person.

"Peter?"

He'd left the line open; he wasn't sure for how long. He stood on the fifth-floor landing of the fire stairs debating whether to call Homicide.

"Peter?" she repeated, her voice warm with concern.

He told her, "Stuckey's dead. My rookie nightstick's lying under him. It's my M.O.—it's Chester Washington all over again. They probably knew I'd called him from New York. They certainly knew I came down here. So now it's made to look as if I lose my temper and pound the guy clear to heaven. Maybe they meant to kill him, maybe not. Doesn't matter now. All they needed to do was steal my stick. The rest was timing."

"You've got to get out of there," she said.

"Run from a crime scene?" asked the former homicide cop. "With this kind of evidence stacked up? Are you kidding me?" He mumbled, "That's the final nail in the coffin. That's what they *want* me to do." He tried to settle himself, for he knew intuitively that the next few decisions he made would dictate the next few weeks, months, maybe years of his life. He said, "Either way, I'm screwed. If I call it in and stay, they win: I'm out of the picture, which is what they want. If I run, and this thing's connected to me, which it's going to be, I'm a fugitive. I'll tell you one thing: they must have a lot to hide, Nell."

"Get that nightstick and get the hell out of there," she encouraged. "You must still have friends on the department. Call them. Explain it—" He heard her talk to the driver. "I'm here. Where are you?"

"Stairwell. But the entrance is locked." He could barely see straight.

"Get back to the apartment. Get the nightstick. Buzz me through." He cracked open the door to the hallway. His bloody shoe prints formed a slowly fading route toward the fire stairs. Then he looked down at his hand on the door pull: more prints to worry about. Evidential quicksand: the more he moved, the deeper he sank.

The cell phone still to his ear, he heard the doorbell buzzing from Stuckey's apartment. In the phone he heard, "I'm here. I'm buzzing you. Peter? Get me in. I can help you."

"Don't touch anything," he said. "Wipe down the buzzer. Get well away from here and give me a minute. I'll find you. Must be someplace to wait for me. I'll call you."

"Let me in!"

"No. One of us is enough. You have to be clean, Nell, or they take both of us out. I'll meet you in a minute."

"Peter!"

"No arguments." He disconnected, reconsidering his options. Could he trick them? Get out of the city, leave some crumbs for them to follow, and then return to clear this up? On the surface, taking the nightstick seemed the thing to do—it would no doubt be carrying prints of his, and latent prints could not be dated. He could smear the handprint on the doorjamb, the shoe prints in the hall, and dispose of the nightstick forever. But he had made the long distance call to Stuckey only hours earlier; he'd ridden in a city cab arriving close to here. He could hear a detective like himself making hay over the fact he'd asked the cab to stop a block away. If O'Malley's people made a few anonymous calls, the evidence would stack up no matter how Tyler compromised the scene.

Detective Eddie Vale answered on the second ring. "Vale."

"It's me: Tyler."

"Pete? God damn!"

Tyler cut right through old home week. "There's a body going cold on a floor of apartment five B, fourteen-twenty-seven R, Northwest. Guy has been beaten to shit. Latents matching my prints are no doubt going to be found on what turns out to be my rookie nightstick, and on the doorjamb, too. Shoe prints, in the dead guy's blood, outside the front door will match my size. I stick around, I'm looking at a couple months in and out of court, and probably some serious time in lockup because it'll be viewed as a second offense. And that's if I'm *lucky*."

Vale repeated the address and said, "Where are you now?"

"On the scene."

"Stay there."

"No can do, though I wish I could. It's supposed to mirror Chester Washington so you guys can fit the square peg in the square hole. It's supposed to take me off the case I'm working for Rucker over at NTSB. I'm going to flee the scene, Eddie, but I'm making this call first to try and set things straight."

"Do *not* flee the scene," Vale protested. "Let me get there. Just me. Alone. Let's look at it, Pete. Use your head here. You run and what's it going to look like?"

Tyler theorized, "If a friendly face arrived here first, maybe he'd think I'm too smart to leave my own nightstick under the body, too smart not to wipe down the doorjamb and smear the footprints. I'd have to explain how so much blood got on the outside mat when there's only splatter on and around the doorjamb. How'd all that blood walk itself outside onto the mat? I'll tell you how: it was transferred there to make sure I left shoe prints for you guys." He added, "Never mind that I don't have a drop of blood on my clothing. If I stuck around, it would be to show you that. I rode the Metroliner from New York tonight—you can check on that—and chances are someone on that train or the cabbie who picked me up at Union Station and dropped me here might remember these same clothes I'm wearing." He paused a moment, giving Vale time to take the notes that Tyler knew he was taking. "But all that's a little thin, you know, Eddie? That's not exactly ice I want to skate on. And no matter what, if I pause a moment—even to make this phone call—whoever did this wins, because the object is to tie me up so badly that I bail on the case I'm working."

The connection hung between them, neither man speaking.

"I ain't your attorney, Pete, but it's damn stupid to flee the scene, and you know it."

"I'm going to flee the scene, only to pull these guys off. They have the power to arrest. They could move me away from my friends like you, Eddie. I made this call first, and I want that in the jacket."

"The nightstick? Your place broken into?"

"I haven't been there in a week. It must have been hit. Is there evidence of that? I would doubt it. That would make the case against me pretty thin, and that's not the intention here."

"Who *are* these guys?"

"Northern Union Railroad's security guys."

"That's a joke, right?"

Tyler answered, "I wish."

"Apartment five B. Fourteen-twenty-seven R, Northwest," Vale repeated.

"I owe you, Eddie."

"No shit, Sherlock," said Eddie Vale.

Tyler walked briskly for a dozen blocks, trying to second-guess what means either his former colleagues or Northern Union would use to track him down. Eddie Vale or not, they would want him in for questioning. He hit an ATM and withdrew the maximum four hundred on three cards. A credit trace would be initiated. The withdrawal of this money within a short walking distance of the murder might be later used against him, but he saw little choice. If they locked out his cards, he wouldn't have access to any money. He played a bird in the hand and took his chances.

Twelve hundred dollars, plus the sixty he was carrying. He reached a pay phone and placed a landline call to Nell, not wanting his own cell phone record to show this call, not wanting to suggest she might have been an accessory. A plan was already forming in his head: Nell could distance herself from him, reestablish herself within. If there were any answers, they most likely lay within the corporate headquarters. Above all, they needed access.

With luck, Eddie Vale's involvement might buy Tyler some time, but the lieutenant in charge, Bridlesman, would never allow a good friend of Tyler's to lead the investigation once Tyler had been identified through his prints and nightstick. Tyler's cellular phone records would already link Tyler to both Priest and to Vale's home—mistakes he'd made in haste and wished he could take back. Nell would be sought for questioning. Vale might be asked about why he was the first cop to arrive on the scene. Tyler was making trouble for everyone, and he had put barely twenty minutes between himself and that bloodied apartment.

O'Malley's tactics enraged Tyler. No matter what Stuckey's involvement had been in the Genoa tragedy, he didn't deserve death at the end of a nightstick. That O'Malley would go to such extremes served to reinforce Tyler's sense of the stakes involved. Whatever the company's culpability in the Genoa accident, it had to be enough to bring down at least Keith O'Malley, if not William Goheen and the board of directors along with it.

His no longer using credit cards and his cellular phone would frustrate investigators. *But what else?* Tyler wondered, using the quiet time of the walk to see this from the side of his former job. Communication, expenditures, transportation: the three axioms of a manhunt. He'd taken care of two of these. Transportation would be far more difficult. *How to remain invisible?* Having pointed to Priest by calling her cell phone from his, Tyler realized that if they fled together, she could not use her credit cards, either. That meant no rental car. Planes were out because they required picture ID. That left stealing a car, hitchhiking, trains, and buses. Both bus stations and train stations had security cameras—Tyler had used them to track Alvarez. *How far would they go to find him?* he wondered. *How much of this could O'Malley get his hands on? Whom should he fear more, O'Malley or the cops?*

Finally, the thought came to him. The Potomac. The docks: a place where he had a couple of contacts, a place that lived on cash, a place where people knew how to keep their mouths shut.

His plan continued to take shape, but all the while he found himself thinking that beating Stuckey to death did not come lightly. Perhaps the idea had been to put him into the hospital, O'Malley sending a message of silence. This, in turn, led him to wonder again about the stakes at play. And then—and only then—did it dawn on him that *three* employees had left NUR with unusual compensation. The other two—Milrose, if alive, and Markowitz—might be as valuable to the investigation as he'd believed Stuckey had been. The obvious question remained: Had O'Malley already beaten him to them?

CHAPTER 22

"Nice view," Nell Priest said from the starboard walkway of the two-hundred-foot-long container freighter *The Nannuck*.

Tyler wasn't thinking about the view. He'd been reading the names off the chart, marking their progress: Goose Island, Fox Ferry Point, Fort Fotte Park, Mount Vernon, Gunston Cove, Hallowing Point. Now a rose-colored horizon bled a bruised orange hue onto Craney Island. As a fugitive, Tyler found nothing to celebrate.

"Are you sure you're okay with this?" he asked.

"Would you remain loyal to O'Malley?"

"It's no small thing," he reminded her.

"The man had a former employee's head bashed in. Regardless of whatever's proved, that's what happened. And I'm an employee, soon to be former employee, don't forget. Am I madly in love with you? Swept away? I'm sorry, Peter, but that's not what's behind this decision. I happen to have taken sides, that's all. I won't work for him. I still feel loyalty to the company, but not O'Malley."

Tyler considered some way to get back at O'Malley, some way to turn the tables, but he had little reason for optimism. "Don't quit. If you continue to work for him, we can use it to our advantage."

"If there's something I can do to help you, I'll do it. Absolutely. If that's what you're saying, Peter, I'm okay with that."

He touched her cheek gently with cold fingers, attempting to convey both his appreciation and the fondness he felt for her. The last five days had begun as part-time work and had gone on to abruptly alter his life, quite possibly forever. A manslaughter charge tacked on to his previous assault would mean definite time behind bars. And a former cop behind bars was a dead man, which made it a life sentence no matter how many years were given.

Tyler's standing on a cold walkway at sunrise had nothing to do with navigation charts but instead was a contrivance for him and Nell to get out of earshot of the captain and crew. The raw wind stung his face despite the two-day beard. Tyler disconnected a call he'd placed using Nell's cell phone. Again, he churned over O'Malley's tossing away Stuckey's life. How badly the man must have wanted him off the Alvarez manhunt! He'd obviously gotten far closer to the truth than O'Malley believed possible. And this in turn thrilled him because it indicated a vulnerability in O'Malley that Tyler might yet exploit.

Handing Nell's mobile back to her, he wondered how thorough their manhunt of him would be. Would O'Malley or his former colleagues on Metro think to monitor Nell's mobile? Did they know already that her phone had just placed a call overseas? Tyler had avoided public transportation, had avoided use of his credit cards. As a cop, he knew the traps to avoid. But again he questioned his use of Nell's phone. Maybe he'd come to regret that as well.

"I woke him up," he told Nell. "Markowitz," he added, naming the NUR accountant who had unexpectedly retired overseas.

"Did he volunteer anything about Genoa? Would he talk?" She remained on edge. He understood the agonizing that must have gone on in making her decision to join him. *Regrets?* he wondered, despite her proclamations made only moments earlier.

The peaceful, slow grinding of the ship through the dark water belied the tension between them.

He said, "Markowitz kept his options open, let me do most of the talking. I stepped him through what we currently knew about the crossing accident, and that we suspected a cover-up. I told him that Stuckey was dead, that Milrose had probably left a widow behind, and that I believed O'Malley was involved in at least Stuckey. I cautioned that O'Malley might be cleaning house. I reminded him that lying to a federal agent was a federal offense. He proved a good listener."

She wore a dark green oilskin jacket that the captain had loaned her. Oilskin had never looked so good.

"He negotiated some limited immunity, actually believing I had anything to do with that, and finally opened up some. His retirement was not his idea. Surprise! It was handed to him along with a golden parachute. To his knowledge no one, including Goheen, if that's who's ultimately found responsible, is guilty of an actual crime. Negligence, maybe, as legally defined. But not a crime."

"Meaning?"

He wanted to reach out and stroke her cheek again—yearned for some kind of physical contact with her—but felt foolish about taking her hand. He'd quit smoking twelve years earlier but suddenly longed for a cigarette between his fingers.

"He claimed ignorance but went on to say that he thinks that a number of people probably saw a piece of the puzzle. Maybe that puzzle could be reconstructed, maybe not. When they volunteered his retirement for him, he collected as much information as he could as quickly as possible. There apparently was plenty of creative bookkeeping. He has copies of some of it."

She crossed her arms, visibly upset. "You're telling me we're not going to get anywhere with this?"

Misunderstanding her tone as all-out regret, Tyler said, "Listen, when we dock, you can walk away from this. You can play it however you want—"

"Shut up, Peter. It's not that at all. Stop taking things so damned personally. I made my decision. I'm not going back on that."

"But if you wanted to—"

"Just *drop* it!"

Tyler grinned out of nervousness. He and Kat had settled into a lovers' routine. He wasn't used to this early stage of a relationship in which the boundaries were continually tested. "It will apparently require a full audit. Court orders. Subpoenas. Even then, Markowitz repeated that he doubted there was any criminal offense. Cooking the books will cost them a hand slap from the SEC and maybe a fine. That's all, folks."

"How does crooked accounting dovetail with the crossing accident? Did someone try to pay off Alvarez under the table? That doesn't make sense, given an attempt at a settlement."

"Unless Alvarez's attorney was paid off for convincing his client to settle."

"But the case didn't settle!" she protested.

"And the attorney didn't live," Tyler reminded her.

That won a moment of silence. He hadn't wanted a cigarette this badly in years. "Markowitz used NASA as his analogy—the space shuttle program. He said that every so often the space shuttle program hits these major hiccups, unanticipated problems that require huge infusions of cash. They can't go running to Congress because even if Congress responded it would take months to see the actual cash."

"So," she said, interrupting him, "they borrow from other programs. Mars landers—that kind of thing."

"Mars landers. Exactly. He said the same thing."

"And we were doing that? Budget-dipping?"

"Markowitz says so. Furthermore, he believes the decision to borrow internally like that would have been made by either Goheen personally or the board collectively."

"And this connects to Genoa how?"

"Goheen is apparently maniacal about this bullet train technology."

"F-A-S-T Track. I can confirm that," she said.

"Sees it as the future of public transportation."

She nodded. "It's basically all anyone talks about. It's as if the company has only the one project."

"Markowitz says the program has been a financial black hole from its inception."

"It's the track."

"Meaning?"

She explained, "Europe rides on welded track. Much of our track in this country is still not welded. Worse, our tracks are not banked enough for high speed. There was no way we could bank existing track without spending billions. So Goheen had the vision to have the Metroliner route relaid with welded track and then imagined a guidance program engineered to bank the individual train cars in advance of turns. That's where the money has gone. Without the technology, the unbanked track would throw the cars off at high speed. The train then flattens out again on the straightaways. It's all satellite-guided, GPS technology that needed special military rating to be pinpoint accurate. How much of this do you know already?"

"None," he said.

"Rumors is all I've heard," she said, "so I shouldn't pass it off as fact. We talk about the technology as if we know, but no one but a few insiders does for sure. They've kept it secret to avoid patent infringements." She added, "That much I *do* know, because a big part of our job in security has been to police possible leaks."

He said, "Markowitz's NASA analogy is that when the space shuttle needed the funds the Mars lander program lost out. In NUR's case, the pension funding couldn't be touched because of union supervision, so they raided maintenance."

She turned her face directly into the wind and closed her eyes. "It might explain the derailments. Maintenance is constant. Twenty-four, seven, coast to coast. They have an enormous department. Huge budget. They're responsible for everything from track wear and bed maintenance to—" She gasped.

"Yes?"

"Crossing guards."

Tyler felt the wind as particularly cold on his face. The landing lights of a plane shone brightly on the horizon.

"Oh, God," she moaned, "it makes so much sense."

"Does it?"

She said, "Stuckey was an *electrical* engineer."

"As in maintenance," Tyler completed.

"As in crossing guards."

"Markowitz was familiar with Stuckey's name because Stuckey bitched to accounting about his money drying up. Markowitz's job was to stall him and make promises that couldn't be kept. The truth was that the maintenance budget was being used for the bullet train."

She said, "Routine maintenance was probably suspended. That would have included crossing guards."

Tyler said, "So after Genoa, Stuckey gets handed a dream of a retirement package. Markowitz, Milrose, and Stuckey forget they ever heard about maintenance problems or that funds were ever diverted." Tyler felt he had most, if not all, of the pieces now, and he wondered what to do with them. He still felt he needed the NTSB files on the crossing accident. The details. And then a sickening feeling, like nausea, twisted his gut—the suspicion that Loren Rucker, his boss, was somehow involved with Northern Union. What if Rucker had been the investigator assigned to the Genoa crossing accident? Perhaps there had been a few favors granted. Tyler recalled that Rucker had known O'Malley a long time—since they had served in the Marines together. The same Loren Rucker who had made this spur-of-the-moment job offer.

"Peter?" she said. "What are you thinking?"

Tyler spoke calmly, though inside he churned. "Rucker gave me this job because O'Malley asked for someone he could blow up."

Priest turned and faced him, her hair partially obscuring her face like a curtain.

Tyler theorized, "If I led them to Alvarez, they would kill him, just as they did Stuckey—beat him to death—and make sure that I looked good for it. Their dirty little secret dies with Alvarez, and anything I say gets taken as the ranting of a desperate man."

"That's a little paranoid, don't you think?" If she crossed her arms any more tightly, she was going to stop all circulation.

"Is it?" He asked, "Why else did Rucker bail me out with this job offer? Me, of all people?"

"Your experience on homicide," she said, reminding him of his own explanation.

"Yeah?" he asked sarcastically. "Now I wonder."

She reached out and touched his arm, "One thing at a time. We stay focused. Can we get Markowitz to testify?"

"To what? He doesn't believe any crime was committed. And now that I've tipped him off?" he asked disappointedly. "He has a lifestyle to protect. Either O'Malley will get to him, or he'll go underground and no one will ever hear from him."

"Then what?"

"Alvarez," Tyler answered. "As long as Alvarez is alive, the Genoa accident can't go away. If O'Malley gets to Alvarez and Markowitz, the cover-up will hold."

"Are you saying what I think you're saying?"

"If we're going to beat O'Malley," Tyler said, grinding his teeth between his words, "we have to get Alvarez before he does."

Under a slate sky and steady rain, Baltimore, from the river, looked eerily deserted. A refrain from a song passed through Tyler's head, "Ain't no one in Baltimore no more." Later, the freighter docked, with deckhands busy making preparations, and Priest hung up from a call to a taxi company. "Ten minutes or less," she told Tyler. "What now?"

"A room. Some sleep. A shower. We start fresh."

"I hate to state the obvious, but O'Malley will make every effort to make sure you're placed in custody A-S-A-P."

"Will he send your colleagues or the police?"

"Both. With you off the case, and Stuckey dead, there aren't going to be any grand revelations."

"There's always you," Tyler pointed out, turning his collar up. "What do you suppose he has in mind for you?"

"If he suspects I know something, he'll either try to buy me or discredit me. I should resign effectively immediately."

"No, I don't think so," Tyler protested. "We're far better off with you inside."

"You're kidding, right, Peter?"

"You could wear a tape recorder. Maybe we get him trying to compromise you."

"I've chosen sides," she reminded him. "I like the team I'm on."

Tyler repeated, "They *must* be liable for those Genoa deaths—it must be provable—or they wouldn't have taken it this far."

Priest asked, "But *why* take it this far? Have you asked yourself that? A case like this always settles, never goes to court. You raise the offer high enough, and eventually it settles. Ten, fifteen million for Alvarez's wife and kids? What's the big worry here for Northern Union?"

"The big worry is that it ends up more like eighty or a hundred million."

"No way!" she protested.

"Not if they'd admitted their mistakes up front, no. Not if they could win a settlement. But what if Alvarez was demanding a trial— a stage to air his suspicions? The press. A jury. A Latino crushed by a corporate conglomerate." He thought this out. "You can bet they've destroyed documents along the way. We know for sure they've given early retirements in exchange for silence. That kind of behavior on the part of a corporation pisses juries off, I'm telling you. They would pay through the nose for that kind of attitude."

Nell picked up on this. "What if we carry Markowitz's NASA analogy a bit further? What if the company is broke? What if Goheen has leveraged the company to the hilt for F-A-S-T Track?"

"A lawsuit like this could start the dominoes tumbling," Tyler answered. "Questions start getting asked, stockholders demand an audit. Weirder things have happened."

Priest's mobile rang yet again. She didn't answer it. The leash that connected back to NUR was tugging at her.

"Maybe next time you answer," Tyler said. "We give them something tiny to suggest where we are. It can't be too obvious."

"Why?"

"Time. For both of us to get some answers."

She reached down and took his hand. They watched as the longshoreman began unloading the containers. She said, "In my heart of hearts I want to believe that Bill Goheen is honest. He has a vision. He's charismatic. He's one of those guys you cheer for. Would he condone beating Sam Stuckey to a pulp? Not on your life. I know the man, Peter. That had to be O'Malley, and my guess is, they didn't mean for him to die. They wanted him like Chester Washington, *exactly* like Chester Washington: alive for the cameras to capture all the gory detail when the guy leaves the hospital with a face the size of a hot-air balloon. This went south on them. They wanted to scare Stuckey into keeping his mouth shut and to get you out of the way in the process. Now they're cornered, and it's their own doing. If Goheen's smart, he offers O'Malley's head and wipes his hands of it."

"If he was clean, he'd have already done it," Tyler offered. "A guy like O'Malley—he's got something on everyone."

"That sounds a little paranoid to me."

Tyler gently let go of her hand. "Cab's here," he said, pointing.

"I'm sorry," she apologized. "Luxury of hindsight. We are where we are."

"Indeed we are," Tyler agreed. "Listen, temper or not, impatience or not, why on earth would I beat up Stuckey? At some point that has got to occur to somebody investigating this. Why would I kill a possible witness? Why club him as he answers the door? Why would I do that? Truth be told, I'm not so worried about the long-term outcome of all of this, I'm worried about the short term. I know how slow police work can be, believe me. If I get back down there, I can speed it up."

He asked rhetorically, "You want some irony? At this point, my job is not only to stop Alvarez from derailing this bullet train—and I know that that's what this is about—but to protect him, to *save* him. *He's* the witness we need, the voice. If something happens to him, then whatever went down at that rail crossing will never be heard, just as you said. O'Malley sent Harry Wells on a search-and-destroy. They don't want him in custody, they want him out. And if they kill a domestic terrorist? Hell, they'll get medals." Tyler signaled the cabbie, and he and Priest walked off the ship.

They were about to split up. He'd lost control over events. Or maybe he'd never had any. Cops had a corner on the market when it came to arrogance.

"Thanks for being here," he said over the roof of the cab as they were about to climb in. Honesty was as good a place to start as any.

"Wouldn't miss it for the world," said Nell, smiling at him in a way he felt to his core.

It was called the Maritymer, but judging by the decor, and the ceiling-mounted mirror, it might as well have been the No Tell Motel. Forty rooms on two floors. Anchors at the bottom of the outside stairs, with white-painted chains for handrails. Anchors as door knockers as well. The minibar refrigerator stood empty, a patch of green mold in the back like a birthmark. Tyler took a ground-floor unit, in part because it had a sliding glass door leading out the back, where a covered swimming pool hid under snow.

Tyler sent Priest out to buy him a new pair of shoes so he could toss his own, hedging his bets in case the police did catch up with him. The bloody shoe prints outside of Stuckey's would not match with the new shoes. When she returned, nearly two hours later, with a pair of leather boots cut low at the ankle, a freshly showered Tyler protested over the cost. "I only gave you eighty bucks."

"Never mind. They're a gift. I couldn't see you in running shoes in this weather." She handed him back his four crisp twenties.

"And you paid for them how?" he inquired, his nerves on edge. He feared she had accelerated his plans.

She didn't answer right away.

He asked, "You *did* remember what I said about not using any credit cards?"

"It wasn't exactly a credit card," she said. But she looked guilty as all hell.

"Tell me you didn't use a credit card." Tyler was already gathering his jacket and some change he'd removed from his pocket. Unable to reach her on her cell phone, O'Malley would be using every means to track her. "Tell me you paid with cash."

"Not a credit card."

"Thank God." He relaxed some.

"I have an account at Nordstrom. I charged it to my account."

"You charged it." The room grew progressively smaller, the walls coming in toward him. This was much too soon. He hadn't planned his trip back to Washington.

"But not to a card!" she protested.

He closed his eyes and breathed deeply. He explained, somewhat calmly, "Your credit rating will show the Nordstrom account," he informed her. "They'll be watching that account if they're smart."

"I know you were a cop, and I don't mean this the way it sounds, but I think you give them too much credit."

"I'm not talking about the cops," he said. He stepped toward her and took her purse strap. She pulled back to stop him. They struggled. Tyler won the purse. He pulled out the cell phone and held it in the air as he switched it off. "When was the last time you used this?"

"The cab," she said. "I called a cab from the boat. Remember?"

"Ship," he corrected. Some things he couldn't help. He dropped the phone back into her purse and returned the purse to her. "My call overseas? It doesn't help them any; it doesn't place us. Even the call to Milrose. But a call to a Baltimore cab company? What the hell was I thinking? We're screwed," he said. He glanced at his wristwatch. "Hell . . . they could already be out there waiting."

"*My* cell phone?" she asked. "I understand they might watch yours, but—"

"If they're alerted to the Nordstrom charge—and they very well could be—then they'll know you're in Baltimore. That call to the cab company cinches it. O'Malley can use his clout to get our drop-off from the cab company."

"Well, let's hope like hell that you're a better cop than they are. And I suggest that we get the hell out of here."

"How? Call a cab?" he snapped.

"Elite," she said. "The rent-a-car company. They pick you up and bring you back to the rental agency." She added, "We watch for anyone following us."

"To rent a car we have to use a credit card, and we can't do that."

"I rent it, and I call in, and I head back to the city. I drop you somewhere. I tell them that I stayed with you, wanted to get word to them but couldn't because you had my phone. You ditched me at a gas stop."

He nodded. It was good thinking and he told her so. He sat down on the bed, flipped through the Yellow Pages, and made the call.

Tyler kept watch from the window, a lone eye peering out alongside the blinds. Dusk fell early, to where everything was a shade of gray, and the air seemed thick with dust. A few minutes before he expected the rental pickup, a Baltimore PD cruiser pulled into the parking lot and one uniform went inside the office while a second kept the structure under surveillance. He had hoped to lure NUS away from Washington but on his terms, not this way. O'Malley must have tipped the local police to their location. No stone unturned.

Tyler's reaction was immediate. He grabbed hold of Nell Priest, held her close to him, and gripped her wrist behind her, their chests touching.

"Your dry cleaner," he asked her.

"What?" Their lips were nearly close enough to kiss. Her eyes seemed enormous at that moment. He held her arm pinned.

"The name of the dry cleaner you use," he stated.

"Ming Ling. Twenty-third and—"

"If you get a message on your answering machine from them, the invoice number will be the area code and prefix of the number I want you to call. The amount you owe is the last four digits of the number. That's all you have to remember: combine the invoice with the price."

"Got it," she said, her face a knot of worry.

"Call me at the number from a pay phone." He smiled, "And remember to leave off some dry cleaning. Even if you're being watched, or if your phones are tapped, we're cool."

He yanked the phone out of the wall and used its wire to bind one wrist and spun her around sharply, explaining above her protests, "I took you onto that ship against your will. I left the motel twenty minutes ago." He hooked the room's only chair with his foot and dragged it so that Priest would be facing the door. "Peter!"

Working frantically, he tied both wrists together, behind the chair. He kissed her on the cheek from behind. "Remember to act pissed at me."

"That won't be too hard!" She strained at the wire.

"Sorry if it hurts."

"It *does* hurt!" she complained.

"I said I was sorry," Tyler replied. Grabbing the room's spare blanket from the open closet's shelf, he hurried out through the sliding glass door, taking one last look at Nell Priest from behind and wondering if it was the last time he'd see her.

Tyler lay on his back on top of the blanket that he used as an in-
sulator against the solid ice surface of the motel's winterized swimming pool. Above him, by only a foot, was the underside of a section
of the reinforced pool cover, installed for the winter months to prevent accidents.

Tyler counted the voices shouting back and forth—three, maybe
four cops out searching for him. In this cold, they would be impatient
to quit. Beat cops rarely pursued anything beyond a reasonable effort.
They'd be thinking about the warmth of their cruisers.

Suddenly, one of the voices sounded incredibly close. A man's
deep voice said, "Too many goddamn tracks out here."

If the cops thought this through, they would see that the vast
majority of the tracks were small—left behind by kids playing out
in the snow. They might notice a particular set of larger tracks
that led from the room where they had found Nell Priest tied to a
chair. They might observe that those same tracks vanished at the
pool.

"Nothing over here!" shouted another man.

The voice near Tyler faded as the man moved away. "Maybe he
went over the back fence. Jimmy!" the man ordered. "Get your
cruiser out back on Cardiff. And call into dispatch to put it out over
the MDT that we think the suspect's on foot in this area." MDT:
mobile data terminal. To Tyler, that meant that every cop in every
cop car in Baltimore had his description. He tried to think, but the
smallness of the space, the confinement, got the better of him. He
closed his eyes, trying to hold off dizziness and claustrophobia. The
darkness helped. The acute cold, too, by winning his attention and
distracting him, seemed to help. Nonetheless, the anxiety continued
to build inside of him. He felt as if he were suffocating. He felt
trapped.

The talk between the cops faded as they returned to the room.

Or was that deep-voiced cop still nearby? With the sound muffled, Tyler couldn't tell.

As he rocked his head to get a better listen, he heard instead a sharp, loud rap—like a hammer pounding down. Then another. And yet another. At first, believing it was the patrolmen, Tyler wondered what they were doing out there. But then, as another, even louder small explosion filled the tight space, he identified it as coming from beneath him. *Cracking ice!* The warmth of his body, trapped in the confined space, had set into motion the laws of physical science. *Crack!* Another one.

These triggered a bout of nauseating anxiety as his claustrophobia raged.

Tyler knocked away the plywood cover and came out of the pool like a dead man out of a grave—paste pale, sweating, and shaking.

One of the cops, much closer than Tyler had expected, spun around, reaching for his weapon. Tyler lunged, grabbed him by his weapon arm, and flung him toward the open pool cover. The cop went over the edge and broke through the ice in the shallow end. Tyler glanced in the direction of the motel and saw Priest standing in the door there, two cops questioning her. He found himself momentarily paralyzed. This woman had wormed her way under his skin. He didn't want to leave her, didn't want to strike out on his own. Didn't want to run like some fugitive. They met eyes, making a connection, and then Tyler took off. He heard the warning shouts: "Stop!" "You, stop!" These patrolmen were at a disadvantage: Tyler knew they wouldn't shoot unless fired upon. They could chase, but he had a head start. He also knew that their sense of brotherhood would require them first to save the man in the pool. He'd gone in hard, fully dressed. They would probably split up, one staying with the pool, one or two coming after him on foot.

He ran.

At the end of the small parking area he cut left, along a cracked sidewalk bordered by a wood fence.

He heard the sound before he fully identified it: *cha-cha-hmmmm, cha-cha-hmmmm*. The clatter of a slowly moving freight, traveling toward the north edge of Baltimore's downtown.

From over his shoulder he saw one of the uniformed cops, still a distance back, running for him but clumsily because of the artillery and hardware on the man's belt.

Tyler turned left at the end of the fence and ran through the snow parallel to the moving train. Ran hard. Ran fast. Grabbed hold of a handrail on the far end of a car and hung on. Pulled himself up.

By the time the cop rounded the corner, there was no one to see, the train now going fast enough to make the man think twice about jumping.

Tyler, above a coupling, hung on for dear life, marveling at the fine line that now separated him from Alvarez. He had become the man he was after.

Tyler's fingers felt frozen as he clung to a metal rung of the ladder bolted to the rumbling freight car.

His toes were numb from the steady forty-mile-an-hour windchill of the train's progress, his ankles were stiff, his neck was sore from craning to watch the passing landscape. He had lost sight of Baltimore an hour earlier, consumed by suburbs and finally engulfed by the starkly barren dark tree trunks of the endless deciduous forest that blanketed western Maryland.

He wanted off this train, needed to be off it before those cops back at the motel made the necessary calls to determine which train it was and went about stopping it. Maybe they wouldn't care enough about him to go to that kind of trouble, but Tyler couldn't take any such chances.

His focus had to be the bullet train. He needed to know more about this test run than Nell had mentioned. On or off Rucker's payroll, it didn't matter to him now—he had to reach Umberto Alvarez before Alvarez derailed that train. Perhaps the freights, with no passengers aboard, were nothing more than test runs. But the F-A-S-T Track was a media event, a publicity spectacular, including dozens of dignitaries. O'Malley had to know it was the ultimate prize.

Several times he'd been tempted to jump, but the broken and frozen body of Harry Wells reminded him that this was dangerous sport.

However, weighed against the prospect of encountering small-town, trigger-happy police the first time this train stopped, Tyler had to decide not whether to jump but when and where. He knew nothing about jumping from a moving train, only that the one time he had faced such a jump, he had frozen.

He studied his situation: there was a pipe handrail mounted to the side of the freight car, just around the corner. He thought it might be possible to stretch from where he stood, around to this handrail, grab hold, and drop from the train, but timing would be everything.

His cold fingers gripping the steel rung of the ladder, Tyler waited for the train to slow, for the blur of the ballast that formed the railbed to come into better focus. Five minutes passed, ten, twenty, the pain in his fingers and toes excruciating, and yet the image of Harry Wells preventing him from jumping.

Finally, the train slowed significantly as it began ascending a hill, cutting its speed in half. Tyler stuffed his cell phone deep into his front pocket, attempting to protect it. In the middle of nowhere, as he was, if he broke a leg, that phone might be his only way out.

Before he made the move, he thought of Nell, and how he wanted more time with her, he thought of the derailed train outside Terre Haute, and of Harry Wells. Then, he lunged for the pipe rail around the corner, his left foot and hand firmly gripped to the ladder as the rest of him hovered over the blurred railbed below. He missed, swinging like a door from the hinge of his left hand, perpendicular to the train car, suspended out over the blurred railroad ties. He crashed back against the car, his unwilling fingers groping for purchase on that handrail and catching hold. He let go with his left hand, pushed away with his foot, and swung to the outside of the car.

He lifted his knees, scouted up the track, and let go, pushing off the car like a swimmer starting a backstroke.

Cha-cha-hmmm . . . Cha-cha-hmmmm . . .

He crashed onto the frozen earth and rolled down the embankment. He rolled, collided with something hard, and tumbled into a bramble patch that tore at his skin.

Finally he came to a stop, every joint aching. After a moment of a prayer or two, he caught his breath and slowly checked his aching joints and bones to see what worked and what didn't.

Everything responded, and though painful, it all moved.

The train chugged past him, *cha-cha-hmmmm, cha-cha-hmmmm. . . .*

He had no idea where he was, but he knew where he was going.

CHAPTER

23

"You're a photographer," Alvarez said.

"I'm a starving artist. Everybody starts somewhere."

He had not noticed the appointments of Jillian's apartment on his first visit. He'd been consumed with fatigue and with this sweating, sensuous woman he'd taken home from a dance club at four in the morning. But the black-and-white photographs of New York's homeless, of the subways, the cab drivers, and the street vendors, struck him as both gritty and accessible. She had talent. The studio apartment was crammed with paperback books. The sparse furniture, begged and borrowed mostly, was eclectic, pleasant to the eye and revealing of a woman comfortable matching contemporary with Junko Victorian.

Jillian had met his arrival at her door first with shock to see him, then with outward indifference. "You left without a word. I thought—" but she stopped herself, her eyes glassy and unwilling to look at him. She motioned him inside and then locked all four door locks. "I don't know what I'm doing," she admitted, upset with herself. "Your wife and kids . . . When we first met at the restaurant, I think I felt sorry for you. And then our night together, I felt something different—much different. But now? I don't know what to think."

She collapsed down on the bed, emotionally exhausted. Alvarez stood a few feet from her in the center of the room. He had hoped for a spark, a connection. Instead he got confusion, even despair, and he felt ill equipped to handle it. They met eyes. "I don't expect you to understand," he said.

"Understand what? We slept together. It was fun. Right? But if you're back for more—"

"No!" he interrupted.

"Who are you? What is going on here?"

He glanced toward the door, considering walking out, knowing this was the thing to do. But instead, he stepped forward and sat down close to her.

"They killed my family," he said. "An accident, they said. Greed and ignorance is what it was. And then they went and blamed my wife."

"You've lied to me."

"Yes," he admitted. "About some things," he added.

A prolonged silence hung between them.

"What's going on?" she asked.

He told her of the accident, that he believed the crossing guard and all its lights had failed, and that he had been sandbagged. "When you lose a child," he said somberly, "when you lose *two,* it is not something that you can ever explain to someone. You wake with it, you walk with it, you can die of it. Should I feel ashamed I don't feel this same grief for my wife? I miss her, yes, but I somehow *accept* her loss, whereas not with the children."

"You should leave," she said firmly.

"It's complicated," he said.

"You should have told me," she said sadly.

He shook his head slightly, finding he couldn't explain himself, his fantasy of togetherness with her shattered.

"Am I supposed to forgive you?" she asked, grabbing him by the arm and preventing him from standing.

"My lies, not my actions. Whatever hurt I've brought you."

"And?"

He simply stared at her, a wry smile forming on the edges of his mouth. "You asked me to leave."

"My mistake," she replied quickly. "Listen, you came along at the right time for me. You know, between men. Bored with my job. Bored with the scene. Even the clubbing—I'm bored. But you? You're mysterious. Exciting. You got me going. I want more." She leaned back onto her forearms. "I want you to stay. To be with you, even if it's just for the night." He wanted so badly to give in to that urge.

"You want to save me," he said. "And it isn't going to happen."

"Can you be so sure?"

"Yes."

"I can be persuasive."

"No argument there," he said.

"And if it's no strings attached?" she asked.

"They're already attached," he pointed out. "Why do you think I came back?"

"Don't flatter yourself," she said.

He handed her a VHS copy of the hotel room video. "If something happens to me, this gets sent to the *New York Times*. Under *no* circumstances do you watch it. This, you've got to promise."

"I promise."

"For real," he said, "a promise that is for real."

She sat forward and took his arm again. "I have needs right now."

He let her pull him down to her, allowed himself the luxury of settling atop that body, into her warmth. He whispered into her hair, "I can't do this."

"That's not the signal I'm getting."

He was, in fact, aroused. He rolled off her and stared at her ceiling where a single strand of cobweb had collected dust and rocked in an unfelt breeze. "This would be another lie," he said.

She reached out and turned his head toward hers. "This would be right now. Nothing more. A memory. We make a memory and we leave it at that."

"A memory," he repeated. She nodded. "I have too many," he informed her.

"Then a new one to replace the old," she suggested. Her eyes smiled at him. It was a willingness, an offer to take her, to have her, to be lost in her, no matter how briefly.

And he took it.

CHAPTER 24

Hiding in the shadows outside Rucker's R Street brick town house, with black shutters and a red front door, Tyler wasn't sure if this was the right thing to do. The quiet street, lined with eighteenth-century brick homes, reminded Tyler of all the things he loved about this city: the history, the heritage, the politics and power, the architecture, the arts, the free museums, the summer festivals and celebrations. He felt he'd been driven away. Ostracized. Resentment boiled inside him as indigestion. He smelled the burning wood of a fireplace and longed for even one peaceful moment. Rucker represented everything wrong with the system, the decay that precipitated from the misuse of one's position.

More to the point, Loren Rucker was careful. Careful to protect himself. Tyler believed that even if Rucker had worked with O'Malley to hide what had happened in Genoa, Illinois, the man would have stashed enough evidence against O'Malley to cut himself a deal with prosecutors, if it ever came to that. The person with the most information won the sweetest deal. Certainly Rucker, as an executive in law enforcement, knew that only too well.

Sounds of traffic whined in Tyler's ears as he waited, the temperature hovering near freezing. His only reprieve from the cold had been the two bus trips he'd taken after jumping from the freight— the first, a Greyhound back into Baltimore, the second, an express that ran hourly between Baltimore and Washington. Following the payoff for passage aboard the ship, Tyler had just shy of eight hundred dollars in his wallet. He'd bought a turkey sandwich from a to-go shop and had eaten half, the other half wrapped and in his left coat pocket. Two cups of Starbucks coffee had briefly given him an energy boost, but that was starting to fade.

A heated gutter dripped rhythmically. The late-nineteenth-century pseudo-federal spread holiday cheer with electric candles in each of its eight windows, and an evergreen cone-and-berry wreath was wired to the front door's brass knocker.

A big car parked in a space down the street. Tyler tucked himself deeper into the bushes as he recognized Rucker: the slightly stooped shoulders, the halting walk, the old, brown leather briefcase, over-stuffed.

Now it was either the coffee or just adrenaline, but Tyler's heart pounded in his chest violently. This would have to be a blend of confrontation and accord; Tyler had to play both good cop and bad if he was to win a rapport with Rucker and come away with the evidence.

Tyler climbed out of the bushes. "Hello, Loren," he said from behind, startling the man.

Rucker turned and stared, dumbfounded. "You're in a pile of trouble," Rucker said.

"That makes two of us."

"Metro wants you for questioning."

Tyler said nothing.

"What the hell's going on, Peter?"

"We're going inside," Tyler informed him. "I'm half frozen to death."

"You look like hell."

"Now you're getting the picture."

"And I'm supposed to cooperate? Why?"

"Because you know I didn't do Stuckey."

"Do I?" Rucker asked.

Tyler then played the one card he felt could open that door, a card that was no more than an educated guess. He tried to make it sound convincing. "We're going inside because you oversaw the investigation into the Genoa, Illinois, crossing guard fatalities. And this would not be an opportune time for me to tell the world about that, would it, Loren?" He gave the man a moment to digest this. Then, fearing he had missed, Tyler added, "As I understand it, the final F-A-S-T Track test is scheduled for the day after tomorrow, in the afternoon." He smiled, though his cold face made it look like something of a snarl. "Maybe Bill Goheen and I could make it a joint press conference."

Rucker stared at Tyler, seething. Then he turned and walked toward his red front door. "I'll put some coffee on," he said.

Tyler followed, sensing that he'd scored a direct hit.

Rucker had won the house in a divorce from a wealthy wife. He'd clearly lost a good deal of the furnishings. Great holes of missing pieces and artwork called attention to themselves in the sitting room and dining room that opposed each other across a hallway painted a lush green.

Rucker switched off the security alarm and set down his briefcase by the door, a man of habit. He turned and hung up his overcoat as Tyler looked on. He'd said nothing, except his offer to put coffee on, since Tyler mentioned Genoa, Illinois.

"We're friends." Rucker offered Tyler a look that told him to keep the sarcasm to himself.

Rucker punched the coffeemaker's switch a little too fiercely. Some water sloshed out of the back. He stepped back, met eyes with Tyler, and said, "You're suspended, pending an investigation into Stuckey. It's pro forma in a situation like this. I can still get you your paycheck until it's resolved." The coffee machine made beeping sounds. *Everything* was computerized.

"You may want to reverse that suspension," Tyler said. "I can walk out of here now, but it won't be good for any of us. Especially not you, Loren. Because I'm walking out of here with the Genoa file, and anything else you have stashed away."

Rucker's face paled. He seemed to struggle for the appearance of control.

"And if I don't leave with at least a *copy* of whatever you have, then everyone involved is in for a long and protracted legal battle."

"I think you're misinformed, Peter," Rucker said, coming to life. "What is it exactly that you think I've done?"

"The Genoa, Illinois, crossing fatalities."

"I know the case," Rucker confirmed.

"Northern Union tracks."

"Yes."

"Keith O'Malley's turf."

"Goes without saying."

Tyler felt dread. Either Rucker was too cool, or Tyler had it wrong. "You did O'Malley a favor," Tyler suggested.

"I had nothing whatsoever to do with that accident. I recused myself because of my friendship with Keith. You're in left field, Peter."

Tyler's hand shook slightly as he brought the coffee to his lips. He said, "You've been involved with all the derailments. You didn't recuse yourself from those investigations."

"That's true enough."

"So why the difference?"

"I was promoted," Rucker explained. "At the time of Genoa, I was an investigator. Now, I'm admin. That's the only difference. I oversee *all* rail investigations. I'm a train buff, Peter. I love trains."

Tyler ran through his options. They seemed precious few. "They effected a cover-up," he stated. "NUR was liable for the Genoa accident, and they covered it up. One Hispanic family weighed against the bullet train, and they opted for the train."

"F-A-S-T Track?" Rucker placed down his cup of coffee, suddenly interested.

"I'm sketchy on all of this," Tyler confessed. "Publicity? Money? I don't know. But they couldn't afford what happened at Genoa to be blamed on their negligence. They'd been shorting maintenance funds, that's what Stuckey had for us before *they* got to him."

"You can prove this?"

"An accountant inside the company says their monkeying with the budgets won't get us to anything illegal. I'm not so sure about that. To me, it gets us to three guys who were each given way too nice a retirement package following Genoa."

Rucker looked dumbstruck.

"What is it?" Tyler asked.

Rucker mumbled, "I set you up for Stuckey." He sounded ashamed.

Tyler attempted to digest this.

"Keith suggested you for the boxcar investigation. I played right into it."

Tyler recalled Banner, the St. Louis detective, questioning the timing of his and Priest's arrival at the boxcar—how it was that two people from East Coast cities could arrive only an hour behind the local police. O'Malley had orchestrated everything to give his team the best shot at protecting the identity of Harry Wells, alive or dead. O'Malley had manipulated him from the start. Struggling against his rage, Tyler said, "Suggested me how?"

"He thought it a good idea that someone with homicide experience take lead on that bloody boxcar. We discussed the possibility of a Railroad Killer copycat. How no one needed that. He'd read about your misfortune and went on about how half his men were formerly policemen and how they make for good employees, especially investigators. I called and got you on that flight."

This fit. Tyler wanted to break something. Anger grated his voice. "O'Malley liked me for the job because Chester Washington left him an easy pattern to copy if he ever caught up to Alvarez. His guys beat him to death; I take the fall." He repeated what he'd discussed with Nell. "Stuckey wasn't supposed to die. They wanted to put him in the hospital, to keep his mouth shut, leaving me to take the heat. Ten to one, the cause of death comes back a heart attack, not trauma."

"You've got to get out of here," Rucker said, perspiration breaking out on his brow. It wasn't the coffee making him sweat. Before Tyler had a chance to speak, Rucker pulled out his cell phone. "I called nine-one-one as I was making the coffee."

Tyler recalled hearing the beeps and mistaking them for the coffee machine.

Realizing Rucker was giving him a chance to get away, Tyler said, "You believe me."

Rucker nodded. "When Alvarez's prints kicked off that airline ticket, and we found out who he was, I wasn't feeling too good. It was obvious that Keith had kept this from me and from the Bureau for months. He had to suspect who was rolling his trains. So the question was why he wouldn't have wanted our help bringing this guy in? Why hide it? Interestingly, he hasn't returned my calls. My guess is that we could build obstruction charges at the very least."

Tyler saw there was no love lost between these two. O'Malley had violated their friendship, and Rucker wasn't forgiving.

Rucker repeated, "You've got to go."

"Can NTSB stop that test run?"

"Is it possible? Yes. Will they do it on such short notice? I doubt it," Rucker admitted. "It's too political. Way over our heads."

A patrol car's blue flashing lights splashed onto the hallway walls.

The doorbell rang. A loud knock followed with the announcement of the police. They weren't going to kick a door in this neighborhood until they had played out their options.

"Coming!" Rucker shouted.

Tyler elected to stay. "O'Malley knew you would have to suspend me. He *wants* this. He wants me on the run." He'd been on the run for twenty-four hours. It felt to him like a week.

Rucker nodded earnestly, "So we don't give him what he wants. Believe me, that feels good."

Tyler felt like a marionette. Then he reached into his jacket and withdrew his weapon, reversed the knurled handle, and handed the gun to Rucker. It felt like a surrender. It terrified him. "This had better work," he said.

"Amen," said Rucker, already moving toward the front door.

Detective Eddie Vale was too handsome, too well dressed, for police work. A year earlier he had traded in two weeks' pay for a pewter gray Armani suit. Wore the thing damn near every day. The right sleeve was going threadbare, but Eddie chose not to notice. He spent another fifty every other month on a Hollywood haircut, wore it wet-shiny and slicked back. At night he left his red and black tie knotted, slipping it over his head to preserve the perfect length, the two pointed tips of fabric meeting exactly. Civilians who passed by him in the hallways nearly always mistook him for a famous pro basketball coach. Vale wore the lime cologne a little too thick, especially for the confined space of an interrogation room. He rapped a knuckle against the edge of the Formica tabletop, beating out the rhythm to a melody that only he heard.

They were into their second hour of questioning, Tyler holding firmly to the order of events of that night. He had glimpsed Rucker just outside the room's door several times as people came and went. He knew that things looked good, because Vale had not officially charged him with any crime, although a few had been mentioned in passing, among them, leaving the scene of a crime.

Tyler finally challenged, "Did anyone bother to check my house?"

"Of course we did."

"And there was, or was not, any sign of a break-in?"

"Why do you think you haven't been processed?"

"You tell me, Eddie."

Vale pursed his lips. "Your home security system reported a violation at seven forty-four P.M."

"I was still on the train," Tyler protested.

"So you say. We don't know that for sure."

Tyler could produce Nell Priest to corroborate but decided to hold off on that. Priest's fleeing with him could produce problems for both of them, and he didn't want her talking to these guys. "And?"

"Secor security guards responded, found the home secure, and put it in the books as a false alarm. Ninety-five percent of all such responses—"

"Are false alarms," Tyler interrupted. "I know the stats, Eddie. Come on!"

"So there you go. It could have been you entering your own house and leaving it locked for the sake of the false alarm."

"Except I was on the train."

"So you say."

"I'm probably on video arriving at Union Station. I gave you my receipt."

"You can pick a receipt up off the floor. Besides, the train stopped in Baltimore. You coulda done this assault, driven to Baltimore, ridden the train into town, all to look clean. There was time for that. ME has a three-hour window on this." Vale added, "And don't tell me you're not smart enough to think of that, because that's exactly the kind of thing you woulda done if you'd done this, and we both know it."

"And we both know I didn't do it."

"So you say."

"Put me under the light, Eddie. For the blood splatter."

"There are ways to beat that, and you know it." Vale smirked. "You being a cop? That's working against you right now." He said, "You ditched the shoes, didn't you? How stupid was that?"

"Don't know what you're talking about." On this, Tyler was clear. They couldn't link him to his earlier pair of shoes, even though changing the shoes might make him look guilty. He'd sat in that other chair before. He took a deep breath and said, "You can't hold me, Eddie. Even if you want to, you can't."

"You fled a crime scene."

"It's a twenty-five-dollar fine."

"You're pissing me off here," Vale complained.

Tyler lowered his voice and placed his thumb over the tiny microphone hole in the tape recorder. He whispered, "Why did I call you, Eddie? What was the point of that?"

"Can't go there, Pete," Vale whispered back. Up close, the cologne was just this side of sickening.

Tyler leaned back and gasped for air.

Vale said, "Take me through it again."

"For the fourth time? No thanks. I'm about to lawyer-up, Eddie. Is that what you want?"

"You're putting this off to suspects, unnamed, with no descriptions. Some kind of conspiracy that you're not willing to discuss—"

"Not at the moment," Tyler corrected.

"And we're, of course, supposed to trust you on this."

"My boss is behind me," Tyler reminded him. "As in the federal government. As in, we're supposed to all be working together. Isn't that right, Eddie? What, you think I'm a risk for flight? They've foreclosed on my house, but I'm fighting it. I'm not going anywhere. My boss, Loren Rucker, will know where I am at all times." Addressing the room's mirror, for the benefit of Vale's superiors, Tyler said, "You want me, you tug on the leash."

Vale said, "You should have come in last night."

"I used to work here, remember? Would you have spoken with Secor Security last night? Would the ME have given you a window of time? Would the blood guys have already gone over the scene and spelled it out for you?" Tyler added, "And don't forget, I *did* come back of my own volition."

"Says here it was a response to a nine-eleven call. How does that end up in your column?"

"A technicality. Loren Rucker will back me up on that."

"You're lucky he's on your side."

"I know that," Tyler admitted. He now felt foolish for not trust-ing Rucker. Vale. He'd been up all night and all day. The suit needed a press. And fumigation.

Still facing the one-way glass, Tyler said bluntly, "If you hold me, we never get any answers." He raised his voice, "The NTSB wants me out there working this, and so do you. Do you think you're going to clear Stuckey by holding me? That's what you have to ask yourself."

There came a light tapping on the glass. It drew Vale from his chair. The man brushed down the length of his suit coat and touched the knot of his tie.

"You're looking good," Tyler allowed.

"Screw off!" Eddie Vale smiled widely.

Tyler took that as a good sign.

CHAPTER

25

40 Hours

With forty hours to go until the bullet train trial run, Alvarez faced himself in Jillian's mirror, wondering at the age and fatigue he saw in and around his eyes, the slight scowl to the forehead that had not been there eighteen months earlier. Jillian reluctantly had headed to work, leaving Alvarez briefly with a sense of home, of a relationship, and he found it subtly disruptive. Whole worlds could come and go in a matter of minutes—as a science teacher he knew his astronomy—and his world, too, seemed now on the verge of finality as he moved himself toward a final confrontation with William Goheen. *I am no better for what I've done,* he thought disappointedly. *No fuller, no more complete. Nor will I be for what I'm about to do.* Nonetheless, he felt compelled, driven, to see this through. Somewhere between the delicate beauty of justice and bloodthirst was something his wife and children cried out to him for. And for them, he would do anything.

He understood that the next forty hours were to comprise one of the longest days of his life (though nothing compared with that first day after the accident) and that he was likely to go without sleep, eating only energy bars and drinking water from a plastic bottle.

His first task was to get his duffel inside Newark's Meadows rail yard without detection.

The Internet had provided him with freight train schedules for the East Coast, including arrivals and departures for the Meadows, where, according to internal NUR documents, the bullet train was presently sidetracked.

Alvarez checked through the duffel one last time, leaving nothing to chance. With each item, he checked its name off a handwritten list. He was not new to this—he considered himself a veteran—but failure came with slipshod planning, and he had taught himself to maximize his own resources and never to underestimate his enemy. Twenty-seven items in all: some as small as a flexible-neck penlight, a computer card, or a pair of tweezers; others large and bulky, like a customized window shade or a pair of electro magnetic "clamps" invented to hold Navy undersea welders to the hulls of ships as they worked. For the third time that day, Alvarez placed all these into the duffel. One forgotten item could spell disaster.

He was dressed in heavy, sand-colored coveralls, a fleece vest for warmth, and work boots. He wore a blue knit cap pulled down over his ears as he rode the subway to the Bronx and a small rail yard where, bearing his duffel over his shoulder, he set out to find freight line #717, a line of five empty flatbeds headed tomorrow into the Meadows yard. Once there, #717 was scheduled to be side-tracked.

He clipped on his New York Central Railroad laminated ID tag, courtesy of an Internet site that displayed images of all such tags. It was thirty-some degrees with a steady wind out of the north, but still he could have walked for hours, not minding the bitter cold. He was completely focused. He snuck through the yard's flimsy chain-link, taking advantage of one of its many gaping holes. The Bronx was not a place of high security. He passed dozens of abandoned subway cars, some cannibalized for parts. There were six sidetracks, each several hundred yards long: flatbeds, freights, and tankers. Some looked as if they'd never roll again. Others stood with their doors wide open, having only recently been emptied.

A dark winter night, the moon struggled to emerge behind high wintry clouds like a dim bulb. Alvarez could faintly see before him without his flashlight.

It took him a while to locate the #717 line. Walking alongside it, he marked the car he wanted: the thirteenth from the back of the train. Unlucky or not, he felt elation at locating it.

Dragging the duffel, he crawled beneath the car, a CB scanning radio playing into an earpiece in his left ear.

The scanner paused five seconds on any frequency containing radio traffic then continued on to the next active frequency. Alvarez endured channel after channel of Arab-accented limousine and taxi dispatch, for at this time of night the frequencies were almost entirely devoted to such traffic. But when an incredibly clear voice (indicating close proximity) asked, ". . . anybody see a guy just now over on track fourteen?" Alvarez tripped the radio to remain on that frequency, wondering if the 717 was on track 14, and if *he* was the subject.

A lower voice came back, "You want to check it out?"

"Roger, that."

"I'll take the north side of fourteen," returned the lower voice.

"Billy, you take the south side."

A smoker's voice responded he would indeed take the south side of track 14.

The following day Alvarez could not simply walk into the Newark Meadows yard carrying this duffel. He had to attach it to a car on line 717 so it would be carried inside for him, hidden like a suckerfish, no one the wiser.

But the possibility of security already being on to him made him wish there were some other way.

He reached the center of the car, where overhead there was a spot well hidden from inspection angles. Without surveillance mirrors or someone actually crawling beneath the car and looking up into the space, the duffel would not be spotted. He stuffed it up there, attaching nylon straps to hold it.

Ominous orbs of light from flashlights washed over the ground on each side of the train. The guards approached from opposite ends, squeezing him in and negating any chance for him to escape. To run now, even if he got away, would attract attention to this particular car, and the duffel would be found. He watched those flashlights carefully and realized both guards were stopping at each car and shining the light *beneath* the car.

He glanced up at the duffel, reached up to test the strength of the nylon strapping, and pulled himself up between the twin I beams and into the dark space there. His face pressed against the nylon, his arms trembled as his muscles fatigued. He awaited the telltale sweep of a light. The pain grew. His biceps and back cramped.

Faint twinges of light. He pulled himself up higher.

The light drew closer, brighter.

He held absolutely still—it would be movement more than anything that would give him away.

The flashlight's yellow beam passed just below him, shadows dancing. Sweat ran into his eyes, blurring his vision. He held his breath.

The footsteps faded. The light moved on. Alvarez started to lower himself, his muscles grateful, when he heard their voices nearby. He sucked himself back up, arms quivering.

"Nothing!" one of the voices said.

"Same here," came the other.

The men spoke to each other across the coupling, between cars, less than ten feet away.

"We should continue on—down both sides—and check that all the cars are still locked."

"It's cold as a witch's tit out here."

"You want to check the rest of the cars or not?"

"Yeah, what the hell? Why not?"

"Okay, then."

Still on opposite sides of the train, the guards continued their respective routes, this time with footfalls coming to Alvarez's right. Again a beam of light swept below him, slowly moving forward.

Footfalls grew more faint. He lowered himself down to the chipped-rock railbed and lay motionless, noting the locations of both guards. He remained absolutely still for several minutes, until the guards were nowhere to be seen. He then rolled over, came to his knees, and rechecked the duffel one last time.

He slipped out from under the train, stayed in shadow, and hurried along the side of line 717, searching and finding a hole in the fencing. He checked behind himself one last time, ducked through the fence, and took off at a run.

CHAPTER 26

A ffecting an Asian accent, Tyler left a message on Priest's answering machine that her dry cleaning was ready and could be
picked up. Included was an invoice number and the amount she
owed. With most pay phones in New York blocked from receiving
incoming phone calls, Tyler sat at the end of Murphy's Bar on 23rd
Street, only a few blocks from the Flatiron Building in lower Manhattan.

The bartender at Murphy's was a thick-armed guy named Chuck.
He had a graying beard and a ruddy complexion. At 8 A.M., Tyler
was one of three at the bar. He drank coffee. The other two were
drinking beer and booze, and they looked it. Chuck had pocketed
one of Tyler's twenty-dollar bills to play the double role of telephone
operator.

Tyler was reading through the entire NTSB file on the Genoa,
Illinois, accident for the fifth time. Rucker had supplied it before
their departure by private jet to New York. Rucker, who had been
scheduled to attend the test run of the bullet train, now intended to
meet with O'Malley prior to the event. Tyler doubted he'd be granted
that interview.

From the Genoa paperwork, the investigation looked straightfor-
ward enough. The vehicle in question was believed to have stalled
on the crossing and to have been struck when it couldn't move off
the tracks in time. The tenor of the report seemed to be that this

wasn't the first time this had happened, and it wouldn't be the last. Over a thousand people a year were struck by moving trains. Both crossing gates were shown in photographs in their lowered positions, supporting the claim that the auto had been out on the tracks—either intentionally or accidentally—when those gates had lowered automatically, signaling the arrival of the freight. There was nothing in the file to suggest the warning lights or one of the gates had failed to lower properly. The *only* mention of a 911 Emergency Communications call was an entry listed under Means of Notification. In Tyler's mind, this indicated there would likely never be any proof that the tape of this call, long since missing, had contained incriminating evidence against NUR. He wondered if the train's driver, Milrose, had made that call himself and what, if any, observations that call had contained.

To read the file, Alvarez's wife was at fault. Listed anonymously as the "vehicle operator," Juanita Alvarez was said to have failed to get herself and her children out of the vehicle and off the tracks in time. NTSB photographs showed the crushed minivan's ignition switch in the "on" position, indicating either that the car was running or that the driver was trying to start it at the time of impact, and thus the ambiguity about responsibility for the vehicle operator's failure to "secure a safe distance from the approaching train."

The phone rang and the bartender, Chuck, answered. He listened and passed the receiver to Tyler. "Your call, pal."

"You're here," Nell Priest said, somewhat desperately. "In the city, I mean. Two-one-two."

"You're on a pay phone?" Tyler inquired.

"Yes, of course."

"We have a lot to catch up on." Tyler said, "We need a favor from you, some files."

"Did you say 'we'?"

"That's part of the explanation."

"It certainly is." She named a breakfast place near Union Square.

Tyler named the Marriott at Times Square. "Room eleven-twelve." The return to government payroll had its privileges. "Make sure you aren't followed," Tyler stressed.

"Give me two hours," she replied, not challenging his choice of the hotel.

When Nell Priest knocked at room 1112, no one answered. She waited and then knocked again. Behind her, the door to room 1111 opened, though she paid little attention until she heard Tyler's voice say, "In here." She turned around, stepped across, checking both directions first, and was quickly admitted.

Tyler wanted to hug her, to tell her how good it was to see her. Instead, he introduced her to Rucker as he locked the door. She looked to Tyler as he showed her to a chair. Confusion filled her face. Tyler explained that he'd turned himself in to Metro Police and had subsequently been released. Rucker had dropped the suspension, reinstating him.

"But he lacks the power to make arrests," Rucker filled in.

"Which is where I come in?" Priest's eyes searched Tyler's.

Tyler said, "If O'Malley gets Alvarez, it's the last any of us will ever hear from him."

She reached into her purse and withdrew copies of the files Tyler had requested she bring. "Do you want these?"

Rucker stepped forward and blocked the exchange. He explained, "We're asking you to cross over, Ms. Priest, and work for us. I can offer you legal protection—immunity from anything Northern Union might throw at you. In terms of your personal security, it's your own risk, I'm afraid."

Still looking at Tyler, she replied, "I crossed over a while ago. There's no need for any of this."

Not sensing the connection between these two, Rucker insensitively plowed on. "It needs to be made official. Essentially, I'm recruiting you as an NUS insider to provide information against Keith O'Malley, to inform me of his plans and to assist Agent Tyler in the arrest of Umberto Alvarez."

Tyler said to her, "As you and I discussed, we're assuming O'Malley will do everything to ensure that Alvarez is *not* arrested."

"Agreed," Nell said, her eyes pleading with Tyler. She didn't want to be put through this.

Rucker added, "What we're asking has risk for you, both personally and professionally."

She said sarcastically to Rucker, "I pretty much figured that out for myself."

"I've drawn up a paper for you to sign," Rucker explained. "It's to protect you, since I'm assuming you've signed a nondisclosure agreement with NUS."

"I have." The files still remained gripped in her hand. "Am I the only one who's worried about Peter in all this?"

"The way we help Peter," Rucker said, in a patronizing tone, "is to bring down Keith O'Malley. These papers make the exchange of any inside information at the official request of the NTSB. Whatever penalties are named in your NDA are overridden by this."

Her eyes once again found Tyler's and asked why it had to be done so formally. He felt a sadness, a heaviness in her, and wanted to rush to an explanation. "We may not beat him to Alvarez. It may come down to a conspiracy charge. Loren wants every precaution taken to nail him on whatever we can."

"You want me to sign papers, I'll sign papers." She signed the documents and then handed the NUR paperwork over to Tyler. "He won't derail the F-A-S-T Track. He won't even *get* to it," she injected. "This is not some freight running a Midwestern route. We've been focused on the security of this train from its inception. And not just because of Alvarez. It's a great target for any weirdo out there, and O'Malley has taken every precaution there is. It's inspected, top to bottom, several times daily; it's watched by a dozen guards around the clock; when it rolls, a lead locomotive will run on ahead of it,

to trip any devices that may have been set on the rails themselves.
The invited guests have been screened and will be required to pass
through two separate security checkpoints before getting anywhere
near the train. That goes for maintenance, catering, even Penn Station
employees. I'm telling you, this is a military operation. No way he
gets this train."

Neither man chose to speak, Priest's words hanging in the air.
She glanced at Tyler, and he felt a connection with her that he trea-
sured.

Rucker, oblivious, took up the signed document and thanked her.
"If I can push the necessary warrants through, will you plant a listening device for us? Today, if possible."

"I could try. But he sweeps the offices regularly. It won't last
long, and when it's found he'll know someone is onto him, and
whatever he has will be shredded or destroyed. FYI." She added, "If
it hasn't already been. He's one careful man, I'll tell you what."

"We'll reconsider," Rucker announced. Collecting his things, he
requested Priest's mobile phone number and she supplied it. He said,
"I want to know where both of you are at all times and what you're
doing."

"Hopefully, yes," Tyler said.

"Hopefully, nothing," Rucker protested. "You keep me in the
loop." He shook Priest's hand and hurried out. Tyler locked up behind him.

He sensed her spinning head. "You okay?"

"This was not what I'd expected."

He apologized and said, "We have different agendas, Rucker and
I. O'Malley's a friend of his, and he feels used. He agrees that these
earlier derailments by Alvarez were possible warm-ups. That with
this bullet train, he'll make his statement."

"He's wrong. The trains operate off of completely different tech-
nologies. Alvarez is not going to sabotage the journal bearings on
F-A-S-T Track. No way he'll get that chance. So practicing on those

freights won't get him anywhere. That theory just doesn't make sense."

He stepped up to her, leaned over, and kissed her gently. Then he pulled up a chair to face her. She looked uncomfortable with the kiss—or was that longing, he wondered.

"You're going to ask me for something," she said in a hoarse whisper. To him, her lips, wet from their kiss, begged for another. He nodded. The air seemed still, the short space between them pulled at him.

"That's what you want—another favor."

"It's not all I want," he said, equally softly.

"No?" She moved a little closer. The air seemed quite still.

He reached out and ran his fingers from her ear down her neck, and then wrapped his hand around her neck and pulled her to him.

She checked him just as their lips were about to touch. "We're mixing business with pleasure," she cautioned. "Why don't you ask me for whatever it is you want first?"

Tyler let go of her neck, his fingers slipping down her chest and running over her breasts and finally finding her arm and her hand. As she leaned back, they held hands. Her eyes were glassy and she held a faint, winsome smile on her moist lips.

She squeezed his hand. "If you're trying to bribe me, this isn't going to sit well for us."

"I need you to get me onto the bullet train," he told her bluntly. "The F-A-S-T Track. Well in advance of the test run."

She let go of his hand and sat up straight. "How do I manage that?"

"There must be a maintenance group aboard the train. If I go on with them, maybe I go unnoticed. Who pays attention to guys in blue jumpsuits?"

She nodded slightly, "And maintenance would give you access to every part of the train."

"Exactly."

"And if O'Malley finds you?"

"I understand it's not without risk," he said.

"You're kidding, right? Twelve guards. Everyone, everything screened."

"There must be special badges," he guessed. "You lift one of those and a maintenance jumpsuit. I dress for the party underneath the jumpsuit."

"What if I don't want you on that train?"

"I thought you said Alvarez couldn't roll it."

"Even so."

"Are you going to be on it?"

"I was scheduled to be Gretchen Goheen's personal bodyguard. She was to be on Daddy's arm for the event. But now word is that they've had a little falling out, and that he doesn't want Gretchen on the train. I'm still planning to take the ride, but who knows? O'Malley likes to change things at the last minute, and I'm not sure what my standing is at this point."

He couldn't talk business anymore. With Rucker gone he wanted to get down to what mattered. "I missed you, for what it's worth."

"You just bought yourself a pass and a maintenance jumpsuit," she said. For a moment, he thought she was teasing. But then she came into his arms, and the room spun, and he didn't care about Alvarez or Rucker or even Chester Washington. He didn't think it could be love—not this soon—but whatever it was, it felt pretty damn close.

CHAPTER 27

24 Hours

The challenge was to derail a train carrying a hundred journalists and dignitaries, all moving 180 miles an hour, without any injuries or fatalities. Every teacher knew the importance of study, and Umberto Alvarez was no exception. His risky forays into NUR's Park Avenue headquarters the past few months had armed him with data on the guidance and stabilizing systems, security procedures, and even the scheduling and routing of NUR's vast freight fleet.

At 3:58 P.M., Thursday, December 18, the premature sunset of early winter cloaked the Meadows rail yard in a hazy dusk. Alvarez had selected the 4 P.M. shift change because of this gray light and the way the eye had difficulty picking up details in it. If he had any chance to slip through the front gate, it was now.

He had endlessly debated how to enter this well-guarded yard and finally decided deception outweighed stealth. He knew that all arriving trains were being thoroughly searched. He had risked placing his duffel on one of those trains but would not risk his life. Hiding a small black bag and a man were different altogether.

Posing as a security guard at shift change on a cold winter evening seemed a more unlikely way to enter the yard and therefore should be less expected.

To his advantage, O'Malley's overtime rosters called for a dozen guards in the yard at all times, triple the usual. The more the merrier—the easier for Alvarez to get lost in those numbers. Ironically, a smaller crew might have meant easier detection of an intruder.

Standing in an alley facing the yard entrance, Alvarez unzipped the black nylon jacket he'd bought at the Salvation Army, uncovering a navy blue security uniform. That, combined with his identification tag, were to be his passport inside.

Leaving the ski coat unzipped so that his ID tag showed, Alvarez took a deep breath to settle himself. There would be twelve guards heading home in the next few minutes, thirteen arriving. He carried a red metal lunch box containing a tuna sandwich, a Coke, and a small bag of chips. The steel thermos held Blue Mountain coffee, perhaps the only clue to the man's true identity.

If anything went wrong, he had contingency plans. This, too, was why he chose to enter on foot. If caught on an arriving train, he would have been inside the fenced yard. If busted at the gate, he could run a carefully planned route to a waiting cab, the driver of which had been paid fifty bucks for a ten-minute wait that was about to expire.

The plastic laminated ID, clipped to his breast pocket, flapped with each step, rhythmically clicking against a button. Still twenty yards away, he looked on as two entering guards grabbed hold of their IDs, displaying them for someone unseen who occupied the entrance booth. Clearly, there was no formal inspection of these tags going on; they passed through without breaking stride, without saying a word. His surmise had been accurate: this was not where they anticipated a penetration. It appeared, too, that the rank and file was simply going about its job in the way a mason or garbage collector does. Security guards were, for the most part, former college athletes who had bet too hard on professional sports advancing their minimally educated lives. Brawn, but not a lot of brain. If NUR management was concerned its train might come under attack, the guards here appeared more concerned with clocking in on time and staying warm. All the new arrivals were heading straight to an elevated office trailer.

The combination of the ID tag and the proper uniform appeared to be enough to get him through. He swallowed dryly, reached to hold up his tag toward the booth's window, avoiding looking in, and kept walking as if he'd entered here a hundred times.

No one stopped him. No one called out. No one was counting heads.

As two arriving guards in front of him headed for the trailer, Alvarez turned right, into the yard and the endless lines of train cars. Sodium-vapor lights burned a bluish glow over the yard, struggling against the dusk. At a distance, in the haze, Alvarez saw a mangy dog duck under a freight car and take off. Fifty yards down the tracks, Alvarez himself disappeared.

Over these past months he had spent countless hours in rail yards just like this one, and yet this one was like no other. He believed it would be his last. Here, he'd board the bullet train for a first and a last time. From here he'd launch a final blow to Goheen and his corporation, one from which they could not recover. If all went well, not a single person would be hurt, but a billion-dollar corporation would fall.

It took Alvarez nearly two hours to locate train #717, in part because he felt obligated to act out his role as an NUR security guard, to be seen patrolling, in part because of the daunting enormity of the Meadows yard. The handheld radio scanner clipped to his waist, a Uniden BC245XLT, was barely larger than a cell phone. It scanned three hundred channels, including those used by the dozens of limousine and taxi dispatchers. After nearly a half hour of scrutiny through an earpiece that ran the sounds continually, he had finally identified the channel in use by the NUS guards and had locked into this frequency. Each guard checked in with a dispatcher referred to as "Control" on a regular basis—every ten minutes—and reported his exact location within the yard. Alvarez found the regularity of these reports surprising, and disturbing. It meant the dispatcher was well organized; she could map out the deployment of their team for the best possible coverage of the site.

So, even after identifying 717 on the outskirts of the yard—nearly a half mile from the bullet train—Alvarez walked this freight train in its entirety two full laps as he attempted to role-play dispatcher and track the movements of the guards. The last thing he needed was to be spotted hauling that duffel out from underneath.

After about twenty minutes, he picked out a short window of time when no guards were in his immediate area. But his nerves were rattled by this impressive coordination of O'Malley's guards. While communicating with each other the guards also used two flashes from their flashlights to acknowledge one another. These looked like huge white fireflies in the cold night.

Seizing the moment, Alvarez rolled under the freight and felt his way along the underside of the car. As he touched the duffel bag, energy sparked through him. He would have to move carefully now, one train to the next, bearing that duffel along with him. If a guard closed in, he hoped to cover himself by leaving the duffel behind and returning to it later. It was all a dance now, a fragile choreography. He watched for flashes. He listened for locations. The map of the yard—so carefully studied that he had even memorized Internet satellite photographs of it—remained imprinted in his brain. The dispatcher moved her chess pieces. Alvarez moved one train to the next, ever cautious, ever closer to the bullet. He'd waited eighteen months for this. He couldn't blow it now.

Something was dreadfully wrong. Alvarez had studied the specifics of the bullet train from top to bottom—*inside* Northern Union's own offices reviewing blueprints of the mechanicals and electronics. After nearly three hours of crawling track to track, the duffel in tow, the engine he now faced matched none of those specifications.

The train itself held half as many cars as NUR had scheduled for the test. The engine might have fooled someone less studied than he, but despite the aerodynamic nose, the sleek lines, and the silver paint, its modified coupler revealed its true identity. That coupler was a trademark of the early prototype locomotive, installed so that a variety of American-manufactured train cars could be connected to the French-built locomotive. That coupler had been abandoned in the latest model as the lightweight, guidance-controlled passenger cars had arrived from plants in France and Belgium. This engine he was looking at was a descendant of France's TGV turbo diesels—a beautiful specimen but not the Japanese powerhouse that would drag the country's fastest manned test run from New York to Washington.

This train was a ruse. His heart nearly stopped. All the guards, all the lights, the radio traffic: all in place for his benefit, and his benefit alone. Dumbfounded, he crawled out, leaving the duffel, and looked down the length of the train. O'Malley had tricked him, had moved the real F-A-S-T Track to another location.

"If you've got nothing to do, help load the test dummies." The voice came from a big guard behind him. The man had caught an agitated Alvarez flat-footed. This guard had a dark beard and shoulders as wide as a doorway.

Alvarez said, "My dinner didn't agree with me. Maybe it's time for a visit to the blue box." He'd seen the Porta-Potties when entering the yard.

Tricked! Heat flooded his face. *Where the hell had they hidden an entire train?*

The guard said, "Just get back here and put yourself to use. This thing rolls in a couple hours."

Even the guards had been tricked! This man didn't know the train he was guarding was a fake. And then, looking closer, Alvarez reconsidered. The guards were filling the cars with mannequins and crash-test dummies. The cars were, in fact, the ones Alvarez had expected to see. Only the engines were different. But the Japanese locomotives and their guidance computers were essential to him. So what the hell was going on?

"Back in a minute," Alvarez said, walking up toward the loco-motive.

He glanced back toward the duffel bag, lying in shadow. He needed that bag. He would leave on the next shift change. Who would stop him from bringing a bag *out* of the yard? he wondered, a headache creeping into the front of his head and seizing him at the temples.

CHAPTER 20

"Are you sure you want to do this?" Nell Priest asked from the other side of a white Formica table in a turnpike rest area McDonald's south of Newark. Both she and Tyler drank black coffee from white Styrofoam cups. They shared a large order of fries.

Tyler answered sarcastically and a little nervously, "The worst that can happen is they beat me to a pulp and attribute it to Alvarez."

"The man murdered his own attorney, don't forget," she chided. "Don't make him out to be Robin Hood."

"He's a suspect in that murder. The crime is alleged," Tyler corrected.

"You're defending him? I'm trying to warn you. If you go under O'Malley's radar and you happen to find Alvarez, you're on your own. And he has absolutely nothing to lose."

Tyler savored the coffee, surprised at how good it tasted. But even more satisfying was the company. "Don't you see the problem O'Malley created for himself?"

"Maybe I don't," she admitted.

"He offered explanations for those early derailments—drivers on booze, on pot, maintenance problems. He issued reports to the NTSB and made it all official. At the time it probably seemed like a good idea, clever even, a way to throw Rucker and the NTSB off Alvarez's scent, because O'Malley didn't want Alvarez caught by anyone but his own people. But the upshot is that legally Alvarez isn't responsible for those derailments. It would have been one thing if O'Malley had worked with the NTSB to go after Alvarez while putting on a different face to the press, but that's not what happened. Those derailments, those bearing failures, are not going to be blamed on Alvarez. For O'Malley, that means he has to solve it himself; he dug himself into a hole."

"So why didn't he want him caught? Why not involve the Bureau, you guys, whoever he could?" she said, more thinking aloud than asking a question.

"That's the big, unanswered question," Tyler said. "The obvious answer is that he didn't want Genoa coming to the surface again. But that's what keeps it interesting."

"It's a game to you?" She sounded disappointed. Angry even. "You know, just as I'm thinking that this thing between us, whatever it is, is worth pursuing, you come out with something like that."

"Well, then I wish I could take it back."

"You can't," she said. "You're too smart, Peter. I like smart."

"And I thought it was my dashing looks," he interrupted.

"See? There you go again!"

"Dumb," he filled in for her. He appreciated her honesty, wasn't sure why he reacted sarcastically.

"Listen," he said, "I was hired because O'Malley had picked me for this job, not Loren Rucker. O'Malley needed someone who could take the fall, someone new to NTSB and therefore untested, unknown." She was shaking her head, but Tyler wouldn't allow her to interrupt. "Believe me, I *know* all this now. I'm not making this up. My point is that it is about something else for me. It's about proving my worth, about taking the job seriously. Taking it farther than the original assignment called for. I got shafted in the Chester Washington thing. And yes, I carry a chip on my shoulder about that. And if Harry Wells and Keith O'Malley give me a leg up, a chance to win back some of what I've lost, then screw it: I'm taking it."

"Peter, you can't undo that stuff, the negative stuff. It's what people remember. And if you allow it to stick in your throat like some fish bone, it's going to choke you and kill you. Booze. Ulcers.

Whatever. You let go, and you move on. And if you do, you're a survivor, and if you don't, you're a victim." She added, "Whether he's caught or not, by you, by O'Malley, by the Bureau, a week later no one will remember." She shook her finger at him. Her nails were painted a metallic deep purple, an eggplant, that went beautifully with her skin. "And don't go sappy on me," she scolded. "Don't tell me you'll be the one to remember, because that makes it about you, and only you."

As she'd predicted, Tyler had been about to tell her that he'd be the one to remember, so he held his tongue on that. "The point is," he said, "O'Malley has been unwilling to share Alvarez's identity with law enforcement. He doesn't want him caught, he wants him dead." He lowered his head sheepishly, wondering if he dare share his inner thoughts. "For a few short hours, after the motel in Baltimore, I was Umberto Alvarez. On the run, hanging on to a train, my hands and toes half frozen. A fugitive. Nowhere to land. I felt like I was in some parallel universe—don't laugh—where I was given a chance to feel some of what he must feel. As ridiculous as it may sound, I connected with him. And it was fear. Pure, visceral fear. No place was safe. This kind of disconnection, detachment, that I don't think you, or anyone, can understand until you're there, and hopefully you'll never be there."

She said nothing. She ate another French fry and finished her coffee. Finally she said, "Why sneak onto that train if you're convinced he's going to derail it? I just don't get that."

"But you're convinced he won't. Can't. Whatever."

"Maybe I'm less convinced than I was."

"This time, there are passengers. This time he will be blamed. Everything O'Malley has created about this guy will be justified. Whatever is supposed to happen on this train can't be allowed to happen."

"You're just trying to impress me," she said, allowing a smile.

"How'm I doing?" asked Tyler.

12 Hours

Raritan Center Parkway. Some called it Red Root for the creek that ran through it. Some referred to the rail yard as New Brunswick, or Edison, the nearest towns of any size. It was a vast stretch of former wetlands, absorbed into industrialized America, where dozens of sidetracks and spurs ran out from a central line like needles on an evergreen branch.

Alvarez wasn't sure who controlled the miles of track there any longer, but he hung up the pay phone convinced that the bullet train was hidden there. The deception had been simple enough, and he never would have been able to dope it out without his prior subterfuge at corporate headquarters, where he had obtained the necessary phone numbers. He had called the private internal number for the bullet train project, reporting that he had a truckload of crash-test dummies and that no one at the Metuchen yard would sign for them.

"That's because they're supposed to be delivered to Raritan," the woman had said disapprovingly, asking him to hold while she connected him. Alvarez had hesitated only seconds before hanging up, the new location written in ballpoint in the palm of his hand.

Slipping out of Meadows yard had required a diversionary tactic he would have preferred not to use, but with time being of the essence, and unwilling to wait for another shift change, he had burned a cigarette as a delayed fuse to ignite a signal flare he'd set between trains. By the time the flare lit up, Alvarez was across the yard. The resulting commotion allowed him to strap on the duffel as a backpack and hurry out the yard's front gate.

Now, standing in the cold outside an Airstream diner on Route 1 in Edison, Alvarez faced a mile walk to reach Raritan. With twelve hours until the bullet train test, he felt rushed. He'd lost nearly half a day to O'Malley's cunning. Worse, his duffel was no longer secreted beneath a train but on his back. He couldn't afford any inquiries as to its contents, so he'd have to enter Raritan on foot, and without being seen. Crawling, if he had to. With dawn quickly approaching, he had to rush.

Fortunately, the mapping software on his laptop revealed several ways to cross the New Jersey Turnpike from Route 1. Both Meadow Road and Woodbridge Avenue were shown to have underpasses connecting to the Raritan side. More important, a dead-end spur of rail track, south of Martin's Landing, clearly crossed under the divided highway. It was this route that Alvarez took, and at 4 A.M., he entered the enormous Raritan complex from its south end.

Reading a map and seeing over fifty quarter-mile stretches of railroad track in person were two entirely different experiences. With the winter sun beginning to pale the morning sky, with seagulls swooping aimlessly over Crab Island and the Raritan River, Alvarez observed the 150 acres of remains of disused passenger cars, their wheels nearly welded to the tracks in their unmoving decay. Windows broken. Graffiti encrusted. Dead weeds poking through a thin slush of last week's snow.

Seeing sterile electric light reflecting off the low clouds, his fatigue washed away. He stashed the duffel beneath a rusted car and made note of its location. Fingers cold. Cheeks stinging. He wore the uniform. He had an ID clipped to his pocket. He steeled himself, knowing he needed the right attitude above all: slightly hostile, cold, tired. It wasn't so difficult a stretch.

He heard the distant hum of a power generator and knew beyond any doubt that he'd found the bullet train. *Who else would be in this godforsaken place at four in the morning?*

Nothing could stop him now. Or so he hoped.

11 Hours

Alvarez hid in a shadow of a rotting caboose, beginning to wonder if his uniform was more of a liability than an asset. Unlike the Meadows yard, where the uniform had helped him to blend in, Raritan was being watched by fewer guards.

This time there was no mistaking the bullet train. The Japanese engine car was pure elegance, space-age aerodynamics, smooth, sleek, even sexy. With just five cars total—an engine, followed by two passenger cars and then two dining cars—this configuration was four cars short of its scheduled size. This difference worried Alvarez. His plan had been devised around a longer train. He guessed that O'Malley had divided the passenger cars between Raritan and Meadows for the sake of stealth. The question remained whether or not the four at Meadows would be added back on to this train prior to its arrival at Penn Station. Alvarez believed they would be added, simply because the NTSB required a minimum of nine cars for the historic test run. He decided to count on it: the two dining cars at the back here would end up roughly in the middle of the train that would make the maiden run.

The crisp, wet air smelled faintly of fresh paint. The horizon shimmered in expectancy of the morning sun. The sounding of geese could be heard from out over the black swirling waters of Red Root Creek.

Alvarez studied the routine and movements of the few guards on duty. Nearing 5 A.M., he counted no fewer than eight maintenance men and six guards. He watched as a pair of them carefully inspected the exterior of a dining car—brakes, axles, cables—and then, apparently pronouncing it sound, stickered each of the car's four doors. They then moved on to the next car, also a dining car.

Alvarez liked seeing those stickers being applied; they would go a long way toward convincing the team at Penn Station that the train had been properly inspected only hours before.

Alvarez concluded that the Raritan yard was meant to serve as a staging area for the final checks. The F-A-S-T Track was said to offer airphone service from every seat, Internet connections, and in-seat videos and entertainment consoles. It was here, at Raritan, that all that would be double-checked one last time. With the national media aboard, everything had to run smoothly. Perhaps there would be preparations made as well for the entertainment of the guests, although he knew from documents that the catered food and beverages were to be brought aboard only after the train had arrived into Penn Station.

He continued to track and to time the movements of the guards, and when the opportunity presented itself, he ducked and sprinted across the short open space, the duffel on his back. He ignored his uniform, fearing that the members of this small security team would all know each other.

Quietly, he slipped beneath the last car, a dining car, marveling at the elegant mechanics of the train's undercarriage. Until that moment, he had only read blueprints.

Now, from memory, he worked quickly. He had practiced this procedure a dozen times, sometimes in virtual darkness, coming to know the tactile qualities of the various pieces of equipment. It came together for him, not like a dress rehearsal but like the performance itself. He executed it flawlessly.

Scooting forward and centering himself, he located the dead space created by the sewage holding tank and a compressed air reservoir used for braking. He hoisted the first of his two magnetic clamps to the car's underbelly, threw the switch, and attached it to the car's undercoated steel. Setting a second clamp roughly six feet down the length of the car, he then draped a webbed net, made of black nylon strapping, between the two. Within two minutes, Alvarez had created a hammock that held him and the duffel parallel to the railbed. Once inside it, he adjusted the two end straps, pulling himself higher, within inches of the car's undercarriage.

A guard inspecting the car from either side would see only the bulkhead of the steel sewage tank or the compressed air cylinder. That security man would have to crawl all the way to the center of the car and look straight up to spot him. Within a few more minutes, he would have the camouflaged window shade in place as a screen, further concealing him. Carefully painted to look like the car's underside, the window shade would hide him well. This, because NUS had plans to use boom-mirrors to inspect the train's undercarriage. O'Malley had picked up the idea from military checkpoint security.

Tucked up in his hiding place, Alvarez now faced the most difficult task of all: waiting.

C urled up inside the trunk of a Ford Taurus, suffering claustro-
phobia, Tyler feared he might pass out. Adding to his discom-
fort was that the ride had grown increasingly bumpy over the course
of the last few minutes, leading Tyler to believe Priest had nearly
arrived at Edison's Raritan yard. The car's trunk was unlatched, the
mechanism rigged so that it could not lock. Tyler held it closed with
his right hand, struggling to keep it from popping open on the bumpy
terrain.

When the car stopped, he heard the purr of the engine followed
by the hum of a window going down. In his cramped space he
tensed, fearing discovery. He fought the claustrophobia, fending off
the next wave of nausea, the next dizzy spell. The muffled voices he
heard through the car body suggested a checkpoint, perhaps a gate,
perhaps nothing more than a couple of orange cones in the road and
a cold guard impatiently verifying IDs.

Nell Priest spoke to the guard, the window hummed, and the car
rolled. Tyler closed his eyes and tried again to fend off his anxiety.

"Almost there," Priest called out loudly to him.

He pounded on the steel in response. God, how he wanted out
of there.

She hollered, "Bright lights to the right. Train cars everywhere.
Mostly abandoned. The guard back there wore a uniform and carried
a handgun. Unusual for our guys." The car slowed. She was pulling
over.

Tyler wore a pair of NUR maintenance coveralls over black slacks and a white shirt and tie. With a navy blue knit cap pulled down low over his ears, he exposed as little of his face as possible. To complete the disguise, Priest had suggested he carry an aluminum clipboard. She said all NUR maintenance guys carried them. The idea was for Tyler to have the run of the place; he'd seen Alvarez on the Crawfordsville Amtrak, however briefly, and felt hopeful he might identify him from the man's build or the way he moved. In the early morning half light, with only six security personnel working the site, it seemed doubtful much attention would be paid to one more maintenance man walking around with his clipboard.

Tyler's knees ached, and whenever he opened his eyes the claustrophobia got to him. With his leg muscles cramping and his stomach sour, he held the demons at bay through concentration and determination; this minor victory felt to him like a major accomplishment.

Nell had been gone from the car for at least ten minutes. It felt much longer to him.

First, she would explain her unscheduled arrival at Raritan. Her line would be that as Gretchen Goheen's personal bodyguard for the test run, she had arrived to take a firsthand look at security preparations. She believed her recent promotion, along with the early hour, would limit the opposition she encountered—she would outrank anyone here.

Minutes later, Tyler twitched as Nell knocked on the trunk. He threw it open and sucked in the fresh air as he slipped out, his cramped legs failing him as he sank to a crouch. Priest kept watch, scanning the area.

Her voice sounded like a clenched fist. "Go!" she said.

The calling of geese drew attention to the black V as it arced out over the river and a hundred birds set their wings for landing.

Clipboard in hand, Tyler hurried to the far side of a line of abandoned train cars, dropped into a lazy walk, and slowly approached the F-A-S-T Track, a sleek, silver monstrosity, looking like a space shuttle without wings.

The closer he came, the more people he spotted: a pair of uniformed security guards to his left but walking away from him; a pair of maintenance men inspecting the suspension of a forward car. Tyler stopped beneath the huge locomotive with its angular twin windshields of tinted glass. Its sleek design lent it a menacing presence.

He kneeled by and stuck his face half under its frame, as if inspecting. Only then did he realize its huge electric diesel engine was idling, its gentle rumble barely a purr.

Though dressed in maintenance coveralls, he had no desire to encounter other maintenance personnel. He hoped to reach the boss first and make his case. He circled around the front of the locomotive and walked down the busier side of the train, his heart pounding, his stomach still upset.

Everyone had a job to do, and this helped him. The area hummed with activity. Maintenance personnel, inside and out, inspected various elements of the train while just behind them a team of security guards made a final sweep of each car. This task completed, the guards applied Day-Glo stickers to the train car doors, sealing them.

At the far end of the train, Tyler spotted a guard handling a German shepherd, presumably a bomb-sniffer. Tyler glanced up at the first passenger car and quickly lowered his head, tricked briefly by the eerie, unflinching eyes of crash-test dummies. Only a few rows of seats in this forward car were occupied, but their presence gave him a chill. Male, female, children, and infants, the effect was too real not to be jarring: some publicity person's idea of lending realism to the "test run," the effect was haunting.

Tyler kept his head bent, his clipboard out in front of him. He kept walking, knowing that moving targets were more difficult to hit. He could not afford to be identified as an imposter.

He picked up movement to his left and glanced up to see Nell Priest carrying a large pink box that he knew contained doughnuts.

She approached an abandoned train car being used as a temporary office. With its lights powered by a noisy generator, its windows were fogged, obscuring any of the activities inside. A moment later, a man whistled loudly and announced, "Doughnuts and coffee for anyone who wants them!"

The diversion worked brilliantly. At five-thirty in the morning, most, but not all, made for the temporary field office.

Tyler attempted to put himself into Alvarez's head, looking for a hiding place despite the security. According to Nell, no train had ever undergone this kind of security and thorough maintenance inspection. As he witnessed the sealing of each of these cars, Tyler became convinced that Alvarez would have to try to board the train, probably in disguise, just as Tyler was. He assumed this attempt would come on the platform at Penn Station—perhaps Alvarez intended to assault and take the place of a reporter, or a caterer. Or perhaps he, too, was dressed in maintenance coveralls and carrying an aluminum clipboard.

As the doughnut feed went on, Tyler noticed a small group of maintenance personnel gathered below the door of the locomotive.

Among these three was a tall, burly man who wore khakis and a dark blue jacket bearing large yellow lettering on the back: F-A-S-T TRACK CREW CHIEF. One of the three looked down the line, noticed Tyler, and signaled him. Tyler lifted his clipboard, returning the wave. The crew chief was just the man he wanted.

The most effective place to hide is out in the open, the cop in Tyler reminded. This had been drummed into him as a rookie patrolman— suspects were typically not found hiding in basements or crawl spaces, more often they were standing on the street corner or occupying a bar stool. He walked toward the locomotive, closing the distance with the maintenance men, his stomach in a knot. As the maintenance team, including the crew chief, climbed a ladder into the locomotive, Tyler thought through his approach. Maintenance would not be too surprised by the arrival of an NTSB agent. Nor would they expect to have been forewarned. Surprise inspections were commonplace. By now they might have been shown a photo of Alvarez, being asked to keep a weather eye out. But they wouldn't know Tyler's face, nor should they be shocked to learn the feds had sent in an undercover agent.

Cupping his federal shield in his right hand, Tyler stepped up to the two maintenance men still on the ground and displayed it. "I need to speak to your crew chief," Tyler announced. These two looked him up and down, that badge and his NUR coveralls clearly convincing. One of the two nodded.

"Sure thing," he answered.

"Without a fuss," Tyler said. "We want to keep this as low profile as possible."

"No sweat," the man returned. "You are?"

"NTSB," Tyler replied. Of all the federal agencies he might have mentioned, none would sound alarm in a maintenance crew more than this one.

The man climbed the ladder—aerodynamically built into the side of the huge locomotive—and opened the door. A moment later the crew chief appeared and said down to Tyler, "What's up?"

"In private," Tyler said quietly.

The man nodded. "Come on up." He, and the man who had announced him, switched places.

Tyler climbed into the cab and closed the door. The space was warm, the engine's satisfying purr felt as a slow rumble in his legs. The forward panel, a mass of small lights—LCD and LED indicators—reminded Tyler of a commercial jet cockpit.

The driver, a thin-faced man in his late thirties, wore corduroy pants, a white shirt bearing the Northern Union Railroad F-A-S-T Track logo, and a company tie—a far cry from the soot-smeared face and goggles of steam engine days. He was flanked by a skinny, fortysomething Frenchman wearing an Armani suit, a brakeman, and the big bear of a crew chief.

All four of them wore laminated security tags either clipped to their clothing or hung around their necks. Tyler did not, and he wondered if this might stop him before he ever got started.

The crew chief said, "You've got some ID?"

Tyler passed him the shield and then unbuttoned the coveralls and withdrew his fed creds. The crew chief looked them over and then introduced himself as Coopersmith. "So what's an NTSB agent doing dressed as one of my team?"

"In private," Tyler reminded.

The crew chief looked irritated but acquiesced. "Engine room." He showed Tyler into a loud room filled floor to ceiling with complex machinery. It smelled bitter, of electricity, not diesel fuel. "Now what the hell is going on? You're pulling a surprise inspection at five on the morning of a test run?" the man asked angrily.

"I'm a criminal investigator, not an inspector," Tyler corrected, watching as the man's anger subsided into a stunned surprise. "You can verify my presence here by calling Deputy Director Rucker. I'm sure you and your crew have been briefed to keep watch for the Latino, Umberto Alvarez," Tyler said. "That's what this is about, and it's crucial that Northern Union Security not know I'm here, which is why I'm wearing the maintenance coveralls." He was making this up on the fly, but it sounded convincing, even to him. He pressed on. The crew chief nodded, clearly somewhat overwhelmed. Tyler began to sense he was in control. "To pull this off, I'm going to need a little cooperation out of you and your men," he said.

"Why not security?" Coopersmith asked, regaining his composure and sounding somewhat suspicious.

"Are you familiar with the term Need to Know?" Tyler asked.

"Don't hand me that shit. I need to know, or else security is going to know, pal. Count on it."

"I have reason to believe Alvarez will attempt to board this train," Tyler said, "if he hasn't already." Hurrying, to stay ahead of the other man's thoughts, he continued, "And if that has happened, or if it is even *possible,* then which department would have to be part of his plans?"

Coopersmith's face blanched and his eyes went wide. "You're bullshitting me!"

Tyler shook his head, his chest in a knot. The walls of the engine room began to move toward him. He felt hot and short of breath. He pushed against this, and it eased. It was the first time in many months that he had controlled it, not the other way around.

"I need two things out of you and your people," Tyler said.

The big man nodded.

"One is to get a message to the woman who just arrived on-site: Ms. Nell Priest. She *is* security, and she's the only one who knows I'm here. She's expecting to hear from me, through you. The second job is for you and your men to find a place on this train where I can hide until it's under way, preferably in the passenger cars, because that's where we believe Alvarez is most likely to strike." For authenticity, he tried to sound like he knew what he was talking about. "The rear dining cars should have been sealed by now. But if so, they've been sealed by security personnel, so you can see the reason for our concern."

"Holy shit!" the big man barked. "You're telling me this guy may already be on board?"

"Security is the last to check the cars before sealing them," Tyler replied. Fueling this man's paranoia, he added, "How perfect is that?"

"We can break any seal we want," the crew chief advised Tyler. "We have full access to this train."

Tyler found his first smile in days. "Now we're getting somewhere," he said.

CHAPTER

31

Suspended beneath the bullet train in what amounted to a hammock made of nylon strapping, Alvarez had a bad case of nerves. He heard the scurry of dog paws as well as the banter of excited voices nearby. The chassis shook. Excitement rippled through him. The bullet train was moving.

He quickly worked to remove the window shade that concealed him. He rolled it up and stored it alongside himself, ready to deploy it at the next stop, whether the Meadows yard or Penn Station. He'd rehearsed this procedure many times, and he pulled it off smoothly.

The train picked up speed, the railbed blurring only a few feet below him.

If his plan held, he would remain in his hiding place until the bullet train entered the tunnel as it departed Penn Station.

The train traveled at lower speeds for its short trip north; Alvarez's handheld GPS, a satellite mapping device, indicated a ground speed of sixty miles an hour. As he'd anticipated, the train stopped in the Meadows yard to take on additional passenger cars. Taking no chances, he replaced the camouflaged window shade during this down time, although as it turned out, only the newly added cars were inspected. Shortly after its arrival at Meadows, the complete F-A-S-T

Track departed for Penn Station. The gala test run was now only hours away.

"What makes this work for you," Coopersmith, the maintenance crew chief, informed Tyler, as the two stood in front of a passenger car's mechanical closet in the forwardmost passenger car, "is that this space can only be locked and unlocked from the outside, the aisle side, meaning that the security guys will simply check to make sure it's still locked. They won't bother opening it. I've seen their routine."

The French-built passenger cars housed a mechanical room adjacent to the wheelchair-accessible lavatory. This mechanical space was itself divided into two sections by a thick plastic floor-to-ceiling barrier protecting a rack of sensitive electronics. Behind that divider there was just enough room for a man to stand.

Coopersmith continued, "These goons? I doubt they're even aware of these electronics compartments."

"So essentially I'm locked inside."

"Until me or one my guys comes along and unlocks you. Yeah. But that's the beauty of it, right? I mean, who would think to look?"

"I'm claustrophobic," Tyler explained. He wondered if Alvarez might know about these spaces. "This just isn't going to work."

"Then you tell me," an annoyed crew chief stated.

"You passed my message along to the woman agent?" Tyler checked.

"Yeah."

"Will you, or any of your team, be aboard the train during the test?"

"Me, plus four. Two up front in the engine room, two back in car five. In case we're needed."

"Can a person get between the locomotive and the passenger cars once under way?"

"Sure. No problem."

Tyler suspected security would not pay much, if any, attention to a couple of on-duty maintenance men riding in jump seats in the engine room. Added to that, they were looking for Alvarez, a Latino, not an ex-cop working undercover, whereas anyone in the passenger cars—even maintenance men—were likely to come under more scrutiny. Tyler said, "Can you put me with your guys up in the locomotive?"

"Claustrophobic or not, you're way better off in this mechanical closet. It's small, loud, and hot up in that engine room."

"Just the same, it's the engine room," Tyler said with finality.

The crew chief viewed him oddly. "I hope you know what you're doing."

Tyler was tempted to give a snide answer, but he kept his mouth shut.

15 Minutes
Track 7
Penn Station

"I hesitate to attempt to rework well-worn clichés about breaking new ground or ushering in the new millennium, but the fact is, clichéd or not, this is an historic moment. We—all of us—stand on this platform, Pennsylvania Station's track seven, about to embark on a journey made possible by a new technology that could revolutionize train travel both in the United States and abroad, for decades to come. I'm proud to say that Northern Union owns patents on the GPS gyro-stabilizing mechanism in the new F-A-S-T Track system, and that this technology, which allows high-speed trains to run on existing track, is, and will remain, uniquely American. But at the same time, I must tip my hat to our French consultants and manufacturers, *Vitesse,* as well as to the hundreds of Japanese designers who conceived of, and carried out, the dream of electric high-speed train travel decades ago." Goheen's voice reverberated into the chilly cement bunker in the bowels of Penn Station, furious that at the last minute the rail station manager had decided against letting his speech be delivered in the central concourse upstairs, where it belonged. The media, the mayor, the senator and her aides, the New York secretary of transportation, and a host of investors all shivered, pretending to look toward the podium with interest. Goheen realized brevity ruled the day and cut his speech short by nearly two-thirds.

Keith O'Malley stood just behind Goheen and to the man's left, his eyes roaming the crowd.

Long ago, when William Goheen had realized the president of a national grocery distribution network could not rely upon public law enforcement to tend to the needs of private commerce, O'Malley had been called in to "be effective." Collectively, corporations spent tens of millions on private security, and not all of it was clean. Lines blurred. Laws failed to protect. The Keith O'Malleys took charge. On occasion, people got roughed up, threatened, blackmailed, their private lives dragged in front of the media, but the trains kept running and thirty thousand miles of track remained open, just as the stockholders, the consumers, and the politicians demanded. Goheen intuited what went on without knowing the details. He had a railroad to run. From their inception, railroads had been tough. Not much had changed.

For Goheen, this moment in Penn Station was the realization of a great dream, never mind that his speech was being given in an ugly, underground space. He felt shivers, and it wasn't from the cold. He had brought his dream to fruition, overcoming a dozen obstacles that his critics had once claimed were insurmountable. Excitement stirred within him, and he saw it in a few of the faces out there as well. A rebirth. A reinvention. It had not been so very long ago that as a boy he had stood over a Lionel train set and had played with it to his heart's content. Now, thanks to him, the dying industry of passenger rail travel was to be revitalized. Someday soon, people would ride from San Francisco to Los Angeles in just under two hours; Portland to Seattle in forty-five minutes. Chicago to New York in five hours. A joint marketing program with Ford and Honda would put ticket-carrying passengers into electric cars in their destination city at a rate of ten dollars a day. Slowly—he knew it wouldn't happen overnight—rail travel would regain acceptance, the commuter traffic on highways would lessen, and air quality would improve in major metropolitan areas. And all thanks to his wonder train.

This was not a day anyone would soon forget—his public relations people had seen to that. The in-house cameras and video crew were recording every moment. *Dateline* was along for the ride, with the likelihood of their transmitting live footage over broadband data ports provided for passengers in each car. CNN awaited their arrival in Union Station. All the pieces were in place for a bang-up premiere.

Goheen noticed the eyes of his audience shift. As a few heads turned, he sensed he might be losing them. For a moment he tensed, wondering if he'd written the wrong speech, but then, turning to see for himself, a father's pride as well as a father's annoyance pulsed through him as he caught sight of this late arrival. Gretchen wore a black cashmere overcoat—no controversial fur to stir the animal rights people—black Ferragamo pumps, and, as she timed the coat to fall open, a woven black cocktail dress that fit her like a thin sock. A pearl necklace. A pair of Tiffany, princess-cut, diamond earrings, weighing in at two carats each—Goheen knew them well, he'd paid twenty-two thousand dollars for those earrings for her twenty-first birthday. With her blonde hair up and just a touch of eye shadow, eye liner, and lipstick, she carried herself like royalty.

Just days before, she had leveled accusations at him, and he had denied them all. They had fought for the first time in years, both losing their cool. In the end, he had forbidden her from attending this event. Yet here she was—in absolute defiance! He left his own script and made a fluid transition to welcoming his daughter, winning her applause. No matter what, she would not ride this train! He stumbled only slightly as he saw that on his daughter's heels followed the tall, long-legged woman from his security division, Nell Priest, who wore a Japanese-influenced black wool pants suit with a wide tie at the waist and a plunging neckline that followed the tailored lapels. She wore a lined gray raincoat with epaulettes, the hem of which swayed with her rolling hips as she walked. The laced black shoes looked slightly out of place, but she pulled it off. The outfit, especially those shoes, told Goheen that she was on duty: ready to take off at a run at a moment's notice. He forced himself back to the speech while thinking of her connection to the rogue Peter Tyler, who, according to Keith, was the one man who could throw a stick in their spokes. So damn many complications. He shook off these thoughts, never pausing, and jumped ahead in the text and worked his speech to its flag-waving conclusion.

Complications or not, this day would be written in bold on his life's calendar.

Alvarez could hear Goheen's speech from his hiding place beneath the dining car while he readied his thoughts for the five minutes of darkness as the F-A-S-T Track crossed beneath the Hudson River and into New Jersey. During these few minutes, dangling only a few feet above a railbed of crushed stone that would grind him to a pulp if he fell, he would have to climb out of his perch and up and into one of the four rear passenger cars, all peopled with mannequins and crash-test dummies. He needed to accomplish this extreme while in the tunnel in order to take advantage of the total darkness. Prior to the tunnel, but after the train's departure, he needed to move one entire car length while still beneath the train—this, because internal records called for two maintenance men to ride in the front of the car immediately behind the second dining car, the car from which he was currently suspended.

He had his work cut out for him.

When Gretchen Goheen was introduced to the crowd by her father, Alvarez caught her name, wondering if she would be along for the ride, this woman he now knew in the context of a Plaza Hotel suite. In this moment of distraction, he briefly lost his balance, rolled to his right, and lost the headlamp—a camper's light—that had been strapped to his head in preparation for his upcoming tunnel stunt. For such a small, lightweight device, it nonetheless fell loudly, first to the window shade below Alvarez, who reached for it but missed, and then sliding and plummeting unseen to the track's concrete railbed.

Alvarez held his breath and listened, pressing the Uniden radio earpiece firmly in place. "Tommy?" he heard. "It's Keenan."

The voice of an NUS radio dispatcher replied, "Go ahead."

"Something just made a noise over here. Dining car two. Underneath, like. I heard it. You want me to check it out, or you want to send maintenance?"

Alvarez now heard the man's natural voice as well, as this same guard stepped closer to the dining car, up on the platform.

"You hold your position on the platform, Keen. I'll have maintenance take a look." The dispatcher reconfirmed it as being under or about the second dining car.

Maintenance! Alvarez tensed, cursing himself. It seemed possible, even likely, that maintenance might crawl under the car to inspect it, and whereas his carefully painted window shade might trick a security mirror extended into the car's shadow, it would not pass the scrutiny of close inspection. He had either to abort or advance his plans, and he had only a few seconds to make that decision. No matter what, he had to get out from under this train. And fast.

When Coopersmith, with whom Tyler was sequestered in the locomotive's engine room, was summoned by dispatch to have one of his men check out an errant noise overheard by a guard, there was great reluctance and contempt on the man's part to follow up on it.

William Goheen's speech was drawing to a close. Tyler interrupted Coopersmith's assigning of one of the two other maintenance men in the locomotive, asking if he might tag along.

This further aggravated Coopersmith, who then felt obliged to go himself. As a result, all three men climbed out of the locomotive, using the door away from the platform, and walked the gloomy space between the F-A-S-T Track and an Amtrak passenger train adjacent to it.

"Probably nothing more than condensation," Coopersmith speculated.

"Chunk of ice. Absolutely," the other maintenance man, a man named DeWulf, said. He had a French accent and he walked more slowly than the other two.

Coopersmith explained to Tyler, "Any condensation that forms underneath the dining cars freezes en route, thaws here in the tunnel, and sloughs off. The Frenchies warned us about that from the get-go."

"Ice in August," DeWulf said. "I remember thinking that was crazy."

"What's crazy," Coopersmith said, "is bothering us about it now."

There was loud applause from the other side of the train. A jazz trio started into "I've Been Working on the Railroad."

The three stopped in front of the second dining car. Coopersmith pointed out small metal plaques attached to the cars indicating data connection points, manual overrides, and emergency controls, written in both French and English. "If there's one problem with this whole setup," Coopersmith said, "it's that this damn train is bilingual."

"You got that right," DeWulf agreed. "It should all be in French," he teased.

Tyler remained concerned that one of the security guards might confront them and identify him. He kept constant watch for approaching trouble. Amid the litter and debris, he saw a rat the size of a raccoon scamper out from under the bullet train and cross to the Amtrak. Behind them, he also saw a line of tracks left by the three of them—shoe prints in the dirt and dust. These ran from the locomotive down to where they stood.

Coopersmith slipped an oddly shaped key into a hole in the frame of the car and released an air-locked door that opened. "Fredo," he said to the Frenchman, "check for ice or a small puddle."

"How about our new friend here?" DeWulf suggested, believing

Tyler was a new maintenance man, which was how Coopersmith had introduced him.

"You gotta go under there," Coopersmith informed him.

"They have us chasing ice in winter," DeWulf complained.

"I gotta sign off on this now that dispatch is involved. Yes, they have us chasing ice."

DeWulf said, "Whoever catches that rat gets to eat him." He dropped to his knees and crawled underneath.

Tyler heard the opposite doors, those accessed from the platform, spit air as the supertrain was opened for preview. Not all of the guests would make the trip to Washington. Like a departing cruise ship of yesteryear, the train was taking on guests for a brief visit—in this case a champagne cocktail party in advance of the actual departure. All cars were opened for viewing, including the dining car where Tyler's maintenance team was currently working. Looking up at the trailing passenger cars, Tyler saw the static faces of the many crash-test dummies and mannequins, erected in eerie fashion to resemble passengers.

With this aisle-side door open, he could see up and into the area where the two dining cars connected, to the legs, male and female, of the boarding guests. He caught a glimpse of Nell Priest in profile, wearing a long black pantsuit and a gray overcoat, and his pulse quickened. He didn't want her on this train.

"What the hell?" he heard DeWulf call out from under the dining car. The man crawled out holding a backpacker's headlamp in his gloved hand. It was clean—no dust or dirt on it.

"One of yours?" Tyler asked the leader.

Coopersmith shook his head, his mood suddenly sour. "We use goosenecks that clip to a pocket. Everyone's issued the same gear."

Tyler snatched DeWulf's flashlight from the man, quickly opened his own coveralls, and reached in, producing his handgun—a Beretta 9mm semiautomatic.

Keeping in mind that guests were swarming the train, Tyler bootlegged the weapon. He then squatted, edged toward the darkness beneath the car, lowered his voice, and aimed the weapon and flashlight below the undercarriage. "Whoever is hiding under here, I'm a federal agent, I'm armed, and I'm coming under this car! If you do not make yourself known to me this instant, I will shoot on sight. So make yourself known to me."

He felt his body rush with heat, almost as if he were kicking in the door and seeing Chester Washington beating that crying baby's head against the wall. The indignation. The rage. It all came rushing back to him. Tyler had called out a warning then too, only to have the gun knocked from his hand a moment later by an arm that somehow reached inhumanly across the distance of the room.

Coopersmith stared at him.

DeWulf proclaimed, "Federal agent?" in astonishment.

Tyler felt sweat drip down his rib cage. Fear of the unknown parched his throat. He needed Alvarez alive.

"No person is under there," DeWulf advised.

"Notify security. You two spread out and cover this immediate area," he indicated the aisle between the two cars.

Coopersmith got on the radio and told of the headlamp and that "one of his men" was going under to take a closer look.

Tyler appreciated Coopersmith protecting his identity. He ducked and, gun extended in his right hand, flashlight in his left, slipped beneath the train.

Tyler trained the flashlight's powerful beam left, right, up, and down. The barrel of his handgun followed that light, his index finger outside the trigger guard but ready. He knew something no one else did: Alvarez had dropped that headlamp. He believed it absolutely.

From behind him, DeWulf called under the train, "If there was anyone under there, he would have already taken off. Yes?"

Tyler instructed the man to move farther down the train—

DeWulf seemed to play by his own rules. Tyler then aimed the flashlight's beacon up at the car's undercarriage.

"Fredo!" he called out, stopping the man. "I need you under here."

"Moi!?"

"I don't know what the hell I'm looking at," Tyler said. "Get under here and help me, would you?"

DeWulf reluctantly crawled under. Accepting the flashlight from Tyler, DeWulf waved the beam and said, "That's part of the backup system for the brakes. This is the sewage collection tank . . . fresh water . . . mechanicals. . . . Wait just one second!" The wide circle of light reversed direction, and DeWulf scampered backward, away from where the headlamp had fallen. He thumped the back of his head against the undercarriage and dropped the flashlight.

Tyler picked it up and immediately spotted the false floor of the extended window shade. "I'm armed," he repeated sharply.

The jazz trio started into a rendition of "New York, New York," up on platform seven. Champagne bottles popped, and in a nervous reaction Tyler nearly pulled the trigger. There was a surreal quality to the juxtaposition of the caviar-and-champagne party overhead and the litter-strewn filth and feeling of danger here below.

Tyler signaled for DeWulf to hold the light while he moved forward and reached overhead. He took hold of the camouflaged shade and, in one motion, tore it loose. It ruffled like a flag and fell to the concrete floor. The space above held nylon webbing, like a hammock.

"Empty," DeWulf said. "Gone."

"Wouldn't be so sure," Tyler replied, working the flashlight in all directions.

"What's going on under there?" Coopersmith called out.

Tyler called out from underneath, "Can security seal the tunnel?"

"With all the trains coming and going? Not possible."

"Besides, he is long gone," DeWulf speculated, studying the arrangement left behind. "Clever bastard, this one."

Tyler heard Coopersmith making the radio call. He said to
DeWulf, "I need to get started right now. Your boss and I are going
to start at the back of the train and work our way forward. You," he
said to the man, "are going to get a message to someone."

By the time Priest had been located and escorted to the empty side
of the bullet train, Tyler and DeWulf had searched beneath the four
trailing cars while Coopersmith and one other of his men searched
forward. At the same time, security guards worked the interior, randomly checking the IDs of some of the guests while still others
searched the tunnel and the various converging tracks. All this was
done with as little commotion as could be managed, the consensus
being that Alvarez had fled the scene, and whatever threat he had
represented had gone with him.

Tyler was not convinced. He and Coopersmith had already discussed how much time they'd need for a complete inspection of the
train's systems and mechanicals. He knew that O'Malley, who was
leading his troops in the search of the train, would throw him out
with the bathwater, so he kept his head and his profile low.

His coveralls filthy, Tyler crawled out from under the last car as
Nell Priest called out for him. "We've got ourselves a situation," he
told her.

"So I've heard. O'Malley's ordered every guest checked against
the list."

"He was suspended up under a dining car. Who knows for how
long? He apparently avoided the security checks at Raritan."

"That's not possible," she muttered. "I supervised most of that."

"He camouflaged space beneath a car. They would have had to
have practically reached up in there to find him."

"He fled?"

"May have," Tyler answered. "Or he may be somewhere inside.
Up there in the party with the others."

Priest lifted her head up toward the windows that were filled both with crash-test dummies and visitors.

"Everyone wears a visitor's ribbon." She pointed to the purple one pinned to her chest. "Even Goheen. It was a last-minute decision by O'Malley. No matter what Alvarez knows about us, he couldn't possibly know about these ribbons."

"There are a lot of guests. At this point, he could be hiding anywhere up there."

Again, she looked up. She shook her head. "No. He fled," she said. Facing into the dark tunnel, she said, "He knew we'd blown his cover, and he took off." She sounded almost convincing.

Tyler said, "I need one of those ribbons."

She shook her head. "I don't know that I can do that. One ribbon per name on the guest list. That's how O'Malley is controlling it."

"Then give me yours," he pressed. "You tell them it must have fallen off. They'll look for it, but it'll buy me time."

She promptly unpinned the ribbon and handed it to him. Concern creased her otherwise smooth skin. He said, "We've already done this underneath, but let's do it again. You'll work the train front to back. I'll start in the last car and work forward."

"Our people are already working the train, rechecking each guest against the guest list. And that's not great for you. Most of them know your face by now," she cautioned. "O'Malley will have you thrown off."

"Technically, he can't. The NTSB has every right to be here. What he can do is delay me, tie me up with conversation, keep an eye on me. But in this crowd?" he asked. "It's a zoo up there. I'll be fine. What's the schedule?"

"Train rolls in ten minutes."

"Will they delay it, now that this has happened?"

She shook her head. "O'Malley will probably try for that. Goheen won't allow it. Trains leave on time. Company policy."

Tyler looked into her dark eyes and felt his throat tighten. He would never have guessed that he might feel the way he did about her. "I want to kiss you right now," he said, "but I can't."

"You most certainly cannot." She read his face.

"While you're guarding Gretchen Goheen, guard your own backside as well," he advised. "It's a very nice backside."

"Some things are better kept to yourself," she said, allowing a smirk as she turned and hurried toward the train.

The train's public address system announced, "Our guests wishing to remain in New York are invited to please depart onto platform seven at your convenience." This was the first time Tyler realized that everyone in attendance was in fact invited to take the ride but that not everyone would. The crowd thinned, with passengers moving forward toward their assigned cars. Behind the locomotive came a VIP passenger car, followed by a second passenger car for press and media; next were two dining cars with open bars, then four cars of crash-test dummies and mannequins—required by the NTSB for the test run. In the first of these four mannequin cars were seats set aside for Coopersmith's two maintenance men.

Tyler, a purple ribbon pinned to his coveralls, worked the train from the rear car forward, head low, moving through the rows of dummies and milling guests. He studied the shoes of the guests, believing this might be the one piece of clothing to set Alvarez apart: he watched for scuffed or dirty shoes or boots. He inspected faces from a distance while not allowing these guests to get a good look at him, assuming that some guests were NUS guards working in suits.

Suddenly a number of guests craned toward the starboard windows, stretching and bending to see out. Tyler got a look as well: William Goheen had daughter Gretchen by the shoulders, leaning into her, his face flushed with anger. She pressed back, clearly trying to work past him and onto the train, but Goheen blocked her entrance. This was a not a skirmish but a pitched battle, and neither father nor daughter seemed about to yield. The cars were too sound-proofed for Tyler to hear what was being said, but it wasn't pretty, not by any stretch of the imagination. Again it became obvious that Gretchen wanted to board the train and that Goheen would not permit it. Tyler caught the signal from Goheen, and a moment later security stepped in, Nell among them. Gretchen screamed at her father, this time her voice carrying into the train through an opened door. "If it's so damn safe, if you're so damn innocent, then why the hell can't I join you?"

Goheen stepped back, wounded. He motioned to Nell and the others, and Gretchen, literally kicking and screaming, was led away from the train and off the platform. Tyler saw Nell go and felt a wave of relief. Perhaps the same degree of relief Goheen must have experienced, confirming his daughter was to remain behind.

He'd lost track of O'Malley, who was busy with his troops as-sessing the potential danger represented by the discovery of Alva-rez's lair. Tyler believed now that without a doubt Alvarez intended to derail the train. He'd gotten closer than anyone had believed pos-sible. Failure to take him seriously now could prove to be fatal.

Some guests departed the rear cars onto the platform, electing to remain behind. Tyler found the presence of the crash-test dummies disturbing. They had been dressed to resemble passengers. With their eerily realistic faces, and positioned as they were in a frozen tableau meant to mimic the living, the effect was surreal.

The crush of guests slowly moved forward, settling mostly in the dining and beverage cars. Tyler held back, assuming if Alvarez were aboard, he, too, would stay behind and seek out a hiding place. He checked the lavatories of each rear car but found them unoccu-pied. Tyler sagged in disappointment. Alvarez was not going to make it easy.

Despite Coopersmith's claim that the mechanical closets could not be opened, Tyler now wanted a look inside them.

If Alvarez was not found, then, as far as Tyler was concerned, the only explanation was that he'd already carried out his sabotage. Despite the thorough security checks, despite the bomb-sniffing dogs, despite O'Malley's switching the train's location, Tyler gave Alvarez the benefit of the doubt. In a minority of one—not even Nell seemed ready to accept that their security might have failed—he decided he'd better learn as much about this train's operation as he could, and do so as quickly as possible.

Standing amid a group of guests in the vestibule between cars, Tyler turned to see dark suits—obviously security personnel—methodically inspecting the adjacent car. Guest ribbon or not, maintenance coveralls or not, he would be asked to provide a name to be checked against the master list. And he'd be discovered. He thought he might buy himself time by showing his fed credentials, but more likely he would invite O'Malley down on him. He felt cornered—and once again likened his own situation to that of Alvarez.

He tried to push his way into the next car, but the crowd was too thick. When he glanced back a second time, he saw the adjacent car's mechanical closet open and a guard clutching a crash-test mannequin. The man spun around as if dancing and set the dummy into a seat.

This time Tyler moved some guests out of his way and pushed through the mobbed dining car. In the next vestibule a door and stairway to the tracks remained open, allowing maintenance and security quicker access between cars. Tyler stepped down.

"Name, please," called a guard's voice from behind him. Tyler looked up the track toward the locomotive and saw Coopersmith with several of his maintenance crew. He wondered if Coopersmith could save him.

"Chief!" Tyler called out. But the maintenance boss didn't hear him.

"Name, please," the guard repeated, this time closer. Tyler didn't want to turn around and show his face for fear he'd be recognized.

He faked a French accent and said, "DeWulf. F. DeWulf. Maintenance, under Coopersmith." His accent was horrible. He held himself motionless, unable to breathe.

"Got it," the man said.

The duplication would likely be caught soon enough. Tyler would now have to remain one step ahead of O'Malley's guys. He headed up the line of cars toward Coopersmith, waving to catch the chief's attention.

Departure was stalled seven minutes to allow additional inspection. Guests were told that the train was delayed because some guests had been caught in traffic and had yet to arrive. O'Malley was clearly a busy man, working quickly to complete the search.

Tyler reached the locomotive. "Nothing?"

"Nothing," Coopersmith confirmed. "Our guys checked everything: brakes, guidance computers, data flow, communications. All intact. Nothing's been tampered with."

"Not yet," Tyler said.

"The only incident we heard about was that one of the security goons maced a dummy when it fell out of the mechanical closet in car seven."

DeWulf laughed. His presence again alerted Tyler to the security check only moments before.

Coopersmith handed him a set of bright orange plastic earplugs, and together they entered the engine room where DeWulf had already found a seat. Tyler held Coopersmith back and leaned out of earshot of the locomotive's driver. "I gave DeWulf's name in a security check just now."

"Did you?"

"They'll work their way forward. Everyone gets compared to a list."

"You're fine," Coopersmith said. "I'll sit by the door. They'll check with me. I'll okay it."

"One more maintenance man than on their list? That'll send up a red flag, whether or not they check with you."

Coopersmith nodded, seeing the logic in this. "Okay. So Fredo steps into the power supply for a minute or two. He'll go along. And believe me, even security isn't stupid enough to open a power supply closet."

"I appreciate this," Tyler said, feeling vastly relieved.

"A leak in security makes sense to me. And the feds trying to sting them also makes sense. Believe me, if you were even one-sixteenth Latino, I'd have turned you in. But as it happens, I believe you. And I don't want anyone messing with my train."

They stepped inside the warm space. DeWulf was told by Coopersmith that he'd have to hide for a minute in the power supply closet and that the fewer questions asked, the better. DeWulf had overheard enough about Tyler to catch on. He agreed without complaint.

Five minutes later, the same security man paid the locomotive a visit, and Tyler passed as DeWulf for the second time. The man left, and DeWulf joined Coopersmith and Tyler on the jump seats. He was sweating profusely.

The huge train shuddered, lumbered, and eased forward. Now, with the train moving, there would be no more passenger checks, although security was no doubt on alert to watch for Alvarez. If Tyler could reach the passenger section, he'd be free to continue his search for Alvarez or for the man's sabotage.

"Your first time in an engine room?" DeWulf asked Tyler, shouting to be heard. It broke Tyler's thought—that discovery of a crash-test mannequin in the mechanical closet weighed on him.

Tyler answered, "My first time in a locomotive."

"Yes? Well, you're in for the ride of your life."

Tyler grimaced, hoping not to take the man literally.

Believing that Alvarez was on board, Tyler reconsidered all that had gone on prior to departure. Finally he understood what they had overlooked. "I need to get back there," he called out to Coopersmith. "He's on the train. And I think I know where he's hiding."

This won both Coopersmith's and DeWulf's attentions.

The crew chief checked his watch and shouted back, "We'll go together. I need five minutes for us to cross-check all systems. Then we go!"

"The sooner, the better!" Tyler hollered back.

Minutes later Coopersmith handed Tyler DeWulf's set of keys and led him the length of the locomotive, past rectifiers, oil cooling systems, and electrical controls. Again, it reminded him of the space shuttle. They cleared the rear door and entered the vestibule that fronted the first passenger car.

Two smokers, a man and a woman, leaned around the edge of the oversized baggage bin in the area just before the door to this forward car. Coopersmith shouted at them, "Unscheduled maintenance inspection. Nothing to worry about."

Some smoke escaped the woman's mouth as she smiled. Tyler smelled pot. The man offered him a wry smile.

Coopersmith, oblivious, said, "We'll be coming up to full speed now. Enjoy the ride."

"Oh, we will!" the woman coughed out, laughing.

Coopersmith pushed the red plastic bar marked OUVERT/OPEN.

Tyler's skin crawled. The coveralls were sure to draw attention. Any one of O'Malley's people might spot him.

Vivaldi's *Four Seasons* played softly over the public address system. It was such an overplayed piece it sounded more like Muzak. This car, for VIPs, wasn't terribly crowded. Most of the guests stood talking, a drink in hand.

Coopersmith's huge carriage led the way. Tyler followed, head down.

The second car was media. It hummed with loud conversation. Some laptops were out, already testing Internet connections. It seemed a more cheery crowd than in the VIP car.

Tyler felt a burning impatience. He believed not only that Al-varez was aboard but that sabotage was soon to follow. What would be the sense of derailing a bullet train prior to its reaching full speed? And yet waiting to derail it increased Alvarez's risk. The longer the man waited, the more chance he might be caught or his sabotage outfoxed.

"How soon until we cross the Delaware River?" Tyler asked. The earlier derailments had all occurred in remote areas, in or around a large curve or a switch. But there were few such remote areas in the northeast corridor. So Tyler thought Alvarez might target a bridge crossing—about as remote as this train was to get.

"Twenty-five, thirty minutes," the crew chief replied.

"And what's the river north of Baltimore?"

"The Susquehanna?"

"How far to that?"

"Another fifteen. Make it forty-five, fifty from here."

In this brief time, Tyler needed to find Alvarez, uncover his plan, and abort the intended sabotage. He started feeling sick to his stom-ach. "This train is *too* fast," he said.

"It's something, isn't it?" Coopersmith stated proudly.

They reached the first of the dining cars. It was mobbed. Nearly impossible to get through.

Tyler stopped Coopersmith and pulled the man in toward him. He spoke carefully. "In which car was that dummy found?"

"Seven."

Tyler considered explaining his theory to Coopersmith but then thought better of it, electing to wait. "We need to check out the maintenance closet in seven. A-S-A-P."

"Because?"

"Would one of your guys have played that kind of trick on se-curity?"

"I'd never hear about it if they did," Coopersmith replied.

Pushing past a group of champagne-drinkers, nearly through the first of the dining cars now, Tyler said, "But would they play such a cheap trick on a trip like this? This important? The dummy. The closet? All that?"

Coopersmith shrugged. "Not if that guy was hoping to keep his job. I find out who, and he'll be buying a ticket home from Washington."

Tyler let slip, "I think I know who did it." Coopersmith stopped. Tyler added, "And I think I know why."

He looked back through the vestibule connecting the cars, catching a distant glimpse of O'Malley conferring with a couple of his men.

"We'd better hurry," Tyler said.

"You're telling me they're for show?" Tyler gasped. They had just cleared the second of the dining cars, entering the first of the four cars peopled with mannequins and dummies. Some of the guests had wandered back here. Two of Coopersmith's men occupied the front row. It was the first chance Tyler and Coopersmith could speak to each other without shouting.

"These mannequins, yes. Our safety department rents them from a place in Detroit. As you know, you—the NTSB—require us to put about a half dozen in each car, for the safety test. It was some publicity person's bright idea to fill these cars with these things. Supposed to look impressive, I suppose. Looks stupid to me. But then, I've already been on all the other test runs."

"And this new F-A-S-T Track technology? What about it? I've heard rumors, but I need the dime tour," Tyler said. He pointed to the far end and changed subjects on Coopersmith. "Seven is the next one?"

Coopersmith nodded, sensing Tyler's impatience. He let Tyler go first and talked over his shoulder. "We needed a system to account for the fact that we don't have special tracks laid for high speed like they do in Europe. High speed has to have the railbed banked on even the smallest curves. And many of the curves have to be not only banked but laid out in a wider radius, or the high speeds will literally throw the train off the tracks. But we can't get those changes in our track here. There's no space. It's what stymied us for nearly twenty years."

"And this new technology?"

"So, Goheen worked with an existing system where the cars tilt to hold them down onto the tracks. Similar systems are in place in Japan and Europe, but Goheen refined it. A crude version of the technology was used in this country between Boston and New York in the sixties. Now, it's all controlled by GPS technology. We don't get the European or the Japanese speeds, even with the stabilizers—as we call them—but we can more than double what we used to get."

"These stabilizers," Tyler said over his shoulder, reaching the end of the car. "They're GPS?"

"Synched to GPS, yes. The engine car, all the passenger cars, all clock-synched, one to the other. Pinpoint technology. Computers monitor the exact location of each car several times *a second* and send signals to the stabilizers that then compensate real time, physically tipping the cars. The change in the center of gravity drives the weight and the force down, instead of out, and the cars stay on track."

They passed into car seven, Tyler's heart thumping painfully from adrenaline.

He'd gotten Coopersmith started, and now he couldn't shut the guy up. "Ten years ago, the GPS technology wasn't accurate enough, not for commercial use. Military controlled it all. Even today most commercial GPS devices are manufactured for less accuracy, though the technology does exist to make them pinpoint perfect."

Tyler had heard enough. He thought he understood now what

Alvarez had in mind. *A science teacher,* he reminded himself. "Here," he said, stopping at the mechanical closet in seven. He groped for keys, but Coopersmith beat him to it, unlocking the door.

The closet was empty, as he'd expected.

Coopersmith snapped sarcastically, "So how was this worth our time?"

Tyler asked him to open the interior wall, the one behind which Coopersmith had earlier suggested he hide.

Coopersmith couldn't stop lecturing. "There's triple redundancy involved in the GPS tracking *for each car*—all the computers double-checking each other. As F-A-S-T Track approaches an area where excessive ground speeds would throw it offtrack, the stabilizers compensate, one after the other, car after car. And the passengers never even feel it."

Tyler stepped out of the way. Coopersmith unfastened and opened the panel, confirming the rear part, too, was empty. Tyler said, "And if you could corrupt the stabilizers?"

"Forget about it. No way. Too many backups, too much redundancy. And if any one of them fails, the driver is signaled and the locomotive begins an automatic shutdown. If all of them fail, even the driver can't override that shutdown."

"But if you could," Tyler pressed, "somehow trick the system."

"I'm telling you: you can't."

"Theoretically," Tyler tried.

Coopersmith locked the closet. Tyler was already scanning the lengthy array of mannequins. Coopersmith answered, "Then she would hit a turn and either roll or just keep on going."

"At a hundred and eighty miles an hour."

"I'm telling you: it can't be done."

"And I'm telling *you,*" Tyler answered, "that it's about to happen."

Alvarez sat still as the two men approached him down the aisle of car eight. For the past five minutes he had watched them from not twenty feet away, and yet they had no idea of his presence. The train rode so smoothly that at times it gave the illusion of not moving at all. A glance out the window dispelled that fantasy as the foreground blurred and even distant lights tracked past with alarming speed. Goheen had his prize.

Alvarez was dressed, not as a maintenance man, nor as security, but in a crash-test dummy costume he'd bought a month earlier from a mail-order catalogue. He'd loaded this outfit into the duffel—the two halves of the plastic head being the largest pieces he'd had to carry. This costume had been the key to his invisibility. People had blithely walked right past him for the better part of the last thirty minutes.

But panic filled him as these two men walked past, now only three feet away, and then continued on toward car nine, the last car. He clutched as he recognized one of them as being from the Amtrak—the fed who'd been able to delay that train so he could get aboard. Seeing that face set him wildly on edge. He had heard the two talking about the technology, including the GPS guidance. So he needed to act quickly now, before this agent—whoever he was— pieced it together. And they were heading back to car nine, where he'd hidden the duffel.

Thankfully, inside the costume, he was carrying all that he

needed: the digital video camera, the computer card, and McClaren's explosive. But the duffel, now at risk, was also his escape. That damn headlamp had made him change things—and now, like dominoes, those changes were forcing others. *If they find that duffel . . .* he thought, already searching for an alternate way off the train.

Time now was everything.

The crash-test dummy slowly turned its head until the man inside it confirmed car eight was empty. Then he pushed a child dummy off his lap, sat that child in the seat he'd occupied, and hurried down the aisle to seven.

These moments of movement, dressed as a test dummy, were the riskiest. He had a few pat answers down, if confronted: "part of the show—don't tell anyone!" "undercover security, and it's important it remain undercover." But if real security or maintenance stopped him, it would get ugly.

He hurried to the lavatory, shedding the costume in favor of the black pants, white shirt, and tie he wore underneath. To this he clipped the all-important NUS identity tag that from a distance at least looked a decent replica. Under scrutiny it might not hold, and this thought caused him to flush with unwanted heat.

He used his set of keys—the shapes and dimensions stolen from NUR corporate—to unlock the lavatory's trash disposal bin, and he hid the uniform along with the two halves of its plastic head. If needed, he might resort to this costume again. With this change in clothes he could move freely through the train. With each new step in his plan, he felt closer to the end. He stretched for it now, knowing these next few minutes represented a lifetime. Maybe many lifetimes, if things went poorly.

As a security man, Alvarez crossed into car seven and walked its empty aisle, the eerie mannequins staring at his back. He headed straight for the mechanical closet. He opened it, unlatched and opened the divider, and quickly stepped inside, pulling the unlocked door closed.

Here was where the headlamp was to have assisted him. Without it, he worked now in the gray haze seeping under the door and the limited light cast off by a few amber and green LED indicators from the guidance computer. He connected his video camera to the train's audio/video feed without trouble. The timing of his showing that video would depend on Goheen staying on schedule; the tape contained ten blank minutes. Goheen—a man obsessed with staying on schedule—was supposed to greet his guests as the F-A-S-T Track crossed the Delaware, making reference to George Washington and to American ingenuity and glory.

Next, as he'd rehearsed, he used a Leatherman pocket tool to unscrew and remove the face plate from the GPS guidance device, a metal box about the size of a book. He faced a circuit board, a cream-colored resin epoxy board containing dozens of gray chips and other smaller, piggybacked boards, all connected by razor-thin silver lines.

For him, the beauty of the NUR design was the redundancy factor. There was not one GPS board but three, all in sockets next to one another and in the center of the circuit board. If one board failed, the next took over for it in nanoseconds. Had the system contained only one board, Alvarez could not have hot-swapped his replacement. The system would have crashed. But with three, he merely removed the second and replaced it with his own, a board programmed both to misdirect the car's stabilizer and to trick the locomotive's computer into believing all three cards were functioning normally. The replaced board functioned exactly as did the others and therefore would not pass the handling of the car's guidance to the third, and final, backup card. More important, someone looking at this replacement would see no difference when compared to the others. If inspected, it would go undetected. The actual differences between the boards were several: the NUR board was programmed to this train route, designed to anticipate and adjust the stabilizers as the car approached a particular bend in the track. Alvarez's replacement was blank—its GPS memory erased—and yet it would send out a signal to the locomotive's server that all was well. Without the route programmed in, this board would not signal the stabilizers of an impending curve. It would also displace the stabilizers if the train slowed more than ten miles an hour, removing the center of gravity and causing the car to derail. But the crowning achievement for Alvarez was his computer virus. This virus sent itself out over the diagnostics data port and corrupted each GPS board in succession, all of which would then report to the server that they were in perfect order. With the installation of this single board, he'd corrupted the entire guidance system in every car but the locomotive.

If on the outside chance Goheen met his demands, then this card could be identified and removed, the guidance system re-booted from the locomotive's server, allowing the train to slow to a stop without incident.

In less than thirty seconds, it was in place. Alvarez withdrew the portable GPS device that showed him the train's exact location, speed, and time to destination. In forty seconds, the southbound train would reach a straightaway that would be maintained for over ten minutes. Alvarez waited out those seconds in stomach-knotting tension and then ran the metal tip of his screwdriver to the base of the processing chip on the first guidance board, shorting it out. A tiny spark flashed, and the air smelled metallic. Handling of the car's stabilizers passed instantaneously to the replacement board, where an LED continued to glow green, just like the others. At that same instant, the virus began to spread to the other cars.

Alvarez held his breath, waiting, his legs tensing. If the train suddenly began to slow—if his ruse had been detected by the server—then the train would likely automatically shut down. But the vibration remained steady. The purr beneath his feet warmed him.

In the end, it was Northern Union's quest for total safety that made this system vulnerable.

He marked his watch, pushed PLAY on the video, and then peered out of the closet. His ten-minute grace period began to tick off. Seeing the car still empty, he stepped out, replaced and latched the divider, and shut and locked the closet's door. His final move was to fill the lock mechanism with an instant-dry epoxy that would set fully in less than five minutes.

He still had a lot to get done, including his own escape.

Umberto Alvarez prepared to crash William Goheen's party. He grinned at the irony of that expression.

Alvarez gathered his strength as he advanced toward the backs of the two maintenance men, the gear heads, who occupied the two right front row seats of car six. He could approach this one of two ways, but he opted for the bold.

As he came up behind them he intentionally startled them by speaking loudly. "Okay, guys, I got the wonderful job of checking the coupler." He walked right past them, reached the door, and popped the red panic bar that opened it automatically. He offered them only a piece of his profile, but enough to show them that he had a tag clipped to his shirt. "If you hear me yell, come looking."

He stepped out into the vestibule, where casually dressed reporters sucked on cigarettes and shared vodka on the rocks and war stories. A woman looked up and checked him out. He felt her study of him clear down to his toes.

He said loudly, "Sorry, folks, but I've got to ask you to take the party forward for a few minutes. We're getting ready for the press conference. You can smoke in the vestibule between the next two cars."

To his surprise, even the spoiled-looking guy with wet eyes didn't object. They snubbed out their smokes and reentered the dining car. As the door shut behind them, Alvarez unlocked and opened the right-hand section of accordion wall that connected the two vestibules, and he reached outside. He tripped a release lever that allowed a flange of corrugated flooring to be lifted. This flange could move with the turning of the car through curves, but it connected cleanly, one vestibule to the other.

With this short piece of flooring lifted, Alvarez could see down past the massive coupler. Part rush, part terror, he kneeled just four feet above a railbed hurtling maniacally past at 180 miles per hour. For a brief moment he felt in awe of the technology that generated such speeds. For a moment he felt empathy for William Goheen's dream.

Unlike the freight cars, and most passenger trains in the United States, the couplings on the French-built high-speed trains were controlled electrohydraulically. A keyed switch on each car—both of which had to be operated nearly simultaneously—allowed coupling and uncoupling. For safety, the tension between two moving cars prevented uncoupling. In theory, only while the cars were at rest, in a yard or a station, and pushed against each other with a tug or locomotive to remove that pressure, could uncoupling take place.

For this reason, Alvarez reached down and placed the McClaren explosive onto the coupler alongside the main pin. It adhered to the forged steel magnetically. Checking his portable GPS one last time, he threw the two switches, starting the timer and triggering a tamperproof detonation device: if the magnetic bond with the coupler was disturbed, the bomb would explode prematurely.

Life is made of moments, and had Alvarez finished doing this at a different moment, his plans might have ticked along as scheduled. But after replacing the floor flange, as he was locking up the accordion wall, he felt an urgency to look over his left shoulder and through the tempered glass window into the dining car. It was a wholly inexplicable urge. His plans had called for him to hurry back to car nine and the waiting duffel bag. Escape!

He caught sight of the back of a woman's head. A chill swept through him, and now he was drawn to trip open the door and go into the dining car. It smelled some of perfume, with a dash of locker room. His nerves were jangling. Something cut to his gut. He feared his plans had been uncovered. He took another step into the car, his heart beating wildly. He saw sport jackets hanging on coat clips, white shirts and ties and small orbs of sweat; he smelled beer and pretzels, Scotch and traces of cigars; he heard loud voices and laughter. Part high school, part summer camp, part press room. A few of the men appeared to have already reached a sloppy drunk.

Out the dining car windows, he caught sight of a faintly rust-red skyline. *Trenton, New Jersey,* he thought, realizing Goheen would start his press conference any minute.

The people suddenly seemed to be talking louder, their laughter directed at him. He knew he'd made a mistake entering this car. He wanted to turn around but felt himself resisting. What had drawn him in here? Who? A guest? A security guard? Goheen himself? That feeling burned in him—something was terribly wrong. He checked his watch. His video would start playing in less than three minutes.

A waiter bearing a tray of champagne held high was barely able to pass. He squeezed by Alvarez, excusing himself. Alvarez turned to move out of the man's way, and as he did so, he couldn't resist looking up ahead into the crowded car.

He made the move nonchalantly, a polite gesture to allow the waiter through.

There was that same woman, not ten feet from him. She turned her head away, just as Alvarez rotated, as if avoiding him. She wore a dark blue, crushed velvet cocktail dress. She had skin the color of pearls, her face framed in dark hair. Now she turned toward him. It was Jillian.

CHAPTER

35

"You're telling me we've been walking right by this guy?" Coopersmith asked.

"I think so, yes," Tyler answered quietly. They stood in the vestibule between cars eight and nine, tucked around the edge of the accordion connector alongside three carpeted shelves for luggage. "That dummy hidden in the maintenance closet was no practical joke, it was an extra. Extra because Alvarez is now occupying a seat."

Coopersmith, distracted by the gun in Tyler's right hand, didn't seem to hear.

"And I think he's probably monitoring our radios—both maintenance and security frequencies. We can't use the radios."

"You don't know for sure he's even aboard this train."

"I bet we're about to confirm that," Tyler said. "We should be finding a black duffel bag, possibly with clothes inside, possibly with explosives, hidden behind the panel in one of the mechanical closets. That is, if we're lucky. Otherwise he's already moved that duffel to an overhead rack, where it's blending in with the other carry-ons. In that case, whether he's on board or not, this train could already be rigged to derail."

"That's bullshit. Besides, why the mechanical closets?"

"Because he hid the dummy there. We know he has access. A key. Whatever. And that means he has access to *anywhere* on this train—a full set of keys. I'd count on that."

"But that's just not possible."

Tyler had no time to argue. "Normally, I'd try to get word to security. But now without using the radios we can't trust security," he said, returning to the ruse he had invented to protect himself. "That means I personally check every crash-test dummy on this train. And I'll need your guys, the two guys in car six, to clear these four rear cars and block that door at six. We can't let him slip by and reach the forward cars. Too many people there."

"Yeah, okay," Coopersmith said reluctantly. "I can do that."

"We do the mechanical closets both for that duffel bag and for any tampering," Tyler reminded him. "I'd pay special attention to the guidance systems."

"You're way off base on this."

Tyler barreled ahead. "I'll take car nine. You and I already did the closet in eight. But seven, six, and all cars forward have to be thoroughly rechecked."

"No problem."

"For now we'll focus on these rear cars. If we have to move forward, if we start pushing guests around, it's going to get sticky." He asked, "What about *under* the cars?"

"At these speeds?"

"Can he access the electronics down there?"

Coopersmith considered. His face soured. "If he knew what he was doing, if he had the wiring schematics, it's possible he could interrupt the data cables. But trust me, he doesn't have the schematics."

Tyler wasn't so sure, but he held his tongue.

"And a hundred-and-fifty-mile-an-hour windchill? A man wouldn't last ten minutes down there."

For Tyler, it was still a possibility he needed to follow up. He didn't put anything past Alvarez. He knew the man. "If you find that duffel, go on the radio and announce that you found the missing wrench. You got that?"

"Missing wrench," Coopersmith echoed. For such a big man, he looked a little frightened, his face florid, eyes bulging.

Tyler again felt relief that Nell had left the train with Gretchen Goheen. He had a feeling Alvarez was hiding in car nine. If so, perhaps the train was already rigged to roll. The last car—nine— was the farthest from the action and, as such, presented the best hiding place. Tyler moved quickly.

Coopersmith went forward to empty the rear cars of any stray passengers and to block egress from six into the dining car.

Tyler entered car nine, at once excited and terrified. He walked to the far end of the car, to a locked door with a tempered glass window. It was dark out. Tyler couldn't see a thing out there. He walked the car then, taking hold of each of the half dozen life-sized dummies that had been randomly placed about. He shook each of the dummies, ensuring they weren't concealing a person. The mannequins were too small and skinny to hide anyone. If Alvarez was in here, he had to be costumed as a dummy.

Tyler marveled at the number of mannequins, the elaborate masquerade to impress the media, the expense to which Northern Union had gone.

By the time he reached the front of the last car, Tyler felt nauseous, disappointed, and in the throes of self-doubt. Through process of elimination, he'd convinced himself that he'd find Alvarez hiding here. Now, his thoughts strayed back to the undercarriage where they had found his original hiding place. Had he somehow eluded them during their exhaustive search? What if Alvarez had intended to remain outside for the whole trip? Tyler glanced at his watch. He didn't have much time. The train was up to speed. There was no reason for Alvarez to wait. The longer he waited, the greater the chance of being caught.

It took Tyler three tries with the keys to find the one that opened the mechanical closet. He stared into the empty space, more discouraged, and then worked on the latch to the interior panel. It came open. Lying on the floor in front of him, crumpled and standing on one end, was a black duffel bag.

"Oh, shit," Tyler gasped aloud, not a soul within earshot.

The duffel's zippers were not locked together, though a tiny pad-lock did hang there. This told him that Alvarez had been rushed, had left the duffel perhaps half expecting it might be found. A tad of encouragement buoyed him. He unzipped the bag and searched it. The largest of the items came out first, a stuff sack the size and shape of a sleeping bag. *To keep him warm under that train,* Tyler decided. *Does this mean he's still on the train, not under it?* he wondered. The only other fairly large item was a cardboard shipping box, of a size to contain a crash test dummy, since the only bulky part of the costume would be the plastic head. He found duct tape, nylon webbing, a wire cable ratcheted winch called a come-along, flares, superglue, matches, spare batteries, and a laptop computer. But no explosives, no corrosive acid, no GPS devices.

Tyler focused on the computer. He tried to turn it on, but no surprise, it was password-protected. Maybe some lab tech at the FBI could some day access it, but for the time being, it was useless as evidence. His momentary encouragement lost ground to increasing panic: Alvarez *was* on board, and he meant business.

He got on the radio and announced he'd found the missing wrench. Coopersmith called back, "Yeah? Well we need you in seven."

Tyler, anxiety mounting, repacked the duffel and slung it over his shoulder, locking up the closet. He would ask one of Cooper-smith's guys to deliver the duffel to the second dining car, requesting it be locked up behind the counter where it would also be under the constant watch of a bartender. The mechanical closet was bait now—Tyler believed Alvarez would return for the duffel at some point. But did its being hidden in the train's final car hold significance? A person couldn't jump from a train at nearly two hundred miles an hour. Or could he?

Tyler inspected the sleeping bag more thoroughly: it wasn't a sleeping bag at all but a thin, extremely lightweight synthetic ma-terial. He pulled it out further—yards of parachute cord. It was a parasail, a controllable parachute.

Tyler knew at that moment what Alvarez had in mind. The man was going to separate the train in two. The front half would derail. Then he'd parasail off the back to freedom.

Tyler quickly caught up to Coopersmith and his two men, who were all gathered around the maintenance closet to car seven.

Coopersmith saw him coming and said, "He shanked this lock. Superglue, I think. Filled the hole. Can't get a key in." He faced Tyler and apologized, "So maybe I was wrong about his having a set of keys."

"The stabilizers?"

"For this car, they're controlled inside the closet. Yes."

"Could tampering with a single car derail the train?"

"No," Coopersmith answered. "Too many redundancies built in." He added, "At worst, he fries three separate boards and the override kicks in and disengages the engine."

Glancing frontward, sensing he'd missed his chance at Alvarez, Tyler said, "You've got to get inside this closet while I keep looking for him."

"Hell, we'll never get this door open. The French built these things like brick shit houses. They didn't want anyone messing with the gear."

Tyler repeated, "You've got to get in there."

"We should stop the train," Coopersmith abruptly decided, elbowing one of his workers aside and headed for the ceiling-mounted emergency brake.

Tyler accepted that if they stopped, Alvarez at least could not derail the train. He followed on the chief's heels, his mind whirring.

Coopersmith broke the glass barrier and reached for the emergency brake. Tyler grabbed hold of the man's forearm. He asked, "What if that's what he wants us to do? Panic us? Make us hit the brakes?"

Coopersmith stared at him angrily, keenly aware of Tyler's hand restraining his forearm.

Tyler went on, "What if hitting the brakes will roll the car? What if he's rigged it to do that? How can we be sure?"

Coopersmith's eyes seemed to shift in their sockets. His hand remained on the brake as he clearly debated leaning his weight into it, his brow beaded with sweat.

Tyler said, "What if we get the driver to just cut the engine and let it glide to a stop?"

"At these speeds, with no brakes, you're talking miles for this baby to come to a full stop." His hand remained clutched to the emergency chain. "Listen, if he's screwed with the stabilizers, if he knows what he's doing, this thing could still roll at thirty, forty miles an hour on a *straightaway*. It could injure, even kill people. That's a big chance to take."

"What if we uncoupled these rear cars on the fly?" Tyler suggested. This was exactly what he thought Alvarez had in mind, and he wanted to test its feasibility on Coopersmith.

The big man shook his head. "Can't be done. There has to be slack, no tension, in the coupling." He added, "But I see your point, if we could get the guests back of here *before* trying to slow the train, that's a hell of an idea."

"What are the mechanics of this? Help me out here." He dug into Alvarez's duffel bag and produced the come-along, a hand-operated winch. "Could I take enough pressure off the coupler with one of these to uncouple two cars?"

Coopersmith took his hand off the emergency brake, stunned. "That was part of his plan? But why would a terrorist want to uncouple the cars?"

"In order to escape."

Coopersmith nodded, picking up on the thought. "Uncouple nine, yeah, and watch as the train runs off without you." Coopersmith hurried to the front of the car, opened a box, and picked up the phone that connected to the locomotive. "This is Coopersmith," he said.

"Maintenance Crew Chief. Listen up. We've got a situation back here."

Coopersmith hung up, looking bewildered. He told Tyler, "The driver won't do it. Won't disengage."

"He's *got* to!"

"Says he's not stopping the train based on a door being glued shut. He wants Goheen making the call."

As if on cue, a woman's voice came over the public address system, announcing that Goheen's press conference would now take place in the press car and would be carried live on the in-seat videos in all cars, for those interested.

"Goheen is not going to stop this train," Tyler realized aloud. "Not after that. He's not going to move his guests. He's not going to do anything."

Coopersmith, still reeling from the driver's refusal, mumbled, "I should have told him something different. Should've handed him a lie."

Tyler glanced at his watch. "How soon can you get this door open?"

"We could drill it. Jig it around the lock. Ten . . . fifteen minutes."

"Make it five," Tyler urged.

Tyler stared at the small door that had been jammed shut. The train was set to derail—he knew this beyond all doubt. He couldn't ignore this closet, but at the same time, he pondered at its obviousness. What if it was nothing but a diversion? He asked Coopersmith, "You said each car separately tracks its own location?"

"Yeah."

"Speed. Direction."

"Right."

"And the stabilizers react accordingly," Tyler said.

"Which is what keeps it on the tracks."

Again, Tyler felt the pressure of the approaching river crossings and Goheen's upcoming press conference. Time was running out. He shut his eyes and tried to focus. He tried to see the train's design in his head. "The guidance systems must report to each other."

"Of course."

"And to the locomotive." Tyler continued, "So our guy not only knocks out the guidance on a couple of the cars but does something so the driver never knows about it."

Coopersmith shook his head. "A server in the locomotive constantly monitors the data lines. Anything goes south, the engine does an auto-shutdown. We checked those systems again at Penn Station, full data port checks. Everything was go."

"But if he knew that would be your last inspection, it would explain why he risked boarding. Right? He did whatever he did while under way so as to avoid detection." Tyler suggested, "With the sabotage in place, he disconnects car nine and rides it to safety."

Coopersmith stood absolutely still, drained of color. "Who the hell *are* you?"

Tyler replied, "You've got to inspect all the data cable, the guidance systems, the server in the locomotive, anything that's part of the control of these stabilizers."

At that moment, a repeat announcement about the press conference was made.

Tyler said, "Whatever we do, we've got to be fast."

Alvarez froze at the sight of Jillian. Had Goheen or O'Malley identified her, managed to lure her here? Coercion? False promises?

In her eyes, he saw concern and fear. Upon his making eye contact, she immediately looked away. She appeared either angry or under guard or both. He turned back, took two steps, and through the vestibule spotted the man he believed was a federal agent coming at a run up car six. To his right, Jillian had now turned her back on him.

He stepped into the dining car. The lavatory's indicator read *Vacant.* It described how he felt. Her being here started him on a new train of thought: she somehow represented a future; his Goheen vendetta pointed to no future whatsoever, only a past of grief and anger and a need for revenge. Could he drop all that for a woman he hardly knew?

He went into the lavatory dizzy with anxiety. He pulled the door shut and threw the lock.

A knock came almost immediately. This, despite the *Occupied* sign. *The fed,* he thought, pondering violence or surrender. And he had come too far to surrender.

"Please," came Jillian's muted voice through the door.

Alvarez reached for the lock. Was he being set up? Were they using her? His fingers found the cool metal lock and twisted. The door opened a crack, and Jillian slipped inside.

She pulled the door shut and deftly locked it, the two of them standing in the cramped space. She looked stunning: the velvet dress, her hair up. Her eyes shone. "I didn't believe them," she said, staring at him.

He opened his arms and they embraced, and briefly he felt peace. "How?"

"I couldn't bring myself to tell you, at the restaurant or the apartment."

"Quickly," he urged.

"When I saw the article in the paper, I called the police to say I'd seen you." She seemed to be fighting to hold herself together. "Later, this man came. With the railroad. He said that if I took this trip, if I rode this train, I might save hundreds of lives. I told him you wouldn't, couldn't possibly, do what he said you were planning to do."

"But you came," he said, standing her up, releasing the embrace. "You didn't believe that."

"So why are *you* here?"

"Yes. It's interesting, isn't it?"

"It's over, Bert. It has *got* to be over."

"No one's getting hurt. No one but this bastard and his company."

A heavy pounding on the bathroom door. They both tensed. Alvarez pointed to his lips and then to Jillian. He wanted her to answer.

"Busy!" she called out.

"No problem. Sorry." A male voice. The fed he'd seen? One of Goheen's guards? By coming in here with him, by her answering, she might have just saved him. Or trapped him. He couldn't be certain of anything.

"I can't expect you to understand," he whispered.

"So many lies." She considered this. "So many *lives*."

"The lies started with them."

"Listen to you!" she exclaimed.

He checked his watch. "Any of the cars behind the dining cars will be safe." He added, "Go there now."

"No." She stared at him. "I won't."

In the near silence, Alvarez became aware that there was no rhythm to this bullet train, no cadence. They had robbed train travel of its soul. They had robbed *him* of his soul.

He checked his watch. "You have to decide if you're turning me in or not. I'm on a tight schedule."

"I won't be in the back cars," she affirmed. "Whatever you do, you do it to me. This is not a solution—whatever it is, it is not that."

"It's not your battle."

"There is no battle. Your family is dead. None of this will help."

Alvarez burned with resentment but spoke gently. "You compare us as if we're the same." He waited. "You have a decision to make," he said flatly.

Jillian glared, turned around, and unlocked the door.

CHAPTER
37

Wearing a hand-tailored blue suit and a red, white, and blue tie, William Goheen stood at the front of the press car at a small lectern before an improvised cluster of microphones and a slightly inebriated audience. *Dateline* was one of seven video cameras taping to run the event that evening. Installed into each seat back was a small liquid crystal screen that showed Goheen's face as slightly pink.

Goheen offered a second hearty welcome to his honored guests. There would be even more food and drink right after the presentation. He won a light round of applause for that, which should have told him something about his audience.

"Before I take your questions," he said, flanked by two attractive women from public relations, "we'd like to show you a short video on the F-A-S-T Track's innovative technology and futuristic features. We have this information for you on pass-outs as well. They're available in the catering car, along with some T-shirts and brochures we thought you'd enjoy. It's only about five minutes. We'll run it now."

Behind Goheen and to his left, O'Malley stood facing the camera's glaring lights wearing sunglasses, looking completely out of place. He wore a curly wire in his right ear and a scowl on his face.

One of Goheen's aides spoke into her cell phone, and everyone's attention fell to the video screens. Anticipation mounted as the screens remained black. Some sparkles suggested tape might be running, but no image appeared. No sound.

A perfectionist, Goheen prided himself on presentation, a hall-mark of Northern Union Railroad. This short press conference had been rehearsed several times, the equipment checked repeatedly. Sloppy performances had no place in his camp. He merely turned his head to send his people scampering to solve the problem.

Before his assistants had moved ten feet, a man's blackened sil-houette appeared on the small screens, as well as on the larger mon-itor set up to Goheen's right. When this man spoke, his voice sounded electronically altered—like an imitation of a robot. "Wel-come passengers of the F-A-S-T Track test run. If security personnel manage to stop this video, it is you, the passengers, who will suffer for it. Demand this video be played to its conclusion. As of this moment, your continued safety lies with me. I have a list of demands for Mr. Goheen."

One of the two PR women frantically hoisted a cell phone to her mouth. O'Malley, his face suddenly ashen, had stepped around Goheen to view the screen. Goheen glared down at him from the podium with all the fury a man could muster.

The voice continued. "If these demands are not met, this train will derail in exactly seven minutes."

Panic erupted. The next few seconds of video were lost to all but those closest to the monitor, among them, Goheen and O'Malley. "If the train slows more than ten miles an hour, it will derail auto-matically. Mr. Goheen, I trust I have your attention."

The passengers roared out complaints—one of the more drunk shouted, "This is *not* funny!"

A full third of the reporters had their mobile phones out, already speed-dialing.

"First and foremost," the voice said from the television mon-itor, "William Goheen and Keith O'Malley must confess their crimes of fraud and cover-up and assume responsibility for the three deaths in Genoa, Illinois, which resulted directly from their deci-sions . . ."

Goheen looked as if he'd seen a ghost.

As the video began, Tyler, making his way up car six, watched Alvarez's silhouetted profile in silence. As on airplanes, each seat had a headset, without which there was no sound.

Without using radios, he'd been alerting Coopersmith's men to start checking data cable and to recheck the guidance systems. But now he shouted for them to turn on the sound, and one of the men jumped up and did just that. The sterile, synthesized voice came across, making its accusations and announcing that the train was set to derail. The hundreds of mannequins, all seemingly watching their screens, lent it a surreal feeling.

The electronic voice declared, "CEO William Goheen, and Northern Union's chief of security, Keith O'Malley, have perpetrated a crime against all customers and shareholders of Northern Union Railroad by diverting funds budgeted for regularly scheduled maintenance and later falsifying documents to affirm that that maintenance was carried out. These diverted funds, in fact, ended up as part of the F-A-S-T Track budget, the result of which is unsafe and poorly maintained rail lines, and crossings, nationwide."

Tyler recalled the sight of the derailed train outside of Terre Haute. To his knowledge Alvarez had never killed anyone in a derailment, but perhaps that was all about to change.

He collected the two men and explained their assignments, at which point one of them—Raoul, as per the name stitched into the coveralls—told him that security was a step ahead. "The guy just now got through inspecting the coupling."

"What guy?" Tyler's head was reeling.

"The *security* guy!" Raoul said, restating the obvious.

"Before or after the video started?" Tyler asked. O'Malley might have rallied his troops within seconds of the video starting.

"Before," Raoul answered. Again stating it as if Tyler should have known. He said, "The video, it just started now."

"Show me!" Tyler thundered. Had he guessed wrong about the

crash test dummy? Could Alvarez have been disguised as a security guard? Wouldn't O'Malley's guys have caught that?

If the sabotage was now in place as the video claimed, and with the train already up to speed, there was nothing he could think of that could still be done. So then Goheen had to capitulate to whatever demands were made. But from what he knew of the man, Tyler did not see that happening.

Could he and Coopersmith somehow still prevent this from happening?

The silhouette on the video announced, "Mr. Goheen, I offered you many opportunities to reveal the truth of what happened at Genoa. You declined, putting everyone here at risk. And yes, at last, I even solicited your daughter—as repugnant as that may have been—and again you refused. You are undeserving to be called a father. It was a title I cherished. As you and your guests will now see, you failed in even this regard. You could have prevented all of this. I'm sure the press is eager to ask you some questions."

Raoul indicated the small LED screen mounted to the bulkhead where a partially clothed woman transformed herself in a mirror. Gretchen Goheen turned and looked toward the camera and said, "I've never been asked this. Usually, it's to add something more— a certain look, you know?"

A man, his back to the camera, slowly disrobed her, first removing her bra, then dropping to his knees and pulling down her underwear. The camera caught it all, missed nothing.

There was a discussion of payment.

"Your credit card was charged when I confirmed you were in the room," a naked Gretchen Goheen said. The tape had been poorly edited. "Let's not talk business." Another edit, and the scene repeated, "Let's not talk business." Over and over, this naked woman said the same few words into the camera, a man kneeling in front of her, eye level with her crotch.

Alvarez's silhouette reappeared.

Tyler could only imagine the devastation heaped upon Goheen. How would any father react? A human body could not survive a jump at such speeds, but Tyler wondered if the man wasn't contemplating that fate.

Alvarez's synthesized voice warned all passengers to move immediately to any of the four cars trailing the second dining car. "Anyone in, or forward of, the two dining cars takes responsibility for his or her own safety."

"He's going to split the train in two," Tyler spoke aloud, now understanding how Alvarez planned to spare lives.

Raoul depressed the button, unlocking the car's forward door.

As he did, a stampede of boozed, hysterical people knocked the man over and trampled him. Tyler jumped to the side, shielding himself behind the bulkhead. He reached down, caught Raoul's limp hand, and dragged him out from under the crazed herd of escapees.

The stream of people seemed endless. Thankfully, they fled right through car six en route to the very back of the train. Tyler held himself pressed to the wall and inched his way forward toward the lavatory and the door beyond, the terrified guests still hurrying through.

He had to reach that forward vestibule. He had five or six minutes at the most.

CHAPTER

38

A s Alvarez and Jillian stepped out of the lavatory, the video
began. Alvarez's timing was off.

Everyone in the dining car faced away from them, focused on
one of two TVs suspended from the ceiling. As the screen began to
show a naked woman, Alvarez tugged on Jillian's arm, hoping to
lead her to the safety of the rear and to keep her from seeing him
on video. But once she saw the back of his head, she flushed and
stood her ground.

"No," she gasped. "I think I'll stay for the show."

Alvarez couldn't move, but he knew he would have to be *ahead*
of the forthcoming mad rush for the back cars to have any chance
at the parasail.

Jillian shook her head, her face contorted with anger. "You've
been busy," she said.

"We've got to get to the back of the train."

"Not me."

"Yes!" he said, pulling on her. He now heard his own distorted
voice issuing its warning and, as every guest turned toward him at
the same moment, knew it was too late.

The crowd stampeded.

Alvarez pulled her to him. She resisted with all her strength,
wrestling to be free of him. But then she caught a fleeing passenger's
elbow in the neck and reeled in pain. Alvarez buried her in his arms,

shielding her, as the screaming mob streamed past. Alvarez hated this; he had imagined an organized exodus.

Twisting to avoid getting clipped, he caught sight of the accordion wall that joined the vestibules between cars.

It was unlocked. Open.

Was someone out there?

Tyler unlocked the accordion wall and split the barrier open a crack, wishing Raoul was here now to guide him. Cold air stung his face and caught in his lungs.

The gap between the two cars was less than a foot wide, but either Alvarez or a security guard had been out here, and Tyler had to know why. He moved tentatively, squeezing through and inching outside, reaching for a handhold on the front of car six. He crouched and tipped himself over to get a look.

Directly beneath the accordion was the coupler itself, still out of sight. What he saw were black cables stretching one car to the next— communications, data, and electricity, he assumed. He looked back and forth at these, and to his layman's eye, none had been tampered with.

He moved cautiously, the wind stinging his face and almost freezing his fingers. When bent at the waist and extending himself off the front of the car, clutching to the handhold with only one hand, he could get a decent look at the coupling. But it was too fleeting. He moved down one ladder rung and finally got a heads-up view of the coupling itself. The railbed blurred past at dizzying speeds. Holding fast to the ladder, he leaned out and away, struggling to peer beneath the mated vestibules to the massive coupler joining the cars.

Atop it he now saw a small gray box. It looked either glued or magnetically attached. He leaned out farther for a better look. He saw no blinking lights, no digital clock counting down the seconds, just a plain gray box about the size of a cigarette pack. But Tyler knew he was looking at a bomb, a device meant to explode and disconnect the coupler.

Alvarez must have set the thing while posing as a security guard. Upon its explosion, the four aft cars would disconnect and glide to a stop; the front cars and locomotive would no doubt derail. Alvarez meant to ride his parasail, driven by a hundred-mile-an-hour lift, landing well away from the tracks. Now he was maybe strapped beneath a car, awaiting his move.

Tyler considered trying to remove that box and dropping it to the tracks, but he feared it might be rigged to detonate if tampered with. Worse, he knew it was intended to *save* lives, not destroy them. The best he could do was to get everyone into those rear cars and allow the damn thing to go off.

No evidence of explosives had ever been uncovered at any of the derailments. So explosives seemed out of character for Alvarez. But none of the freights had carried passengers, either, and this, Tyler believed, explained the difference.

Through a long turn, Tyler hugged the back of the car, only feet from the railbed. The train ride felt rocky, as if the stabilizers weren't working. Overcome momentarily by a wave of nausea and dizziness as the cars pinched together, the space narrowing, Tyler discarded the idea of attempting to climb under the cars to search for Alvarez. He felt sick to his stomach.

Then, out of the corner of his eye, he caught movement and looked up. Alvarez stood on the platform between the cars, at the narrow gap in the open accordion wall. The man stared down at Tyler, who felt paralyzed by this sudden confrontation. His face unflinching, Alvarez pushed the accordion shut, and Tyler saw it bite tightly to its mate.

Alvarez had locked him out of the train.

CHAPTER

39.

Passengers streamed from the four forward cars, through, and out the back of the second dining car, through and out the next and the next, until they jammed into the train's last car, some overflowing into car eight as well. William Goheen remained behind at the second dining car bar where the bartender, sweating profusely, remained with him.

"Go on," Goheen said at last, sipping from a scotch.

The bartender, a weathered black man in his fifties by the name of Fred Walker, got the nerve to face up to his boss. "We had better do as the man said, Mr. Goheen. Yourself included. I expect he means trouble for this train."

For several minutes of the evacuation, Gretchen Goheen had appeared naked on the monitors.

"Go on, Fred," Goheen told him. "I'll be along."

The bartender nodded gravely. He'd seen hundreds of drunks in his time. He'd seen women pick up men, men pick up men, and college kids green sick and still drinking. To some he'd offered advice or refused service. With others he'd discussed world affairs. He'd been a shrink, a friend, an adviser to so many strangers that he could speak whatever came to mind with no reservation. But now he hesitated. He'd worked for this company for thirty years. Finally, just before leaving, he said, "Kids get themselves into all sorts of trouble, Mr. Goheen." Fred knew that none of Goheen's despondency had to do with the train. "But it's the parents that got to get them out. Your girl needs you, sir. So don't you stay on this train."

Goheen looked up. "What do you know?"

"More than you'd think, sir." And with that, Fred left, but at a walk, not a run.

Goheen slumped into the leather seat along the wall and reached for the nearest abandoned drink. Scotch. *Just right.* He recalled vividly reviewing the design of these seats, the floor plan of the French-built dining cars. So many details. So many endless improvements. But these thoughts pulled him off only briefly from that horrific image of Gretchen.

He checked his watch. The deadline for his confession was three minutes away. It would come and go, this deadline. The only confession he planned on making was to God.

In minutes he had gone from an all-time high to the darkest place he'd ever been, and the severity of that descent made him want to lie down and die. He had wanted to give America something great and lasting, to put his own name, his family name, into the history books. And all such momentous undertakings required sacrifice. Alvarez had been asked to make his, but that, Goheen had realized early on, had been handled badly. And then it had only gotten worse. True, death and grief were awful, but over and done with, whereas the train was something immortal, important to the country, to all humanity.

"Come on, Bill." Someone had spilled wine down Keith O'Malley's tailored suit. It looked like blood. He beckoned Goheen with sad eyes. "We're still looking for him. If we can find him in the next couple minutes, we still might save this thing."

Goheen shook his head. He glanced up at the dark TV. "You think?" The dining car appeared empty, littered with cigarettes, trash, and empty plastic cups.

"We'll catch this guy," O'Malley said, "and it's the last anyone will ever hear of it."

"Maybe it's some kind of trick. You know what they can do with pictures these days. Paste someone's head onto someone else's body."

"Yeah, that's what it is," O'Malley agreed.

"It sounds like her, but there are ways they can do that, too. Right?" He looked up, a mass of grief.

"None of what went down can be connected to you. Remember that. You're clean, Bill. Even Andersen. If anyone goes down for that, it's me."

"Gretchen is connected to me," he corrected. "I let her down, is the thing. And I've never done it right. Not ever. It just didn't come naturally to me—being a father."

"Bill, we've got to get out of this car."

That snapped Goheen's head up, and he seemed finally to take notice of O'Malley. "Keith?" He downed the rest of someone's drink and looked for another.

"Smart money says to leave these forward cars."

"I thought you were the one with the brass balls."

"Now would be a good time, Bill." He checked his watch.

"You want me to go back there with *them?* You're kidding, right? Do interviews on my daughter, the hooker?" He added, "Let him do whatever he's going to do. I'm through."

"None of this will stick!" the security man repeated.

"Stick?" Goheen glanced up at the black TV. "Were you watching? Do I have your full and undivided attention?" He waited. "It's over."

O'Malley glanced at his watch nervously.

Pointing to the television, Goheen said, "That bastard! He knows everything. He named Genoa. Andersen. And the thing is—you know this better than anyone—the truth will out. Polygraph, whatever. There it is." He pointed to the floor where there was nothing to point at. "I'll keep you out of it."

"Out of it? Bill, you're not thinking straight. You're the one who's out of it."

"The piper will be paid." Goheen nodded and began searching the discarded glasses for something more to drink, sniffing them.

"You can't stay here." O'Malley insisted, "You're coming with me."

"No, I'm not." He sipped another drink, fished a cigarette butt out of the glass, dropped it to the floor, and then sipped some more.

"He can't derail this train," O'Malley said. "Not with the security we've thrown up. The technology. Don't you see this, Bill? He's making a scene is all. Threats. He got himself a soapbox and he got himself heard. A captive audience. It's all he wanted."

"He sure got Gretchen heard," Goheen cried. "Oh, God," he moaned, his head sinking into his chest.

"We've got . . . one minute, Bill." O'Malley's forehead shone with sweat. "I'm going to drag you out of here if I have to. You want to think of impressions? Think how that'll look!"

Goheen had rheumy eyes. "She's getting back at me. You see that? She became the kind of girl she thought I went for." He mumbled, "She's known about . . . *me* for a long time."

"Bill, you're losing it."

"No. I've lost it," Goheen returned. "I've lost her, Keith. She tried to get me to go public with Genoa. I didn't tell you . . . couldn't tell you about it. This is on my watch, Keith. It's all on my watch."

O'Malley began to speak but reconsidered. Then he said nervously, "I gotta check on my guys."

"Sure you do." The men exchanged glances.

A frightened O'Malley hurried for the rear door.

CHAPTER

40

Alvarez had just locked the accordion wall, sealing out Tyler, when O'Malley stepped out of the dining car, shoulders hunched, head lowered. He barked out the order, "Clear the forward cars!" without so much as looking at his minion. He knew the uniform, and that was enough.

Alvarez stood alone in the vestibule connecting the cars, staring at O'Malley's back as the man hurried into six and continued down the aisle. The perfect opportunity had just passed him by. He had stood there, as close as he'd ever get to the man, and he'd done nothing.

He watched as O'Malley stopped, midcar, met there by two of his plainclothes men. Outnumbered, Alvarez saw no point in heading that way. Instead, he hurried into the dining car, knowing the explosion would come any minute.

He spotted William Goheen slumped in a leather chair, chin to chest, shoulders shaking. Goheen looked up, dazed; his face showed his disbelief just before his legs willed him out of his chair and he charged. Alvarez stepped to the side and tripped him and pinned him under his foot. Goheen's head hit the bar, his scalp cut and bleeding.

Alvarez grabbed a champagne bottle and held it high over the man's head. At that moment, he could have killed him. One or two good blows, and by the time the wreckage was pried apart, no one would ever know this man had died a minute or two before the accident. But Alvarez lowered the bottle and said, "Even I won't stoop to your level."

"Bert?" A woman's voice. *Jillian!*

She came around the corner where the stainless steel bar met the wall. She had been sitting on its other side, tucked away from where the passengers could bang into her as they clamored for safety, she refusing to follow, refusing to go along with *him*. Tucked back, where no one could have seen her. She said, "He didn't know I was in here."

"Jilly!" Alvarez said, wanting desperately to get her to safety. "You were supposed to—"

"There was another man." She pointed to Goheen. "With him. I heard it all." She seemed frightened. "Bert, I heard it *all*." She added, "The other one is who killed your attorney, Andersen. You don't have to do any of this. I'm a witness!"

Goheen looked at her. Alvarez couldn't tell if the man was laughing or crying.

Two gunshots rang out like handclaps, their reports distinct and unmistakable. Alvarez instinctively grabbed the champagne bottle and broke it over the edge of the bar, its jagged edge held out as a weapon.

Tyler dared not try to climb beneath the train. Perhaps Alvarez had managed this after setting the explosive; perhaps that was how he had moved from one end of the train to the other, undetected. Tyler didn't know. He just could not do it.

He struggled up the ladder to the intersection of the vestibule's accordioned walls, his hands still slippery, his head reeling.

Below him, unseen, was that gray box, stuck to the coupler. The video had mentioned seven minutes. He checked his watch. Most were gone now: one minute remained.

"Stand back!" he shouted loudly. He paused and called out again to clear the area.

He slipped out his gun and fired a round into the wall lock. He felt a hot pain in his arm as he tugged on the wall and thought that on top of all else, he'd torn a muscle. The wall held firm. Tyler shouted a second time and fired another round into the lock. The louvered wall sagged open.

Tyler reached to open it further, switching hands, but his left arm didn't hold him. He'd shot himself—a flesh wound—catching a ricocheted bullet. With that arm failing, he lost his balance and swung in an arc just as his right hand found purchase. In the process, he dropped the gun. It clanked once on its way down, and was lost.

Painfully now, he tugged the vestibule wall open enough to slip inside. He felt light-headed and still a little sick.

He glanced to his right, through the door's window and into the dining car where he saw Alvarez holding a jagged bottle to Goheen's throat. There was a woman in the car, a few feet behind the men.

Thirty seconds, he thought. *Twenty-five . . .*

Alvarez made eye contact with Tyler and pointed with the broken bottle, directing him back.

Tyler glanced toward the passenger car and saw O'Malley and two others. O'Malley looked up, saw Tyler, clearly recognizing him, and marched forward.

Fifteen seconds . . .

Holding his bloody hand up to stop O'Malley, Tyler simultaneously retreated toward the dining car. Now he raised both hands and motioned O'Malley to go back. Beneath him, he could feel the second hand sweeping toward the top of the hour.

O'Malley, spurred by Tyler's retreat, hurried forward and opened the automatic door. At the same time, Tyler backed up against the automatic door's panic bar and the door slid open.

He backed through, shouting to O'Malley, "Get back!" An angry O'Malley had stepped out onto the platform.

"You?" O'Malley called out.

Five . . . four . . .

The dining car's door hissed shut. As Tyler turned, he saw Alvarez drop to the floor, pulling the woman with him.

Instinctively, Tyler shielded himself.

The bomb went off. And Keith O'Malley with it.

Chunks of tempered glass whipped through the air. Tyler fell to the floor as a massive rumbling swept through the car. In that moment, as he thought he might die, Tyler saw that in his life he was less a victim of a system gone bad and more one of just plain bad luck. Chester Washington had scared him, had frightened him to the point that once he began beating that monster he couldn't stop. He vowed now not to repeat the same mistake.

The rumbling settled out of the chassis. Tyler stood slowly to feel the cold wind rushing through the empty window frame in the dining car's bulging door and the warmth of blood on the back of his neck. He was cut, though not badly. Behind them, on the track, the last four cars had slipped away, and Tyler saw sparks rise from the tracks like fireworks as someone must have leaned on the emergency pull.

Alvarez, too, had come to his feet, his hand bloody from the bottle breaking in his grasp as he fell. Goheen remained down, as did the woman.

Both men fell again as the dining car swayed.

The cry of brakes sang through the steel.

Alvarez ran to the wall phone by the door, picked it up, and shouted into the receiver. "No brakes, you idiot! And no slowing the engine. If we lose speed, the stabilizers will roll the train!" He hung up, everyone looking at him.

He said to the gathering, "At the time, it seemed like a pretty good plan."

The train shuddered again. Alvarez pulled the handheld GPS out of his jacket, glanced at it. "That's the first curve. Three more to go. On the third, she won't make it."

The car settled back down.

Tyler felt his legs beneath him again.

Alvarez grabbed the woman by the arm and led her at a run to the front of the car.

Tyler decided that if Alvarez was heading to the front of the train, then so was he. The car's front window had blown out in the explosion as well, and Tyler saw the forward dining car tilt, Alvarez halfway through it. A fraction of a second later, the car beneath him shuddered so hard that every item on every horizontal surface rained to the floor.

The vestibule and the accordion walls between the two dining cars tore loose and blew apart, carried off by the ferocious wind. The locomotive's brakes screamed, and Tyler fell to his feet before standing, but as the destabilized cars buckled, the driver must have released the brakes. Without a progressive slowing of the whole train, the brakes, he realized, were more dangerous than useful.

Goheen, sobered by fear, followed Tyler. With the vestibule's accordioned platform connecting the cars now torn loose, Tyler stepped out of the second dining car and lowered himself to the exposed coupler. He placed his left foot down, realizing there were no handholds with which to reach the car in front. It required a leap of faith: placing that foot down and pushing off the rear car while reaching through space for a handrail on the back of the next car. Before making that move, he glanced back. Goheen stood above him in the doorway.

"I'm not doing *that!*" Goheen shouted.

"Suit yourself," Tyler hollered back. It was no time for heroes.

He jumped, and his good hand found purchase. He was on the other side. He climbed toward the back door of this dining car.

Below them, he felt the tracks begin a long slow curve. *The second curve.* Again, Tyler felt a sickening weightlessness, as this time the cars actually lifted their right wheels off the welded tracks.

Goheen made the jump across the coupler, caught hold, but lost his balance. Tyler reached down with his injured arm and reeled with pain as he snagged Goheen by his wrist and stood him up. For an instant their eyes met, and Tyler felt nothing from this man. William Goheen looked dead inside.

Tyler hurried through the forward dining car as again he felt the right side of the carriage lift beneath him. It was a precarious, unstable feeling, this lifting and floating of thirty tons of steel. It began to settle but then lifted again. He ran harder and faster, through the forward door—Goheen now right behind him—and into the press car.

The car was trashed with spilled drinks and paper napkins with the F-A-S-T Track logo. Tyler ran down the aisle, the gray blur of a forest running past the windows. In the distance he saw marshland and the suggestion of a river.

Before he ever reached Alvarez at the front, Tyler intuited the man's intentions. Alvarez had sabotaged the guidance system on the passenger cars. (No doubt had the back four cars not applied their emergency brakes they, too, would have rolled.) The locomotive, however—so thoroughly guarded and closely inspected—had never been a part of the man's plans. So, if Alvarez could get himself onto the back of the locomotive, could disconnect the trailing four cars, they alone would jump track without taking the engine car with them.

Tyler reached the vestibule of this forwardmost car. He and Coopersmith had boarded through here only thirty minutes ago. The back door to the locomotive stood open, the woman crouching on her knees looking shell-shocked. Alvarez stood ready to shut that door, and presumably to lock it.

The vestibule began to feel incredibly cramped to Tyler.

The two men stood ten feet apart. "Don't shut that door," Tyler called out to Alvarez. Goheen was slowly catching up. "I know what you want to do, and I can help you."

"Help him?!" Goheen thundered from behind. He stepped forward, but Tyler restrained him. When Goheen struggled, Tyler turned and wrestled him down. He slugged him in the jaw, collapsing the man. His hand ached, but no punch had ever felt as good.

"You want to uncouple the engine," Tyler shouted at Alvarez. "The engine's stabilizers are intact. It won't roll, unless dragged over by these trailing cars." He added, "Can we fix these cars?"

Alvarez simply stared.

"You don't want to kill anyone," Tyler reminded him.

"I'm staying on this train," Goheen announced, recovering and coming to his feet.

Alvarez shouted, "And what, you're just going to hold the two cars together while I turn the key and uncouple them? I don't think so. It can't be done."

Tyler glanced backward. "I have your duffel. I have the come-along."

Alvarez's face lit up. Then it hardened. "You're lying. You just don't want me locking this door."

"I'm not lying!" Tyler knocked Goheen off his feet and warned him not to get up. He raced to the first of the dining cars, painfully leapt over the bar, and searched the storage areas. No duffel. He tore out at a run, dared a jump across the exposed coupling, and again checked behind the bar. One of the storage closets was locked. He scrambled for a pry bar—something to force it open—and came up with a bottle opener. It bent on his first try and he chucked it. His eyes settled on a fire extinguisher, and he ripped it from the wall, immediately bashing the lock. Thankfully, the dining car storage bins did not carry the same hardware as maintenance closets. With the fifth blow, the door sagged open. Inside, he spotted it. He tore through its contents and came up with the come-along, the levered winch and cable.

Seconds later, he was facing Alvarez once again, this time holding up the come-along. With a sturdy hook on either end, the metal cable was coiled around the hand-levered winch.

Alvarez checked his watch and barked, "Hook your end there!" He pointed through the vestibule to the edge of the car.

Tyler ran off a length of cable.

"Give me the other end!" Alvarez shouted.

Tyler pulled out slack and stepped forward tentatively, growing cautiously closer to Alvarez with each step. The two men nearly touched hands as Tyler passed him the hook.

Tyler secured his hook to a steel edge on the passenger car. Alvarez secured his to the back of the locomotive.

With his one good arm, Tyler worked the winch handle, taking up the slack in the cable, one ratchet at a time. As the slack came out and the cable tightened, it raised in the air to waist height. Then, as hard as he pulled, Tyler could not budge the lever handle. He couldn't get another inch out of it. "I need some help here."

Alvarez crossed the no-man's-land of the open vestibule that separated them. He indicated for Goheen to move back and then tripped open the flanged flooring so he could see the coupling. He shook his head. Nothing. The purpose of the come-along was to move the car closer to the locomotive, to remove the tension between them so that they could be uncoupled.

Together, the two men grabbed hold of the lever meant to tighten the winch. Their blood mixed on its handle. Together, they leaned into it. The winch tightened a single notch. Then, no more.

"It's no good," Alvarez shouted. He and Tyler stood face to face, both sweating, their fists gripping the come-along's lever.

Alvarez reached for Tyler, who reacted defensively, lifting his arms to deflect a blow. But Alvarez merely slipped the walkie-talkie off Tyler's coveralls. He turned and tried to hand the radio to Goheen, finally tossing it at the CEO, who caught it. "Call the driver. Tell him to tap the brakes. But gently!"

"Never," Goheen hollered over the roar. "So you can escape?" He looked at Tyler threateningly. "With this turncoat?"

"I'll stay with you on this side," Alvarez bargained loudly. "He goes on the locomotive."

"No way!" Tyler objected.

"Shut up!" Alvarez roared. He looked back to Goheen. "Call him. Remind him whose train this is!"

Tyler leaned in. "Do it!"

Goheen took up the radio, introduced himself—twice—and hollered into device, "Hit the god damn brakes!" He added, "Gently."

As the driver hit the locomotive's brakes, the passenger car lurched forward. They worked the come-along's handle together as a team and took out a good deal of slack. Alvarez inspected the coupler. It was working.

"Again," he instructed Goheen, who briefly looked unwilling to cooperate.

"Again!" Now Tyler yelled at him.

Goheen repeated the order. The car lurched again. The cable tightened further. Alvarez checked the coupling, indicated a thumbs-up, and immediately began fishing for keys. The train cars were held together by the come-along, the coupler tension now slack.

"You have keys?" he asked frantically.

"Yes," Tyler replied.

"Hurry! Find this one!" From a distance he indicated to Tyler which key to use. "You operate it from the engine side."

"You are *not* staying on this train," Tyler objected.

Alvarez checked his GPS. "No time to argue. Do it!"

Tyler jumped across, hurried to the panel, and inserted the key.

The woman called out to Alvarez, "You think you win by doing this?"

"No one ever wins," Alvarez replied.

"Then why?" she cried out across the gap.

To Tyler, Alvarez, having inserted his own key, said, "Go ahead."

Both men turned their keys. The coupling came open, the cars separated, and the cable instantly snapped, whizzing by Alvarez's head and arm and missing by only inches. It would have sliced his head off had it connected.

The cars pulled apart. A foot. A yard. Ten yards. Moonlight poured down. Alvarez, standing, and Goheen, still lying on the floor, grew smaller and smaller in the lit car.

Alvarez shouted to Jillian, "Maybe I win after all."

"No one wins," she cried back defiantly.

Tyler felt the force of a severe turn in the tracks. The locomotive's stabilizers countered to find a center of gravity. He and the woman watched as Alvarez disappeared from the doorway, jumping over the defeated Goheen, who swiped out to confront the man but missed. Goheen struggled to standing.

Five seconds passed. Ten. The trailing train rocked up on one side, then settled, then lifted again. Fifteen seconds had passed. It lifted and fell again. Twenty. Twenty-five. Then the car lifted high, rocked side to side, and broke clean off the tracks in the middle of the long sweeping curve. The steel rails tore like paper straws, and the four cars plowed into a sea of bulrushes, spraying a plume of mud and debris a hundred feet into the air. All four cars roared straight, aimed at the Susquehanna River a mile away. Then, in an eerie slow motion, they began to lean left, the steel trucks and wheels lifting out of the mud and dirt to where Tyler could see the underneath of the lead car.

Unexpectedly, a small, dark object rose briefly into the night, lifting skyward, and catching in the wind, and then ever so slowly floating, rocking back and forth, as it settled into the grasses.

Alvarez had located his duffel. His seemingly noble gesture to remain behind on the train now made sense to Tyler. He had escaped.

The front car rolled completely over, caught in the terrain, and stopped abruptly, throwing the remaining three cars into, up, and over it. They broke apart and scattered, rolled and tumbled, skidding as much as another quarter mile in a grinding, screaming, fevered pitch. And then they were still.

Five hundred ducks and geese lifted out of the marsh and beautifully filled the sky, as if part of some celebration, as if following that parasail.

Not long after, the driver again tested the brakes. This time the locomotive slowed without incident and came to a stop.

Nell Priest's mother owned a two-story clapboard Cape in suburban Maryland, most of whose residents commuted to the nation's capital. After two full days of interviews, attorneys, and debriefings, Tyler was a public hero but a *former* government employee. Loren Rucker promised another job offer would be on the table in a few weeks, but he wanted "the heat to blow over." Tyler wasn't holding his breath.

The FBI search of the crash site had produced Goheen's body, found inside the wreckage of the forward car, and an abandoned, camouflaged parasail found a half mile into a forest east of the tracks. Forty-eight hours, and still no sign of Umberto Alvarez. The press was teeming with stories of investigations by a myriad of government agencies into Northern Union's F-A-S-T Track train, improper accounting, maintenance violations, and misuse of public trust.

Priest knocked as she entered the room where Tyler was reading from a stack of newspapers. "Well, there goes my retirement," she said. "If you were thinking about marrying me for my money," she teased, "you had better look elsewhere."

Tyler, reading from the paper, said, "It's being reported that O'Malley killed Alvarez's attorney, Andersen. One of his guys cut an immunity deal. O'Malley may have tried to cut a deal with Andersen to settle. No one's clear on that. But it went south, and the attorney ate it. The guy who's talking was part of a cleanup crew that staged the office to implicate Alvarez. With both Goheen and O'Malley dead, no one will ever know for sure, but from Jillian Barstow's statement of what she overheard in that bar car, Alvarez is basically in the clear."

"I have this feeling," she said, "like you've been given another chance, a second chance. That *we* have. It could have been you in that car with Goheen, you know?"

Tyler replied with a look, attempting to convey his happiness.

"It's good, isn't it," she declared.

"It's very good," he agreed. "I've lost the house—for good, this time—my Norton, my job, and I've never been happier."

"My biggest regret is that the F-A-S-T Track never proved itself," she said. "Goheen may have mismanaged things, but he was a visionary. It'll be years, if ever, before it runs again, and that's a loss to everyone."

"It was a hell of a ride," he agreed. "But Alvarez got his wish: the press barely mentioned the technology. All the focus has been on the abuse of power."

"It's a shame."

She sat down on the arm of his chair, ran her long fingers along his shoulder, and pointed to the newspaper. "With Andersen's homicide cleared, do you think he'll come out of hiding?"

"Not with the derailments squarely on him. No. Besides, who cares?"

"You do. You're beating yourself up over this, Peter. Is it worth it?"

Tyler answered, "I should have remembered that parasail. *He* certainly did. I thought he was sacrificing himself. What the hell was I thinking?"

"So, go find him," she encouraged.

"Yeah, right. The FBI must have five hundred guys on this, and they haven't found him."

"But they don't know what we know," she said.

Tyler looked up at her. "What do we know?" he asked.

"We looked at what he was doing. We didn't look at how he managed it," she said obliquely.

"Do I have to beg?"

"How did he finance these last eighteen months?" she inquired. "It didn't occur to me until I realized how much I'd lost in stock options."

"But you still have a job. That's better than some of us."

She ignored his complaint. She had insisted the job offers would come in for him. He'd been painted in the press as a hero. She said, "What occurred to me was how much money I would have made if I'd thought to sell short, if I'd bet on the stock falling instead of rising." She snatched the paper from him and leafed through sections of the *New York Times,* extracting the business pages.

"The thing is," she said, "we weren't paying attention to the money. *Follow the money,*" she recited, quoting a law enforcement rule. Pointing out a headline, she smacked the paper loudly enough that he jumped. "Here," she said, leaning toward him and spreading the open paper between them. "They printed the two-year historical today. See?"

"I'm not exactly a business major," he told her.

"Alvarez was a teacher. What, if anything, would he have accumulated in his four-oh-one-K? Twenty thousand? Thirty?"

"If that."

"Exactly. And we know he turned down the settlement, never received a dime because he wanted to take us to court."

"What's that get us?" he asked, clearly frustrated by his lack of understanding. "He was broke?"

"But he wasn't broke. He managed a war against a major corporation for well over a year." Again, she indicated the stock chart. "Look at these dips! The dates. Every time a train derails, NUR's stock tanks. The street reacts to news. You can bank on it."

He turned his head so fast his neck made a cracking sound. "He played the market!"

"He *made* the market. He shorted the stock, based on insider information only he possessed. He knew exactly when the stock would fall, and my guess is that he's been doing it all along. If he sold short on margin, or if he played options, he could be worth a fortune by now." She whispered, "Think what he had riding on the test of the F-A-S-T Track!"

"He would have bet the farm," Tyler said.

"The FiBIes have been trying to follow his trail. They never thought to follow the market. What we need is somebody in the SEC to check Internet trades for us," she suggested.

"So call someone," he said.

"You're going to let this go," she replied skeptically.

"It's not my investigation."

She thought a moment and said, "What if I offer you a job?"

That turned his head. "Has this latest promotion gotten to you?"

"It's still very much in our interest to see Alvarez arrested. He's caused over a hundred million dollars in damages. He killed our CEO."

"You're insured."

"I could hire you on special assignment." She added, "Unless you're uncomfortable working for a woman."

"Loren Rucker knows everybody in Washington," Tyler said, not allowing her that one. "He could open up a contact for us at the SEC."

"Quietly."

"Absolutely."

"Expenses plus a starting salary at what Rucker was paying you. I'll have no problem justifying that."

"Make the call," he said.

"Let's find out what the SEC can tell us first. If we can confirm someone was selling short prior to the derailments, you've got yourself a job."

"No charity, Nell. That won't work for me."

She leaned over and kissed him. He wanted to pull her into his lap, but it wasn't proper conduct for an employee. Between kisses, she said, "Call Rucker. We'll see what we see."

CHAPTER

42

For nearly two months, Tyler sat behind the wheel of a nine-year-old Pontiac convertible—the top up—in front of a bland brownstone on Arcadia Street in Rockford, Illinois. Through a twelve-hour shift he watched winter tighten its grip on the upper Midwest. Slouched low, dressed to fight off the cold, he lived on a diet of fast food and hot coffee, reminded of his years on Metro and dozens of stakeouts. He continued to pay off creditors, including his attorneys, who had generously worked out a long-term payment plan, and he began to see a pinpoint of light at the end of the debt tunnel. He wouldn't own a house anytime soon, but the time would come when he could rent. He might lease an inexpensive car. Get back on his feet. He'd been eyeing the classifieds, hoping to see a 1953 Norton—something to dream for.

Nell Priest remained his boss at Northern Union Security and was rumored to be under consideration for the top slot. She had flown to Chicago for several weekend visits, technically there to supervise an active investigation. But it wasn't all business between them.

Nell arrived on a Friday morning, intent on a three-day week-end with Tyler. She had long since hired a local private detective to take the graveyard shift, believing little activity would occur at the halfway house in the off-hours. She sat in the passenger seat reading the nine o'clock movie listings in the local paper aloud to him. Tyler dropped the surveillance each night from 8:00 P.M. till 8:00 A.M.

At Rucker's request, a forensic accountant at the SEC had in fact identified a series of option trades, all timed around the derailments. The seven trades had netted a total of $927,000 over the last eighteen months, including a $710,000 option following the F-A-S-T Track derailment. All the funds had been wired to England, back to Bermuda, and finally into a custodial account held on behalf of one M. Alvarez, who currently resided at the Bennett House, across the street from where they were currently parked.

"UPS," Nell said, her attention divided between the paper and her door's rearview mirror.

Tyler watched in the driver's door mirror as a uniformed UPS man walked from his truck to the front door of the halfway house. The delivery man walked with a slight limp, and he wore his company-issue baseball cap pulled down onto his head.

Tyler said, "How many UPS deliveries have we seen here?"

"I haven't seen any," she reminded him. She had never spent a weekday with him in Rockford.

Tyler said, "Yeah? Well, I've seen several, and it's always the same guy. Kind of heavy. Sideburns. A smoker." He added, "That is not him."

Sitting up to pay more attention to the mirror, Priest noted nothing about this man that matched that description. "A substitute?" she asked. "Your guy's home sick?"

"This one, I think we follow," he said, checking his watch and making a note of the time: 12:40 P.M.

The UPS man had spent over ten minutes inside the halfway house, at which point Priest said, "It's him, isn't it?"

"Some of those guys can be chatty, but yes, I think maybe it is."

"Visiting his brother."

"It's a decent enough disguise. It gives him a way to come and go."

"The limp. Did Alvarez limp?"

"Could be he had a rough landing in that parasail."

"Should we call for backup?" she asked.

"Scooch down," he advised. And they both slumped in their seats.

The UPS man left the house, boarded the old brown panel van, and drove off. Tyler said, "When those trucks reach a certain mileage, the company sells them off."

"So he bought one, painted it up like the original, and got himself a brown uniform."

"Could be," Tyler agreed. "We know he's good with disguise."

"Then why exactly did we sit here and let him take off?" she asked. "Why not question him?"

"We've waited this long. We can wait a while longer."

"This is Peter Tyler talking, right?"

For nearly ten minutes, Tyler followed the brown step van at a good distance. As they entered a residential area, Tyler backed off even further.

The UPS truck pulled into the driveway of a brick two-story, and the Pontiac rolled past just as the driver lifted the door to the garage. Tyler drove well down the street and parallel parked.

"It's him," Tyler confirmed.

"You saw him?" she asked, her voice nervous.

"No, but he's parking the thing in a garage. It's him." He wondered aloud, "What do you want to bet he's been to the halfway house before this and I never caught on?"

"If you're going to beat yourself up, I'm going to take a walk," she announced. "You've got to cut yourself some slack."

Briefly, he took his eyes off the outside rearview to look over at her. "Is all this advice of yours free?"

"You wish," she said, suppressing a grin. "Too much advice?"

"Sometimes."

"You'll live. What now?" she asked.

"We wait," Tyler announced.

"Why?"

"Did you happen to notice what time it is?" he asked.

"Twelve-fifty," she answered.

"Lunch hour," Tyler supplied.

"You're hungry?"

"*His* lunch hour," Tyler answered.

"You've been at this too long," she said. "No one should do two months of stakeout solo. You're losing it, Peter Tyler."

"Gives a person a lot of time to think," Tyler said.

"You take the front, I take the back. What's to think about?" She added, "Or we call in the local cavalry, get some backup." She reminded him, "I have jurisdiction to make arrests in every state."

"Except Louisiana," he said.

"Point taken," she said. "Lucky for us we're in Illinois." She hesitated and said, "So, do you want the front or the back?"

"Neither. We sit tight."

"Is the real Peter Tyler locked up in the trunk or something?"

"The real Peter Tyler is sitting right here," he said. "The Peter Tyler *before* Chester Washington. The Peter Tyler who has nothing to get even for. No grudges. No chip on his shoulder."

She said cautiously, "Well, that sounds good."

"Maybe you won't like the real Peter Tyler."

"Are you afraid of that? That if you change, I won't like you?"

"I've already changed," he said. "Or maybe I haven't. Maybe I'm just back to the same old me again."

"Does this have anything to do with your not touching me?" she asked.

"I touch you."

"I love sleeping with you. Don't get me wrong. But I mean the other kind of touching."

"I don't want to rush things."

She laughed. "When we first kissed, it was December."

"And you didn't want to rush things. So we do other things,

and they're fun. I don't want you thinking that that's all I'm after."

"I spend four weekends out here with you in the freezing cold, and you're wondering if I'm going to give this a chance? I've got news for you: I don't like western Illinois all that much."

Tyler concealed a grin, but she saw it.

"That's better," she said. "Don't tell me this new Peter Tyler doesn't have a sense of humor, because it's one of the things I love about the old Peter Tyler."

Use of that particular word turned his head. He stared her down. "I thought we were going to be careful about that word."

"I *am* being careful. Or actually, I think I'm sick of being so careful. That word. In bed. Whatever."

Tyler was saved a response by the activity behind them.

"Here we go," he said, indicating the house, where a late-model Volkswagen Jetta pulled out of the drive. "Five minutes of one," he noted, checking his watch.

"He's going the other way. Turn around! We'll lose him," she said.

"Lose him?" Tyler questioned. "We now know where he lives. We're not going to lose him." Tyler waited until the car disappeared down the street.

She said angrily, "What the hell, Peter?"

He pulled the Pontiac off the curb and drove straight.

"He went in the *other* direction!" she reminded him.

"I've spent two months in this town. I know the terrain."

"Are you withholding something from me?"

"What exactly do you want this guy for?"

"As in crimes perpetrated, or what?"

"Or what."

"You're kidding, right?"

"Other than the ego thing of 'I set out to get him, so I'm going to get him.' Other than that." He negotiated the big car through a series of turns. She stared at him in profile. He said, "I've had a long time to think out here, Nell."

"You're freaking me out here, Peter. You really have been out here too long."

He said, "Destruction of property?"

"*Millions* of dollars' worth of property," she answered.

"But you're insured," Tyler responded. "Loss of life?"

"Goheen. O'Malley," she recited.

"He lost three lives," Tyler said. "Northern Union lost two."

"What exactly are you saying?"

"I told you: two months is a long time," he answered.

"So you get cooped up and lose your brain."

He turned left and pulled the car over. They faced a field of grass, a parking lot, and the back of a brick building.

"Where are we?" she asked.

"Westside Middle School."

The dark green Jetta was parked in the lot. It took Priest a moment to pick out the car, but as she did, she asked, "Is that the same—"

"Yes," he answered.

"You've been here before," she suggested, knowing him.

"There are three other public middle schools. Four in all. All named after points of the compass. After a week or so of the surveillance, I started watching one or the other of them when school let out."

"Because?"

"Once a teacher, always a teacher," he said in a dry, hoarse whisper.

"You *knew* he worked here?" She sounded angry.

"No. But Westside is the closest to that house. And it's his lunch hour."

"You're not making any sense."

"To me I am," he said.

"That's the same Jetta," she stated.

"I'd say it probably is. Yes." He added, "I'm guessing maybe he's a substitute teacher. He came into the year late. Maybe that's why I never saw him, even when I staked out the schools. Maybe he works at all the various schools, depending on when they need him."

"He's teaching school."

"Substitute science, and computer science, would be my guess."

"Under an alias," she proposed.

"Some name he bought a while ago and never used. Yes," he said.

"So let's go in and have a little talk with him," she said.

"Are you sure that's what you want to do?"

"Isn't that what *you* want to do?"

He said, "You hired me to find him. I found him. My job's over."

"What exactly are you saying?" she sounded nervous.

Tyler stared at her, allowing a grin to slowly occupy his face. The smile grew wider, as Nell's eyes went wide.

She complained, "You're kidding, right? You're either kidding or you're out of your mind."

"It's fetal alcohol syndrome. Did you know that?"

"The brother?"

"Miguel," Tyler supplied.

"Yes. I know. It's horrible."

"It's horrible, and it's forever."

"Meaning?"

Tyler said calmly, "Who needs Alvarez more? The People? A prison? Or these kids he's teaching and his little brother who has no other living relative?"

"There is definitely another Tyler locked in the trunk."

"How many more trains do you think he's going to derail?"

"That's not the point."

They sat in the car for another five minutes in silence. Nell seemed preoccupied with her own hands. Tyler broke the silence. "I won't stop you, if it's something you have to do."

She snorted derisively and looked over at him. Then she glanced back at the school, taking it in. "I took you for the committed type. Do not tell me you're not the committed type."

"I'm very committed to some things."

"It isn't showing."

"I went through the system, dear woman, and it spit me out the other side. The same system I'd given much of my life to. It's there for a reason, this system. I understand that. And it's a decent system most of the time, but not always. It deals in evidence—what it calls fact—which works fine until you take into consideration that people can't always be judged by the facts. How do you suppose it will judge Umberto Alvarez?"

Again, for a long time neither of them said a word. A gray bird made a lot of noise from a nearby tree. The winter sun shone strongly. Tyler slipped on a pair of sunglasses.

Nell snorted several times during those minutes as she worked through an internal dialogue. She shook her head, looked over at Tyler, and then went back to worming her hands as if she were washing them.

"How'd you do in science?" he asked. She didn't answer. "I liked it," Tyler answered himself. He looked over at her, studying her, awaiting a reaction. It came slowly, but as brightly as the sun over the horizon. She was smiling. He dared to start the car.

"I sucked at science," she admitted.

"Why, do you suppose?"

She grinned. "I probably didn't have the right teacher."

"Probably not."

She took a deep breath, had one last look at the school, and asked, "How long do you think it will take you to pack?"

"What's the hurry?" he asked, pulling the car out into the empty street.

"No hurry, I suppose. But there's a red-eye that leaves at eleven. I'd just as soon have breakfast in Manhattan as Rockford."

"Leaves us the rest of the afternoon," he said, suppressing a grin. He drove into traffic and headed to the motel, where he hoped they might find a way to kill some time.

Please visit Ridley at his website:
www.ridleypearson.com